SKY WARRIORS

Book I: The Star People Series

BY

PAUL A. HANSEN

SKY WARRIORS

Copyright © 2012 Paul A. Hansen
All rights reserved
ISBN-10: 1477429832

Please visit http://paulhansenauthor.com for more information

All rights reserved.
Except as permitted under the U.S. Copyright Act of 1976, no part of this publication may be reproduced, distributed, or transmitted in any form or by any means, electronic or mechanical, including photocopy, recording, or stored in a database or retrieval system, without the prior written permission of the publisher. This book is a work of fiction. Names, characters, and incidents are the product of the author's imagination, except for references to the events of "9-11." Any similarities to persons, living or dead, are purely coincidental. References to certain places, (cities, locales, etc.), history, aircraft, airbases and other equipment and technology may be authentic, but not personal.

SETTINGS
The locales in or near Blanding, Utah are accurate with a few minor exceptions: Comb Ridge, Arch Canyon, Edge of the Cedars Museum, certain motels, restaurants, roads, and streets exist as described. The pocket canyon where the saucer is hangared is fictitious. On old geo maps, there was an "Indian Village" site located northwest of Blanding.

ACKNOWLEDGMENTS

Mimi: My best friend, wife, in-house editor, and partner in life. Without her support, this writing life would never happen.

My Writing Critique Group; Stephanie and Bernice, who listened and gave feedback as this story took shape.

My first readers for their comments, which helped make this a much better book: Gary, Christine, Ron, Dan, Carl,

Cover design: Kathleen Riley, kreilly@krpatentdrafting.com

SKY WARRIORS

Life, death,

Past and present,

Command

The closing of one door and the opening of another

Into

Journeys of healing the heart and soul.

Flights of airplanes, UFOs, and spirit

Probe

The labyrinths of the soul,

The canyons of Utah,

Leading to

New discoveries of self,

Purpose,

Hope,

and Love.

1

1935 The Canyon Lands of Utah

Gasping for breath, seventeen year old Joe Star pulled himself over the rim at the top of the mesa and sagged to his knees. He'd raced to follow the squash sized glowing orb up the steep trail after it had mysteriously appeared at his camp. Moonlight reflecting off the silvery surface of a strange object caught his eyes. What is that? Moments later, the orb disappeared into the bottom of an enormous object as big as their hogan. It looked like a huge inverted bowl on four slender legs. His mouth dry from panting, he stood up and cautiously felt his way across the wind swept mesa on moccasins damp with sweat. A faint humming sound grew stronger with each step of his approach, reminding him of the sound of a bee tree. Keeping a safe distance, he circled this object that showed no line or mark and shook his head. Was it real? A vision? Was it alive? What had he found?

Or had it found him? He remembered how the orb had suddenly appeared at his camp and led him here. Maybe he didn't need the peyote buttons he'd brought along on his vision quest after all. He waited, his eyes scanning the object. After a few more breaths when nothing happened, he sidled closer, afraid, yet curious. He guardedly stretched out his right hand to touch it. Though its surface was as smooth as newly tanned deer skin, a shock leapt from it through his fingers and up his arm. Yelping in surprise, he jumped back, stumbling over a rock, and stared down in disbelief at his still tingling hand.

Was this some sort of spirit creature that bit him? Was it dangerous? He retreated to sit on a nearby rock to ponder the situation. He had been hoping to find his totem animal, such as a wolf or bear, or maybe even one of the great ceremonial masks portrayed in the rock art of the Ancient Ones, but not this thing, whatever it was.

Before climbing up here, he'd been sitting peacefully by the embers of his campfire, listening to a nearby owl hooting a conversation with its brother across the canyon, while a neighborhood pack of coyotes yipped their excitement over some quarry. When the mysterious glowing orb about the size of a squash floated into his camp, he vaguely remembered stories his mother and grandmother told of such a thing. As it came close, he stood to touch it, but it moved away. He took a step toward it.

It moved again. He took another step. Again it moved just out of his reach. After a number of such moves in the direction of the trail up the mesa, he concluded that it wanted him to follow, like the doe that had recently led him to where her fawn lay with its leg caught in a crack in the rocks. He had wondered then what lay ahead if he followed the orb. Now he knew. But what was it?

"*Looks-at-Stars.*" He whipped his head around looking for who had called out his Ute name, the name he was known by in his home village. Joe Star was the Anglo name used by his teachers at the mission school. He saw no one.

"*Looks-at-Stars.*" Again he heard it, but now it sounded almost like it was inside his head. He turned back to the object and watched, amazed as a hatch lifted open in its side, revealing a softly lit interior, and two steps extended down toward the ground.

Now Joe heard, "*Yugay,*" the word his Ute family and villagers used when someone came to their hogan, meaning welcome, come in. Scarcely daring to breathe, he approached, and peered in to discover walls that curved from ceiling to floor, matching the outer form. Tentatively, he eased one foot onto the bottom step. Finding it solid, he brought his other foot up. Again he heard, "*Yugay, Yugay.*" Dare he enter?

He paused to gather courage, all the while hearing in his head, "*Yugay, Yugay.*" Cautiously, he leaned in through the doorway and on his right saw two seats facing a panel of colored lights. Taking a deep breath, he decided to risk it, stepped all the way in, and paused, marveling at what he saw.

A moment later some inner sense caused him to glance behind him. The hatch had closed behind him without a sound. Trapped! He froze, his heart pounding. Again he heard the word of welcome, though now with another added to it, "*Yugay, Supa-uni.*" He knew this word meant "be calm" or "be at peace," but it did little to ease his terror.

As he waited for the hammering of his heart to subside, a strong musty odor assailed his nose. The hair rose on the back of his neck. Where was it coming from? Something was moving in the back of this space! He was not alone! He stared into the dark recess, his body tense, then let out his breath in relief when the dim light revealed one of the great ceremonial masks he had so long sought. Then it moved! It wasn't a mask at all, but the head of a short, skinny creature such as he had seen only in the Anasazi rock paintings. Enormous black eyes slanted up away from its tiny mouth and chin. It vaguely resembled a masked dancer he'd seen at a ceremony some time ago. The creature moved toward him. He shrank back from long fingers that reached for him. No way to escape. The touch of those fingers jolted, then numbed him. Sinking to the floor, he dimly observed the being slip into one of the seats as he began to lose consciousness. Moments later he felt the vehicle rise. With no strength or will to even move, and certain he was about to die at the hands of this monster, he sank into deep blackness.

2

When Joe regained consciousness, he was lying on a padded flat surface. Still groggy as he started to focus, his eyes darted over his surroundings and saw several of the short large-headed beings clustered around him. With his body feeling so heavy that he couldn't yet move, panic and fear gripped him anew. Then he noticed, here and there among the short grey beings, tall people more like himself, or at least that's what he first thought. His mind raced. Where am I? Who are these creatures? What is happening? Neither he nor his father had imagined anything like this for his vision quest. As two of the small beings helped him sit up on the table, he heard in his head, over and over, *Supa-uni, Supa-uni*. How was that happening? He'd certainly not thought that himself.

Almost as soon as he asked the question, its answer came in his head.

I am sending it to you.

Was that his own thought? A moment later, he felt someone touch his shoulder. Startled, he turned to look directly into the blue eyes of one of the tall beings, a human-like person with blond hair, who emanated a great sense of calm.

"Who are you?" Joe asked, still frightened.

I am called Markel.

Bewildered, questions surged in Joe's mind. Where am I? How did I get here?

The answer came instantly, though Joe had heard no sound. *You are on our home ship or Mothership, near your planet. We park it here in a stationary orbit when necessary. You came here in the small Explorer craft you found on top of that mountain.*

"Mothership? Stationary orbit?"

To orbit means to circle the earth, high in the sky, in space. But we adjust our speed so that we remain stationary, relative to your earth.

"Oh," Joe said, though he didn't really understand. The rudimentary science he'd studied in elementary school with the missionaries did not cover such things as orbits and space travel, though he had learned about the planets. More mystery.

Then Joe wondered, *How is this talk happening? I don't hear anything.*

Almost before he'd finished the thought, the answer came. *We no longer need to make sounds to communicate. We use our minds. It is much easier, faster and leads to less confusion. Our thoughts and feelings can be instantly known, though we can choose to limit that, should we wish more privacy. You can do this too, though you have not yet developed the skill. We hope you will soon become accustomed to it and not feel frightened by this way of communicating. You have actually used it in hunting, when you sensed what an animal would do next. You did it naturally and thought that everyone else had the same ability. They don't.*

"They don't?" Joe paused, then asked, "Why do I have this and others don't?"

Have you noticed there are different types of beings here on the ship?

"Yes." Joe scanned the room, noting the various beings.

Just as there are differences between people in your village and white man on Terra, there are differences here too. The small grey ones have large eyes. Others, like myself, look more like you and have eyes like you. Most of us have lived our entire lives here on the ship, though a few who can easily pass as earth beings have lived part of their lives on the surface of your planet. You yourself are a mixture, which gives you your ability to communicate this way.

"Mixture?" Alarmed, Joe spoke aloud.

Your mother, Little Moon, had contact with us, as did your grandmother and great grandmother. To fully understand, I must tell you something of our history, which in a way, is also now your history. A long time ago, atmospheric conditions on our home planet began to deteriorate, making life there increasingly difficult. Our sun is in the process of dying. It became necessary for us to find other alternatives in order for us to survive, though not many planets have suitable environments for our people. Your planet, which we call Terra, came closest to the climate of our planet that we could find, though there is a difference in gravity. Therefore, long ago, we began a program of trying to use genetic information from the people of Terra to augment our own so that we could adapt and live on your planet. You see the results of the program in certain beings on this ship, like me. Long before your birth, your mother shared some of her genetic information with us.

How did she do that? She never told me anything about it. Joe knew how animals reproduced and didn't like the image he formed in his mind of such sharing. It sounded more like she had been forced. A wave of anger rose in Joe's throat. How dare they do this to his mother? He seriously doubted that she would have agreed to be a part of such a program. And what about his father, Swift Fox? Surely he would not have agreed to it.

As if in answer to his thoughts, he heard in his head, *She may not have clear memories of it, but we brought her to this ship several times, beginning when she was a young girl. When she reached the proper age, our people harvested eggs from her to help us with our program. And no, she was not forced. She agreed to help us in our time of need, before she even knew your father, though her agreement was not exactly the same as you use in your everyday life. As a result, one of the female beings here is related to you. You might even think of her as your sister. You will meet her at another time.*

"I am not a space creature," Joe retorted loudly. "I was born of my mother, Little Moon, and Swift Fox is my father. She told me the story of my birth many times."

Yes, you were. However, prior to your birth, her genetic information was mixed with ours, then placed back inside her to grow to fulfillment. Thus, you came into being. Long before you were born, the one I said was your sister was inside your mother for three months and then removed for final development on board here.

Completely stunned, Joe thought it simply could not be true. He'd never had a sister. On the other hand, how could he be here in this place, wherever it was? Surely this must all be a dream and he would soon awaken on the mesa he had climbed in the night, or even back at his camp nearby. He felt scared, angry, and confused all at the same time.

We know that this is a lot for you to take in at one time. Please be patient.

"Take me back! Take me home!" Joe shouted. "I want no part of all this. This must be a dream. Let me wake up and be back home."

Let me assure you that you will return home safely, but we want you to stay with us for a short period of time. Think of this as part of your vision quest. You came on your vision quest to seek out your identity, to become a man amongst your people. Now it is time for you to understand who you really are and how to use the abilities you have. We have much to teach you. We appreciate how difficult this must be for you at the moment. We will give you time to become accustomed to it.

"But if I don't return to my village soon, my family will be worried," Joe countered.

We are sorry for any concern this might cause your family. Please be patient. I will leave you to rest now. Markel turned and walked from the room.

Patient? How could he rest, not knowing what would happen next? He didn't even know where this place was, but he knew he must be a long way from home. When he looked around him, what he saw appeared so totally different from anything he had ever seen, either in his village or in Blanding, that he felt as bewildered as a small child. While these rooms with their curved walls reminded him a little of his hogan at home, nothing else appeared the same. The light came from the walls themselves, not from a lantern. The floor felt soft, like a rug, but was not a rug. The chairs were not at all like those at school or at home. And the people, if that is what they were, were totally strange.

Two days later, after Joe had been thoroughly briefed on his heritage and about the history of the Star People, Markel led him to the cavernous hangar bay where they kept their space craft. Joe's eyes opened wide at the sight. Different shapes and sizes of craft rested there. He saw several shaped like the one that had appeared on top of the mesa the night they brought him here, and some large craft shaped like the long squashes in his mother's garden. Markel led him over to one of the disk craft. Admiring its silvery surface, Joe reached out to touch the ship and instantly felt a mild shock run up his arm. Startled, he jerked his hand back, much as he had that night on the mesa.

You may put your hand on it, Markel said.

Joe laid his hand on it again and experienced the same sensation, but knowing what to expect, didn't react as before.

Markel said, *You might think of this craft as alive, not just an inert piece of machinery. As long as its energy source functions correctly, it is ready to interact or fly.*

Totally fascinated now, Joe peered underneath, and found that rather than resting on wheels, like the old truck in his village, it had legs with solid flat plates on the ends. He didn't see any door or windows, though he remembered that a door had opened in the one that brought him here.

Would you like to learn how to fly it?

"What?" Joe wasn't sure he'd heard correctly.

Would you like to learn to fly this craft? Markel repeated.

He had not even imagined that possibility. Could he really fly this thing? What if he failed? Though scared, Joe knew he could only say yes. Where this adventure would take him, he could not imagine, but it surely would be one he would never forget.

3

Grandmother Two Elks stood at the edge of the village with her daughter, White Dove, and her granddaughter, Little Moon waiting to catch sight of the returning searchers. One of the children had come running to announce, "They're almost here." With hearts full of hope, the women scanned their faces, but saw no smiles, no sign of success. The boy Grandmother knew as Looks-at-Stars, also known by the name Joe Star because the mission teachers had been unable to pronounce his Ute name, had left on his vision quest over two weeks ago. When he didn't come back, Little Moon's husband, Swift Fox, had led the other men of the village out to hunt for him. The small party of silent, grim faced men rounded the corner of the canyon wall and entered the village. Scarcely able to meet the eyes of his wife as he neared them, Swift Fox just shook his head, but said nothing. Their worst fear realized, Little Moon and her mother erupted in wails of grief. Swift Fox reached out to hold his wife. Grandmother's face remained unchanged.

Later, at the evening fire, Swift Fox finally spoke, "We finally found his camp, but the fire bed was cold. He had not slept there for many days." He shrugged his shoulders. "Maybe he fell somewhere. Maybe he was taken by a bear or lion. I hoped that we might at least find . . . something to bring home." He paused, eyes filled with tears, and shook his head. "Nothing. No tracks. No animal tracks either. It's like he disappeared into the air. It has been so long now, with no food or water, he would be . . ." He left the word unsaid. "We finally gave up and came home."

Wrapped in her blanket by the fire, Grandmother sat in the hogan she shared with her family, rocking to and fro. The other two women wept openly, but no tears slid down her own broad wrinkled face. For her, not finding Joe's body was good news. She'd nodded and smiled at Swift Fox's words about Joe disappearing into the air. Had they forgotten who this young man was? Her mind flashed back to Joe's difficult birth. She'd known then who he was.

* * *

After many long hours of labor, Grandmother had been relieved when she first spotted the baby's black hair emerging and knew that it was not turned backward, as they had feared. The baby's unusually large head made the birth quite painful for Little Moon. Grateful when her ordeal was over, Little Moon had simply held the baby and murmured, "Isn't he beautiful? Isn't he beautiful?" What else would she expect Little Moon to say? Grandmother had merely nodded and smiled. But to her, the baby's large almond eyes made him look more like one of the star people than a Ute child. She also recalled how difficult it had been for the baby, with his uncommonly small mouth, to nurse at Little Moon's full breasts. Even with help from White Dove and Grandmother, many frustrating and tear-filled sessions passed before the nursing began to go smoothly.

In her mind, she replayed that first ominous scene many years earlier when Little Moon came running in from the garden at age five to tell of her newfound playmate, the shiny ball that hummed. With sinking hearts, she and White Dove exchanged a knowing glance and shook their heads. It must be happening all over again. Each in turn had known such a ball and knew all too well what it meant. Would the women in this family ever be free from... them? Even now, her stomach clenched at how powerless they had been to protect the little girl.

Later that same day as Little Moon played nearby, Grandmother went to the back of their hogan and brought out something she had never shown to the girl and tossed it to her. Sewn carefully from dried rabbit skins was a ball about the same size as the one she had seen near the gardens. Little Moon caught it and smiled when she held the soft fur to her cheek. Grandmother told of making it many years ago, using milkweed pod down for stuffing so it would land gently, like the real balls did sometimes. She told Little Moon, "I used to play a game with some of the other old ones by tossing it around the circle. We called it the Soft Lander.

Over the years, she and White Dove had gradually shared and pieced together more details of their own memories from the times they had been taken by the star beings in a flying disc to some giant hogan in the sky. Several times, each in turn had thought herself pregnant, only to later to have their wombs suddenly be empty. Both had wept bitterly for the babies who had never suckled at their breasts, never known their love.

Several other times as she was growing up, Little Moon spoke of following such a ball away from the garden and then remembering nothing until much later when she returned, having noticed the odd way that the sun had slipped in the sky and that her woman's parts were sore. More than once, all had suspected she was pregnant, only later to have the baby disappear, just like her mother and grandmother before her. The only exception to that pattern occurred the time shortly before Little Moon's joining ceremony with Swift Fox. That time it had resulted in the birth of Looks-at-Stars only eight moons after their joining.

Grandmother remembered well an exchange between mother and daughter about it. Swift Fox had come to stay in the village before their joining, so that he and Little Moon could prepare for their life together by building their own hogan. All the men and women of the village assisted in various ways. The men helped lay the logs of the walls and roof and brought dirt to insulate the sides and top. The women made pottery and baskets for cooking and eating and wove rugs for use on the floor and as hangings for the walls.

One day, while the hogan was under construction, Grandmother heard White Dove ask, "Little Moon, why are you not eating your breakfast? You need your food to work."

Little Moon responded, "I can't eat, Mother. I feel sick. Maybe later."

Her mother frowned, but said nothing. But as the morning sickness continued daily, she worried, and finally asked, "Have you lain with Swift Fox?"

Little Moon had fired right back, "No! How dare you ask that, Mother? You know I would not do that. I love Swift Fox, but we will not share a bed until after our joining ceremony." Tightlipped and silent, she had stomped away.

* * *

Grandmother remained by the fire and sorted through her memories, the privilege of being an elder, she thought. So now she listened to their grief, sorry for their pain, but did not share it. At the moment, she thought it unlikely that either woman would be able to hear her idea that perhaps Looks at Stars, Joe, might be with the star people. While it was certainly possible that he had died, it was equally possible that he had been taken in the flying disc and would be returned in due time. She recalled his naming ceremony at age four. They had given him the name, Looks-At-Stars, because, as a little one, he had spent so much time looking at the night sky. When asked why, occasionally he would plaintively say, "I want to go home." But they had not understood. She would offer her thoughts another time.

4

A Week Later

Little Moon paused after stepping out of her hogan. High canyon walls, their red color deepened by the setting sun, led her eyes upwards to where an eagle wheeled about in the deep blue sky above. Did it carry the spirit of her son, Looks-at-Stars? Her heart lurched with sadness over the loss of her only child. He'd been gone for over three weeks now. For the last week, after Swift Fox returned, she had slept little and could hardly bring herself to eat anything at all. Day after day, her sadness ruled her life. She still winced at images of the pain that she imagined he must have experienced in whatever way he died. Her heart ached with longing to hold him to her breast once again. If only she could have been there to protect him. With a sigh she resigned herself to the emptiness in her heart and their hogan and continued on to the garden to gather food.

She was so absorbed in her own grief that when the silver ball appeared, after so many years of absence, she felt only confusion and dismay. She had not seen it since before Joe's birth. Why had it come now? What did they want with her today? She knew, however, that she might as well follow it, as she had long ago. It led her to that same small clearing in the cedars, below and out of sight of the village. Arriving there, she heard a humming sound, faint at first, then louder. She looked up and saw more clearly than ever before, the round disc descending slowly out of the sky. As it neared the ground, her hair loosened and floated up, similar to when lightning was imminent. Too fearful to run away, she stepped back to the edge of the clearing and waited while it extended its landing legs and settled to the ground. From somewhere deep inside her mind, she thought that she herself had been in just such a craft, but the memory seemed so faint, she couldn't be sure whether it was real or imagined. In a few moments a door lifted open in the side of the disc and Joe stepped down to the ground. She hardly dared believe her eyes. Maybe it was a ghost playing a cruel trick on a grieving mother's heart.

"Joe?" She called out tenuously, "Is that you?"

"Yes Mother, it's me. I'm home," Joe walked quickly to her outstretched arms. Tears flowed as they clasped each other tightly, until Joe turned back toward the craft, where the door had silently closed, leaving the skin seamless. Joe waved goodbye as the craft silently lifted off the ground, retracted the legs into its belly, and shot up into the sky, disappearing from view.

With a lump in her throat, Little Moon said, "I'll run ahead and tell everyone that you are back, Joe, that you are alive!"

Joe lay his hand on her shoulder, "No, let's go together, Mother," as they started up the path.

The evening fires had been lit and the other women were busy with cooking when Joe and his mother walked into the village. Little Moon saw, by the astonished looks on the faces of the women and children, that they too wondered if what they saw was a spirit or ghost. Not until Joe smiled and lifted his hand in a familiar greeting did they fully recognize him and rush to welcome him.

The men of the village were more reserved. Though extremely rare, it was not unheard of for a young man to abandon his vision quest. After their search, Swift Fox and the other men had believed him dead. Now, to see him walk into the village, whole and healthy, raised the other question in their minds. They could only wait to hear what he had to say for himself. Sometimes after their vision quest, young men would tell stories of their adventures. Other times, they shared little. Joe said nothing at all.

Swift Fox knew the men harbored their suspicions and wanted ask him what he knew, but Joe had not told him anything. They would all have to wait, as it was not considered proper to ask. They all did agree that Joe had a new sense of confidence. He seemed to know himself, which, after all, was the purpose of the quest.

5

Early 1942

Joe turned over again on his sleeping mat near the outer wall of their hogan. The dying embers of the fire gave enough light to allow his eyes to follow the stream of smoke to its exit hole centered above it, then roam along the circular network of logs that held up the roof. On the other side of the room, the sounds of heavy breathing from his mother and grandmothers confirmed their deep slumber. He longed for sleep, but it continued to elude him. Many nights had passed since he'd read in the newspaper at the trading post about the attack on Pearl Harbor. He almost wished he'd not gone to the mission school and learned the white man's language. At the post office, the words, "I WANT YOU," printed under the image of Uncle Sam pointing a finger at him, disturbed him the most. Young men of the nation were asked to join up to fight the war. Was this his war too? Uncle Sam didn't look like his people, the Utes. Should he go? Who would care for his mother and grandmother if he went? His father, Swift Fox, had died two years previously of a sudden illness, only three years after Joe had returned from his vision quest. Since he had no brothers or sisters, Joe had become the sole support for his mother and grandmothers. His mother would have no other family, except for Grandmother Two Elks, who was quite old and needed care, and lived with him and his mother now. Well, they wouldn't really be *all* alone, he reasoned. Others in their village would look after them.

Too restless to remain still on his mat, he rose, slipped on his moccasins and heavy fleece jacket, and stepped out into the winter night. As always, the bright stars drew his eyes upward. In one direction lay the star pattern they called the Archer, the warrior. Did it now call him to war? To the north hung the constellation he knew as the Water Gourd, the one the white man called the Big Dipper. Its outer edge always pointed to the North Star. He'd long ago learned to use it to orient himself when away from the village. He wished it would point the way for him now. Did it want him to remain home to care for his family? And what might the Star People say? He knew they were up there somewhere, though it had been five years since he'd last seen Markel.

He shivered in the cold night air. War meant killing. Could he allow himself to be trained to kill another human being. Though an expert hunter, he hunted only to provide food for his family. He never liked taking a life, even of an animal. Whenever he did kill, he always whispered a prayer of thanks to the spirit of the mule deer or other animal for giving its life in order that his own could be sustained. He understood and accepted this natural order. But killing other humans was a different matter.

Then there was the whole issue of flying. He wanted to fly. Ever since returning from his quest, where he'd learned to fly the saucer, he'd longed to fly again. The military airplanes that regularly crossed the skies above their canyon home beckoned him. But what would it be like to be in the Army of the United States? Knowing how he loved the solitude of the canyons and the quiet life of his village, could he stand to be with so many other people? Could he keep his true identity, his association with the Star People secret? And a final question. Would he himself survive the war? He knew no one could answer that one. He shivered again. Finally, he decided to consult Grandmother and returned to the warmth of his sleeping mat. Perhaps her wisdom could help him resolve his struggle.

The next morning Joe waited until he knew Grandmother was alone in their hogan. He found her sitting on the floor, rocking to and fro by the fire and softly chanting to herself. Her long white braids hung over her favorite wool shawl, which she'd pulled close about her shoulders for warmth. Seeing her broad wrinkled face brought memories of happy times with her throughout his life.

"Grandmother," Joe began as he entered.

Her nearly sightless eyes opened in surprise. "Looks-at-Stars! Yugay." She seldom ever called him by his Anglo name.

Joe proceeded to tell her of his intense desire to fly and of his inner conflict about going away to war, the many concerns that tumbled through his mind and heart, concerns about leaving his family, about fighting and killing. He finished by asking, "Grandmother, you are wise. Though I know I have to make my own decision, I value your advice." He waited in silence.

Grandmother poked the embers in the fire pit with a stick, sending new spirals of smoke up and out the smoke hole in the roof. Finally she spoke. "Why is it that you want so much to fly? You are not an eagle or a hawk. Great Spirit gave them wings with which to soar, but to you he gave feet for walking."

Joe smiled, remembering back to that spring day when it had all started at the mission school where his parents had sent him at age eight. To answer her, he began telling the story of seeing an airplane for the first time.

"It happened the year I was twelve and about to finish school. To celebrate the end of the school year, the missionaries piled all the kids my age into the back of an old truck and set out southeast for a day long trip to the town of Blanding. There, after more than an hour of travel, I saw more white people than I ever knew existed. My exposure to goods at the small trading post near the school had not prepared me for what I saw in the stores in town.

Midday brought the time for eating the food we'd brought with us, the meal the teachers called a picnic. I was playing with the other boys after the meal, when I heard a great racket in the sky. I looked up to see what I thought at first was a giant bird. But as it flew closer, I could see it was a big flying machine with two silver wings on each side and a motor at the front of its bright red body. The loud noise of the engine drowned out our talk as it swooped over our heads. All I could see of the man above the cockpit was his head, with goggles over his eyes and the wind streaming through his hair. I wanted to know what that felt like to be up there, to see the earth from the sky."

"Yes, I remember when you came home and told that story," Grandmother nodded her head.

"Ever since that time, Grandmother, I have wished I could fly."

"I've seen you watching the eagles for hours at a time. Maybe the Great Spirit will turn you into an eagle and then you can fly," She chuckled, and though her eyes were cloudy, her voice sparkled. "But, I don't see you growing wings or feathers yet."

Joe remained silent for some time. There was another story to tell, his other connection to flying. Could he actually speak of it to Grandmother? His vision quest experience? He had never told anyone, though he believed his mother somehow must know, especially after she had seen the way he had returned. Ever since he'd learned to fly that saucer-shaped spaceship, he had wanted to fly here too. The frequent sound and sight of military planes flying overhead, especially since the war began, fed that desire. Every time he saw an airplane, he longed to be at the controls. How would flying such a simple craft with actual wings compare with his experience in the space craft? In the end, his longing to be fully understood won out and he began.

"There is more, Grandmother, a long story."

"I like stories, Little One." She often used the name she'd used when he was a young child before he was named.

Joe proceeded to tell her of his vision quest, his terror at being taken up into the sky, learning about the Star People, and then of being taught to fly their craft. As he spoke, he glanced frequently at Grandmother to gauge her reaction to what he was saying. It must sound unbelievable and he expected that at any moment she would laugh at him. Instead, he noted her frequent nods, as if she really understood. He felt especially anxious when he told her the part about his mixed heritage and that he might even have a sister there. To his surprise, she continued to nod.

"There. Now you have the whole story, Grandmother. I've never told anyone, not even Mother. I know this must sound crazy, but that's the reason I wish to fly."

Grandmother poked the fire again and laid two more sticks on the fire bed, nodding silently as it flared to life. As the silence lengthened, Joe expected to be dismissed. Eventually, she raised her eyes, as if seeing some distant scene, then turned her full gaze to him. "Now I must tell <u>you</u> a story."

"I listen, Grandmother."

"Your face is dim to these old eyes, but I hear in your voice that you thought I would not believe you."

"Yes, Grandmother. I did fear you would laugh."

"I did not laugh, Looks-at-Stars, because I know that you speak truth."

Surprised, Joe's eyes opened wider.

"You see, I too know the Star People, and so do your mother and grandmother, but your father never did."

"But then, it must be . . ."

"Listen, Little One. Just listen." Grandmother went on to describe how she, White Dove, and Little Moon had been lifted to the skies many times. Each time, they were told not to remember, but as the years went by and the women shared a home together, they remembered more and more. At different times, they each had thought they were carrying babies, only to have them later disappear after one of their trips up there. Her eyes grew moist with tears when she told of their deep sadness for the babies they'd never suckled, never held, and never had a chance to love.

"When your mother became aware she carried you inside, especially when she swore that she had not yet lain with your father, Swift Fox, we feared that they would take you from her and keep you, like the others. But for some reason they left you, and though your birth was difficult – your head was big – we were overjoyed. Throughout your childhood, I feared that they would come for you. As a young boy you always studied the night sky. That's how you got your name, Looks-at-Stars, you know. When sometimes I heard you say that you wanted to go home, I knew for sure that you are part Star People, and yes, I can believe you might have a sister up there just like you."

She continued, "I do not have many years remaining on this earth, and I have wanted to you to know this story before I died. When you were gone so long on your quest and then refused to speak of your adventures when you returned, I believed in my heart you had been with them, that you knew who you really are. Now you no longer need to doubt."

Joe sat for a long time, absorbing all that she had said. He gazed at this stooped old woman whom he knew as his beloved Great Grandmother, her skin wrinkled and leathery from long years in the sun. He wondered what it must have been like to keep this story to herself all this time. Then he thought of his mother. Finally, he spoke softly, "And my mother, Little Moon, is she also part of them?"

"No, she was born from the love of your grandfather and grandmother, at least as far as I know." A tear slid down the channels in one cheek. "I look forward to joining Grandfather again soon when I too go to Great Spirit. And you, Little One, you must listen to your heart. Let Great Spirit guide you. Long ago, our people were warriors, but have not been for generations. Perhaps you are called to be a warrior now, a sky warrior. Listen well." With that, she lapsed into silence, her eyes closed, and her chin drooped slowly toward her chest.

After a time, Joe rose quietly to his feet to leave the hogan. At the entrance he turned toward Grandmother and silently thanked her for telling him the story. He vowed to tell his mother that they no longer need to keep secrets between them, even if they chose not to share with others in their village. Then he paused. Were there others in their village who knew the Star People? Or people in other villages? And what of the white man? Did they too know the Star People? Calmer inside, though still uncertain of his path, he felt confident that he could listen to his own heart and to Great Spirit. He would soon know what he must do.

6

March 17, 2000
McPherson, Kansas

Brian Nelson's eyes fluttered open in the predawn half-light. In a sheer panic, he found himself all wound up in his bed covers, sweating and breathless. He knew he had been dreaming, but couldn't make sense of the images. A vague impression of a strange airplane cockpit and instrument panel flashed through his mind. In the dream he'd been flying through a canyon, frantically twisting and turning to keep from crashing. Finally, he could hold it off no longer and his aircraft slammed into the river, jerking him from his dream and leaving him trembling. Some dream! He wished he could recall more details. He disentangled himself and began to breathe easier.

In a ritual familiar to many couples, he slid his leg over to Betty Jean's side of the bed to say hello and good morning, as he'd done every day for the many years they had been married. Not finding her foot and wondering where she was, he slipped his hand over to her side to gauge by the remaining warmth how long she had been up. The sheets were cold. She must have been up for some time.

Then it hit him, like a punch in his gut. He remembered. BJ wasn't there. She hadn't been for many days and never would be again. Now he recalled what lay ahead today. Her funeral. His heart a black hole of pain, scenes of her last days at the hospital flashed through his mind: her body emaciated by the cancer; her final words, "I love you, Brian," before she slipped into a coma; saying his own ultimate goodbye at the funeral home viewing. How would he get through this day? So unreal.

Brian went to the closet to get his dark suit. He buckled his belt one hole smaller than usual. Hmm. His long sleeved white shirt hung loosely on his frame. At age forty four and already slender, his five foot eleven inch frame now seemed gaunt. Not surprising to have lost weight in the last few weeks.

The unreality of the day hit him again as he stood before the bathroom mirror. He'd automatically reached for his favorite red necktie, but stopped himself. Too bright. Best choose the dark blue one. Looking in the mirror, he couldn't help but notice how fatigue had furrowed his forehead and his once dark brown hair now showed more salt and pepper gray. How foreign to put on his suit on a Thursday morning and have both his sister Ann and BJ's brother Roger in the house at the same time, as well as both girls home from college.

It just didn't seem possible that BJ was gone. He should be able to turn to see her coming into the bathroom and say good morning, like always. Numb and with a heavy step, Brian descended to the kitchen to start coffee in their big party pot. Some party, he thought, glancing at the counter nearly covered with food people had brought. None of it even looked good, though he appreciated the generosity of their friends and neighbors.

The 10:00 a.m. service at the First Methodist Church came and went in a blur. They had attended there as a family ever since their girls, Jenny and Jackie, had been born. BJ was so well liked in this town they called home, it was no surprise that people filled the church to capacity for her funeral. He made it through the service, though with difficulty when people rose to speak of BJ in glowing terms. But he almost lost it when he and the girls followed the casket out the east doors of the church, to be seated in the mortuary car, while the casket was slid into the hearse. Though the sky threatened snow at any moment, as was the custom in this Kansas farming community of twelve thousand, nearly everyone attending lined up their cars in the parking lot for the processional to the cemetery south of town. By the time they got there, the first white streaks of wind-driven snow marred their vision. Brian shivered in the March wind as he stepped from the mortuary limo. Jenny, slender and brunette like her mother, emerged next, followed by Jackie, blond, slightly plump, with BJ's heart-shaped face. Brian reached for a hand of each as they followed the minister and the pall bearers to the grave.

Entering the north-facing funeral tent, which did little to protect them from the sting of the wind-blown snow, Brian found their place in the front row of chairs, with Jackie on his left and Jenny on his right. Nearby sat his sister and BJ's brother. Behind were other members of the family. Only one person was missing, Betty Jean, BJ, or 'Beej,' as he loved to call her. And yet she really wasn't missing either. Directly in front of them, covered with the flowers, sat her shiny silver casket containing what was left of her after the cancer. Through tears, Brian looked out across the gravestones to where the tall reddish-brown prairie grasses waved in flight before the northeast wind and the snow. The idea that she would lie in that cold yawning hole forever was almost more than his heart could bear. The words of the minister only enhanced his pain.

And then it was over. They stood and hugged each other, cried some more and accepted the well-meant condolences of friends and neighbors. The snow storm that would normally have had them dressed in parkas, mittens and stocking caps, easily pierced their dress clothes, underscoring the austerity of the occasion. So they returned to the cars before her casket was lowered into the cement vault and covered with dirt. After all, how many times could he say goodbye? In a way, Brian felt glad it was over.

God, as if it could ever really be over! But at least the endless days and nights of B.J.'s dying were over, the sixty mile trips back and forth to Wesley Medical Center in nearby Wichita, where she'd wasted away, slowly at first, and then all too rapidly. They'd found the cancer too late to be able to do anything about it. The surgery attempt had confirmed that the disease had gone beyond those other heroic, but usually futile efforts such as radiation or chemotherapy. Bitterness crept in around the edges of his grief. Why did it have to happen to her? Her absence was an ache that gnawed at him inside, much like the cancer that ate her from inside her uterus.

Back at the house, they sought to warm their hearts as well as their bodies. All the well-wishers that came and went throughout the afternoon only added to the exhaustion that had been building over the last few weeks. Thankfully, due to the snow, his sister and brother-in-law decided to leave early to drive home. By seven p.m., the three of them were finally alone. The girls changed into jeans and sweatshirts and plopped down at the kitchen table.

"You girls hungry?" Brian asked. None of them had eaten much all day, only snacks.

"Yeah, sort of," Jenny said.

Brian surveyed the spread of cakes and pies on the counter, then opened the fridge to see two pans of lasagna, a tuna casserole, a quiche, and a bowl of salad.

"Any of that look good to you guys? We can warm it up in the microwave."

"It sort of looks good," Jenny said, "but not really, if I'm honest."

Jackie spoke up. "Dad, could we just order in a pizza? Maybe have it with that salad?"

"Yeah, why not?" He brightened up enough to smile. It even sounded good to him. He went to the phone.

Over pizza they talked about their memories, alternately crying their grief and laughing at remembered incidents across the years. No one seemed to want to go to bed yet.

Jackie sat on the floor with her arm around Sadie, their old golden retriever. "Mom gave us so much. I don't know how I would have made it through high school without her. Remember that time when all my girlfriends were down on me because I didn't want to go party with them when they were drinking. Mom always encouraged us to do what we thought was right. Glad I didn't go. Lucky they weren't all killed in the car crash that night."

"Yeah, she always made so much sense when I was going nuts over boys, or about what to wear, or how to fix my hair," Jenny said. "Feels like I ought to be able to call out, 'Mom?', and she'd answer, like always."

They talked far into the night, unconsciously reconfiguring themselves as a family, acknowledging without words, that things would never be the same. Finally, their emotions drained enough for sleep to be welcome, with one last hug, they went up to bed.

7

April 18, 2001
Blanding, Utah

Brian Nelson stepped out of his room at the Best Western Motel on the northeast edge of Blanding. He yawned, stretched his arms over his head, took a deep breath of the spring air, and decided that his jeans, sport shirt, and windbreak were adequate for the day. He tugged on the door to make sure it was locked, then headed for his car. He reached his hand up to smooth back his thick brown hair. At least there's something there to ruffle, he thought. Not like some of his friends who were losing theirs already and had a paunch or more to go with it. He was glad he paid attention to his eating and still maintained his trim waistline.

He folded himself into his Land Rover, pulled out of the motel parking lot, drove south from town to the airport, where he turned west on the paved entry road leading to the airport. He parked on the south side of the airport office, stepped out of his Rover, and let his eyes scan the unobstructed view of mountains on the horizon to the west. How nice to be out of the crush of tourists in Moab and breathe the desert air. He had been pleased to see some Native Americans on the street yesterday afternoon when he came into Blanding.

He marveled for a moment that what had begun as a vacation ten days ago had now turned into something much more, a real spiritual quest. The mantle of grief he'd worn from the death of his wife, BJ, last year, felt lighter. He shrugged his shoulders, as if to throw off its last vestige, and surveyed the airfield itself. From the number of planes tied down on the ramp, it looked like an active airport for such a small town. Maybe he could rent a plane and go flying. He reached back into the car to extract his pilot log book from the glove box.

On opening the door of the FBO office, the aroma of fresh coffee welcomed him. Though they didn't match, the green overstuffed couch and grey recliner chair nearby sure looked like they would provide comfort for visiting pilots. The largest window looked west out onto the ramp and the planes tied down there. His eyes scanned the room, taking in the large aviation map of the United States that embellished one whole wall, while on another, a black display board with white plastic letters showed the price of gas and the rental prices for the planes. He could rent a Cessna 172 here for about the same rate that he paid back home in McPherson, Kansas. Only $45 per hour with gas. No one was in the office, so he opened the door into the attached hangar, where he saw a dark haired, khaki clad man bending over the engine of a beautiful yellow Super Cub.

"Hello there," Brian called out. "I'm looking for the airport operator."

"Well, you found him," the man replied, turning to straighten up and wipe his hands on a shop rag. "What can I do for you?"

From the man's brown skin and high cheek bones, Brian surmised he was Native American, though he didn't have the round face he'd seen on others in town. "I'm visiting here in town and I'd like to see about getting checked out in the 172 you have for rent, do a little flying." Brian held out his hand to the tall slender man. "My name is Brian Nelson."

"Joe Star," he grasped Brian's hand. "Welcome to Blanding. Just passing through, or are you going to be here a while? Tourists don't usually stop here to fly."

"I'm not exactly sure how long I'll be here," Brian said, "but I want to hang around long enough to explore the area. I started out from Kansas a couple of weeks ago and stopped in Moab, but I got tired of all the tourists. So I came on down here to spend some time hiking in the canyons and maybe explore Anasazi sites."

"Well, we do have a lot of both of those." Joe raised his eyebrows and hesitated before he continued, "You can't very well do that from the air."

"I'd like to fly over the area to get the lay of the land before I start hiking. Besides, I haven't been up for a while, and want to get back in the air again. I don't want to let my skills get rusty. By the way, that sure is a beautiful Cub you're working on there. Is it yours?"

"Yeah, this is my beauty," Joe admitted. "Just finished up the annual inspection. She's all ready to go now for another year. So, you want to fly the 172, huh? How much time do you have in a 172?"

"A little more than 400 hours," Brian answered. "Though I haven't flown now for almost a month."

"We require a one-hour check ride here to make sure that you're safe in the aircraft. How does that sound?"

"Sounds reasonable to me," Brian said. "When could you fit it into your schedule?"

"Oh, most any time. Give me a chance to button up the Cub here, and we can go out this morning. The winds aren't too squirrelly this time of the morning, so it should be a good time to fly. Help yourself to a cup of coffee there if you want and grab a Denver sectional map out of the rack in the office and familiarize yourself with the area."

Brian went back into the office and spread out the air map that included Blanding and nearby Canyonlands area. Then he poured a little powdered creamer an into a Styrofoam cup, filled it with coffee from the pot, and returned to the counter to study the map. He identified the two eleven-thousand foot mountain peaks he'd seen yesterday about fifteen miles north of town, Mt. Abajo and Mt. Linneaus, and noted something called Comb Ridge a few miles southwest of the airport. As big as it appeared on the map, it must be a prominent feature, both from the air and the ground. He looked forward to seeing all these features from the plane.

* * *

While Joe closed up the Cub and made the required entry in the aircraft log book, he wondered about this stranger. Was he a pot hunter, seeking to steal artifacts from Anasazi sites? Surely he knew it was a federal offense that could land him in jail. Maybe he thought he was smart enough to get away with it. Even some of the locals got caught and ended up in jail for that. We'll see.

After putting the log book away, Joe entered the office and asked, "Do you have your pilot's license and log book?"

"Yes, I do." Brian removed his license from his wallet and passed it across the counter, along with his log book.

Joe pulled the pre-flight checklist for the Cessna from beneath the counter and handed it to Brian. "Here, take the checklist and go on out and do the pre-flight while I look these over."

Joe watched the slender man in blue jeans and long sleeved sport shirt go out the door. His pilot license showed an address in McPherson, Kansas and his Pilot Log book appeared up to date, with 427 hours recorded, most of it in a 172, with some initial hours in a Cessna 152. Maybe he should ask to see the man's driver's license, to compare the photo to see that it matched. The guy looked about 45 to 50 years old.

"Everything looks shipshape," Brian said, re-entering the office a few minutes later. "You keep the airplane remarkably well maintained."

"Can't afford not to. This country is unforgiving. Not as many places to make emergency landings as you have back in Kansas, so I like to keep it in top condition. Let me see your driver's license so I can write down your address on our renter card here."

"Sure." Brian pulled out his wallet again.

"Go on out to the plane and I'll be with you in a minute." Everything checked out. He matched the description on the Kansas driver's license: 45 years old, 5' 10" tall, 160 lbs., brown eyes, brown hair. Well, it didn't hurt to be cautious.

Brian went out and climbed into the left seat of the plane and scanned the instrument panel to familiarize himself with the layout. In a few minutes, Joe joined him at the airplane, returned both licenses and the log book, and then buckled into the right seat. "You ready to go?"

Nodding, Brian asked, "Anything special I should know about the plane?"

"Nope. She's stock Cessna. Crank up when you are ready."

Brian went through the normal startup procedure, then taxied down to the run-up area at the south end of the runway, and waited while the engine warmed up.

"Do you know about density altitude?" Joe asked.

"A little," Brian responded, "enough to know how to lean the engine at altitude."

"Well, here we're already at a high altitude compared to Kansas, so we have to lean before we get off the ground to get the best power. When you do your run-up, lean the engine before you check the mags. Run it up to about 1750 rpm, lean it with the mixture control until it starts to drop in RPM, then enrich it a couple of half turns. After that, go ahead and check your mags and carburetor heat. Our altitude here is 5865 MSL, so this time of year we are already at 8000 feet density or more. In the summer it can get up to as much as 9,000 or 10,000 feet, right here on the ground, so we're a high altitude airport without even trying. Pay attention to that, or it will bite you big-time, especially if you're trying to take off from a dirt airstrip out in some hot canyon. There's not much left but bits and pieces after you fly into a canyon wall."

Brian followed Joe's directions for leaning and mag checks. "Back in Kansas I was taught to take off with full rich mixture," Brian commented, after having completed the run-up check. "We might do better if we leaned there too, especially in summer."

"Yeah, I imagine so. Let's go whenever you're ready," Joe said.

Brian taxied out onto the runway, lined up heading north, and pushed the throttle all the way in. He noticed that the plane did feel more sluggish than back home in Kansas. He was surprised at how much effect the high density altitude had on the airplane's performance, though with a 6000 foot runway, he had plenty of room to take off. At McPherson, he seldom used more than 1000 feet for take-off.

"Let's go on up to about 8000 feet and do some stalls, so you can see how she performs," Joe said. Brian followed Joe's directions. After a series of steep turns, Brian felt his confidence return.

"When you get out over the canyons," Joe said, "it's easy to get confused if you're watching the ground too closely. But most anywhere in this region, you can point yourself north and see those two mountain peaks north of town, or Comb Ridge southwest of town, and reorient yourself. But if you're flying low, watch out for the updraft on the west side of the Comb and the downdraft on the east side, so it doesn't surprise you. The wind usually flows from west to east here. Let's head over there now and see what it's doing."

As they approached Comb Ridge from the east, Brian was startled by how the downdraft plummeted them almost below the top of the ridge. He had to apply full power to climb up over the ridge, at which point the updraft suddenly jolted them upward. "Wow, I see what you mean," Brian stabilized the plane, then wiped the sweat from his forehead. He continued to climb up to the altitude Joe requested and went through another series of steep turns, and both power off and power on stalls.

"Okay, let's head back to the airport and shoot a few landings," Joe directed. When they approached the airport, Joe said, "I'll do the first one, to show you how we like it done out here. You follow through. Just be aware that the air is thinner, so your sink rate will be much higher at this altitude, so we start our final approach at a higher altitude than you might normally use. And don't let it get too slow." Brian kept his hands on the control yoke and his feet on the rudder pedals to feel what Joe did, but surrendered the throttle. After the wheels touched the threshold of the runway, Joe retracted the flaps, pushed in the throttle, and took off again. "Your plane now," handing off the controls to Brian. Coming around the pattern, Brian felt the aircraft sink rapidly as he glided in on final approach for his first landing and had to apply considerable power to keep from landing too hard.

"You'll get used to it pretty soon. Come in a little higher on final to compensate for the higher sink rate." Joe encouraged. "Let's go around again." After a few more touch-and-go's, Brian learned to feel the air and the plane much better and made several smooth landings. "You'll do all right, I think. At least I don't think you'll go out and kill yourself now, or bend my airplane," Joe commented dryly. "You seem pretty comfortable in the plane. But pay attention to your density altitude and watch out for updrafts and downdrafts over the canyons. They can be pretty tricky, so don't fly down in the canyons until you get a lot more experience. Let's go in now and take a little break while I sign off your check ride in your log book. Then you can go fly for a while to familiarize yourself with the area. Okay?"

When Brian took off again, he headed southwest. He had always appreciated the great visibility in Kansas, but it didn't begin to compare to the pristine clarity of the air here in this desert region. He could easily see 100 miles or more. What a thrill! In the distance, he saw the monoliths of Monument Valley rise like giant statues from the desert floor. He considered swooping down to fly between the huge spires, but decided not to take any unnecessary risks today and turned back north toward Blanding. On return, he made another smooth landing and taxied back to the parking ramp. After tying down the plane, he checked in with Joe and recorded the time on the renter card, which he put in the small file box on the counter.

"Whenever you want to fly, sign up here on the schedule to reserve the plane," Joe turned the ledger so Brian could see it. "I keep the key in the desk drawer here. Don't forget to log the time after each flight," Joe said. "You can pay as you go or I can bill you at the end of the month, if you're going to be here a while."

"Thanks, Joe," Brian replied. "I look forward to flying with you. I think I'll be around for a while, so, if it's okay, I'd prefer to pay at the end of the month."

Brian flew every day for the next week, enjoying the new vistas that unfolded before his eyes. Sometimes he glanced over at the passenger seat, half expecting to see BJ, who had flown so often with him, keeping track of maps, looking up radio frequencies, and spotting landmarks. She would have loved this beautiful country. How empty that seat had felt since she died. How empty he had felt. Though he didn't feel as much pain now as when she first died, he still wished that she were here flying with him. It had been over a year since her death, but he remembered as if it were yesterday.

8

> *"Each man must look for himself to teach him the meaning of life. It is not something discovered, it is something molded."*
> Antoine de Saint Exupery, French aviator and author.

April 26, 2001
Blanding Airport

    Joe leaned his elbows on the counter of the airport office and watched as Brian drove up, parked on the south side of the building, and got out of his car. A nice enough looking man, his brown hair clipped neatly in a conventional haircut, he obviously kept himself fit and trim. Joe found himself rather liking the guy, in spite him being new to town. Brian had been courteous and respectful to everyone from the moment he walked in the door. He never ran others down, even during the friendly banter among the guys who showed up here every day for coffee, most of whom were retired and didn't hesitate to express their opinions and prejudices.
    But the look of intense concentration on Brian's face this morning brought questions to Joe's mind. Who was this guy anyway, and what was he doing here in Blanding? He'd been flying every day for a week now. Why? Was he looking for ruins? Maybe he was a prospector, or worse, a yuppy pot hunter in disguise?
    Joe watched Brian walk into the FBO, pour himself a cup of coffee, drop a quarter in the kitty, and sit down on the couch. "Hey, I found a small furnished apartment yesterday."
    "Gonna stay a while, are you?"
    "Yeah, I think so."
    It still didn't make sense to Joe. "So Brian, what really brings you out to this country? You seem to be more than just passing through. Most folks don't spend more than a few hours here at best, let alone rent an apartment."
    After a long moment of silence, Brian said, "Search and rescue."
    "Search and rescue?" Joe asked, more curious than ever. "That's what I do. What do you mean?"
    "Guess I do need to explain that one."
    "It would help." Joe chuckled.

"A year ago in March, my wife died of cancer. We didn't find it early enough to be able to do anything. So, it's been a hard year for me. I own a Toyota dealership back in McPherson, Kansas, but I have a great manager, who finally persuaded me to take a vacation. Only it's turned into more than a vacation." He paused. "I realize I am searching for where to go next with my life, maybe even rescue my soul in the process."

"Oh." That explained a lot . . . and didn't.

"Flying helps me to think, to get perspective. I've never been through anything so tough, so having time alone, away from my business and . . . ," Brian's voice trailed off. Silence held both of them for several minutes.

Then Joe said quietly, "I understand. I lost a girlfriend during the war, as well as lots of buddies. I don't think it ever completely goes away."

Brian looked up at Joe from where he sat waiting, but nothing more came. Finally he went on, "I've always been fascinated by this part of the world. When I was in college, I took a summer course in archaeology that included a field trip out here. We stayed in Blanding for a couple of weeks that summer to do some excavation and restoration of a cliff dwelling southwest of here. The Anasazi mystery has always fascinated me. A long answer to a short question, eh?"

"It'll do."

"What about you, Joe? How did you get here?"

"I grew up here," Joe said. "I was born out in one of the canyons northwest of town on the other side of the Comb. I tried a few things after the war, but ended up back here, so for me, it's always been home."

"There's something else that draws me here," Brian paused, debating whether to go on. "You believe in reincarnation?"

"My family always regarded our ancestors as very important. They teased us kids about whether one of them had returned, particularly when we did something wrong. They'd say, you're just like your grandfather or something similar. Why do you ask?"

"This is probably going to sound really crazy, but I think I might have lived around here in another lifetime. Perhaps I was even an Anasazi in one of the cliff dwellings somewhere out in canyons. I don't know for sure." He paused to gauge Joe's reaction. Seeing none, he continued, "On the way out here, I stopped in Crestone, Colorado, where I met a psychologist who offered to do a past life regression with me. He used hypnosis to guide me back to a past life out in the canyons some place." Again he paused, scanning Joe's face for any negative reaction. Nothing.

"It was a weird experience, Joe. I saw myself sitting by a fire in front of a kiva-like structure under a large cave overhang, when suddenly I felt the earth shake, probably a small earthquake. I heard a cracking sound from the rock over my head, and before I could move, a big rock slab fell on me. I died quickly before they could pull me out. They had to find a pole large enough to pry the rock up enough to get my body out. I know this must sound bizarre to you. I don't know whether I imagined all this or whether that's what really happened a long time ago. It's what I remembered. So to more fully answer your question, I think I may be here to connect with whether I actually did once live a life here, and maybe resolve any unfinished business. From what I've read, some people believe that we can have lives anywhere in the world and anywhere in time. I'm not yet sure what I think about that. I do know that I feel connected to this country. Hope you don't think I'm nuts."

Joe remained strangely silent, but eventually said in a muted voice, "No."

Then after a long pause, Joe finally broke the silence, "I see you have your hiking boots on today,"

"Yeah, I thought I might take a drive out northwest of town and check out the notation on the topo map of an old Indian village. Was that by any chance where you grew up?"

"Not that one, but close. That's where I went to a missionary school though. The old school building is still standing, as far as I know. It was built of stone and made to last. Not much left of the village where I grew up though. It's a couple of canyons further west. The hogans have all fallen in and there's an old cliff dwelling up above the village." He paused again. "I haven't been out there in years. Guess everybody would rather live in trailers near town now. Course, I can't rightly talk. I live in one too, right here at the airport. Hard to make a living out there anymore. Besides, there's no electricity, so there's no TV."

"Sounds interesting. If you showed me how to get there on a map, do you think anyone would mind if I paid a visit to the school and to your village site?"

After a short silence, Joe said, "Nah. Actually, I own all that property now myself, and the canyon next to it. Sort of came down through my family to me. My mother grew up in one canyon and my father's family lived in one nearby. I can draw you a map."

"Thanks. I really appreciate it," Brian replied, and listened carefully as Joe drew a map and explained how to get to the area.

"If anyone asks what you're doing there, tell'em I gave you permission."

Brian's excitement grew as he drove north from the airport back to town. He looked forward to exploring. After stopping by his apartment to get his daypack and some food and water, he'd headed northwest out of town on Elk Mountain Road. The dense cedars that lined the sides of the winding road limited his view, but from time to time he could orient himself with a glimpse to the west of the distinctively shaped mountain known as Bear's Ears. He decided to explore Joe's home canyon first. About a half-hour out of town, Brian turned north off the gravel road into the valley Joe had drawn on the map. Here the road deteriorated rapidly to a barely passable jeep track, forcing Brian to carefully negotiate its twists and turns.

After a while he came to the mouth of the small canyon Joe had indicated. Cedars growing in the track made it impassable. He'd have to walk the remaining half mile or so, like Joe said. He parked his car, stepped out, and paused to inhale the pungent fragrance of the cedars. Retrieving his walking stick, pack, and water from his car, he started up the canyon. Along the trail he saw raccoon and coyote tracks, but no human footprints. He felt a sense of reverence when he came to the village site. Once the ancestral home for Joe and his extended family, the small cluster of hogans had long ago fallen in, leaving only circular mounds of the dirt which had insulated the outer log walls and roof. He smiled at the sight, for they looked rather like large donuts.

He walked on into the village site. A stark weathered-wood door frame still stood in one donut, marking the east facing entrance, though no windows remained. Could this one have been Joe's home? What was life like here almost a century ago? Off to the east, he saw the clearing where they had probably planted their gardens, now mostly reclaimed by sparse sage brush. Nearby, meandered the stream that Joe mentioned was fed by the deep ever-flowing spring at the very head of the canyon. He followed the stream to the base of the cliff and saw the spring rising within a deep blue-green pool resembling a giant morning glory blossom. The only signs of life were the raccoon tracks in the mud at its edge.

Going back toward the hogans, high canyon walls led his eyes upward. He scanned the north side of the canyon for the cliff dwelling Joe had mentioned. He headed across the valley and sighted a faint trail that climbed upward and disappeared around a little projection in the canyon wall. Though he could see nothing from down here on the canyon floor, maybe that led to the cave or ledge where the cliff dwelling lay. Brian began to climb the rock strewn trail. It had obviously not been used for a long time and he had to watch his footing carefully, yet somehow the trail seemed oddly familiar. When he reached the end of the visible trail, he saw ahead and off to the left what looked like either a cave or deep overhang. As he approached, flashes of familiarity increased his excitement. Deja vu? Climbing still higher and over the jumble of fallen rocks, he mounted the ledge from which a cave extended back into the cliff, sheltering the ruins of a dwelling made of stones, cedar logs, mud, and sticks. Then he froze, his breath stilled and a shiver ran up his back. In front of him lay a scene exactly like what he had viewed during his chilling regression back in Crestone. Under the overhang lay a huge slab of stone about 10 feet in diameter that had fallen from the ceiling of the cave. Could that possibly be the one that had dropped on him? Was this where he had died in that life? It seemed almost too much of a coincidence to believe. But as he poked his way through the ruins, he realized he knew the exact function of each room and which family members had lived where. He forced his breathing back to normal as more details of his regression returned.

    The cave dwelling had long been abandoned, but he spotted a few pot shards, and a large three grooved metate obviously used for grinding grain. He walked to the rock slab that he thought had caused his death and looked beneath it. Though he knew his family had retrieved his body, he found it uncanny, eerie even, to stand here and see the place where he felt he had died so long ago. He surmised that the family must have moved out of the cliff dwelling right after that, and never returned. They would have considered it too dangerous to stay, though some of the rooms actually remained intact. He identified the smoke blackened walls and ceilings of the room where they had cooked their food. Ghostly memories floated to the surface of his mind as Brian wandered around the ruin, now empty of all the voices that had once given it life.

    After a long time, just taking in the scene with reverence, he reluctantly turned to head back to the canyon floor. Dare he let himself believe that his death in that life had actually happened right here on this site? He had not expected his quest to yield such astounding results. Questions rushed to his mind. What did all this mean? Had he been led here in some unknown way? Was this all just fantasy? What should be his understanding of death now? He'd long believed there was something more. This discovery seemed to confirm the notion of reincarnation. Did that mean that he and BJ might have been together before and might be again in some future life? Many questions, but no easy answers yet.

    This strange mixture of questions, feelings, and memories accompanied him back to his car and on back to town. He decided to postpone exploring the old mission school to another time. Should he tell Joe about his find? Surely Joe must have been up there many times as a kid and knew exactly what that ledge looked like. What had Joe thought when he told him the story in the first place, when he described the rock fall? Was this some fantastic coincidence? He shivered.

9

Friday, April 27, 2001

    Returning from her early in morning jogging run out Elk Mountain Road, Sally McNeill slowed to a walk as she entered the Edge of the Cedars Museum parking lot on the northwest corner of Blanding. She turned toward her little yellow house at the end of the street near the museum. Sweat dripped off her forehead and darkened her shorts and long sleeved knit shirt. This morning's run had seemed more difficult than usual and for some reason, getting out of bed today to get started had required a little more effort. Perhaps her body knew that next week would bring her big Four-O birthday. Were it not for her well-entrenched daily habit, and knowing that she would feel better afterward, it would have been easier to punch the alarm off this morning, roll over, and go back to sleep.
    Running had become her way of dealing with the dark shadows of her past, the legacy of her divorce and the terror of the night visitors. She had come a long way in the last ten years, from feeling like a failure and hating her body, to feeling good about herself. She hoped she would never get too old to run. Now, after a three-mile run, indeed she did feel better, with all the endorphins coursing through her bloodstream, bathing her body and brain in their 'go juice,' as she liked to call it. Coming back from Westwater Canyon and up the final rise from Cottonwood Wash seemed a bit tougher than usual, but as the sun rose over the mesa east of Blanding, slanting down her street, she once again felt pleasure in her fit condition and looked forward to a hot shower.
    Approaching her house, she spotted the familiar bundle of orange fur on the back step. The cat rose and arched its back up to meet her outstretched hand. It wasn't really her cat, but seemed to have adopted her and showed up daily, meowing to be fed. She'd never discovered where it slept, but assumed it must be somewhere in the neighborhood. Sally let herself in through the back door, flipped on the coffee maker on the kitchen counter, then headed down the hall, pulling off her long sleeved top and tossing it in the laundry basket by the bedroom. Her sweat soaked jog bra was next. Two days of sweat were enough, she thought, as she pulled it over her head. Phew! That's got to go. She stripped off her running tights and underpants, then dumped the basket of

clothes into the washer, started it, and headed for the shower.

She paused in front of the long mirror on the bathroom door. The cool morning air coming in the bathroom window on her damp body raised goose bumps all over and made her nipples erect. Speaking to her image, she declared, "You're getting older lady, but you sure don't look it. You look better now at forty than you did at twenty." She was proud that she weighed 20 pounds less now. Glancing at herself again, pleased at what she saw . . . not only her firm breasts, but also her flat belly and smooth, taut leg muscles. Turning sideways toward the mirror, she pulled her shoulders back, twisted a little each way, and tightened her belly muscles a bit more to enhance her youthful image. "Not bad, not bad at all!"

She turned the shower on to warm up and gave thanks for the blessing of exercise. Showers were always such a luxury. She enjoyed vigorously massaging her scalp as she shampooed her hair. Toweling down briskly afterward, she felt clean and alive all over, inside and out. A good way to start the day, especially a Friday. While she dressed and brushed her thick auburn hair into a loose semblance of order, her mind jumped ahead to the day with her twenty-three third graders. She reminded herself to call the airport manager when she got to school and ask him about bringing her class out on a field trip next week.

Back in the kitchen, with a cup of fresh coffee at hand, she popped her oatmeal into the microwave to cook for breakfast. While it cooked, she put out food for the cat and hung out her laundry. She had a dryer, but preferred the fresh smell of sunshine in her clothes when the weather permitted. The sight of the snowcapped mountains to the north helped lift her spirits and take her mind away from the dark shadows from her past.

10

April 27, 2001

When Brian arrived at the airport, he debated whether to tell Joe about what he'd experienced yesterday. Would Joe think he was a kook?

"You find the ruins okay?" Joe asked when Brian came in the door at the airport.

"Yep. Very interesting. What a beautiful spot you grew up in, Joe. You must have loved it."

"Yeah, I've even given some thought to building a cabin out there when I retire."

"It would make a great place to live. Could you get electricity out there?"

"Yeah, probably. But it would be expensive. It's a long way from existing power lines. It would probably be cheaper to put in some sort of solar electric system." Then after a pause, "Did you find what you were looking for?"

"Yes, I did."

Silence followed this exchange. Neither appeared eager to pursue the subject. As Brian watched, Joe tipped his mug to drain the last of the coffee and looked over at Brian for several long moments, as if he were considering something important. Brian braced, still worried about what Joe would think of his story. Finally Joe said in a rather quiet, but serious tone of voice, "You want to learn to fly?"

Surprised, Brian looked up at Joe. What does he mean by that question? Surely, there must be more to it than appears on the surface.

"Hey, I already know how to fly. You checked me out in the 172 ten days ago and I've been flying almost daily ever since, as you well know. What do you mean, do I want to learn to fly?"

"Well, I wondered if you'd like to *really* learn to fly, not just drive around in the Cessna, looking at the scenery."

Intrigued now, Brian paused a moment, then asked, "Exactly what do you have in mind?"

"When you showed me your log book, I noticed that you don't have any tail dragger time. I thought you might like to learn to fly the Cub."

"Your Cub?" Brian's eyebrows shot up.

"Yep, my Cub." He spoke in a matter-of-fact tone of voice.

More than a little surprised, Brian rolled that idea around in his head. Joe's Piper Super Cub was a legend around the airport. Not only did Joe keep it immaculately maintained, but he had a reputation of never, ever letting anyone else fly his Cub. Always hangared, its yellow fabric skin got dusted every day, pampered like a member of the family, which it was to Joe. It was his primary plane for search and rescue. Rumor had it that Joe had done things with that 150 horse Super Cub that no other pilot could, that he could land and take off from what others called impossible places, to rescue downed pilots or lost and injured hikers. He'd heard that the sheriff had called on Joe's skill many times over the years.

One eyebrow still raised, Brian looked at him. Was Joe pulling his leg? He saw no hint of a grin on the man's stoic face, so he finally said, "You're serious, aren't you?"

"Yep."

Amongst the guys who came to the airport for coffee each morning, Joe had a reputation as a superb flight instructor and Brian remembered Joe's sure hand on the controls during his check ride in the 172. Learn to fly Joe's Cub? Brian could hardly believe such an offer, but he could not turn it down either. "When do we start?" he asked, sounding calmer than he felt.

"Whenever you're ready." Joe reached under the counter and pulled out a well-worn Owner's Handbook for the Piper Super Cub. "Take this home and study it so's you know it forward and backwards. Don't just read it through. Really study it! Come back when you know it," Joe said as he turned toward the shop.

Before Joe made it through the door, the phone rang. He returned to the counter to answer it. Brian only half listened to the conversation, but heard Joe confirm something for May 5th. After Joe hung up, he said, "Local 3rd grade teacher. Gonna bring her class out to look at airplanes next Friday. That oughta be interesting." With that, he turned and went through the door back into the hangar, returning to whatever task he'd interrupted.

When Joe had handed him the manual, Brian recognized something more than a suggestion. It sounded like a command. With this astounding offer, any thought of flying the Cessna disappeared. He returned to his apartment, where he debated whether to study the handbook or go out to the canyons. Deciding to do both, he made a lunch, stuffed his binoculars and a jacket into his day-pack and headed west out Elk Mountain Road.

At the trail head, the canyon country stretched west as far as he could see. He parked, turned off the engine, and sat listening to the quiet. High and to his left a golden eagle wheeled, riding a thermal, and further in the distance, not much more than a black dot against the clouds, a vulture hunted for its lunch. For such a sparsely vegetated land, Brian saw it as very much alive, especially here in the springtime when wild flowers were popping up and the sage brush turned bright green with new growth on its tips.

This formed the perfect setting to study the Piper Cub Handbook. It wasn't very big, and Brian read it through once in an hour. And then a second time. It actually contained a lot of very valuable information. Charts specified the performance data for the plane, and diagrams showed the control system, the fuel system, and the electrical system. A lot to know for such a simple airplane. Perhaps that's part of what Joe meant about really learning to fly. Though small, Brian began to see why Joe had demanded that he really study the handbook. He tried to commit it to memory, expecting Joe to quiz him on the smallest detail.

When he thought he had absorbed the manual, Brian put his water bottle and lunch in his pack, and started hiking up the trail. While taking in the view and inhaling the fragrance of the cedars warmed by the sun, Brian mentally reviewed, over and over, the contents and diagrams of the manual. He acknowledged a few points he would need to look up and study when he got back to the car or to his apartment, but having seen the Cub several times in the hangar, he had enough of a mental context for the diagrams to make sense.

As he walked, more questions came to mind. What had prompted Joe to want to teach him to fly the Cub? He'd sensed from the beginning that Joe was at least a little suspicious of him and his intentions. He recalled conversations with the waitress and some other customers in the restaurant he liked for breakfast about the risks of pot hunting. He'd even met one man, a local, who'd spent time in prison for doing just that. The locals were suspicious of him too, thinking he might be a government man looking for pot hunters. It wouldn't be surprising if Joe suspected him of being a pot hunter too. That was the last thing on his mind, though he had enjoyed seeing some artifacts at the cliff dwelling in Joe's canyon. What had caused the turn-around? More questions without answers. A mystery for sure.

The next day, Brian arrived at the airport at 7:00 a.m. Through the open hangar door, he saw Joe already at work on the engine of a Cessna 180, one of the planes hangared at the field. Short commute, he thought, noting the fifty yards or so from the door of Joe's trailer at the edge of the parking lot. He went into the hangar and waited silently until Joe brought the cowling down in place and fastened it securely.

"There," Joe said, and turned to Brian. "You ready to fly?"

"Yes. At least I hope so."

"We'll see," Joe said drily, and walked over to the Cub. "Grab a strut and give me a hand." Joe grasped the wire braces on either side of the tail to steer the plane out of the hangar, while Brian pushed on the right wing strut. It rolled easily on its big balloon tires.

"Go ahead with the pre-flight," Joe took the checklist from the pocket on the back of the front seat and handed it to Brian.

"Okay." Brian proceeded to do a very careful pre-flight inspection. Throughout the plane, he saw evidence of Joe's meticulous attention to the plane. Before finishing, he pulled the prop through to feel the compression in all four cylinders. When Joe returned from the office with headsets in hand, Brian said, "She's ready."

Brian waited as Joe climbed in the back seat, donned his headset, and then motioned Brian into the front seat. Joe then guided him through the starting procedure: pump the primer to load the engine cylinders with fuel, turn the magneto switch to both, feet on the brakes, and then press the starter button. The engine caught on the second revolution of the prop and settled down to a steady idle of 1000 rpm.

After taxiing out to the runway threshold, Brian went through the run up procedure, adjusting the mixture for the current density altitude. Holding the brakes during the run-up, his leg muscles trembled unexpectedly. Hmm. Must be more excited than he realized. Then as they taxied out onto the runway, Joe said, "The Cub was originally designed for a much less powerful engine than the 150 hp Lycoming in this plane. Expect considerable "P" factor. The propeller rotation will tend to push you off to the left, so you'll need to hold right rudder on the takeoff roll."

Brian heard all that and thought he understood, but soon found out that understanding wasn't enough. He started the plane moving down the runway by pushing the throttle all the way forward and lifted the tail by pushing the stick forward. O God! The plane started to veer off the left side of the runway! He counteracted with the right rudder, but overcorrected, and the plane now headed off toward the right edge of the runway. He feared he was going to wreck Joe's beautiful airplane before he ever got off the ground. He felt the throttle move back rapidly under his hand as Joe pulled the power all the way back and felt Joe's feet on the rudder straighten the plane out. Thank God for dual controls! They slowed to a stop and Joe turned the plane around to taxi sedately back to the beginning of the runway.

"I think we better try that again," was Joe's only comment. When they arrived back at the beginning of the runway, Joe asked, "What do you think happened?"

Sheepishly, Brian replied, "I guess I didn't correct properly for the P factor."

"What did I tell you?"

"Use the rudder to maintain directional control on the runway."

"So what do you think you ought to do differently?"

"Dance on the rudder pedals more lightly?" Brian didn't know exactly what to do.

"Right," came the firm reply, "And this time, keep the stick back and leave the tail on the ground until you get rudder authority. Remember the prop wash? That blast of air from the prop will let you raise the tail long before you have positive rudder steering, so keep the tail wheel down longer for steering."

Vowing to do it right this time, Brian started the takeoff run again, accelerating more gradually. He held the stick back, keeping the tail wheel firmly on the ground, and used the rudder pedals to steer the plane, making small corrections, zigzagging only slightly. Gathering speed, he cautiously moved the stick forward and lifted the tail. Now he had positive rudder control. The Cub quickly accelerated. Brian gave a small pull on the stick and they became airborne, surprising him at how quickly they lifted off. After climbing out, he did a few gentle turns to get the feel of the plane and leveled off at 8500 ft.

"The Cub likes turns to be led with the rudder, so feed in a bit of rudder before you move the stick." Joe said. "Real flying has to be intuitive. Anyone can drive a plane around the sky, with their head somewhere else. I want you to learn to fly like the eagle. He may be looking for food, but he is always in his body, flying. If he encounters a thermal, he'll feel it on his wings, in his body, and respond instantly. Next time you get a chance to watch an eagle or even a buzzard, pay attention to how they fly. Follow it with your binoculars so you can really see. Notice how he is always moving some of his feathers, making minute adjustments with his flight feathers on his wings, his tail feathers moving like a rudder."

Brian recalled seeing both those birds yesterday, but hadn't paid attention to such small details.

Joe continued, "You can do that too. I have the stick set for a light touch, so you can feel the plane better. Make some turns and this time really feel the plane. Feel every little shift of pressure on the wings, ailerons, elevator, or rudder. Hold the stick with only two fingers."

Could he really control the plane with just his fingers? Brian's excitement grew as he felt the minute sensations in his fingertips. The plane was talking to him!

"Now take your hand off the stick. I have trimmed it for level flight. Let her fly herself."

Doing as he was told, Brian saw how the Cub made its own corrections to changes in pitch or roll, though with a slight delay. Only when they encountered an unusually strong gust did it require any intervention. Joe took Brian through a number of maneuvers with the plane. From time to time he would call out over the intercom, "Where's your head?" Each time Brian realized his thoughts had drifted to somewhere other than right there in the airplane. How difficult it was to concentrate and stay focused strictly on flying.

When Joe asked him to do a power-on stall, with all that extra horsepower, the plane's nose went to such a high angle of attack that when it stalled and stopped flying, the nose fell abruptly into a turning dive to the left, heading almost straight down. Brian initiated the recovery, pressing on the right rudder to keep the plane straight and not enter a spin. Then gradually he pulled back on the stick to bring the plane out of the dive. He let out his breath. "Whew!"

"Scared you a little, eh?"

"Yeah." Brian admitted reluctantly.

"Know where you are now?"

"Not exactly," Brian confessed. Below them he saw a crenellated panorama of canyons, but nothing distinctive. But then he scanned the horizon, and off to the northeast, he sighted the two big mountain peaks. The green smudge south of them must be the town of Blanding, with the airport south of town. He turned the plane to head back.

"Let's go in and shoot a couple of landings," Joe instructed.

Adjusting the trim to angle down a little, Brian reduced the throttle so that the airspeed didn't build up too much on their descent. Turning to enter the pattern at 6,700 ft., he slowed the plane to 70 M.P.H., the best glide entry speed listed in the manual. As they turned onto final approach, he felt Joe's hand on the stick, "I'll fly the first one. You follow through, but don't fight me on the controls."

As they approached the ground, he marveled as Joe leveled off only inches above the runway and eased back on the stick to keep it from settling too soon. Finally, with the nose high enough to obscure their direct view of the runway, the tail sank until all three wheels gently touched the runway at once, the squeak of the tires audible. Brian felt the rudder pedals moving under his feet as Joe reminded him to always dance on the rudder to keep it straight. Before they slowed to a stop, Joe pushed the throttle forward, the tail came up, and soon they were flying again. "Now you try one," Joe said. Thus began Brian's training in the Cub.

Two days later, after only six hours of instruction, Brian felt both excited and nervous when Joe turned him loose to solo the Cub. His broad smile continued after his flight when Joe signed off the tail wheel certification in his log book.

He flew every day for the next week, and with the exception of a couple bounced landings, he landed the plane smoothly on all three wheels. If it was windy, he landed on the main gear, maintaining control with the tail up by keeping an aileron into the wind and holding opposite rudder, until it slowed enough that the tail sank to the ground of its own weight, where he controlled it with the tail wheel. Day by day, he became ever more one with the airplane, similar to what Joe had suggested. Perhaps it felt that way because of the narrow body of the Cub, with one seat behind the other, instead of side by side seating in the Cessna. He felt more like he imagined a bird in flight might feel, less like he was piloting an airplane around the sky.

When Brian arrived at the airport Friday morning, May 5th, expecting to practice flying the Cub again, he was surprised to find it tied down outside on the ramp. Had Joe pulled it out for him? When he found Joe in the shop, he said, "Thanks for getting the Cub out for me."

"I'd like you to hold off on your flight for a while. That teacher who called last week is going to bring her third grade class out to look at the planes. I want to use the Cub to show how an airplane flies. That okay by you?"

"Sure. Not a problem," Brian said, and walked over and sat down on the bench outside the office to wait for the arrival of the school kids. He wished he had brought along something interesting to read while Joe did the show and tell.

11

**Friday morning
May 5, 2001**

Sally leaned both elbows on her kitchen table, savoring the taste and fragrance of her second cup of coffee. Hard to believe she was forty years old today. Nostalgia for her mom, who had died five years ago, and her childhood birthday parties, brought a smile at first, then a frown and sadness. That's when it had all begun, when they first came. When they first took her. Up there. Oops! Don't let your mind go there, not when you have to go to work today. She drew the curtain on those memories, forcing herself to think about the field trip to the airport this morning. She reminded herself of her plan to go out to dinner this evening with her friend and co-worker, Helen, to celebrate her birthday.

Sally threw the lock on the front door as a matter of habit, though she often wondered why she bothered, since she usually left the back door unlocked, as did most of her neighbors. That was life in a small town, where you knew everyone and trusted most. Climbing into her ten year old Toyota pickup, she heard again her mother's parting words the one time she had come to visit, "Why don't you get yourself a decent car?" But this one did the job and its four-wheel drive came in handy in winter snowstorms, for trips to the canyons, and for hauling stuff.

At school she addressed the task of getting twenty-three excited, chattering youngsters lined up to get on the bus for the field trip to the airport. She'd long ago discovered that she did not like to yell at her kids to get their attention or to line up the way some teachers did. Kids easily tuned out yelling. Instead she used the trick of humming. When she wanted them to all be quiet or get their attention, she would start to hum, which the kids closest to her would pick up and in a very short time it had spread throughout classroom. Humming required that the mouth be closed. Any kid not cooperating quickly became obvious. Occasionally, one or two of the rowdy ones resisted for a bit, but usually they fell into line. She liked to think that she invited the kids into harmony. Maybe it didn't matter that much, but humming got their attention, and in a gentle way.

When the school bus pulled into the airport parking lot, she was happy to see Joe Star come out of the office to greet them. He had a long, narrow face and stood taller and slimmer than most of the local Utes or Navajos. He was one of the few locals she had never actually met. She'd heard that he'd grown up around here somewhere. He'd seemed soft spoken and reserved on the phone, when she'd arranged this outing. She wondered how he would relate to the kids.

She needn't have worried, for the children were obviously soon at ease with him. One little girl took his offered hand as he led the entire class into the office to show them the huge United States air map hanging on the wall. When one of the boys noticed a string hanging from the map at the point of Blanding, Joe demonstrated how to stretch the string to measure the distance to his destination, using the little black marks on the string. Holding the string up to Moab, he said, "See, it's only 85 miles up to the Moab airport."

"How far is it to Denver?" a little girl asked.

"You do it." He helped her stand on a chair, stretch the string, and count the marks. "Three hundred miles!" she proclaimed.

"That's right," Joe confirmed. Then he led the class out the front door to the ramp, which he explained was the name for a parking lot for airplanes. Among the planes parked there was a bright yellow fabric-covered plane with its tail on the ground.

"Why do they have ropes tied on them -- so they don't run away?" One little boy snickered, bringing laughter from some of his classmates.

"Exactly," replied Joe, "only they won't run away, but they could blow away. Remember how hard the wind can blow out of the canyons? That wind could pick this plane up and toss it over the fence like a toy, so we tie it down." The little boy seemed duly impressed.

At that moment the phone in the office rang and Joe excused himself. He called to a man sitting on the bench outside the office. "Brian, could you give me hand here? Show these kids the parts of the plane and how they work."

The man rose from the bench and came over to their group. Sally watched from the edge of the circle of kids. She knew almost everyone in town, but didn't recognize this man, so she assumed he must be a new arrival or a pilot just passing through. He introduced himself to the children and quickly captured their attention as he invited them over to the yellow airplane with the black lightning stripe on its side. He walked around the plane, naming and pointing out the control surfaces, and explaining what each did.

"Who would like to help me demonstrate the controls of the plane?"

Six hands shot up. He selected one shy little boy and helped him climb into the plane. "Now, put your feet on these rudder pedals, and push on them gently. Look back and see how it moves the rudder back at the tail." The little boy seemed thrilled. "Now move this control stick a little. Everyone watch how it moves the ailerons on the wing and the elevator on the tail. That's how you control the plane in flight."

"Cool," several kids said at once.

Brian went on to tell how eagles and buzzards use their wing and tail feathers to control their flight, which fascinated the kids. A few said they had seen that very thing themselves.

He pointed out each of the instruments and explained what function it performed when the airplane was flying. Though the kids had studied the diagram of a plane in class, Sally liked how closely they followed Brian's explanations and how much it added when they could touch each part of the plane. Nothing beats hands-on learning, she thought.

She liked his easy way with her students, but worried that they might be imposing on his time. Still, he seemed willing to engage with them, as if he had all the time in the world. She rather liked his looks, the sound of his voice, and wondered again how he happened to be here in Blanding. At that moment, they heard the sound of an approaching airplane. Several of the kids pointed it out and asked if it was going to land. Their excitement grew as it passed low overhead and turned to line up with the runway. Brian spread his arms as if to surround the group, saying, "Let's all go out the gate and stand behind the fence, so we don't get in the way of the plane." By the time he had shepherded them all through the gate in the chain link fence, the plane had landed and taxied onto the ramp, both propellers a spinning blur, the shrill sound of its twin engines loud enough to hurt their ears.

"Why does it make such a scream?" One little girl shouted over the sound, as the plane braked to a halt in front of the terminal and the engines wound down to a stop.

"That's the sound that a turbo engine makes," Brian replied, without explaining further.

The way Brian had gathered the children and ushered them to a safe place impressed Sally. She liked the gentle, no-nonsense way he got the children to do what he wanted. Fascinated, the children watched two well-dressed men exit via the miniature stairway that swung down from the side of the twin engine plane. Someone from town met them in the parking lot and they drove away. Meanwhile, Brian led the children back to the small yellow plane to conclude his demonstration. Then he invited their questions and comments. They had plenty.

Later when they finished, Sally said, "Thanks for your patience with our class, Mr. Nelson. We've been studying air transportation and I made arrangements with Mr. Star for this field trip. Too bad he got called away. Hope we didn't take too much of your time."

"No problem," Brian said. "I like kids. I have two of my own, though they are in college now. By the way, what did you say your name is?"

"I'm sorry. I forgot to introduce myself. My name is Sally McNeill." She extended her hand. "I teach 3rd grade at the elementary school here in Blanding. Thanks again." Then she scurried off to round up a couple of boys drifting away from the group. In a short time, they all boarded the school bus and headed back north to town.

When the school day ended, Sally went home for a break before returning to school to join her colleague Helen, to finish the work on their rain forest project. She looked forward to their dinner out. In the back yard, taking down her laundry, she reflected on her journey to her fortieth birthday. What a long way she had come, not only from her hometown in Ohio, but even more in terms of her life experiences. Her eyes moistened with tears as she sorted through those long buried memories. What a vulnerable young girl she had been when it had all started, that night after her ninth birthday. She remembered all too clearly.

12

**9:30 p.m. Sunday Night,
May 3, 1970**

Nine year-old Sally McNeill held up the new nightgown her mom had made her, admiring its pink and white candy stripes before slipping it on. Pulling it over her head, she caught a glimpse of her gangly, slender body in the mirror. The gown's soft flannel felt cozy as she tied the pink neck ribbon, careful to make the loops of the bow perfect and even. Sally leaned in close to the bathroom mirror and brushed off a cake crumb stuck to the end of her nose. Even though her birthday was actually on May 5th, they'd had the party on Saturday the 2nd, so her friends could come. Tonight she'd savored another piece of cake, left over from her birthday party yesterday. Her mom had baked her favorite, chocolate with vanilla frosting.

Sally peered into her greenish-brown eyes in the mirror, curious, as if getting acquainted with a new face. She gave her auburn hair a few swipes with a brush, then skipped down the hall to Mom and Dad's room for a hug and a kiss. Returning, she bounced into bed, pushed her feet under the covers and sat waiting for her mom's ritual tucking in. How she loved these close times with her mother.

"Thanks again, Mom, for the wonderful party yesterday. I had so much fun." She flopped back onto the pillow

"I'm glad, Sally," her Mom replied, pulling the covers up to her chin. "Now it's time to get a good night's sleep so you'll be ready for school tomorrow."

After a kiss on her forehead, her mother turned out the bedside lamp and left the door open a crack for some light from the hall. It didn't take Sally long to relax, with her happy memories of yesterday. Several of her fourth grade friends had come to help her celebrate. They had all enjoyed such a good time as they laughed and played. She thought of her presents: new clothes for her Barbie doll from her friends, a new bicycle from Dad, and the new nightgown made by mom. She'd been so excited last night she could hardly sleep, so when it came time to brush her teeth for bed tonight, she could barely hold her eyes open. With one last glance at the door, she curled up on her side with her favorite teddy bear tucked into the crook of her arm.

Sally awoke in the middle of the night. Someone or something was in her room! Something that didn't belong! At first the faint light from the street lamp in the alley behind the house revealed nothing, but as she turned toward the closet, something moved in the shadows and she froze with fear. Suddenly, an intense blue light flooded through the windows. Sally now saw three small figures coming toward her bed. They had arms and legs, but beyond that they didn't look like regular people. Their heads were the scariest part. Much larger than normal, they had huge black eyes that wrapped part way around their heads, slanting up at the outsides. They wore what looked like close fitting long underwear. She had never seen anything like these creatures. Terror choked her scream until only a tiny squeak escaped her lips. When one of them reached out long fingers to touch her, Sally tried to draw back, but had no place to go. The instant the fingers touched her arm, Sally felt an electric shock zing through her body and everything became fuzzy. Semiconscious, she first sensed more fingers under her, and then felt her body lifted up off the bed and floated right out through the window.

Later, Sally wakened to feel a cold metal table on the bare skin of her back and legs. She reached for the comfort of her flannel nightgown, only to discover it missing entirely. Embarrassed at being naked, she tried to cover herself with her arms. Though she couldn't see very well, she had the impression of a round windowless room lit by soft dim light. Several of the weird creatures surrounded her. Most were about her own height or less, except for a taller one who had a female shape and looked a little more like a real person. When that one came over to her, she shrank back, her heart in her throat, and so scared she couldn't move.

Don't be afraid. We will not hurt you. We are only going to examine you.

It sounded as if someone was talking inside her head. Then her body twitched as the being touched her with its long fingers and, in spite of the fear that gripped her, Sally lapsed into sleep again.

The next thing Sally knew, she was waking up in her own bed, shivering with cold and fear, the blue light outside her window was fading. She started to cry, whimpering at first, then sobbed loudly. She stiffened at the sound of footsteps in the hall and turned to see what new threat might be approaching. To her relief she saw her mom, who came in, sat on the bed, took her in her arms, and held her while she cried.

"Did you have a bad dream?"

"Monsters," was all she could choke out at first. Then she cried harder, clinging hysterically to her mother.

Finally, as her shuddering body quieted a bit, she whispered,

"Monsters with big heads and big eyes came into my room and got me."

"You must have had a bad dream, Sally," her mom said, turning on the bedside lamp.

"No, Mom. They took me out the window. I got cold. They put me on a cold table. Mom, I was so scared."

Sally's mother paused, "Don't be afraid, Sally. It was only a dream. See, the window is closed! You're safe right here in your own bed."

"No, it was really real!" And she sobbed some more.

With her mom holding her tightly, Sally felt her mother's comforting hand on the back of her neck. "Why, Sally, look at you. You put your nightgown on backwards. You even tied the ribbon in a bow on the back of your neck instead of the front. How did you do that?"

It took Sally a moment to realize what her mom had said. Sally reached up to her neck and felt the back side of her gown tight against her throat. "But Momma, I put it on right! I remember tying the ribbon in a bow on my chest. I made the loops perfect and even. I can't tie it behind my back!" Again Sally fell into a paroxysm of sobbing, clinging even more tightly to her mom.

* * *

Maryann McNeill shivered in a moment of fear. What really had happened to Sally? Was it only a bad dream, or did something else happen? Had someone broken into their house? Had intruders entered Sally's room? Had her beautiful daughter been molested in some way? No answer readily appeared, but for now the important thing was to comfort Sally. Sitting on the side of the bed, she held her daughter close, much like when she was a baby, rocking gently to and fro.

Sally's sobs gradually subsided, until at last, Maryann felt her daughter's body relax, though Sally's face remained buried in her chest, absorbing the reassuring beat of her heart and the warmth of her body. When Maryann first tried to ease Sally down on the bed, her young arms gripped spasmodically once again. Gradually, Sally became limp as she relaxed into sleep, her breathing deep and even. As she laid her child down a second time, Sally's eyes fluttered open momentarily. "Can we leave the light on, Mom?"

"Sure, we can." Maryann pulled the sheet and blanket up under Sally's chin. "You'll be okay now, honey. Nothing is going to happen to you. And if you need me, just call out." Maryann stayed until she was certain that Sally was sound asleep, then eased herself off the bed and returned to her own room.

Sleep eluded Maryann McNeill for a long time. What on earth could have happened? Surely it must have been just a dream! On the other hand, she had never seen Sally so terrified. She'd had bad dreams before, but nothing like this. And what about the nightgown being on backwards? How did that happen?

13

May 5, 2001
Blanding Airport

After Sally left with her class, Brian walked back into the office where he saw Joe busy at his desk with some paper work. He wondered what had kept Joe from returning to the job of explaining the airplane to the group of kids. Not that it had been unpleasant or difficult. Actually it had been fun, and he'd enjoyed meeting Sally McNeil.

"Hey Joe, what happened? How's come you left me out there to fend with all those kids? They could have used your expertise."

"Oh, I don't know. You seemed to be doing all right when I looked out. Besides, once I finished with the phone call, I didn't want to interrupt. I thought you might like to meet Sally. Looked like you were doing all right there too."

"What are you trying to do, Joe, be a match maker? Just because I've been a widower for a while, doesn't mean that I need you to set me up." He paused. "Who is she anyway?"

"She's the third grade teacher in town."

"Yeah, I know that much already. Come on, is that all you know?" Brian teased.

"Well, officially I just met her today. Unofficially though, she's a newcomer to town. Only been here about eight years."

"Eight years! My God, how long do you have to live here to not be a newcomer?"

"Oh, at least fifty, I reckon, or maybe be born here." They both chuckled. Brian understood that mindset, having come from a relatively small town himself. No doubt everyone in this small town of Blanding maintained an informal mental register of anyone new in town versus the old timers.

"I also heard that she's divorced and single. I heard she came here from Ohio on a vacation one Christmas, 'bout eight years ago. One of the school teachers took bad sick in the middle of that year and Sally offered to fill in and take over the job. Just sort of stuck after that, you might say. Sort of unusual for a non-Mormon to make it in a Mormon town. But she's a good woman from what I hear, and well liked around town."

"Oh," Brian replied, all he could think to say at the moment. Then, to break an uncomfortable silence, Brian pointed to the slightly yellowed black and white framed photo hanging on the wall behind the office counter, showing a man standing beside a World War II P-47 fighter plane, and asked, "Who's that?"

"Come take a look and see if you can guess." A slight smile played on his lips.

Brian stepped around the counter to examine the photo up close and saw a tall, slender young man in uniform with dark hair and a happy smile. He glanced back and forth from Joe to the photo, noting similarities to the tall man in the picture. Joe had less hair than the man in the photo and had slightly stooped shoulders, but he still stood at least 6' 1." He wore a few lines around his eyes, but the smile looked the same. "Well, if I didn't know any better, I'd say it was you, but that would have been way before your time," Brian replied. "You're way too young to have flown in World War II. Is it your father?"

"Nope. You're wrong there. That's me back when I had more hair on my head. I was a gung ho fighter pilot at that time."

"You flew in World War II?" Joe didn't look a day over sixty, if that. Was it because he was Native American? Seeing Joe nod, Brian asked, "What theater of the war did you fly in?"

"Europe. Late 1943 through '45. Flew out of Duxford, England with the 78th Fighter Group."

"Wow, you saw your share, didn't you? I'd like to hear more about that."

"Yeah, someday maybe," Joe muttered as he turned toward the shop.

Brian realized he probably wouldn't hear much any time soon, so after another interval of silence, said "Guess I'll go fly around a while." He went back out to the Cub, made his pre-flight inspection, strapped in, cranked up, and took off.

* * *

Joe stood in front of the FBO office, where he'd returned to view Brian's takeoff, and watch the Cub out of sight. Brian's question brought back memories. Maybe he should put that old picture away. But the memories remained. Images from the past flashed through his mind, some exciting, some painful beyond all imagination. He usually tried not to think about the war. Sometimes he was successful. Sometimes not. He went back inside and just sat, staring at the picture, remembering back to when it had begun.

14

February, 1942

Even as he walked into the U.S. Post Office in Blanding, Utah to sign up, Joe felt the voice inside almost screaming at him. He hoped he would someday get past the feeling of being torn apart by this decision. It took great courage to step up to the table, above which hung the poster of Uncle Sam pointing his finger at the viewer, saying 'I WANT YOU!' Acutely conscious that Uncle Sam didn't look at all like him, Joe again questioned if this was his war too. Of course, Uncle Sam would look funny if he were painted as an Indian.

His mind went back to his days in the mission school, when he was about eight. His first days there, he was scared and lonely. Though he liked meeting other Ute boys and girls, so many new rules governed all parts of their day and night that he thought the teachers wanted to make him into a white man. The food was very different and far too salty. He had to sleep on an uncomfortable cot crowded into one large room with all the other boys. Even the clothes they made him wear felt strange and uncomfortable, white boy's clothes.

The mission teachers had such difficulty pronouncing his Ute name that they gave him an Anglo name, Joe Star, and demanded that he learn and speak English. Shifting from the guttural sounds of Ute and not being allowed to use the subtle non-verbal expressions that said so much with so little, baffled him at first. At first, he relied on the other students to find words in the new language to express himself. The hardest part was trying to think in this new language, rather than in the more visual metaphor of his own tongue. Joe grimaced as he remembered that after the first few weeks at the school, the teachers punished and shamed any child caught talking in his native language. It had happened to him more than once.

He recalled his conversation with Grandmother, and her comment that maybe he was called to be a warrior. Maybe, maybe not, but he did want to fly. This was the only way he could see to do that. Filling out the form to enlist in the Army Air Corps, Joe came to the place where it asked for his age. He truly didn't know his exact age. It had never been a topic of discussion within his family. Life just went on in a natural progression. His community didn't celebrate birthdays as they did in the white man's world. But he could not ignore the comments over the years about how young he looked. He knew he looked similar to other young men in their teens or twenties. At the mission school he had been made aware of the calendar by which the missionaries lived, but it had never been particularly important to him. Thinking that most of the men going to war were young, he finally put down the number 20, and placed the form in the special envelope provided. He did not even have to use the usual three cent stamp, as it was considered government mail. He then headed back to his village.

Some weeks later, the mail man who plied the dusty trails to the canyon country villages in his ancient truck, rolled to a stop outside their village, already thoroughly announced by the barking dogs. As usual, the children crowded around him, eagerly anticipating what he might have brought. The villagers prized Sears and Roebuck catalogues as dream books, which became a source for many important things for them, such as clothes, household goods, or hardware and tools. They marveled that one could even order a kit for a complete house. Thus, whenever the mail man brought a package, it was like magic. From his bag of packages and letters, the mailman extracted a long brown envelope for "Joe Star." One of the boys took the envelope and raced off to find Joe.

Excitedly opening the letter, Joe read his orders to report to the Army Air Corps base at La Junta, Colorado in two weeks. The letter enclosed tickets, the first for a bus from Blanding, Utah to Grand Junction, Colorado, and a second ticket for the train that would take him from there to Denver, where another train would take him south to Pueblo. Then yet another took him east to La Junta to the airbase. When the day came for his departure, neither he nor his mother could hold back the tears. He rode into town with the postman in his old truck. Waiting at the gas station for the bus, Joe wondered what life would be like when he returned, if he did, finding it hard to admit he might die in this war. The cloud of stinky blue diesel smoke that belched from the engine of the old bus leaked in through the windows to mark the first stage of Joe's journey. He had never seen a train before, so getting on one in Grand Junction provided another new adventure. On the last train, from Pueblo to the base, he saw many other young men he suspected were going to the same place he was.

Checking in at the base, Joe followed the shouted orders to join a line of young men, where an officer 'invited' them to take their oath of allegiance. He then congratulated them on being 'in the Army now,' and next directed them to a building identified as the base hospital. There, ordered to strip off all his clothes except his underwear, recently ordered from the Sears catalogue, Joe got a glimpse of military life he did not like. Being ordered to stand nearly naked in a line with other young men for their physicals, violated all boundaries of privacy and propriety for Joe. He was glad he at least had his underwear, something he didn't usually wear at home. He could only retreat inside himself to endure such humiliation, though the other boys laughed and joked to cover their own embarrassment.

After that ordeal, Joe learned with disappointment that the first six weeks of basic training had nothing whatsoever to do with flying. Marching everywhere in a group, even to meals, while being yelled at by a drill sergeant, offended his sensitive and quiet nature. He looked across the field with longing at the biplane trainers lined up on the ramp and flying overhead. Seeing them kept his mind off the daily insults of the Army and left him hope for what might come next. He eventually became accustomed to being called Injun Joe by everyone, and because he could usually outperform the other young men in his squad in the physical training, he was soon looked up to by many. At six feet, one inch, Joe stood tall for his people, the Southern Utes, though he didn't stand out in the white man's world. For all that, he thanked not only his ancestors in Utah, but those above as well.

Graduation at the end of six weeks basic training brought a sense of pride in what he had accomplished. Moving to the other side of the field, where the pilot cadets were housed, felt like moving to a new world, though the barracks were exactly the same as the hastily constructed wooden buildings he had been living in. But now his life took on a new purpose. To fly! Each cadet was assigned to an instructor. Their training began with a cheery lecture about being in the Army Air Corps, and informed them that not all of them would make it to become pilots. Their dreams of being fighter pilots, which they privately admitted when alone, were seriously threatened, but not completely shattered. Even being told by the instructor that he considered it his job to wash out (fail and dismiss) the non-pilots, did little to dampen the enthusiasm of this group of young men. They were boys now only to their families, left behind in towns and farms all across the country.

The second day of being a cadet took Joe to the flight line to meet with the instructor for his small group, Lt. Will Farber, a slender, short young man who wore a thin mustache on his upper lip and maintained a stiff, erect posture. He was known as Killer Will, or just Killer, among the cadets, due to his reputation for being so tough on the cadets assigned to him for primary flight training. Inspection of the sturdy yellow Boeing made Stearman PT-17 trainer created a magical hour of relief for this group of would-be aviators. They gathered around the biplane to hear Lt. Farber's briefing, feel the smooth taut skin of its fabric covering glistening in the Southern Colorado sun, and inhale the faint dope smell and the aromas of the engine and aviation fuel. Then they went back to the classroom to sit with other teachers to thoroughly learn the ins and outs of this airplane, in what was known as Ground School. Studying the manual, learning all the details of the plane, its structure, what each part did, its engine, and its flight regime held Joe's interest, though it was nothing like the engineering complexity of the previous craft he had flown and had studied in a far different way. They also studied meteorology, map reading, and navigation. The end of their second week brought a written test over all these details. Sad faces hung on those who did not measure up and had thus already washed out of pilot training without ever having set foot in an airplane. Those remaining felt sorry to see a few of their fellow cadets pack their bags to be transferred to some other part of the Army. They had struggled together long enough in basic training to already feel a sense of loyalty to one another.

Once past the hurdle of the first written test, the cadets went to the Ready Room, where they crowded around the bulletin board containing the schedule for their first introduction to flight. A few of the guys had some flight training prior to joining the Army. Those with a few hours training in a Piper J-3 Cub initially thought it promised them an edge over the others. Killer Will made it his job to convince them that not only was this no advantage, but in fact he intended to make it even harder on those who claimed it. "You're gonna learn to fly MY way, or not at all!"

First, a flight with Lt. Farber. When it came time for his own introductory flight, Joe walked out to the plane with his parachute pack bumping the back of his knees, adding to the feeling of weakness he already wore there.

"So you think you want to fly, huh?" Lt. Will Farber's grating voice challenged.

"Yes, Sir!" came Joe's stiff answer.

"Ever been in a plane before?"

"No, Sir!"

"And I 'spose you want to be a fighter pilot, like all the rest of this sorry bunch?"

"Yes, Sir!"

"Well, you might as well know now that very few make it as fighter pilots. And most of them that do, get killed doing it, if not before."

"Yes, Sir!"

"So, get your sorry butt into the airplane. Think you can do that?"

"Yes, Sir!" Joe had been watching other cadets clamber into the front cockpit, and followed their example. He did not want the embarrassment of 'mounting the horse' the wrong way.

Lt. Farber followed him into the rear cockpit and signaled the lineman to pull the prop through to load the cylinders. Then he called out, "Contact" as he switched the magnetos on. The lineman then swung the prop down vigorously and with a few coughs of exhaust smoke, the engine caught and soon ran smoothly. Feeling the power of the engine and prop reverberate through the entire plane, and even in his body, thrilled Joe. Over the one way Gosport speaking tube between the two cockpits, he heard Will's voice telling him to put his right hand on the stick, left hand on the throttle and his feet on the rudder pedals and follow his movements. "But let me fly the plane, you hear?" He felt Will's sure hand on the controls as he followed through on the movements required to bring the plane to its place in the line of other Stearmans, also known as The Yellow Peril, en-route to the active runway. Joe's mind flashed back to his first sighting of the biplane flying over his school picnic so many years ago, and felt excited to be in a plane for the first time.

Lined up on the runway, the nose pointing into the wind, Joe felt the smooth forward movement of the throttle under his left hand that caused the engine to speed up and start the plane rolling down the runway, hearing Will's reminder in his ear to remember the P-factor. Joe had read about it in the manual. Now he felt the momentum of the propeller push the plane to the left on takeoff. "Dance on the rudder!" Will shouted. The rudder pedals moved under his feet, with more pressure on the right foot than the left, to keep the plane going straight. Then in his right hand he felt the stick move forward to raise the tail to horizontal. A few more moments of acceleration, a slight nudge of the stick aft, and they were airborne! Flying! Joe had no time to compare the flight of this craft to the one he had previously flown, for Will threw the stick to the left, cranking the plane into an immediate hard left bank to turn out of the line of planes taking off behind them. Joe found himself looking over the side of this open cockpit plane straight at the ground and felt momentary panic at the wings being vertical to the ground instead of level over it. Smoothly, Will rolled the plane back to level flight again, heading directly away from the runway and the airfield.

At Will's bidding Joe gingerly experimented with the controls. Just as he began to get a sense of what each did, Will yelled at him, "Don't be an old lady!" and aggressively flipped the stick all the way to the right, with only a slight touch on the left rudder, and Joe found himself hanging upside down from his seat belt and about to slide out, as Will rolled the plane into inverted flight. Panic and fear froze Joe momentarily.

"Now ya know what that seat belt is for, and why I said make it tight!" Will said with a malicious chuckle. "Don't ever forget it. It will save your life. Now, you fly the airplane," as he rolled back upright.

Once again, but now with more firmness, Joe took the stick in his hands and found the rudder pedals with his feet again, after having had them fall away during the inverted maneuver. He sneaked a moment to tighten his seat belt even more. That quick roll reminded him of learning to fly the space craft and the time he had stood it on its nose. But the systems of that craft kept the gravity at one so he felt none of the body sensations he now experienced in this plane at the hand of his instructor, who had announced his intention to do his best to wash Joe and his fellow cadets right out of pilot training. That memory brought him back to his senses, where he could begin to apply what he knew from ground school and knew intuitively about flying from the saucer, even though that was a different environment and a totally different type of craft. Soon he could make coordinated turns and feel he had the aircraft under control.

"OK, let's go back," Came the voice in back. "Think you know where the field is?"

Joe's many years of living in the canyons served him well, as he knew their exact location in relation to the field and pointed the nose straight towards it.

"Humph" Joe heard from the rear cockpit.

"My plane," Will called out through the speaking tube, as they approached the field. "I'll fly the first landing. You follow through." Once again Joe took the role of learner, as they came in at a 45 degree angle to the runway to turn down wind. When opposite the end of the runway on which they were to land, Will suddenly pulled the throttle back, and in the silence of the now idling engine, Joe heard the whistle of the wind through the wires that held the wings in tensioned symmetry with each other. He could sense their airspeed, as well as see it on the gage in front of him. Will's crisp movements of stick and rudder turned them left onto a gliding approach through the base leg, perpendicular to the runway and left once again to where they lined up on final approach to the runway.

"Remember, the object is to make the airplane quit flying at the exact moment it touches the runway, not before, and not after."

The heavy airplane dropped rapidly toward the ground, and in the last few moments Will pulled the stick back, flying level for a few seconds as it continued to settle. With the main wheels just inches above the runway, Will used the last bit of airspeed to pull the nose to an even higher angle until the tail wheel was also just inches above the ground and with a gentle plop, they rolled onto the runway, dancing on the rudder pedals again to keep the plane going straight. Turning off at the next taxiway, Will instructed Joe to taxi back to the threshold of the runway and get in line for take-off.

Two planes waited ahead of him now, but Joe felt excited to realize that he had the plane under his control, even though he was just taxiing on the ground. He watched in minor horror as he observed another student starting a take-off run and immediately began zigzagging back and forth on the runway, putting the plane dangerously at risk of scraping a wingtip on the macadam and doing a ground loop. He could tell when the instructor took control and straightened them out. He did not envy that cadet and the verbal abuse he was no doubt receiving at that moment. Joe hoped he would not make the same mistake, for he knew that Killer Will would not be kind to him nor cut him any slack. But Joe, quick in his body and mind, had already stored a body feel and memory for the motions on the controls he had experienced on the first takeoff. "Your airplane!" came through the speaking tube with a slight smirk.

Lined up now, nose pointing down the runway, Joe moved the throttle forward, brought the tail up, and nudged the right rudder just enough to keep the airplane straight down the runway with only a slight drift to either side. As soon as they achieved flying speed, he gently pulled back on the stick to lift them off the runway and begin climbing out. Remembering the sharp left turn Will had made, he threw the stick to his left to make that same sharp turn. What he did not remember was Will's immediately reversing the movement, bringing the stick back to neutral to halt the roll to the left. Almost before he realized it, he had rolled, not only into a 90 degree bank left, but on around until they were upside down, and still further to a position with a bank to the right, starting a turn now in the opposite direction from which he intended to go.

"What the Hell do you think you're doing?" As Will rolled the plane level in the correct direction, "You trying to kill us? Turn downwind."

Joe obediently banked left again, but this time halted the roll, held a 45 degree banked turn, and rolled out straight on the downwind leg.

"Now see if you can get us somewhere near the runway!"

Again, Joe used his body memory to duplicate the movements he had felt Will make, chopping the throttle when parallel to and opposite the end of the runway where he wanted to land. A few more movements of the stick, coordinated with the rudder and nudging the nose downward to maintain flying speed, just as the manual had said, Joe brought it in over the threshold, flared to just a few inches above the runway. He held the stick back further and further, bringing it right into his lap, until they touched down on all three wheels with only a slightly bigger thump than Will had made the time before. Though he could feel Will's hand there on the stick too, he was keenly aware of flying the plane himself. Dancing on the rudder pedals, with ever greater movement as they lost momentum and the rudder lost effectiveness with the decreasing airspeed, Joe kept them relatively straight down the runway.

"Humph!" The only comment he heard from the rear seat. He turned off on the same taxiway as before, but this time Will directed him toward the ramp, where they taxied into a line with the other planes. A slight touch on the brakes brought them to a halt. Will cut the switches to stop the spinning prop. Joe let out his breath and took a deep new one. He knew he had done OK, and felt inwardly pleased with his first flight in the Yellow Peril. He climbed out, surprised at how rubbery his legs felt, once his feet touched the ground.

"You sure you never been in an airplane before?"

"Yes, sir."

"Beginner's luck."

"Yes, sir."

As Joe walked back to the other cadets, he thought he heard a barely spoken "Not bad" from Will. But Will's question had disturbed him. True, he had never been in an airplane before, but he had learned to fly the saucer, though it had been almost seven years ago now. Later, as he lay in his bunk, trying to go to sleep, his mind drifted back to that time when he had lain on an entirely different bunk, excitement keeping him from sleep, ready to fly the saucer

15

1935, On Board the Mothership

Though pleased that Markel had offered this opportunity, Joe still had his doubts. Could he really learn to fly this thing? What if he failed? How did these things fly, anyway? There was no motor he could see.
That will be part of your instruction, if you decide to learn to operate this craft, came the answer.
Well, if you think I can do it, I'll try.
Very well. After your next sleep period we will begin.
He wasn't tired and didn't like being sent to his room. He paced, unable to settle. He wanted to begin right now. Learning of his Star heritage over the past two days had been so intense Joe had even begun to consider himself one of them, especially those that looked human. He'd only briefly met the one Markel said was his sister, but hoped to spend more time with her in the future, for he'd sensed an immediate connection.

He finally made himself lie down, but was so excited revisiting the incredible experiences of the past three days, he couldn't get to sleep. How would he ever explain it to his family at home? When he didn't return from his vision quest after three or four days, the men of the village would be out looking for him. The complex array of caves, rock falls, and cliffs, all held hazards to the unwary person. In addition, predators such as mountain lions and bears could carry a man's body off to their dens. It was not unheard of to stumble across the bones of someone years after they had disappeared. Before long, he knew his family would assume he was dead and be grieving for him. With these thoughts whirling through his head, he finally fell into a restless sleep.

Upon waking, he refreshed himself and used the receptacle which was so different from the outdoor toilets at home or at the mission school. He then wandered out into the large public area to eat. The food tasted unusual, but not unpleasant. He saw others like himself eating, but he never saw the small grey ones eat anything. In fact, they scarcely had any mouth with which to eat. He wondered how they sustained their small bodies.

By the time Joe finished his meal, he saw Markel approaching. *Greetings. I will be your instructor for flying the craft we call the Explorer. To you, it has what will seem like remarkable capabilities. However, before you actually assume control of the vehicle you must completely understand all its functions. Are you willing to do that?*

Of course, Joe replied, but he had no idea what he might be in for. He assumed he would be studying books, like he had done at the mission school. What he really wanted was to get into the driver's seat and fly it, but he didn't want to disappoint Markel. He vowed that he would study very, very hard.

Follow me. Markel led Joe down a corridor to a small room with a single padded chair. Joe sat down, wondering what would happen next. Shortly, one of the small grey ones entered. How could he hide his revulsion? It was so ugly.

Markel began, *This is one of our Information Keepers. We find it much more effective for our knowledge to be carried by one of these, rather than storing it on paper as you do in your world. Actually, he is like your story tellers, the keepers of the legends of your people. Please prepare yourself to receive the information.*

Well, that made sense. His people held generations of their history through oral stories. He'd often thought he should write down some of the stories, fearing they would be lost as the old story tellers died off. He expected it to be a long arduous task to keep all the information straight in his mind. Joe shrank way back in his chair as the Information Keeper leaned over with its big eyes less than a hand's breadth away and its musty odor filling his nose. He'd been taught it was disrespectful to ever stare directly into another person's eyes, let alone from this distance. He twisted his head first one way, then the other, shutting his eyes tightly. When he finally relaxed and opened his eyes, a strange thing happened. He began to drift away from his body, the image of the big eyes replaced by that of one of the Explorer craft, almost as if he stood right beside it. When he realized that this creature must have projected the image into his mind, he relaxed a little more and soon other images began to flow, showing the craft from all sides, above it, and even from underneath it. Then, stranger still, the surface of the craft became transparent and he could look right through it and see what lay beneath. Again, the being enabled him to see all aspects of the craft at this layer, including the circuitry embedded in or near the skin of the craft. Joe eagerly absorbed as much detail as possible.

Then Markel signaled the being, to step away, allowing Markel back into Joe's field of vision.

Rest, then review what you have learned before we continue.

What a surprise! Joe had total recall of all that he had seen, down to the smallest details of each electrical circuit and what it did. Without studying, his mind grasped and held it all.

"How do you do that?" He asked aloud of Markel.

For us it is simple, though for you it must seem strange, almost miraculous. I asked our Information Keeper to pause. I don't want you to get overloaded or frightened. But now that you have experienced it and understand that you only have to relax and let the images and information flow into your mind, we can move ahead. You will retain the information in your mind throughout your life.

Will I become an Information Keeper too?

You will retain the information you need, but you will not be able to impart it like this one. He has been specially created and trained for this function. Even in this form, we have to limit how much we give you. If we gave you too much at once, you might have severe pain in your head and would not be able to hold it accurately. I want you to monitor how rapidly and how much you can take in and let us know when you have had enough in any one session. Now I would suggest you return to your sleeping place to rest and review. When you are ready to continue, simply send out the thought, 'I am ready.' I will be notified and will come to get you.

In his room Joe reflected on what he had just experienced. It seemed as if both Markel and the Information Keeper were shamans who performed magical feats. Indeed, this whole experience seemed mysterious. Though at one level Joe knew he was awake and not dreaming, on another level it felt so unreal that he sometimes thought of it as a dream. He understood now why Markel had insisted he have this information before flying. Though excited, Joe's body felt suddenly heavy and his brain and mind begged for relief. Sleep was a welcome respite.

Upon waking, he followed his usual pattern of washing and eating, then said in his mind, *I am ready.* Not long afterward, Markel appeared and this time took him to the hangar bay where the Explorer sat. Though he had been fascinated by aeroplanes since he first saw that biplane with the silver wings, no aeroplane on earth could compare to the sleek, circular craft before him. The Information Keeper arrived shortly, ready to continue the training. Now however, he could apply it directly to the craft sitting in front of him. Joe resigned himself to the odor and eyes of this gray being Markel called an Information Keeper. He wanted to get through it so he could fly. Maybe today would be the day.

Though difficult at first to avoid his disgust, gradually he let the images flow and found himself where they left off yesterday, moving from one layer to the next as they penetrated deeper into the craft, its construction, and its operating systems. He experienced himself inside the craft, inside each successive layer, actually looking at each and every component and its function, not limited to mentally trying to connect a drawing to the actual component.

After a while, Joe felt overwhelmed. Dizzy with the images tumbling through his mind, his perception shifting back and forth between systems, from one layer of the craft to another, he signaled Markel that he wanted to stop. He had taken in enough for the day, perhaps more than enough. He had not imagined how complex this craft would be nor how much he would have to stretch his mind to understand it. Maybe he shouldn't try to fly it after all. He wanted to escape to the clear, clean air and blue sky of his home, where he could look up at the canyon walls and smell the fragrance the cedars emitted on a warm sunny day. .

Instead, after a brief rest, Markel led him over to the craft he had been studying. *Come with me.*

Joe followed. *Is it okay to touch it?*

Certainly.

Joe cautiously reached out his hand to the craft. The surface felt soft. He had expected something very hard or slick like glass. His fingers detected a slight tingle. Markel stepped over to the craft and placed his palm on the outer rim. A moment later, a section of the skin parted and lifted, revealing a doorway for entering the craft.

How did you do that? Nothing happened when I touched it.

It has been programmed to recognize my energy pattern, so that when I touch the outside of the craft, it opens, allowing me to enter.

Do you have to touch it on a special place? Joe asked, thinking of the door latches he knew at home.

No, touching it anywhere on the rim will enable it to recognize me and allow access. When you are ready, I will program it to accept your energy pattern as well. By limiting access, individuals who are not prepared to fly the craft may not enter it without being accompanied by someone who is trained. It is for your own safety. Come inside.

Joe's spirits climbed as he followed Markel into the craft, where he had to bend his head to keep from bumping the ceiling. Surely now he would at last get started flying it. Markel motioned Joe to one of the two seats and took the other. Markel then touched a spot on the sloping panel in front of them. Instantly the panel lit up with a variety of lights and indicators and, even more amazing to Joe, the blank surface above the panel in front of them became transparent, enabling him to see out into the hangar bay. He'd wondered how the pilot could see to fly the saucer, because from the outside he hadn't seen any windows.

Each seat had wide arms that adjusted to the length of the pilot's arms. He easily reached the hand shaped indentations at the end of the arms.

Place your hands firmly on the marked places and keep them there until I indicate you can move them.

When Joe did so, the hand print began to soften and melt, and then quickly re-conformed to his exact hand shape. The hand print felt warm to his touch, with a slight tingling sensation. The spots under the finger tips were now accurately positioned to respond to the slightest movement or pressure from his fingers.

It is now reading your energy pattern and will recognize it from now on.

Does that mean I can open the door now too?

Not until I program it to do so. When you know how to operate all its systems and to fly it, I will do that. You still have much more to learn about the craft from the Information Keeper before we begin flight. However, I wanted to introduce you to the actual feel of the craft, as well as having the information in your brain.

Disappointed, Joe's face fell. When would it be enough? He could just imagine what it would feel like to fly this thing. Would it ever happen?

Markel switched off the electrical systems of the saucer and stood up to leave the craft, motioning Joe to do likewise. Once outside, Markel touched the rim again and the door closed, making the surface absolutely seamless again.

Markel explained, *The speeds at which this craft travels when it is in Terra's atmosphere require that the skin be very smooth to eliminate friction. If it were not, it would create turbulence and intense heat, which could damage the craft."*

Walking away, Joe's eyes roamed the large hangar bay and the variety of craft resting there. Many were circular like the Explorer disc, but a few were quite large, long and cylindrically shaped. What might their function be? He hadn't expected Markel to answer his query

Those are our transporter craft. Though this Mothership is essentially our home, there are occasions when we need to transport people and supplies to or from other planets and other ships. Thus we need craft larger than the one you are studying. For now, however, I wish to not extend your study to them, so that you do not become confused. Rest now

Okay, Joe acknowledged and headed for his room. How much

longer would it be before he would get to fly it? Disappointed, and with no sense of day or night, he had no idea how long he slept. Upon waking, he felt quite refreshed for the next session and sent a mental signal that he was ready. He hoped this would be the day.

Markel shortly arrived with the Information Keeper. *Ready for your final session with the Information Keeper?*

Joe nodded eagerly, glad this would be the last one. At long last he might fly.

Markel announced, *This time you will become acquainted with the power plant and the anti-gravity system.*

Though eager to start the flying, Joe had wondered what fueled the craft. He knew that it didn't run on gasoline like the cars and trucks he had seen in Blanding. The one man in their village who knew how to drive had an old International truck whose engine required frequent attention to keep it running. The roof of the truck, made of wooden slats and covered with tattered black-painted canvas, provided the platform where the man's dog loved to ride, lying with his paws draped over the front edge. The dog had a large black patch around one eye, creating a very comical one-eyed appearance when seen from a distance. Though ancient, the rugged truck negotiated the rough track into the canyon that served as a road.

In this session, Joe learned that the energy cell powering the craft was smaller than the engine of the old truck. When it needed replenishing, they simply removed it and replaced it. Especially fascinating was the anti-gravity system, which enabled the craft to rise and descend silently. The saucer used power from the energy cell, but created no exhaust gases like the old truck. He learned that in space, with no atmospheric resistance, once the craft accelerated to the selected speed, it continued without any expenditure of energy. Joe learned how to set the gravity within the craft to whatever level its occupants desired. With the gravity on board the Mothership slightly less than that of earth, Joe frequently found himself bumping into things because he used more strength or energy than necessary.

When the Information Keeper withdrew, signaling the end of the many hours of information transfer, Joe felt relieved and also a little scared. He had enjoyed the intensity of taking in the information about the craft, but what would it be like to fly it? His apprehension increased now that the time had come. He signaled Markel.

Returning to the hangar bay, they approached the craft, which Markel opened with his touch. Markel pointed Joe to the same seat as before and instructed him to place his hands on the hand prints, then explained, *The first step is to conduct an energy adjustment on your body which will make flying in this craft easier for you, especially during phase-change operations.*

His foot tapped spontaneously and forgetting that Markel could hear his thought, *Oh no. Not something else. When would he ever get to fly?*

With no acknowledgment, Markel continued. *Your energy is already at a higher vibrational frequency than most of the people of Terra, but it is still less than optimal for flying this craft. What you will experience is a sensation of energy flowing into your body through your hands, which will in turn cause your body to vibrate, gently at first, then with increasing frequency and intensity. You absolutely must maintain contact with your hand prints. This may be uncomfortable, but under no circumstance break contact. If you do, it could be quite painful. Do you understand?*

Yes, Joe thought fearfully.

Good. We will start now.

What began as a slight tickling sensation in Joe's hands soon grew in intensity. His hands felt glued to the hand prints, as if by some powerful magnetic force. He doubted he could have broken contact, even if he had wanted. Then it accelerated rapidly, first causing his arms to tremble, then his shoulders, torso and legs, until his whole body vibrated so rapidly he thought he might fly off the seat. His vision blurred and he clamped his jaw shut to keep his teeth from chattering, determined to ride it out. Sweat dripped down into his eyes. He was so scared, he felt like throwing up. Then the vibrations accelerated until they felt like one continuous infusion of energy and he wanted to scream. Just when he thought he could stand it no longer, the energy subsided and in less than a minute, stopped.

Now you can release your hands. You did well. Are you all right?

I guess so. That was scary, Joe wiped the sweat from his face with his sleeve, his nausea subsiding. He was pleasantly surprised to note that instead of tired, he now felt energized and wide awake.

Now your energy system is adjusted to sustain the challenges it will meet in flight. In a few hours this change will become permanent. You will not need to repeat this adjustment.

That's good, Joe thought.

While you are in this elevated state, I think it would be suitable to go for your first flight. Are you ready?

At last, though Joe didn't want any more surprises like the last one.

We will begin our flight now. Markel said.

As Markel engaged the anti-gravity system, Joe felt the craft rise a few inches, rock a little, then settle in a steady horizontal position.

Markel retracted the landing gear and rotated the craft so they faced the large door at the rear of the hangar bay, which slid up, revealing a smaller chamber with another door beyond that. Markel maneuvered the craft into this chamber, then pressed a button which closed the door behind them. With that door securely sealed, he pressed another button which caused the dual panels in front of them to retract to the sides, revealing the yawning vastness of space. Slowly, Markel flew the craft out of the chamber into open space and away from the Mothership. Joe stared back in awe at the immense size of the Mothership.

Joe's stomach rose to his throat. Worse than standing on the edge of a cliff back home! Nothing under him! *I don't think I want to do this,* Joe said fearfully.

His fear brought no response from Markel.

16

"Wow!" Joe exclaimed aloud on the first day of his flight training. He'd not imagined how thrilling it would be to fly the ship. The saucer responded to his slightest touch as he imitated the maneuvers Markel demonstrated. To Joe's quick mind, it became a form of play, and he was pleased to now link what he was doing with all the information he'd taken in. He couldn't stop grinning, especially when Markel transitioned him into the next phase, learning to control the craft with his mind. By first clearly imaging what he wanted the craft to do, Joe learned to execute the maneuvers without using the hand controls at all. He felt increasingly one with the ship, like it was an extension of himself, and his confidence grew.

Eventually Markel headed the craft back and instructed Joe how to home in on the Mothership so that he could find it whenever he wanted.

Once there, Markel demonstrated the procedure for docking, explaining how the outer bay formed an airlock to protect the inner environment. *The inner door to the hangar bay will not open until the outer door has been fully secured and the atmosphere within the airlock matches that inside the hangar.*

After they were safely in the hangar bay, Markel complimented Joe on his flying skills with the craft. *You are a natural flyer, Joe*, Markel said. *It won't take you long to learn to fly this craft. You are doing well for one so young.*

Though happy and proud, Joe said nothing. His first flight lesson had been an incredible thrill. He wished he could rush home and tell his friends all about the wonder of his flight. But he knew he couldn't, for not only would they not believe him, but Markel had already cautioned him that he must tell no one about it.

Markel continued, *Tomorrow, I will introduce you to flying within the earth's atmosphere. It will be different, due to the resistance of the air within the atmosphere which is absent here in space.*

That evening before going to sleep, Joe wondered why they were going to all the trouble of training him to fly the craft. Yes, in a sense, he now felt like one of them. But what did they want from him? Why did Markel want him to learn to fly the Explorer? It was not as if he could keep one at home in the village or even tell anyone about it. He frowned, certain that by now his parents and the village all thought he was dead.

He regretted the pain he was causing.

The next morning Joe blurted out, "Why are you teaching me to fly the Explorer?"

Joe was disappointed and frustrated when all Markel said was, *We will explain that later.*

Joe spent the next ten days in intensive flight training, including learning to fly within earth's atmosphere, which did feel different than flying in space. Markel guided him through landing, taking off, hovering and other special maneuvers and he frequently reminded Joe of the need for secrecy. Joe knew that Markel was right, for his world back home scarcely knew any aircraft at all, let alone something like this sophisticated spacecraft. Markel also demonstrated phase change in the craft, making it instantly invisible should that be desired or necessary. Joe felt the phase change as a jolt, a little scary. But Markel explained that it had no permanent effect on either the occupants or the capabilities of the craft. With so many new things to learn each day, Joe soon moved beyond the stage of awe, and simply advanced to the next step. It would only be later, long after he had returned home, that he would reflect again on the awesome nature of the spacecraft and his experiences.

Finally, one day as Markel and Joe approached the craft, Markel communicated, *"I think you are ready to fly the craft yourself now, without me on board with you."*

Surprised, Joe spoke out loud. "You really think I'm ready?"

Yes. Essentially you have been flying the craft entirely on your own the last few times. I have just ridden along to make minor suggestions for improving your skills. I believe that you will be totally safe in flying the craft. So go ahead and fly now. Return in about an hour.

Aren't you going to open the door? Joe said, standing by the craft.

You may open it yourself. I have changed the code to respond to your pattern as well as mine. Now it is your ship too.

Joe's hand trembled as he placed it on the rim of the craft and he was almost surprised to see the door open to his touch. He entered, sat down, and pressed the button to close the door and activate the craft. He saw Markel's small wave of encouragement through the flight window. Then he focused on the task of flying the craft safely, piloting it carefully through the airlock and out into space. He knew that Markel had instruments in the Mothership to track him in his flight, so he used great caution in his maneuvers to ensure that he didn't do anything dumb or risky. He wanted to justify Markel's trust and confidence in him.

His first solo! An incredible thrill coupled with a deep sense of satisfaction. Was this what it was like for the young eagle? Born to fly? The beauty of space, its deep black sprinkled with a myriad of stars, beckoned to him. Loving the freedom of flight, he felt powerful, and at the same time infinitely small, as he gazed at the vastness around him. Later when he noticed that it was time to return to the Mothership, he had a moment of sadness, for he supposed that he must soon return to his village. Learning to fly this craft had been the most exciting thing to ever happen in his life. He couldn't imagine anything more wonderful than this adventure.

17

April, 1942
La Junta, Colorado

After that first orientation ride in the Stearman, Joe threw himself into his primary flight training, putting all his energy into studying and learning with Lt. Farber. In spite of endless trips around the pattern, practicing his take offs and landings, he never got bored. He was flying, and that was all that mattered. Though Killer Will seemed to always be on his back, Joe didn't mind, as he recognized that Will was teaching him to be more precise with his flying, and at the same time more intuitive. Joe realized he was learning to feel the airplane, in a different, yet similar way to how he felt the saucer, gradually becoming one with it. The plane began to feel like an extension of his own body, even his own mind.

Over those first few days, Will Farber reluctantly came to the conclusion that Joe was one of those natural born pilots and secretly admired this new student of his. He seemed to have a highly developed intuitive feel for the airplane. Only twice did Will have to ask him what he was thinking about when he had botched some maneuver. Thereafter, when Joe strapped himself in, he did not so much wear the airplane as Will did, it was like he 'became' the airplane. His thinking always flew even with or a little ahead of the plane. One day, after only 10 flying hours, and several successful landings, Will tersely said, "Let me outta here. And don't bust my airplane!"
"You mean you want me to take it solo?"
"Yeah, what'd ya think I meant?"
"Yes, SIR!" Joe replied.
"When you get back, taxi back to the line, if you're able."
"Yes, Sir"
With that, Joe taxied out to the runway, got a green flag from the flagman, and rolled on out onto the runway. With Will out of the back seat he noticed a difference in how quickly the plane lifted off and how it flew. But Joe liked that difference. Even though he was just going around the pattern one more time, he felt a great thrill. When he smoothly touched down again, with only a very slight bounce, due to

lack of fine adjustment for the weight change, he found himself breaking into a smile that wouldn't stop. When he had parked the plane in the line on the ramp, he climbed out still wearing the grin. Will walked up to him, and gave one of the few compliments Joe ever heard from him.

"Nice job." And after a pause, perhaps to cover his own embarrassment, Will continued, "And wipe that stupid grin off your face."

"Yes, SIR!"

Would they ever have a normal conversation? Joe doubted it. But he was glad for the brief compliment and Will's moment of digression from his stern demeanor. Will continued to press him further in his flight training, moving rapidly into aerobatics. Sometimes it seemed to Joe that Will indeed deserved his Killer nickname, as he pushed and challenged him relentlessly. Joe didn't know then that Will believed he had the makings of a superb pilot and was determined to make him the best pilot he had ever turned out of pilot training, if he didn't kill himself in some accident of pilotage or equipment failure.

But to Joe it felt different. He knew nothing of Will's true feeling and intent. He constantly wondered why Will seemed to hate him so much, always telling him what he did wrong. When graduation time finally came, after logging sixty hours in the Stearman, Joe had the highest number of points in his class, and in fact the highest ever earned at that training base. In addition he had garnered the respect and admiration of the rest of the cadets in his class, not only for his flying skills, but also for his support and leadership amongst the cadets. They voted him the honor of "Outstanding Cadet", which meant as much to Joe as the graduation ceremonies. As Joe walked through the line of officers, saluting and shaking hands, he came to Will, who merely grunted, "Come see me in my quarters when this is over."

Joe wanted nothing less than one more chewing out by this man. He'd had his fill of him during these weeks of pilot training. Will more than deserved his nickname of Killer Will in Joe's mind. What more Will could want with him, he couldn't imagine.

"Thought you'd seen the last of Ol' Killer Will, didn't ya?"

"Yessir!" Joe's jaw dropped, surprised that Will knew of that term, for he had never ever used it to his face.

"Well, I got a few more things to say to ya." Joe wilted a little, even in his dress uniform. "I've been tough on you, Joe Star. Not because you did so badly, but because you did so well. After that first intro flight, I said to myself, now here's a real pilot! I'm gonna make him the best damn pilot I can. And you know what?"

"No sir?" Allowing himself a bit of cautious optimism

"I think I did. Or rather we did. Joe. You got the makings of being one of the best pilots in this whole damn Army. You've got an intuitive feel for the plane I've never seen before. I preach to these kids that they gotta wear the airplane. But you, you not only wear the plane, you ARE the plane. Never saw that before. I've recommended that you be assigned to skip Basic Training and go on to Advanced immediately. Your next training will be in the T-6, (North American AT-6, the Texan). It is a lot more airplane than these birds we've been flying, so study it well and treat it well. BE that plane too and it will take care of you. I don't need to tell you to respect your plane. You already do that." He paused. "I also gotta tell you that I've come to respect you as a man. You seem to have more maturity than most of these kids. Hell, I'm only 26 myself. You sure you didn't lie about your age, that you're not older than the 20 you put in your records?"

"No Sir . . . I mean yes, sir."

"Well, I'm not sure I believe it. You look young, but you act older. Maybe it's just 'cause you're Indian or sumpin,' your quiet nature. But go ahead. Be the best pilot you can. Giv'em Hell, Joe.

"Thank, you sir. I can sure agree that you were tough. In fact, at times I hated your guts. I became convinced that you hated me and couldn't wait to wash me out, one way or another. But I also have to admit that you were fair, and a good instructor. I thank you for that." After a pause he added, "And thanks for the compliments."

Joe wished he could tell him of his other flying experience in the space craft a few years previous, where they trained him to not just wear the craft, but to become one with the craft. To properly fly it, he had to let his mind, his nerves, and body sync with the craft. The Boeing Company built a good strong flying machine in the Stearman, but it had nowhere near the level of sophistication he had known aboard the space craft. During his training here he quickly learned to apply the same skills to the Stearman, at least as much as he could with this simple airplane. Joe didn't think Will would understand if he told him about the Explorer craft. He felt sure Will had no knowledge of the existence of any such vehicle, and would only think Joe was crazy, so he kept it to himself.

18

September 1942

Joe, like a few others in his cadet class in Primary who had done well, received his orders to move on to Advanced Flight Training in the AT-6, rather than go through Basic Training in lesser aircraft, such as the BT-13, as the next step. The Army needed pilots now and ordered instructors to push them through the training system as rapidly as possible. When he opened his orders, he saw a posting to the army airbase at Marianna, Florida. The envelope included train tickets to take him there. After all the flying he'd been doing, he wished that he could take a plane and fly down there, but that was not the fate of cadets and trainees. Perhaps after he had finished his training, he could fly rather than ride the rails. As he packed his duffle bag to leave, he realized that he would miss the friends he'd made here during his training, and he also knew that, like it or not, some he would never see again. In a world at war, where training accidents happened, and where the enemy shot at you with live ammunition to knock you out of the sky, many were never going to come home again, except in a box and maybe not even that.

Sometimes, late at night, he and his bunk mates talked quietly about what it might be like to die in combat. As young men, they typically wanted to believe that it would never happen to them, that they would always be able to evade the enemy and his trigger finger. But each secretly knew that they were going to be vulnerable, now that they would soon be going into situations where they would kill or be killed. They all agreed that if their number came up, they hoped it would be over quickly, and especially to not ever burn in the air, the worst way to go. Always a fairly private person, Joe had never become very close with any of his friends among his class. Maybe that was better in the long run. That way, if someone got killed, maybe it wouldn't hurt so badly.

When he boarded the train in La Junta, Colorado, happy to have done so well in his Primary training, Joe was excited to think about the training to come. He knew that the AT-6 Texan was a powerful plane, a whole different beast than the PT-17 Stearman biplanes he had been flying. His excitement faded though, as his trip took him through many train stations, often with long waits between trains. It didn't take him long to decide he hated traveling in smoky, crowded, noisy trains. Trying to sleep in a chair car on the train or on hard wooden benches in a train station with only his duffle bag for a cushion made sleep difficult if not impossible. Wichita, Dallas, Shreveport, Mobile each exacted their toll on his body and mind. Startling also was his first real encounter with racial discrimination. In Shreveport and Mobile, he saw separate toilets for the Whites and Coloreds. Though in uniform, when he started into one of the restrooms with a white soldier he'd met, a civilian man yelled at him, telling him to get out of there and go to the Colored restroom, which was dirtier, smaller, and less well kept. He felt humiliated and a strange sense of shame. Though it would be hard for anyone to take him for a Negro, he did have a darker skin than most of the soldiers, and certainly had a different look to his face. It was a painful introduction to the South. He wished they had sent him somewhere else.

 He entertained himself during the long hours of the trip with imagining how long it would have taken him to fly it in one of the Stearmans. He had picked up a map of the US so that he could track his progress. As the hours passed, he grew more and more tired, more in need of a shower in the increasingly hot temperatures of late summer in the south, and sweated in a way he'd never known before in his life, having grown up in a high altitude, desert climate. Even La Junta, Colorado, was better than this. After two days and two nights, he smelled so bad he could hardly stand himself, let alone the other guys around him in much the same state. By the time he got off the train mid-morning of the third day at Marianna, in the Florida panhandle, the fresh air of the open troop truck, sent to bring them to the Marianna Army Air Field outside of town, seemed inviting.

 And what a small town Marianna was. With little more than two thousand in population, it didn't have much to offer the boys. For Joe, that didn't present much of a problem, but for many of the boys, getting off base to go drinking, and hopefully dancing with girls, seemed important for their morale. A little older than many of his fellow trainees, Joe was grateful he didn't need to get drunk every Saturday night.

 The truck bounced over potholes in the seven mile gravel road out to the air base, making for an even rougher ride than the train. By the time they arrived, they were covered with dust, as well as stinking from their long train trip. The sweat which ran down their faces and soaked their clothes served to trap the dust swirling around them.

 Upon arrival they slung their duffle bags over their shoulders and jumped down from the truck, where a sergeant ordered them to fall in line for roll call. The confusion that arose over someone missing kept them waiting longer in the hot sun than any of them wanted. After the names of those present all got checked off, they were finally dismissed to their quarters. Joe felt so relieved to get to his metal Quonset building and find his bunk that he scarcely noticed the heat of the sun beating through the corrugated tin roof over his head. On the way, a glimpse of rows of gleaming silver T-6's on the flight line to the north of their barracks area, revived his spirits a little. But all he wanted at the moment was a shower and sleep. The latter wouldn't arrive for several hours yet, but he thoroughly enjoyed his time in the shower house near his Quonset.

When he presented himself at the mess hall for lunch, he was unprepared for the greasy, southern style food that would be his fare for the next few weeks. He couldn't bring himself to eat much of it, so he remained hungry, even after his meal. Endless waiting in lines, orientation, and paperwork took up the afternoon. By the end of the day he agreed with his fellow trainees that they should take most of their paper work and use it in the latrine. By the time Joe finally got to his bunk that evening, the fatigue of two days and nights of train travel weighed him down, body and soul. Exhaustion had devoured his normal resilience and he slept, knowing that daybreak would come all too soon.

Morning brought a new outlook on life and with it the beginning of a new ground school. The training manual for the T-6 was much larger than for the old Stearman, but Joe dived into it with relish, knowing that what he had available in his mind would serve him well when he got into the aircraft itself. He saw happily that they would have radio communications now, instead of the old one way Gosport speaking tube that connected the instructor in the back seat to the student in the front in the PT-17 Stearman, and allowed no communication with the ground. With the Gosport he could only listen to the growling of Killer Will. Now he had a mike and a helmet with earphones, he could talk to the control tower as well as listen. Students still sat in the front seat, where they could more easily see the ground for landing. The instructor took the backseat, where the wing obscured that view. After two weeks of ground school, which included meteorology, navigation, as well as the T-6 manual, all cadets were tested again. Joe studied hard, knowing that he could still be washed out at any time, ending his flying career. He dreaded the possibility of going to the infantry and becoming what the cadets called a ground-pounder, but he passed his ground school test with high marks.

Joe's third week at Marianna brought him his orientation ride in the T-6. Often nicknamed the Pilot Maker or Old Growler, the Army used the AT-6 for training most of the fighter pilots for World War II. His instructor, a man named George Dawson, was tall, slender, and friendly, but all business. Joe thought he'd get along well with him, while at the same time receive good instruction. He was eager to begin flying. Their pre-flight inspection brought the routine review of safety and emergency procedures, with the reminder that if he ever had an engine fire, to never bail out on the right side of the plane, where the exhaust exited and where any fire would be concentrated. Since they usually entered the plane on the left side, he found it easy to remember that side for exits as well, emergency or not. Once in the cockpit for familiarization, George cautioned him to never pull the hydraulic lever on the left side while on the ground, which retracted the landing gear. It would be terribly embarrassing to retract the gear while on the ground, and if the engine was running, ruin the prop and engine. Eager to get going, Joe felt impatient with all this briefing, which he'd already memorized from the manual.

After start up and taxiing out to the runway threshold, George spoke over the intercom, "I'll fly the first take off. You follow through on the controls to get the feel of her." Moving the propeller into flat pitch for takeoff and holding tight on the brakes, George advanced the throttle until the plane strained to move. Brakes released, it started down the runway. Joe could feel George dancing on the rudder pedals. As soon as he had positive control on the rudder from the air flow, he pushed the stick forward, raising the tail to a horizontal position. The plane quickly gathered momentum behind the huge 550 hp Pratt & Whitney engine. Joe was thrilled at all that power in front of him. In what seemed like no time at all, they were airborne and climbing at an angle that would have been impossible with the Stearman. Thus began a love affair with a machine, for this plane would become a firm friend in the next few weeks.

Joe learned rapidly the skills of flying this particular aircraft. After only five hours of dual, George turned him loose to solo the plane. Here too, even in this heavy airplane, Joe could feel the difference between having only himself on board, vs. having his instructor in the back seat. It became slightly more nimble and agile, though not as great a difference as in the Stearman. The next few weeks were filled with flying, studying, flying, instruction, and more flying. Aerial maneuvers, emergency procedures, aerobatics, night flight, navigation, cross country, formation flying, simulated gunnery, (the AT-6 was not armed) and combat tactics all formed part of the training. As the days went by, Joe felt increasingly confident in the plane and in himself. In what seemed like a very short time, Joe lined up with his fellow pilots for graduation from Advanced Training. Now he had his coveted wings and his second lieutenant's bars! He felt proud to be a commissioned officer in the

Army Air Corps. As before, he received his new orders at the end of the training, this time to Randolph Air Field near San Antonio, Texas to learn to fly the P-47.

The train ride from Florida to Texas was not as long as the last one had been, and Joe was both more seasoned and confident by now. He knew he was a good pilot and felt ready to work hard to become a better one. He felt excited to get to fly the P-47 Thunderbolt, the heaviest and fastest of the fighters, often called the "Jug," because of the thick shape of the fuselage, with its huge engine and propeller. It also was known to be able to take incredible amounts of punishment and damage in combat and still get its pilot back home, one small comfort to the boys flying these planes.

The first day on base, their introductory lecture sobered all the trainees, all newly minted officers. The Commanding Officer (CO), an experienced combat fighter pilot with three kills of his own, spoke to the assembly of eager young men. "Six months from today half of you pilots will be dead! That's right. I said dead! Fighter pilots die for many reasons, and most of them are needless. However, one of those reasons WON'T be because you did not get good training. Here you will get the best training in the world, which should make you the best fighter pilots in the world. Some of you will be. Some of you won't, and mainly because you didn't listen to your instructors and flight leaders. From this moment on, you should eat, sleep, and breathe fighter flying. Follow the instruction you are given and you will not only survive, but maybe come home with a notch or two in your belt. We intend for you to be able to take on any adversary. And make no mistake about it, you will have some of the best. The Luftwaffe is no pushover. They are well trained too, and very, very disciplined. You cannot afford to be anything less. If you go to the Pacific, the Jap Zeros are incredibly agile and can turn inside anything we have. You must develop tactics to compensate, or you die.

Each of the young pilots in that assembly vowed that he would not be one who would make those stupid mistakes, nor forget what he was taught. But inevitably some did, and did not survive. Each looked nervously and secretly at those around him and wondered who that would be. Joe vowed to himself that he would learn as much as he could. His very nature, to be slow and deliberate, would serve him well in the weeks and months ahead. But he was ill prepared for one adventure on the horizon. A girl named Amy.

19

That evening brought Joe's first time as an officer in the officer's mess hall at Randolph. As he familiarized himself with the new surroundings, he filled his food tray and scanned for an empty seat. Spotting one, he turned abruptly and launched himself in that direction, slamming into another pilot who had started around him. His momentum knocked the other's food tray to the floor, spilling its contents and its holder on the floor. Joe made haste to apologize.

"I'm so sorry, sir," speaking to the figure on the floor, he reached to help him up, when he suddenly realized that it was a girl . . . in a flight suit!

"Why the hell don't you look where you're going?" The girl yelled from the floor in frustration and fiery anger, batting away his offered hand.

All the more apologetic, he now got down on his knees and to help her deal with the mess. Already he'd made the first mistake of his fighter pilot career, not scanning for hazards. Joe momentarily flashed on his CO's lecture and wondered if this was an omen of more serious things to come. In trying to make amends, Joe felt awkward and embarrassed. He offered to go get her a new plate of food. Two other girls, similarly dressed, stood nearby, laughing at the scene which became more and more comical the more Joe tried to apologize.

His face felt hot as he stammered, "This is my first day on base, my first day in an officer's mess. I was looking for a place to sit and didn't see you coming. I'm very sorry." Then, as he became aware of how extraordinarily pretty this girl was, he got even more flustered. Finally, as if remembering his manners, he just stuck out his hand, well laced with the remains of her dinner, and said abruptly. "Second Lieutenant Joe Star."

"Amy Hutchins," she responded, declining his sticky hand. "And these are my friends Betty and Donna," indicating the two girls coming up behind her. "I'll go through the line again myself, thank you, and after YOU get that cleaned up, why don't you bring your tray and come join us at our table in the corner? You can tell us what they let you fly with that kind of coordination."

Now Joe saw the girls less through a haze of embarrassment and noticed that their baggy flight suits did not totally hide their feminine attributes, though they didn't quite look like the pinups of Betty Grable he'd seen. He later learned the girls called them zoot suits. Joe couldn't help admiring the girls. Amy was especially pretty, with dark auburn hair that curled down around her neck. She looked strong and fit, as well as having curves in all the right places. Betty's bobbed blond hair seemed to match her short stature. Tall and slender, Donna wore her brown hair pulled back in a ponytail. All three looked full of life and energy.

Joe turned and got a wet towel from one of the mess aides to mop up the spill, thinking nothing at all of his being an officer engaged in such a task. Only recently advanced from the lowly position of cadet trainee, it never entered his mind that he shouldn't do it himself. After all, he had caused the accident. But what were girls doing here? And in flying togs? Were they pilots too? He had heard scuttlebutt about the Army training girls somewhere in Texas to be ferry pilots. But he'd hardly expected to meet any of them. When he arrived at their table, his food by now cold, he sat down, felt his face flush, then felt embarrassed by that too. The girls, already seated, giggled at his discomfort.

"Well, soldier, what brings you here to Randolph?" Betty asked, though clearly aware of the new bar on his collar and the wings on his chest, indicating he had graduated from Advanced Training.

Joe, more confident now, said, "I've been posted here for my final phase of training, to fly the P-47. I feel really lucky to get to fly what I hear is the best fighter we have."

"Well, good luck. It's a lotta airplane. We just flew in some new ones from Republic for you guys to bang up. You gotta watch it all the time or it can get away from you. You sure you're up to it?" Amy teased. "You gotta keep your eyes open all the time, you know."

Joe didn't know what to say. The idea that these girls already flew P-47's seemed more than he could imagine at the moment. After all, they were just girls, no older than himself, if as old. He hadn't missed the pilots wings pinned on their blouses, but didn't know what that really meant. Unsure whether they were joking with him, playing him for a fool, or were serious, he finally spoke, "You mean you already know how to fly the Jug?"

"Yeah, been doing it for quite a while now," Donna said, still chuckling to herself, "Like Amy said, you gotta watch it though. It's kinda twitchy on the ground in landing."

Silent for a minute, Joe then said hopefully, "Nah, you girls are just playing with me. You don't fly the P-47."

"The hell we don't!" Amy retorted, exposing her fiery personality. "If you don't believe us, get your butt out to the flight line tomorrow morning and you'll see. We're stuck here for a few days anyway, so we might as well fly and have some fun." The girls all waited in silence to see what Joe would say next.

"So, what all planes do you fly then?" Joe asked.

"You name it, we fly it," Betty said. "PT-17 and 19, BT-13, T-6, P-47, P-51, P-38, P-39, P-40, the Bamboo Bomber, B-25, and the B-26, and of course the Gooney Bird. Oh, yeah, and some of us are checked out in the B-17 and B-24. Like I said, you name it, we fly it."

Joe could hardly believe what they were telling him. They flew all the heavy iron! He realized that he had fallen into the trap, like a lot of guys he'd trained with, of assuming that women were less capable, less skilled than they themselves were. The capabilities and accomplishments of these girls was a lot to take in.

"You fly bombers too?" Joe's disbelief was apparent.

"Of course, though we tend to specialize somewhat. Some of us girls fly fighters more than the bombers, just as a practical measure. Others tend to fly the bombers more, though we trained on all of them," Amy added with emphasis. "Maybe you haven't heard about us. We are WAFS, Women's Army Ferrying Squadron. Some of us are called WASPs, Women's Army Service Pilots. Usually we deliver new airplanes to bases all over the country. Once in a while we get stuck with the shitty job of flying tow targets for gunnery practice for you new fighter jocks, or for ground shooters. We all hate getting shot at on purpose. We worry all the time about the bozos who might be bad shots. More than once we've come home with holes in our planes."

Joe looked at the girls with a new sense of appreciation, and especially Amy. In fact, he couldn't take his eyes off her, though he didn't want be so impolite as to just stare at her. Her long hours in the cockpit had brought a healthy tan to her face and arms, and her eyes fairly sparkled when a smile lit up her face. And when his eyes dropped to her bosom, he forced himself to look back at her face and at the other two as well, so as not to offend. He felt a stirring that he had never known before. He had never dated, never even spent time alone with a girl. Back home in his village and in the little town of Blanding there had been little time or opportunity for that. His awareness of his 'other' heritage had made him even more hesitant about approaching girls. But here he sat, having supper with three lively, interesting girls who were pilots as well. He felt lucky, but also very, very shy.

Sitting across from Amy, he wondered how he could get to know her better. Unsure what to say or do next, he felt relieved when their table conversation returned to flying stories, weather, the latest news of the war, and friendly bantering. When they finished eating, Betty and

Donna stood up to go. Joe said, "Amy, I apologize again for knocking you to the floor. I'll keep my eye out for you next time . . . that is, if there is a next time."

"Well, there might be, but I don't think I'll let you knock me over again." Still seated, Amy turned to Betty and Donna and said, "You guys go on, I'll be along soon." Betty and Donna gave each other a wink. They had not missed the spark that seemed to be happening between Amy and Joe. But they knew she could take care of herself, on the ground with guys, as well as in the air.

When they were gone, Amy spoke first, not one to lose an opportunity. "Tell me more about yourself, Joe. Where did you come from, and how did you get into flying?" She, like most others in the military, grew accustomed to constantly meeting new people. Directly asking for personal background and history simplified getting acquainted. Joe told her of his life-long desire to fly after seeing a biplane fly over his home town in Utah when he was in grade school, culminating with enlisting in the Army Air Corps. He didn't go so far as telling her about his experience with the flying saucer, though he did share his experiences in primary and advanced training.

* * *

Amy sat across the table from Joe, impressed with his quiet way. He seemed confident, without the brash bravado that she usually saw when guys tried to make points with her and the other girls. As women pilots in a man's world, men treated them a little differently than the girls at the USO clubs. Guys often didn't quite know how to take them, but that didn't slow them down for long. They tried to make an impression by bragging about how good a pilot they were, rather than how manly. Now, here was this guy, not even trying to make an impression. She thought his shyness rather cute and appealing. But she couldn't quite place him ethnically. He'd said he came from Utah, but that didn't mean much to her. Due to his dark skin, she wanted to ask about his race, but thought that might be offensive, so more tactfully she asked, "Where do your ancestors come from, Joe?"

Surprised at such a direct question, Joe paused. Amongst his people such a question would never be asked, especially by a woman. But in the military, people often asked about his background and his unusual appearance. Most people had not seen Indians anywhere but in Western movies, which portrayed them as stupid or inept, and who always lost out against the white man. Joe never spoke of his 'other' ancestors. So he simply explained to Amy that his ancestors had lived in Utah and Colorado for centuries, and that his family now lived near Blanding,

Utah. That seemed to satisfy her.

Amy, he discovered, had grown up in Illinois, and learned to fly at an early age with her dad. She grew up something of a maverick and had joined a barnstorming group after high school and even performed at air shows before the war. She had actually been flying much longer than he had, but took her military training at Avenger Field, near Sweetwater, Texas with all the other girls in the WASP. LIFE magazine had even done a feature article on them in July.

In the next few days, Joe and Amy tried to see each other as much as possible, though Joe had intensive ground school classes, preparing to fly the P-47, so he didn't have much time. A single place airplane, Joe knew his first flight would also be his first solo flight in the plane, and he needed to be as well prepared as possible.

Since the girls were stuck here for a while between ferrying assignments, the base commander asked them if they would be willing to fly tow targets while they waited for their next ferrying job. Reluctantly, they agreed. Amy had mixed feelings. She hated flying tow targets, but she welcomed the opportunity to remain and hopefully get to know Joe better.

When Joe climbed into the cockpit of the P-47 for his first flight, he felt awed by the fact that it was a lot more airplane than the T-6, a whole lot more. It looked and felt like one big engine, with just enough of a fuselage and wings attached to allow the pilot to control it. Sitting in the cockpit, he took his time in familiarizing and memorizing every control and instrument in it. When he started it up, he loved the feel of all that power rumbling in front of him. When he finally reached takeoff point and pushed the throttle in, the power of the big prop and engine thrust him back against his seat. His first flight was one to remember.

He took to the plane rapidly and felt so at home in it that it surprised even his instructors. Days flew by, filled with flying during the day, and trying to meet Amy at the mess hall when they both happened to be on the ground at the same time. They tried to spend as much time together as possible in the evenings. Joe was surprised to find himself falling in love with Amy, the last thing he had expected. His normal reserve and private nature as an Indian began to melt away in the face of this vibrant, assertive young woman. He was even more amazed that she seemed to be falling for him too. They both found it frustrating to realize that their future was so uncertain, that they had so little time together. A week later, on Thursday evening after dinner, when Joe walked Amy back to her barracks, their kisses ignited a desire for more. Amy asked Joe if he thought he could get a 24 hour pass to go off base Saturday. Joe promised to put in his request the next morning.

    Relieved and happy the pass had come through, Joe was nervous when he and Amy caught the Saturday afternoon bus from the base into San Antonio, but excited to be spending so much time with Amy with no one looking over their shoulders. Their sudden romance had caught them both off guard, but was welcome as the tempo of the nation's involvement in the war increased. It seemed that the whole country had been swept up into consciousness of the war. It permeated everyone's life, civilians, as well as military. They were not immune to the feeling of having so little time.
    Arriving at their hotel in downtown San Antonio, Joe blushed when Amy registered them as Mr. & Mrs. The desk clerk just smiled at their obvious deception and offered them a top floor room with a view over the city, in what he called the honeymoon suite. They left their small shoulder bags in the room and went back downstairs to walk around the city, hoping to find something to eat. By asking among the many other military personnel on the street, they eventually found a restaurant which promised delicious steaks and delivered on that promise. They lingered over their drinks, both a little nervous about their coming night together. Having satisfied one hunger, Joe didn't know what to say or do next, though his mind darted ahead, imagining what might come next. Finally, Amy said, "Let's go."
    Darkness was falling by the time they stepped out of the restaurant and headed back to the hotel, both pretending not to be in a hurry. They picked up their key and went upstairs. Once in their room, though excited, Joe's shyness escalated into feeling jittery. He started to turn on the lamp, but stopped when Amy asked him to leave it off as she bent to turn on the bedside radio to some music. He looked at the bed, then at Amy, his anxiety a rising lump in his throat. Finally he said, "I've never been with a woman before. In fact, you're the first girl I've ever kissed."
    "I know," Amy whispered as she moved into his arms. "That makes me pretty lucky girl." She reached up to undo his khaki tie, then began to unbutton his shirt. Joe's breath became shorter as he stared out the window over her head. The lights from the city street below slanted through the open curtains at the windows, forming two long panels on the ceiling, ample light to see the girl he held. After removing his shirt and hanging it on the back of a chair, Joe's fingers trembled as he tried to undo the small buttons of her blouse.
    "Here, let me help you," She said, working the buttons quickly with her nimble fingers, and in a moment pulled her blouse off. Joe's breath

stopped as he beheld the beauty of her breasts, supported by her white bra with its concentric circles of stitching that went from its tips back to her chest, something he'd never seen before. "You probably don't know how to work one of these either," she giggled, as she reached around behind her back, unhooked her bra, allowing her breasts to spill out, slipped it off her shoulders and flung it on the chair nearby. Joe was so entranced by the beauty of her body, her breasts, he couldn't even speak.

As she came into his arms, her breasts felt warm against his chest. She molded her body to his, stimulating his growing erection. He bent his head to meet her upturned face, her hungry lips matched his, feeding their passion. His breath so shallow he was unable to speak, Joe slid his hands down onto her hips, found the button on the back of her skirt, undid it, and tugged down the zipper below it. Released, the khaki skirt slid to the floor, where Amy stepped out of it, hooked it with her big toe and kicked it toward the chair as well, never leaving their embrace. Joe felt the movement of her firm buttocks through her cotton underpants. They danced slowly to the music of Guy Lombardo on the radio, and Joe, not knowing how to dance, only moved as if in a trance, marveling at her soft curves undulating beneath his fingers.

When the song ended, Amy unbuckled his belt, then unbuttoned his pants and pushed them down his legs, where he stepped out of them. He gave a gasp as she reached down through the waistband of his shorts and grasped his erection in her right hand, while her left hand pulled his head toward hers. As their kiss deepened, Joe hesitantly brought his hands up to cup her breasts in his palms, bringing a little moan of pleasure from Amy. They couldn't stop their kisses, mouths hungry for each other. Finally, Amy broke their kiss and pulled his head down toward her breasts, whispering, "Kiss them."

Joe leaned down and hesitantly touched his lips to her left nipple. Amy, her hand still behind his neck, pulled him in tighter. Joe spontaneously opened his mouth to take in her nipple and her breast, automatically sucking a little and massaged the nipple with the tip of his tongue. Amy groaned and pulled him in even tighter, arching her back to thrust her breast deeper into his mouth. Time stood still for Joe, his mind scarcely able to believe what was happening. He pulled back once to catch his breath, but Amy coaxed him back onto her breast, with little resistance on his part. By now Amy was breathing hard too. Time seemed to speed up, even disappear. Then Amy disengaged his hand from her other breast and guided it slowly down her firm belly and inside her underpants to her mound of hair, and on lower, to between her legs, where he felt her slick wetness.

Breathless at this new level of intimacy, Joe felt a rush of desire, more powerful than anything he had ever known. Without consciously thinking, he slid her underpants down off her hips, and she did the same for him. Now fully naked, their bodies pressed together so tightly they became one body, breath coming in short intakes, they moved quickly to the bed. Amy fell backward, pulling him down on top between her legs. He felt Amy guide him inside her. Their mutually thrusting hips pressed together, as if they could not get enough of each other, until they both came to their release with sharp cries, first Joe, and then Amy a few seconds later. They clung to each other for long minutes afterward, words inadequate and unnecessary, their skin damp with the sweet sweat of their exertion.

Finally, Joe rolled to one side, pulling back enough that he could gaze into Amy's eyes. After long moments of silence, he finally spoke. "I never imagined that it could be like this! That it could be so wonderful! I never really thought I could be in love with anyone like I am with you. I know it's wartime and I don't know what the future will bring, but I want to be with you for the rest of my life, Amy."

"Me too, Joe," she said, snuggling into his neck and kissing his ear.

After a long while, in which they drank in the closeness and intimacy between them, Amy climbed out of the bed and headed toward the bathroom, which had a large tub. She paused at the door, looked back at Joe. "This looks inviting. Let's take a bath. . . together. I think our tub is big enough for two." She giggled, and continued, "Maybe they planned it that way... for the honeymoon suite." She walked on into the bathroom and started the water running. In awe, Joe watched her naked body move with grace and confidence. She came back to snag her bag and reach in for a small bottle. She poured the entire contents into the tub and said, "Bubble bath. I've been saving this for a long time, for a very special occasion. This is it!"

It wasn't long before the tub filled with pillows of foam floating on the warm, inviting water. She climbed in, then called out to invite Joe to join her. He hesitated, unsure whether to cover himself with a towel or just boldly enter the bathroom and climb into the tub with her. Already in the water, Amy's breasts floated near the top of the water, just showing as small mounds through the foam, her grin mischievous and inviting, "Come on in, the water's fine!" Joe shyly stepped in at the opposite end of the tub and sank away into the foam, something he had never experienced before, let alone with a girl.

By the time they finally emerged from the tub, having shared more of their hopes and dreams, and other more intimate touches, Joe felt more comfortable with Amy and himself in the nude. Damp towels encircled them only temporarily as they collapsed back on the bed, feeling sated, refreshed, and lazy. Joe lay propped on one elbow and let his eyes drink in the beauty of her body in the soft light. His arm drew her to him, where he continued to touch her, gently caressing her breasts, her legs, and her triangle of curly hair. Her fingers traced patterns on his chest and down across his belly. Their closeness and exploring eventually led to another long, slow love making, bringing new peaks of ecstasy and pleasure for both.

Finally sleep claimed Amy, her head on his shoulder with her legs wrapped around his. Joe remained awake longer, listening to her steady breathing on his chest. As he pondered this wondrous gift from Amy, he worried about their future. He knew that they couldn't count on much. What would the war mean for them? Would he survive? Would she? He had seen how quickly men died in training accidents, let alone combat, which he knew would be coming all too soon for him. In spite of his being Indian and her being white, he wanted to marry Amy. Though as he thought about it, he feared that circumstances might prevent them from ever reaching that point. Damn the war! Would her family accept him? He hoped so.

In the early morning light, Joe woke to Amy's lips on his, drawing him slowly back to consciousness. Though a little groggy from their night's exertions and delights, one kiss led to another, and soon they held each other tightly, almost as if afraid to let go. Their young bodies responded with renewed arousal. This time Amy knelt astraddle him, easing down onto him and began a rocking motion that grew exquisitely pleasurable to both. Joe found it exciting to have her meet his movements with equal passion and energy, while at the same time being able to watch her beautiful body move. Their release came and went like a sudden Texas thunderstorm. Passion dissolved into tenderness, excitement into a deep sense of joy. Seeing the happiness radiant on her face and in her their eyes as they looked at each other, Joe said, "I wish these moments could go on forever."

Amy fell into his arms, "Me too. I feel both full and drained at the same time. And I love how safe I feel with you."

The wholeness Joe felt inside was different from anything he'd ever known. He wished he could always keep Amy safe. He didn't want to break the magic of the moment. He didn't want to think about returning to the base and their flying responsibilities and challenges.

But even magic has its moment in time and passes. Finally Amy said, "I gotta go pee," and clambered out of bed and off to the bathroom. After another quick bath, each began to reluctantly pull on their clothes, while fully enjoying the vision of watching the other getting dressed. Their uniforms were only slightly wrinkled from the previous day and night.

"I'm starved!" Amy exclaimed, once she had dressed. "Let's go down and get something to eat."

"I'll buy that," Joe replied. "And no army chow, either!"

Breakfast in the hotel dining room was a treat for both, made the more special by the white cloth napkins and gleaming silver on the white table cloth. Having someone wait on them and bring their food felt so different from eating in the mess hall on the base. Sitting next to each other at the table, they couldn't keep from touching one another, as if their contact was too sacred to be broken, too wonderful to release, and wanting to make it all last for a lifetime.

After breakfast, they strolled around the city for a while, window shopping on the quiet Sunday morning, dreading the moment when they would have to board the old olive drab school bus to take them back to the base. The final break in the magic came as they sat on the thinly padded bench seats of the bus with many other soldiers and airmen, most of whom were hung over and disheveled from their Saturday night revelry, including a not so faint odor of vomit permeating the air. Their real world of war, flying, and fighting reclaimed their minds, but their hearts would hold this night and day sacred, a precious moment in time.

As they approached the gate to the airbase, Amy turned to Joe and whispered, "I'll remember this forever, Joe, no matter what happens."

Joe spoke softly, his heart full. "Me too, Amy. I know it is probably too soon, but will you marry me? I want you by my side forever."

"It's not too soon for me. And the answer is yes, yes, yes!"

"Maybe we can get the base chaplain to marry us soon. I'll find out what we have to do to get our marriage license. Oh Amy, I can't believe how lucky I am."

"No more than I," Amy said, clasping his hand tightly in hers.

20

Monday morning came early for Joe, his mind still half with Amy at the hotel, the other half in his world of airplanes. Today he and his fellow pilots would be flying the gunnery range for the first time, learning to approach and shoot at tow targets with live ammunition. He was excited to meet this new challenge. He saw Amy across the flight line in her flying fatigues and wondered where she was going. Dismayed when he saw her walking toward the old BT-13 used to tow the target, he felt a lurch of anxiety. They waved to each other as they went to their separate planes.

* * *

Hours later Joe sat, totally numbed at what had happened on the gunnery range out near the auxiliary field, its reality almost beyond his comprehension, but the images he carried in his mind had been seared there for eternity. The boys in the P-47's were beginners with their shooting. One had caught Amy's plane in one of his passes at the tow target. Amy released the bright red tow target and headed down to the aux field, a thin stream of white smoke trailing her plane. The bullets must have severed the oil lines in the engine. The cockpit was filled with smoke. Joe saw her plane descending, with the smoke trailing. His throat filled with anxiety as he followed her down to the strip, landing and coming to a stop not far from her plane. As he jumped from his own plane, he saw her wrestling with her canopy, trying to open it, when her plane suddenly burst into a fury of flame. The last image he had of her alive was her frantically beating on the canopy, surrounded by flames, panic and terror in her face. By the time he got close, the plane became a wild mass of flame and exploding fuel, with Amy's head only a huddled black form, barely visible in the inferno's center! He couldn't get any closer. She was gone before he could do anything to help, leaving him stunned and numb.

He barely remembered the rest of the day and didn't even recall now who had landed to pull him away from the burning wreckage. A radio call to the base brought help, but far, far too late. They transported Joe back to the base in a jeep and sent someone else to fly his plane back.

Several days passed before Joe recovered enough from the shock of Amy's death to function. What was left of her body was sent home to Illinois for burial. Joe wanted to go with her on her last journey, but his

C.O. would not release him. To Joe it was as if they had already married, linked together forever, but to the Army, they were just two individuals in a vast war effort. A small amount of sympathy came from his buddies who knew of his relationship with Amy, but little or none from the brass. An unfortunate accident the Army said, and went on about its business of training pilots for war. Joe was ordered to get back in his plane and fly.

And fly he did. He filled his days with a burning anger and hatred that threatened to consume his very soul, hatred for the war that destroyed this beautiful girl, hatred for the enemy that made this war necessary, and even hatred for some of the officers who directed him. But Joe bridled his hatred and anger and turned it into a force within, making him a man to be reckoned with. He flew relentlessly, training and practicing even more than asked, determined to make someone pay for her loss, though he never said that aloud to anyone. He became the best pilot in his training group, aggressively pursuing even the best of his instructors in practice, taking chances, honing his skills to a razors edge. He was recognized by one and all as the best, his fighter plane merely an extension of his mind and body, the combination a deadly killing machine. He held nothing back, and demanded all that the plane was designed for and more. Twisting and turning in dogfights, climbing to heights and diving at speeds far past the design speed of the plane, he pushed the limits of both the plane and his body to the max.

As Joe lived through the final days of his training, the image of Amy trapped in the burning fuselage and beating on the canopy seldom left his mental screen and made his heart heavy with grief. Focusing on his training helped distract him. He left the image behind only temporarily when boring down on a target, with his machine guns blazing or when he engaged in a mock dogfight, straining to get the best of his opponent. His grief, which had no boundaries at first, finally began to ease a little.

21

As soon as Joe graduated from his P-47 training, he went to his Commanding Officer and asked to be assigned to a combat unit immediately. He wanted to get as far away as possible, in both distance and time, from the terrible experience of watching Amy die. When his CO offered him the chance to go home before being sent overseas, he declined. He was geared up to get into the fight. Thus, he quickly found himself on a train bound for New York City, where he embarked on a troop ship for the trans-Atlantic voyage to England. Though the trip across the ocean was mostly uneventful, it was punctuated by drills for possible submarine attacks in which he, along with the hundreds on board the ship, practiced putting on life vests and going to their assigned life boat station, in case they were torpedoed. Joe hated being on board that troop transport. For a pilot it was torture, being jammed into a small space with so many others, sleeping in tiers of bunks four high in cargo spaces with hundreds of other men. He hated the fetid air, with its mixture of diesel exhaust, cigarette smoke, and the odor of so many unwashed bodies. He felt totally powerless and vulnerable to any attack that might come from the sea. He wished he could have flown across, but the P-47 could not carry enough gas for such a great distance, even with drop tanks. Now he could do nothing but endure.

They arrived at the bustling port of Liverpool, England, where ships were unloaded of the men and war materials they had carried across the Atlantic. As his ship docked, Joe saw the fuselages and wings of P-47's and other planes being lifted out of the holds of nearby ships and onto the docks to be trucked away and assembled for flight. Not only fighter planes, but bombers, tanks, jeeps, trucks, ammunition, and bombs all found their way out of the bellies of the cargo ships and onto the docks. A constant stream of men and vehicles hauled the mountains of material away to make room for more.

Joe traveled by train from Liverpool to Cambridge where he transferred to a truck for the ride out to the aerodrome at Duxford, a short distance southwest of Cambridge, to join the 78th Fighter Group of the 8th Army Air Force. This once sleepy little English town had been transformed into a beehive of activity. Joe groaned when he saw that the airfield runway, originally a plain grass field, had been plated with those perforated steel plates commonly used throughout the theater of war to provide stability on unimproved fields. Though he had once flown off steel plates on a practice field in the states, he didn't like them. He thought them too prone to slippage and they created a lot of noise on landing and taking off, as the tires rattled over the steel plating. It did however make a firmer base on the grass field for the repeated landings and take offs of the many, many aircraft on this field, especially in the wet weather so common in England. Without them, the field would have been a sea of mud.

The 78th Fighter Group, known as the Duxford Eagles, took up most of the space here. Joe was one of a group of new pilots arriving as replacements for pilots who never came back from their missions and the few who had finished their tour of duty. After only two days of orientation, Joe was assigned a plane and began his life as a combat fighter pilot by accompanying groups of bombers on their missions to the continent, flying cover to try to keep enemy fighters away. He came to understand personally the saying that their missions were hours and hours of sheer boredom interrupted by moments of sheer terror. Winter flying in England and over the continent was brutal on men and machines. The high altitude at which the bombers had to operate for safety and fuel efficiency taxed the capacities of everyone, requiring that they be on oxygen most of the time. By the time they returned, after long hours on oxygen in freezing temperatures, pilots were so stiff and exhausted they could scarcely climb out of their cockpits.

When they encountered German fighters, the Messerschmitt ME 109 proved to be a challenging adversary. Joe used the superior speed of the P-47 to his advantage, diving out of the sun to flash through the enemy fighters, guns blazing. The first time Joe encountered enemy fighters brought both terror and exhilaration. His group was flying top cover for the fleet of bombers when five ME-109s came slashing up from below to attack the bombers. He pushed his P-47 over into a screaming dive to get down to the enemy fighters as soon as possible. He managed to get on the tail of one who attempted to dive away from him, but it was no match for his heavier plane, well able to exceed 400 mph in a dive. As he closed on the plane, he waited until he was sure, then held down the trigger on his eight 50 caliber machine guns for five seconds, pouring 600 rounds per minute into the enemy fighter. One second was supposed to be sufficient to take down a plane. After five seconds, the 109 was shredded, and as Joe flew through the debris field, he felt his own plane take hits from the pieces. He vowed he would not do that again if he could help it, that is, if he got back safely. He should have peeled away sooner. His plane seemed to be functioning all right, so he climbed back to the bomber formation to assist his buddies, but found that the other enemy fighters had fled. One of the other pilots claimed a probable. Sadly, he observed one of the B-17s streaming smoke from burning fuel and before any of its ten man crew could bail out, a massive explosion tore off a wing, throwing it into an uncontrolled tumble. He knew that he had killed the man in the German fighter, as there had been no chute. Only later would he reflect on the day and feel angry that he had been drawn into this war in which he had killed another man and also watched so many of his own people die too. And yet he also felt a little relief that he had struck back for his loss of Amy. Back at Duxford, when his crew chief pointed out dents and holes in his plane, Joe explained that he'd flown through debris from the fighter he'd shot down.

"And what about those?" The crew chief asked, walking back to the tail and pointing up to six holes in his tail, obviously made by machine gun bullets. "That sure weren't no debris. I'll patch these, but you be careful next time, you heah? This here P-47 is a helluva a machine, but you get enough of these hits, it will take you out or down, sho nuff."

Joe just shook his head and walked away, aware now of how lucky he had been. It could have been him that went spinning down in a spiral of black smoke to plow into the earth below. He'd drawn his 'first blood' in combat, but had also drawn his first hits. Was there a peculiar kind of balance in that? When he started to think about what the other pilot had experienced in the attack and also what it must have been like for the guys on the bomber, he just shivered and forced his mind away from it all. This day was only the beginning.

Many times, on the way back from bomber escort missions, they strafed targets of opportunity, such as trains, convoys of trucks, and anything else that looked interesting, including dive bombing bridges. Joe found that such hits were almost more satisfying than the high altitude dog fights with enemy fighters. Here he felt like he was directly assisting the guys on the ground, by destroying supplies that the Germans would have used to fight the allies. Strafing missions of close-in ground support where allied troops were toe to toe with the enemy or even hemmed in felt doubly good. Here he could see the immediate results of his attacks, and sometimes even see the grateful waves of the guys below.

Within a few months he became an 'Ace' with five official kills to his credit. Each time brought that mixture of pride and sadness. The other men were probably young pilots much like him, who just wanted to fly, trying to do a job. He actually felt good when he saw a chute blossom after the hit, even though he knew that it left the possibility that that pilot could come back to attack him another day. He couldn't go back to his ritual as a youth when he killed a deer and gave thanks to its spirit that it gave its life for him. Each time now, he consoled himself as having done one more for Amy. After his first five, he purposely quit counting, though his crew chief kept painting symbols on the side of his fuselage, one for each kill he made. Thus, each time he mounted his bird, he was reminded of his record, one of the highest in his unit.

Many times, as he flew, he thought of Amy and often felt connected to her. He wondered if somehow her spirit flew with him in some way. On one mission he had a kind of confirmation that she was with him. He was involved in a twisting, turning dogfight with a pair of Folke-Wulfe 190s. He was closing on the tail of one of them when he heard in his head, almost a scream, "Dive away. Now!" He didn't hesitate and slammed the stick forward to the right and stomped on the right rudder, and caught a glimpse of 20 MM cannon shells streaming by his plane. Had he not acted when he did, he would have been shot down. He heaved a sigh of relief and whispered a thank you to Amy.

As the months wore on through winter of '43 to '44 and on into summer of '44, each succeeding mission took its toll. Joe knew a fatigue deeper than he'd ever experienced. Part of it was the grinding schedule of flying mission after mission, each many hours long. But another part went deeper. Combat was eating away his very soul. Seeing so many of the bombers burst into flames and go down was heart wrenching, knowing that each time ten men died if no one bailed out. And he was supposed to be protecting them! But he could do absolutely nothing about all the flak thrown up at them by the German anti-aircraft guns. Several times he brought home souvenir flak holes in his own plane, but none so serious that it disabled his plane and took him down. The time he saw one of his buddies crash and burn up in his plane on landing after getting all the way back to the field, brought back all the horror of Amy's death. To survive so much trauma, Joe withdrew into himself and just did his job. He purposely made no close friends, never knowing when that friend might not make it back from a mission. When the war finally ended, Joe felt grateful to be able to go back to the States alive, but knew that he had left part of his soul behind in the skies over Europe. He wondered if he would ever recover.

Upon returning and being released from the service, Joe wanted to get a job flying for one of the airlines. He, like many others, converted his military pilot training into a commercial pilot's license. But with so many well-qualified pilots returning, the competition was extremely high, and with air travel in the U.S. being in its infancy after the war, the demand for pilots was low. He found that if you didn't have an inside connection to one of the airline executives, you basically had little or no chance of getting such a job. A short visit home to his family convinced him that there was no place for him there at the time. So he proceeded to get trained as an aircraft and power plant mechanic. At least he would still be around airplanes. He applied for and got a job with TWA and was sent to Kansas City to work on the Lockheed Super Constellation, the beautiful, sleek four engine airplane that became the luxury airliner of the skies after World War II. While satisfied with the job for a time, Joe eventually began to feel constricted. He didn't like living in the big city with its pollution and noise, and he missed his beloved canyon country, with its clean dry air.

Joe began to see that if he wanted to make anything of his life, he needed more education. He still had his GI Bill rights so he decided to go to college. He took a bus from Kansas City to Boulder, Colorado, to enroll at the University of Colorado. There, he joined a multitude of other young men back from the war attending classes, most wearing their GI khakis. No stranger to hard work, by the end of four years Joe had earned a degree in business, with some engineering courses added to the mix. Graduation from the university was one of the few times in his life that he felt a sense of personal pride in his accomplishments.

Now, even with a college degree, he found getting a job no easy task. He really wanted a job that had something to do with aviation. But again, the competition remained extremely high. After a while, he grew discouraged and eventually headed back to Blanding. There, he naturally spent time at the airport, where he eventually got a job helping out with maintenance and flying occasionally. Not long after he started working there, the man running the airport had a heart attack, so Joe filled in for him as both mechanic and flight instructor. He was so well received that when it became clear the other man would not be able to return to work, the city fathers offered him the job. He presented his credentials, a degree in business, his FAA certificates for flight instructing and maintenance, and willingly signed a contract.

A few years later, when the war in Korea broke out, he received a call from the U.S. Air Force, requesting him to come back and fly the P-51 in that conflict. He remembered that not long after he left Duxford, his unit, the 78th Fighter Group, known as the Duxford Eagles, had received the P-51. Though he had always wanted to fly the P-51, he decided that he'd had enough of war and killing. He doubted his soul would survive another war and said no. When he later learned of the hundreds of P-51's that fell in Korea, either to ground fire, or to the superior Russian MIG-15, he was glad for his decision. He would have liked a chance to fly the new F-86 jet fighter that came into use later in that war, but again felt happy to be home, and safe from all that trauma.

Joe eventually bought a small house trailer and moved it to the airport, where he led a simple life, living alone. He never really got over the loss of Amy. On those rare occasions when he thought of dating, by that time most of the young Indian women, the only women accessible to him as an Indian, had already married. He never made any serious attempt to form a relationship with a woman at Blanding. His mother died not too many years after the end of the war, leaving Joe alone and without family. After her death, the few remaining people in their village moved to town, living in trailers or simple homes on the outskirts of town.

22

May 5, 2001

While flying out over the canyons, Brian couldn't help thinking about Sally, and noticed that for the first time since BJ's death, he felt a spark of interest in a woman. He tried to dismiss it, figuring that he must have appeared pretty dull to her. Yet the thought of her remained in the back of his mind, somewhat like a Kansas weed seed known as a 'stick tight,' which would stick in his sock and not let go.

Later, back at his apartment, he spent the afternoon on the phone with Bob, his manager at his car business in McPherson, after receiving reports and spreadsheets via email. He was grateful for the wonders of electronic communications which enabled him to keep tabs on the business back home. He also sent off an email letter to each of his daughters, to encourage them as they neared the end of their school year.

By seven p.m. when he finished his paper work, he didn't feel like cooking, so he headed out to get something to eat. Though he often went to Kenny's Restaurant at the north end of town, he now turned toward the south edge of town and the Old Tymer Restaurant. He pulled into the parking lot, whose perimeter was decorated with antique horse drawn farm implements, giving silent witness to the hard labor of Mormon pioneer farmers here in bygone days. Pausing a moment to look around after entering the restaurant, he saw a friendly hand wave from a booth to the rear. Walking that way and recognizing Sally seated across from another woman, he said, "Hi there!"

Sally spoke up, "We've just arrived. Want to join us . . . unless of course you are meeting someone else?"

"I'd be more than happy to. Not much fun eating alone."

"Brian, this is Helen Mattox. She has the fourth grade at the elementary school where I teach third. We've been working on a project at school all afternoon since school let out and decided to take a break and treat ourselves to dinner out. Helen, this is Brian Nelson."

"Hi, Helen. Glad to meet you," he reached out to shake her hand. "And thanks for the hospitality." Brian sat down beside Helen when she slid over to make room for him.

"I hear you gave Sally's kids a great introduction to airplanes today," Helen said.

"Well, I did the best I could. Joe got interrupted with a phone call, so I filled in for him. Do you like airplanes?"

"Only from a distance . . . preferably long distance," she joked.

"I've been spending quite a bit of time out at the airport these days, getting in lots of flying," Brian reached for the napkin at his place. "Say, I would be glad to give you ladies a plane ride some time. Either of you interested?"

"Not me. It's all I can do to keep my feet on the ground these days anyway," Helen quipped. "But old Sally there might be." And turning to Brian, "After all it is her birthday. She turned forty today. But don't tell anyone I told you." She cupped her hand beside her mouth, pretending to hide what she'd said from Sally. "Time to do something daring, Sally.'

"You don't have to reveal all my secrets, Helen," said Sally, though with a smile.

"No, just the important ones. Besides, you deserve a little attention on your birthday."

"Well, may I be one of the many who will want to wish you a happy birthday. But don't worry, I won't tell more than half the town, not that they don't know it already," Brian bantered. They all seemed to equally enjoy this quick paced game of trading quips and laughter.

"And just how old are you, Brian?" Sally asked, taken unawares at her own daring, surprised that she really wanted to know more about this man.

"I'm really just a kid. Only been on this planet for 45 years. But I've got a few good years left yet. How about you, Helen?"

"I guess I have to take a back seat to you two old folks. I'm only 35, and barely that."

"Still wet behind the ears, eh? Bet you still have to supervise her pretty closely, eh Sally?"

"Yeah, we scarcely let her out of the play pen," Sally chuckled, with a twinkle in her eyes. She enjoyed this conversation more and more, getting into the spirit of teasing and kidding. Their fun was interrupted by the waiter, Eric, arriving at the table to take their orders. He greeted each of them by name, including Brian, who had eaten here before. Eric's family owned the restaurant, as well as the motel next door, and they all worked in the family enterprise. And of course he knew everyone in town, having grown up here. He only had to learn the names of the few new people who came to town. They quickly gave him their orders, which he wrote on his pad and took to the kitchen, returning with a glass of water for each. "Anything else to drink?"

"I'll have a cup of decaf," Brian said.

"Me too," Sally added.

"Well, I reckon I'm too young to drink coffee, so I'll have lemonade," Helen giggled, continuing the teasing game they'd begun.

Later, after an enjoyable meal and conversation, Sally spoke up, "I'd like to take you up on your offer to go flying. I've never been up, except in airliners. I've always wanted to see what the canyons look like from the air."

"It would be my pleasure, ma'am," said Brian with exaggerated gallantry. "What about tomorrow morning, when the air is nice and smooth? Get your birthday off to a flying start, so's to speak."

After groans from both women at his pun, Sally said, "That sounds good. What time shall I meet you?"

"Well, that depends on whether you want to see the canyons with early morning shadows, or when the sun is high, poking into every corner and crevice."

"Morning shadows sounds good to me," She said, trying not to sound too eager.

"Morning shadows it is then. Say about 7:00 a.m.?" Brian tried to hide his excitement at the prospect of spending more time with Sally.

"Okay!"

"Just don't fly over my house and wake me up," Helen interjected. "I'm sleeping in tomorrow. Come on, Sally, we better get back to finish up our rain forest project, so we'll be ready for the kids Monday morning." And to Brian, "We don't want to keep this old lady up too late. We're decorating one of the hallways at school to look like a rain forest. Of course the trees are cardboard carpet tubes with construction paper leaves. But it gives the kids the idea. Anyway, we're having fun with it."

Later, at school, Helen looked over at Sally and saw her just standing, staring at the wall with a blank expression her face. "Hey, space cadet. Making plans already? I saw you perking your ears up with Brian this evening. The old spark of romance must not be dead after all, just sleeping soundly!"

"Don't you give me a hard time, Helen," Sally came back. "Just because you're all settled down with a husband and three kids doesn't mean you have to push me into anything, unless you can't stand to have a single woman around."

"Oh, no, you're okay just the way you are, Sally." Helen grinned. "Still, I couldn't help noticing."

"Well, he probably just thinks I'm this dorky old teacher, dull as cold toast, and not at all interesting."

"I doubt that. He scarcely took his eyes off you all through dinner. I sat right beside him, and he sure didn't ever look my way. Not that I minded, of course."

"Of course," Sally responded.

* * *

Later, as she got ready for bed, Sally found herself wondering about Brian. What was he doing here in Blanding? She'd noticed he wore a gold band on his left ring finger. Probably has a wife somewhere. He said he had two kids in college. Must have married young if he's only 45 now. Well, at least he'll be good for an airplane ride. He must be a safe pilot if he is flying one of Joe's planes.

Turning out the light, she was a little surprised at herself. Ever since her divorce from George years ago, she'd had little interest in men. She'd tried dating a few times during the first couple of years after her divorce, but found the guys she'd dated were mostly just interested in getting her into bed, but not in getting to know her. That had little appeal to her, so she'd stopped dating. After a few years, she got used to being alone and single, though she felt lonely from time to time and longed for companionship. And oddly enough, the dreams of abduction that had caused so much upset during her marriage, had nearly stopped, much to her relief. Only on occasional odd moments did she even think about it anymore. "Oh, well," she said, as she drifted off to sleep.

Brian, on the other hand, left the restaurant mildly stirred up, his usual calm demeanor changed by his encounter with Sally, not once, but twice in one day. Ever since BJ died, no woman had seemed particularly interesting or attractive. The time or two he had invited women to dinner in McPherson after her death, had confirmed for him that they were friends, not potential anything else. He'd been happy to leave it at that. Until now! He noticed feeling slightly excited and yet uneasy at the same time, aware of wanting to get better acquainted with Sally if she was open to it. The image of her at the restaurant, her rich auburn hair framing an attractive face sprinkled with a few freckles across her cheeks and nose, would not leave his mind. Her smile and the twinkle in her hazel green eyes lit up her countenance. He remembered the easy way she moved in her obviously fit body. He couldn't help noticing what a nice figure she had. He looked forward to the airplane ride with her in the morning more than he'd expected.

23

May 6, 2001

    Groggy and heavy with fatigue, Sally emerged from deep sleep at the insistence of her alarm clock. She and Helen had not quit working at school until quite late, so she didn't get her usual quota of sleep. With no time for her usual morning run, she did some floor stretches to limber up. By the time she finished, she was awake enough to feel somewhat excited at the prospect of going flying with Brian. Never having flown in a small plane and not knowing what to expect, she decided to pass on a full breakfast and only have toast and coffee. She didn't want to have her stomach too full, though she didn't expect to have any real problem with getting airsick. Were the butterflies in her belly about the prospect of flying or about the idea of spending time with Brian? Maybe both. "Whatever," she said aloud, as her kids would say.
    When she left the house at 6:45 a.m. to drive south out to the airport, Sally saw the wonderful deep blue desert sky, without a cloud to mar its pristine beauty. The sun, creeping over the horizon, pushed long shadows ahead of it, while the town still slept quietly, except for an occasional dog barking and a rooster crowing in the distance. What a peaceful place to live, she thought. I know that I won't want to stay here forever, but it sure has been a good place for me to heal from all my turmoil back in Ohio.
    Her truck started easily and in a few moments she turned south on main street. Traversing this small a town took little time and soon Sally had passed the three miles or so to where the red brick National Guard Armory marked the entrance into the airport. Pulling up at the airport office, she parked beside a Land Rover bearing a Kansas license tag, which she figured must be Brian's. She wondered where Brian might be when she walked into the office and found it empty. The sound of the hangar door being raised drew her through the door leading from the office into the hangar, where she saw Brian at the tail of the yellow Piper Cub, starting to push it out the door. He acknowledged her arrival with a nod, but remained focused on pushing the plane out, careful to not bump the wing tips. She followed him outside. Once he had the plane out, he stepped back inside, pressed the switch to lower the hangar door, and exited as the door started down.

"Good morning, and happy birthday again."

"Thank you."

"We'll be ready to go shortly. I have to do the pre-flight inspection first."

"What's that?" Sally asked.

"It's both a required procedure and a good habit. Always look everything over to make sure it's all shipshape. Better to be safe than sorry!" Brian said with a smile.

After the inspection, which Sally followed carefully, Brian invited her to climb into the back seat of the plane. "Put your bottom in first, then swing your legs in. Easier that way."

Following directions, Sally slipped into the seat with ease. Brian showed her how to fasten the two shoulder straps into the seat belt, then clambered into the front seat.

"Reach up, grab the headset off the hook and put it on. Adjust the microphone boom so it's close to your lips, but not touching," Brian said. Sally followed his instructions, feeling like she was suiting up for a space trip or something.

After putting on his own headset, Brian swung up the bottom half of the split door and latched it, but left the upper half out and clipped to the bottom of the wing. After priming the engine, he pressed the starter button. The engine caught with only one revolution of the propeller and settled into a steady roar. "You okay?" Sally heard over the headphones. She was surprised, but welcomed how much engine noise the headset muffs over her ears filtered out. "I guess so," she replied.

"We'll be talking over the intercom radio. Don't be afraid to speak up if you have a problem with anything at all. Just let me know. Another part of the standard pre-flight briefing is to tell you that if we have to make an off-field landing, all you have to do to open the door is pull down on that black handle to your right by the door. It will open and drop down if needed. In fact, if we have to land anywhere but here, I want you to open the door just before touchdown. That way it can't get caught and keep us in. Understand?"

"I think so," Sally spoke hesitantly, but clearly.

"Okay, we'll taxi out to the runway."

Once there, Brian did the rest of his pre-flight preparations, running the engine up to cruise rpm and setting the mixture control for the density altitude. When finished, he asked, "Ready to go?"

"Yep. But aren't you going to close the top door?" Sally asked cautiously. Even though the frame only contained a plastic window, somehow she felt less safe with the door open.

"We can if you'd like, but we don't need to," Brian said reaching out to pull the upper part of the door down to latch into the bottom half. "There we go. Better now?"

"Yeah!" Came the reply.

On reaching the runway, Brian smoothly advanced the throttle and the little plane began to roll down the runway, gathering speed. He pushed the stick forward to bring the tail up to a horizontal position and a moment later lifted the Cub off the ground, surprising Sally with how quickly the airplane climbed in the early morning air, yet how stable and smooth it felt to her. Initially, fear kept her hands clamped firmly to the frame, but gradually she relaxed her grip and her body, letting out a breath of tension. The first time Brian banked the airplane for a turn, she felt afraid again, though she knew there was no way she could fall out with all the straps on her. Still, feeling the tilt, she spontaneously leaned in the opposite direction. Brian noticed her movement, and said, "You'll soon get used to it and won't need to lean in the opposite direction. Just relax and let your body ride with the plane. You'll discover that it will stay centered with the plane quite easily. If you look around me to the instrument panel, you'll see a little curved tube with a black marble in it. We call that the ball. In flying we try to keep that little ball right in the middle for coordinated flight. That makes for an easier and more pleasant flight. So sit back, relax, and enjoy the scenery."

Heading southwest from the airport, Brian commented, "Look out to your right and you will see Comb Ridge coming up. It's quite noticeable from the air." That they should so quickly reach the Comb, which lay several miles west of town, amazed Sally. "Don't be surprised if we get a little bump when we cross over the Comb. When the wind blows from west to east, it has to climb up over the Comb. It keeps on going up for a while before it goes down, like water over a log in a river. When we fly through that air moving up and then down, it gives us a bump. But it's nothing to worry about. You doing okay?"

"Yeah. I was a little nervous at first, but I'm getting my sea, or rather my air legs now. It is so beautiful! I never knew what I've missed by not seeing this from the air. This is such a treat," Sally said, feeling more relaxed now.

"Up ahead to the northwest you will see Bears Ears." Sally heard Brian's voice in her head set. "But I think I'll head south now over Grand Gulch Primitive Area and on down to where we can see Monument Valley." They flew along for some time without speaking, each taking in the beauty of the setting, until at last Sally broke the silence.

"I'm so glad we came early," Sally said. "The early morning sun sure does set off the canyons. It's incredible! I had no idea it would look like this. I love morning shadows!" Then changing her gaze from looking down to looking forward, she exclaimed, "Oh, wow! Monument Valley! How did we get there so quickly? It seems like we took off only a few minutes ago."

"Well, we've been cruising along at about 110 miles per hour, so we cover a lot more ground than you can in a car, plus, we don't have to follow a road." Brian flew on south, soaring over the broad expanse leading to the monoliths of Monument Valley. Since it was so early, he descended down to only a couple hundred feet from the ground, circled around and flew between two of the giant pillars, before pulling up and climbing back to a more comfortable altitude and turned back northeast toward home. Sally sat wordless, enthralled with the experience and the scenery. Soon Mexican Hat, Utah passed under their wings, with the little town of Bluff following not long after. Climbing higher to gain more clearance over the bluffs, namesake for the town, Brian pointed them north toward Blanding, which showed up as a smudge of green trees on the horizon. Sally appreciated the comments from Brian, pointing out the various features of the landscape and towns along the way. Things look quite different from the air, she decided.

"Shall we give Helen a wakeup call this morning?" Brian asked as they approached town.

"Nah. I think her sense of humor would be severely lacking this morning!" Sally responded. "She's not a morning person."

"Okay. You're probably right. Anything else you want to see?"

"Could we fly over the Edge of the Cedars Museum on the west side of town? My house is next to the museum parking lot. It would be fun to see it from the air."

"Sure, no problem," Brian said, swinging the plane around over the west edge of town so that Sally could look down for an unobstructed view. He circled around the museum so she had time to focus on it, then headed back to the airport south of town.

After they landed and taxied back to the hangar, Sally climbed out of the Cub, surprised at the stiffness of her legs. In fact, she felt somewhat stiff all over. I must have been holding a lot of tension during the flight, she thought. They had been flying only a little more than an hour. Such a brief time for covering so much territory. Amazing! She watched as Brian pushed the Cub back into the hangar and closed the door.

"Don't you need to put gas in it?" Sally asked.

"No, not yet. It was full when we took off, so there's still almost three hours of fuel left," Brian said as he wrote down the time of their flight in the log book on the little desk in the corner of the hangar. "This logbook enables us to keep track of everything that happens with the plane, including how long we fly. That way Joe knows when he needs to do routine maintenance on the plane."

Continuing, Brian asked, "By the way, did you have breakfast before you came out?"

"No, not really. I only had toast and coffee."

"Would you like to go get some breakfast?" Brian asked hopefully.

"I have an even better idea. Let's go back to my place and let me fix you some breakfast. That's the least I can do after you giving me such a wonderful ride. I really enjoyed it, more than I ever thought I would. Morning shadows is definitely the time to go. Thanks so much, Brian." A happy smile lit her face.

"You're welcome. You're suggestion sounds great to me. By the way, where do you live exactly. You mentioned it is close to the museum."

"Yep, right on the corner next to the museum parking lot. You can follow me, not that you could ever get lost in this town," Sally quipped.

"Let me go speak to Joe before we go. I'll be right out," Brian called as he walked into the airport office.

He spotted Joe hunched over the desk in the inner office. On hearing the door open, he looked up and greeted Brian with a grin, "Not wasting any time with her, I see!" More a statement than a question. Brian flushed a little as he groped for an appropriate comeback. Turning to go back out the door toward his car, he mumbled, "I logged one hour and ten minutes. We're going back to town to get some breakfast."

"Well, have fun!" Joe called back, a little too loudly.

Why does he have to make such a big deal of it, Brian thought to himself. We're only going to get some breakfast. But at the same time he denied its significance, he felt his pulse quicken at the thought of spending more time with Sally.

24

Driving back to town, Sally was still excited from her flight and yet nervous about Brian coming to her house. Her inner critic began to torment her. You idiot! Why on earth did you invite him to your house? Too chicken to go to a restaurant with him again so soon? Are you afraid of what people will say? You know you can't do anything in this small town without everyone knowing about it. Are you scared to admit to you're interested in Brian? And what about that wedding ring on Brian's left hand? Though he didn't seem like the kind of man who would cheat on his wife, maybe she'd better cool it.

By the time Sally turned on to her street and approached her house, with Brian following her in his Rover, she definitely felt on edge. As she pulled into her driveway, Brian parked at the curb, exiting his car moments after Sally did hers. "Come on in," she called out as she strode across the lawn and up onto the small front porch. Stepping inside, she held the front door for him, then dropped her purse on the table nearby and went on into the kitchen, words tumbling out in a rush, "Maybe this wasn't such a great idea. I'm not even sure what I have here that I can fix us for breakfast. Want to make us some fresh coffee? I made a small pot before going to the airport, but it's pretty old by now. Coffee and filters are in the cupboard just above the coffee maker."

If Brian noticed her nervousness, he chose not to comment. He emptied, rinsed, and refilled the coffee pot, then dumped the filter with its old grounds in the waste basket. Sally peered into the refrigerator and missed seeing the slight tremor in his hands as he went about his task. Pouring water into the reservoir, he asked, "How do you like your coffee, mild, medium, or strong?"

"Medium, I guess. I don't want to get too much caffeine on a Saturday when I'm trying to relax. Six rounded tablespoons should do it for that pot."

"Let's see here now," she continued from the refrigerator. "I have five eggs left, a little bit of ham, a tomato, and some bread, butter, and jam for toast. Will that do?"

"Sounds like a winner to me. If you want, I could run back out to the store and get anything else you need."

"No, I think this will do, if you aren't too hungry," Sally said, putting the food on the counter by the refrigerator, and anxious about

Brian's thoughts. Somehow, what had seemed initially an innocent, mundane get-together for breakfast, had become more than she had anticipated. Being in the kitchen together felt intimate. She already felt a little sweaty under her arms.

Ease up, she told herself, while to Brian she said, "Pour us each a cup when it's ready. Cups are up to the left of the sink." She continued preparing the food, cutting up the ham, the tomato, and getting out a skillet. With a small blob of butter sizzling in the skillet, she whipped up the eggs with a little salt and pepper and dumped them in. While the eggs cooked, she put bread in the toaster.

"Brian, will you butter the toast when it pops up?"

Brian rose from the kitchen chair to stand beside her at the counter.

When the eggs were almost done, she sprinkled the chopped ham and tomato on top, and folded it over into an omelette. A moment later she slid it out onto a plate, still sizzling and releasing its aroma. While Brian buttered the toast, she set her small table for two and brought the omelette to the table. Brian joined her with the toast, jam, and their coffee cups.

"Looks like a breakfast fit for a king! You're really handy with that skillet," Brian said.

"Thanks. Guess it comes from a lot of years of cooking for myself," Sally said, as she divided the omelet and slid half of it onto Brian's plate.

As they ate, their conversation centered around the morning's flight, remarking on the unique sights they had seen. But after they had eaten and were sipping their second cup of coffee, they fell silent. Then both started to talk at once with the same words, "So what are you doing here in Blanding?" They both laughed. "I asked you first," Sally said.

"You want the short version or the long version?"

"How about a medium version?" Sally replied, not wanting to appear too nosy.

"Well, I am on a sort of journey, though it started out to be a vacation. But as time has gone on, I realize it is more than just a vacation trip. Maybe I should go back a little further."

Sally listened attentively as Brian related some of his story. When tears filled his eyes as he told about BJ's death, Sally spontaneously reached across the table and laid her hand on top of his, causing him to look up at her, surprised and yet grateful for her compassion. She felt relieved to know the meaning of the ring.

"It is only now that I am beginning to feel whole again, not running around with this big hole in my middle. I still miss her, but I think I am beginning to get through my grief, thank God. It was pretty rough for a while." Glancing at his left hand, he said slowly, "Maybe I'm finally about ready to take this ring off."

After a moment he continued, "I've been here in Blanding for about a month now. I stopped in Moab first, looked around a bit, but after a while it felt a little crowded with tourists, so one day I came down here on a whim and after I met Joe, I decided to stay for a while. I've been flying quite a bit and I've explored some of the Anasazi ruins in the back country on foot. They are less disturbed here than further north or in Colorado, plus I rather like the quiet pace around here. Last week I rented a furnished place over at the Butte Apartments, a couple of blocks south of your house here." Then after a pause, "So how about you? What's your story? Joe told me you have only been here about eight years."

"Yeah, still a newcomer. I think you have to be born here to not be a newcomer. This is a pretty strong Mormon community and has been ever since this area was first settled way back in the 1800's. I am one of the few non-Mormons in the community."

"So how did you get out here?" Brian asked.

Sally paused, unsure how much to tell Brian at this time. She wanted to be open, but didn't want to overwhelm him either, so she gave a brief sketch of her life story, but omitted anything about the ET experiences. When she told of finding her husband George in bed with another girl, she stopped, took a quick breath, and looked up at the ceiling, her eyes full of tears.

"Ouch!" Brian said softly.

"Yeah, ouch is right," Sally said after a pause to regain her composure. "Well, we didn't last too long after that. So a couple of years after the divorce, I decided to take a break from teaching and headed west. I arrived in this area around Christmas of 1993 and spent some time in Moab hiking and biking. On a lark one day, I drove down here to Blanding, to get away from all those tourists . . . like me! After being here a couple of days, I happened to be at the library and overheard the principal of the local elementary school telling the librarian that one of his teachers was having problems with her pregnancy and would have to drop out for the rest of the year. He wondered how he'd find someone to fill her spot on such short notice. I'm not sure why, but I walked over, introduced myself, and told him that I was an elementary teacher and currently unemployed. Guess I'd had enough of the vagabond life, after wandering around for almost six months. He asked me to come out to the school for an interview that afternoon, and after reviewing my credentials, which I had thrown into my suitcase, he hired me on the spot. I've been here ever since. I wasn't sure I'd like it, Blanding being a Mormon town, but most folks here are pretty nice. I've made friends here. I probably won't stay here forever, but for now it's okay. So there you have my story. Nothing too exciting."

"Thanks, Sally. Sounds like both of us have had painful losses," Brian said, letting his gaze drop to the wisp of steam rising from his coffee.

They lapsed into silence, each remembering their own hurt, but also conscious of the anguish of the person sitting across the table. Each cradled their coffee cup with both hands, perhaps in an unconscious attempt to draw some of its warmth into the emptiness inside. As the silence lengthened, awkwardness began to replace their mutual brush with familiar old feelings, each waiting for the other to break the silence.

Finally, Brian spoke quietly, "Sally, I feel almost as uptight as I did in high school." He paused again, looking at her sitting across from him. Taking a deep breath, he continued, "Frankly, I've not been interested in any woman since BJ died. Friends tried to set me up a few times, inviting me to dinner or a summer picnic, including single women they thought I might find interesting. And while they were interesting people, I just wasn't ready to be. . . interested, if you know what I mean."

"Yeah, I do know what you mean."

"At first after BJ died, I thought I would never marry again, or even find another relationship. But I've healed a lot. I still don't know if I am ready, but when I met you yesterday, something happened, at least for me. I had so much fun with you and Helen last night at dinner. Then taking you flying this morning, and now having breakfast with you . . . well . . . I like you, Sally, and I'd like to get to know you better!"

Sally sat still, her mind racing. Relieved to hear of Brian's interest which matched her own, now she felt nervous and excited again. How should she frame her thoughts and feelings? She reached out across the small table to touch his fingers curled around his coffee cup. "Your story is similar to mine, Brian. I too never found anybody I wanted to spend much time with. Until now. Yesterday at the airport, I was impressed with the way you related to my kids. Last night at the restaurant, I truly enjoyed the humor flying back and forth. I felt lighter and had more fun than I've had in years." She paused.

"This morning, when I came out to the airport, I had second thoughts. I'd never flown in a small plane before. I felt scared and I wasn't sure I'd like it. But honestly, I wanted to spend more time with you. Flying out over the canyons, and then down to Monument Valley was a thrill in itself, after I got over being scared, that is." She laughed nervously. "It was also wonderful to share something that you obviously love so much." She hesitated again. "I'm not sure I know how to even put this in words. Flying with you gave me a sense of you that I'd not expected. As if, in feeling your hand on the airplane, I could feel your gentleness and strength all at the same time. I felt close to you, Brian, even sitting behind you in the plane." Sally stopped, as tears welled up in her eyes.

"I think I'd given up on ever feeling that again with anyone. It's never happened since my divorce. Maybe I've been too guarded, too many barriers up. It's taken me a long time to heal that awful betrayal. I doubted I ever would. On the way in from the airport a little while ago, I felt more scared about inviting you to breakfast than I did about going flying. What I had in the fridge had nothing to do with it. I worried that you'd think I was being too pushy." She looked down at their hands to give herself time to think. How far could she go in revealing herself and her feelings? How does a forty year old woman do this?

"Touching your fingers makes you real to me, Brian. So real that even that scares me! And I'm normally not scared of much, except rattlesnakes," Sally said with another nervous laugh.

Brian responded by lifting his hand from the cup and interlacing his fingers with hers. After what seemed like a long time of looking at each other, Brian said, "It's nice to have hope again, isn't it."

"Yes, and nice to feel alive again inside."

"If it's any comfort to you, Sally, I was scared on the way in from the airport too. And right now I'm getting scared again, with the rush of closeness I'm feeling. Moving this fast, when I've been on hold for so long, is pretty heady . . . and well, scary. So I need to slow down a little. I don't know what's ahead for us Sally, but I'd like to find out."

"Me too," Sally said, "Me too."

After another period of silence, Sally rose, saying, "More coffee?"

"No, I think I better be going," Brian said, getting up from the table. "Thanks again for breakfast. You wield a mean skillet." At the door, Brian hesitantly said, "Maybe we could risk a hug."

"Yeah, I think we could."

Reaching out to each other, they clung tightly for a moment, then released, each skittish with the feelings inside. Sally spoke first. "Thanks for the wonderful airplane ride this morning, Brian. It was a thrill I will never forget. I hope to have more. Do you have a phone at your apartment?"

"Oh sure, and I'd like yours too" Brian said quickly, and proceeded to give her his number. After exchanging numbers, Brian stumbled past his own awkwardness, "Well, gotta be going." From the front porch, he turned with a final wave and walked resolutely to his car.

25

    Sally leaned her forehead on the small pane of glass in her front door and watched Brian's car disappear around the corner. What am I getting myself into here? Do I dare let this go any further? I want to, but maybe I shouldn't. Her mind flitted back to her past, back to those times, those 'dreams' that really weren't dreams at all. She remembered how those experiences had interfered with her relationships, first with her boyfriend Greg, and later with her husband, George. She wished she could erase them from her memory forever, but they seemed permanently glued into the pages of her mental album. She decided she needed to go for a run after all. Maybe that would help lift the heavy feeling that had invaded her. She changed into her running clothes and shoes and slipped out the back door, heading for her favorite run out Elk Mountain Road.
    At first the fresh air lifted her spirits, but as she settled into her rhythm, pacing herself for a long run, the memories stole back into her mind, unwilling to be dismissed easily. Even as she jogged along, she scarcely saw the road or the passing scenery, seeing not the present but going back in time, back to when she was sixteen. If felt as real as if it was happening all over again.

* * *

    Sally had never told any of her friends about the incident on her ninth birthday, afraid they would all think her crazy. . . as she herself did sometimes. She'd felt normal until shortly after she turned sixteen, when things changed dramatically. Neither Sally nor her mother could have anticipated what happened next.

    June 27, 1976 dawned a busy day for Sally. In the afternoon, she went swimming with her friends and in the evening she went to a movie with her boyfriend, Greg. They returned home, sat in the car for a short time, and enjoyed a few kisses. When it came the time to go in, she hopped out of the car and ran up the steps of the house. As she closed the front door, she said, "Hi Mom, hi Dad."
    Her Dad replied, "How was the movie?"
    "Fine."
    As usual, Sally did not elaborate, but went into the kitchen, took the

milk carton out of the refrigerator and poured herself a glass of milk. After finishing it, along with a chocolate chip cookie, she rinsed her glass, set it in the sink, and went upstairs to get ready for bed. Summer time in Ohio is pretty warm, so she undressed and put on a light weight cotton tank top and a pair of short ruffled sleeping boxers. She brushed her teeth, pinned her hair up a little and then plopped onto the bed, propping herself up with extra pillows, to read more of the book she had checked out from the library. She became very sleepy by the time she had read only one chapter. Laying her book on the bedside table, she turned off the lamp and pulled the sheet up over her, letting out a big sigh as she relaxed into sleep.

Around two a.m. something pulled her from deep sleep. She surfaced to consciousness, aware of light in her room. Glancing at the lamp and finding it off, she turned toward the window and saw blue light streaming into the room. Apprehension suddenly swelled in her throat and tightened her chest. Had they come again? She was scared to turn and look toward the closet, but forced herself to do so. When she did, her whole body stiffened as she saw, once again after all these years, the small beings with the large heads and eyes. "Mom . . . Dad!" She tried to call out, but her voice made no more than a whisper.

When the beings saw her waking up, one of them came over closer to her, escalating her terror. As it reached out long fingers to touch her head, she tried once more to call out, but this time couldn't make any sound at all. Frozen into silence, she could only endure. Its touch on her forehead brought paralysis in her body, though no relief from her terror. She remained conscious of everything happening. She felt the sheet drawn down from her body, then felt many hands under her, after which she felt herself floating in the air, off the bed. Suspended in midair, they floated her out through the window, where she saw the intense blue light and felt the cool night air on her body, followed by a sensation of floating up. Before she could fully comprehend what was happening, she lapsed into unconsciousness.

She awoke to find herself on a cool metal table with no clothes on. She attempted to cover her nakedness, first crossing both her arms over her breasts, then extended one hand down to cover her crotch. When a tall being in the room noticed the movement, she came closer and touched Sally again on the forehead. Sally felt her arms go leaden and immobile, but she didn't lose consciousness. She 'heard' this one's voice say in her head, *"You are okay. We will not hurt you."* Sally was surprised to perceive this one as female, though she didn't look like any woman Sally had ever met. The being stood taller than the others, had some hair on her head, and had large dark almond-shaped eyes, though not as large as the small ones. She wore a tunic made of a soft white material.

    Sally fought the mental pressure from this creature who tried to make her go back to sleep. Though unable to move or resist physically, she managed to keep her eyes open and observe. Situated in a round room, in which light came uniformly from the walls and ceiling, she watched a device with several attachments being lowered from the ceiling toward her body until it pressed on her stomach. Sally felt them move her feet apart, raise her knees, then endured an overwhelming sense of violation when they inserted something into her vagina.

    No! No! No! How could they do this? Why were they doing this to her? Who are they? What did they want anyway? She wanted to ask these questions, but she couldn't make a sound. Suddenly it hurt. She unsuccessfully tried to say "Ouch" at the pressure and pain in her lower abdomen, which was shortly replaced by a sharp drawing or pulling sensation. The female being went about her tasks with an apparent callous disregard for Sally's pain. Sally's paralysis left her unable to voice the terror and rage she felt inside at this terrible intrusion. Though she felt drugged, she still sensed things being done to her body 'down there,' things she didn't understand. She tried again to say "Ouch" when she felt a sharp pain on the inside of her right leg, just above her knee. It burned for a moment and then grew numb like the rest of her body. Helpless tears flowed silently from her eyes, ran down her cheeks, and dripped off her ears onto the table.

    When the being completed whatever procedures she was doing, she came up to Sally's head. Leaning down, she positioned her large black eyes very close to Sally's and said several times, *"You will not remember any of this."* To Sally, the words sounded as if they were inside her head. Not long after, she lapsed back into unconsciousness.

    Sally awoke in her own bed, trembling with terror. She knew something terrible had happened, though she couldn't recall exactly what. A glance at her bedside clock showed four a.m. She needed to go pee really bad. Slowly, she managed to get out of bed on her jelly-like legs and made her unsteady way into the bathroom, where she sat in an exhausted stupor on the toilet. Though her bladder felt full, she could only make a few drops come. When she reached down to wipe, the toilet paper came away bright red with blood. What had happened? She'd had her period just two weeks ago. Now even more afraid, adrenalin crashed through her body, leaving her trembling.

    Slowly and carefully she rose, clutching the doorjamb for support, and leaning against the wall, moved cautiously down the hall to her parents' bedroom. Opening the door, she called out in a hesitant voice, "Mom?"

"Mom," a little louder. Going into the room and over to the bedside, she called out sharply, "Mom!"

"What is it honey? What's the matter?" Maryann answered sleepily.

"Mom, it happened again."

"What happened, honey?" Her voice alarmed, she sat up and reached out to Sally.

"They came again, Mom. This time they hurt me." Sally collapsed into her mother's arms and began to sob, softly at first, and then louder and louder, until her body shook with deep sobs and wailing. Her dad, immediately alert, sat up and reached out to his daughter also. The three of them huddled together on the bed for comfort.

Maryann and Dick knew that something terrible must have occurred, but didn't know what it might be. Gradually, in between sobs, Sally choked out what had happened, starting with seeing the short beings with the large heads and eyes in her room. Her parents listened, incredulous. But when Maryann noticed that Sally's nightshirt was on backwards, she flashed back seven years to that other time when she'd made that same discovery, and she believed.

"Mom, they hurt me," Sally wailed. "I'm bleeding--down there--but it's not time for my period. I just had it two weeks ago."

A shiver passed through both Maryann and Dick, as they took in this new information. Just then Sally happened to look down at her right knee. "Oh, no! Look!" Sally cried with dismay, as her hand moved to an angry red scar on the inside of her leg, just above her knee, where a precise half-inch-square chunk of skin and flesh had been scooped out. Overwhelmed, Sally started sobbing all over again at this new discovery. All her parents could do was hold her as she sobbed her heart out, angry at this violation of their daughter and intrusion into their home. The first hint of daylight began to creep into the room through the curtains before they felt any calmer.

26

When Sally returned from her run, she went to her hall linen closet and dug out her picture albums and journals that she'd not opened since moving all her possessions to Blanding after her mother died. Might as well do it right, she thought, as she carried them to the kitchen table. She made a cup of tea and waited until it had steeped and she'd plucked the tea bag out before she sat down to look at them. In a way she didn't want to do this, didn't want to see pictures to remind her of those times, yet felt she had to.

She opened the album from her college years and, seeing pictures of her friends and roommates, wondered what they were doing now. Then she came to a picture of George, taken the night she had met him at a party early in their senior year, though she had already been vaguely aware of him in one of her classes. Pictures of the two of them on the beach in Florida on spring break reminded her of the good times they'd had together. George had proposed to her there, complete with a diamond ring. Not long after, they'd made love for the first time, enabling her at last to feel like a normal woman. Humph! That sure didn't last long. The continuing intrusions of the aliens had seen to that. Their wedding pictures from 1981 were in a separate album. She didn't want to open that one, at least not yet.

Sally smiled when she came to the page with the picture of the kids in her 2nd grade class in her first teaching job. All she'd wanted was to be together with George, but in order for them to have enough money to live on while he got his M.A. and Doctorate, she'd had to get a teaching job. The only one she could find was in Chillicothe, forty-five miles from Ohio State in Columbus. She rented an apartment and lived there during the week, and they spent weekends together, alternating between their two apartments. Maybe if they could have been together all the time it would have worked. That's what she'd told herself then. But now, looking back, she wasn't so sure. They began drifting apart early in their marriage when those 'dreams' made her so distant from George.

Turning more pages, she realized that the beauty of the mountains on their honeymoon in Aspen, Colorado had seeded her desire to come west. During those years with George, each time the aliens took her, they tried to make her think the abduction was just a dream, but she always found it so difficult to respond to George afterwards, she knew they were not just dreams. She didn't even want to be touched, let alone have sex. That was especially true after that one horrible episode in November of their third year of marriage, when they showed her the babies. She shuddered as she remembered. That time her 'dream' took on a new and disturbing twist.

During that abduction, the beings showed her some babies and young children and asked her to hold them and play with them. The room smelled so nauseating and the babies and toddlers looked so skinny and emaciated that she found them repulsive and wanted nothing to do with them. They didn't look like any children she had ever seen. They had much larger heads and eyes than normal. In fact, she didn't see how they could even hold their heads up, their necks being so skinny. Yet the beings pressured her to touch them . . . saying the babies needed her touch to survive and grow. She tried to run out of the room, but one of the beings grabbed her arms, gripping them so tight that it hurt. She fought them mentally, as well as physically. They tried to tell her one of the babies was hers, a notion she immediately rejected. She thought they just wanted her to feel guilty if she didn't do what they asked.

At the time Sally didn't understand any of it. It made no sense to her that she should continue to have such bizarre dreams. She felt unsure whether they were real experiences or just dreams. However, after that episode with the babies, her terror escalated when she found bruise marks on her upper arms where she remembered being grabbed. The bruises looked like small oval marks of someone's fingers. At first she hadn't wanted to believe it. This just couldn't be! Maybe she had bumped into something. Yet she knew the bruises had not been there the night before when she went to bed. Another time, when taking a morning bath, she had found similar marks on her upper and lower legs as well. Seeing those marks left her even more frightened, but no less mystified and confused. What was going on now, she'd wondered? Usually extremely tired after one of those episodes, she'd wanted to just pull into herself and hide, just retreat from the world.

Tired or not, she still had to get up and go teach school in the morning. In a way, that had helped. It forced her to get outside herself, to pay attention to something and someone other than her own racing mind. Being with the children in her class felt normal. She could let the whole issue rest until she returned home from school in the late afternoon, when the wave of fear would wash over her again and threaten to sink her. The only thing that helped her calm down and get a grip on herself was writing in her journal, though she still had no answer to her question of why this was happening.

Things with George had finally all come to a head one night. God, what an awful night! The images were still seared in her memory. How naive she'd been. It happened in November of 1985, on a Saturday night when they had agreed to each stay at their own places, instead of getting together as usual. Sally felt extremely lonely and increasingly worried about what was happening to them, almost as if some monster, totally out of her control, was devouring their marriage. In the past few months the distance between them had grown huge. She renewed her vow to not let it beat her, nor destroy her marriage. On the spur of the moment, she decided to drive up to Columbus to be with George, hoping that closeness would come later. She picked up the phone to let him know she was coming, but at the last moment before dialing, she decided to just surprise him. She vowed to herself she would be open to him sexually. That should please him, she thought, after all the times she'd turned him down. After that, we've got to talk and turn this around. We can't just let everything we've worked for go down the drain, she told herself.

    On the drive up there she thought about how she would seduce him and try to restore some of the old feelings between them. At 10:30, when she drove up to his apartment, another car sat in her spot in the driveway beside George's car, so she drove down the street and parked in the first empty place she found. She didn't think anything about it at the time. Walking up to the door, she saw a light behind the drawn shade in the bedroom window, but not in the rest of the apartment. Good, she thought. He's probably reading in bed. All the better for what I have in mind. Using her key, she quietly let herself in the back door and tiptoed into the kitchen. She heard music coming from the bedroom. Smiling with anticipation, she slipped out of her coat, laying it with her purse on a chair nearby. Softly she stepped down the short hall to the bedroom door, opened it wide, and said, "Surprise!"

    Time stood still! It was a toss-up as to who was the most shocked, Sally who stood in the doorway with her mouth agape, speechless and stunned to the point of being unable to even breathe, or George, his eyes suddenly wide in horror and embarrassment, or the naked young woman kneeling on top of him in bed, her motions clearly showing their lovemaking. She had apparently not heard Sally's greeting at first, but now turned her face to the door and suddenly froze. When the clock started again and reality crashed through, the girl grabbed up the sheet to cover her body and her head. No one spoke.

    With a little moan, Sally turned away on legs suddenly rubbery, trying to catch her breath. Leaning against the wall, she felt as if she might faint at any moment. Regaining her equilibrium, she stepped back into the kitchen, silently picked up her coat and purse, and numbly left the apartment. Tears started rolling down her cheeks, making the cold wind feel even sharper. She could not have stopped them even if she'd wanted to. She found it hard to get her breath, her chest and stomach squeezed by some powerful force. Still dazed, she forgot where she had parked her car and had to spend several moments searching for it, resenting the one parked in her usual place.

Once she regained the sanctuary of her car, she sat, numb and unable to think. Slowly she let the reality of what she had seen return, and with it, an incredible sinking feeling of betrayal and pain. How could he do this to me? The words played themselves over and over in her mind, more an expression of shock than a question seeking an answer. Numbness gripped her whole body as she tried again and again, without success, to shut out the images burned onto her eyes and her brain: the candles by the bed, a bottle of wine nearby; their naked bodies rocking together in that familiar rhythm. Try as she would, she found no easy way to make them quit. She tried to force her mind to go elsewhere, anything but dwell on the scene, as if blotting it out would make it go away, make it to not have happened.

Eventually she mustered the courage to start her car and turn back in the direction of her apartment in Chillicothe. The drive home that night was the longest she had ever experienced. Her mind raced in circles, trying desperately to make sense of everything, trying to decide what to do next. Nothing came together. When she stepped into her apartment, she moaned with the loneliness that tore at her soul and cried at the pain in her heart. She collapsed on the bed, buried her face in the pillow, and cried. And cried. And cried some more. Just before dawn and still fully clothed, she fell asleep on a pillow wet with tears and hopelessness.

* * *

Sally wiped unexpected tears from her cheeks as she sat with her album now, so many years after that night. Hadn't she cried enough? Maybe she would always feel some sadness about her loss. Their marriage hadn't lasted long after that. George had wanted to go on, said he still loved her, but she couldn't forgive him, couldn't trust him to be faithful. "Guess I'm just an old-fashioned girl," she'd said. His plea that his affair with the girl didn't mean anything seemed as weak and hollow now as it did then. She closed the album, shutting the images away from her direct view. Maybe it was time to purge her albums of all the pictures in which George appeared.

She remembered her decision to quit her teaching job in Chillicothe. She'd stayed through the divorce and a couple of years after, grateful to have something stable in her life. Then, knowing she needed distance from the past, she'd packed up her Toyota station wagon and headed out. Not quite sure what she was searching for, but longing for the peace she thought she might find in the mountains, she'd gone west, first to Colorado and then to Utah.

She drained the last of her cup of tea, not surprised that she still felt sad. Her mind turned to Brian. The beings had not taken her for a long time, but did that mean they would never come again? Why did they do that to her? What did they want? Why did they choose her? Did she dare let herself fall in love with Brian? Would they interfere with a new love relationship as they had with George? Should she just cut it off now before she got any more involved? So many questions. No answers.

27

Brian walked from Sally's house to his car at the curb. As he opened the door to get in, he turned and looked back at the house. Painted light yellow, with white trim around the windows and front door, it looked pretty. He thought he saw her watching him from the door, but due to reflections, couldn't be sure. In a way he wanted to go right back, but knew that wouldn't work. He sat for a moment, unsure whether to go to his apartment or go back to the airport. The latter won out as he realized he didn't want to be alone quite yet. Even Joe's inevitable teasing would be better than sitting around by himself.

On the way, he reflected on how he'd come to this place in his life. He felt excited about new adventures and possibilities. What had begun as a vacation trip had changed into something much, much more. Life had taken on a whole new direction and it left him unsettled. Where was he going now? He felt so disconnected from his life in McPherson, Kansas, from his auto business there. He thought back to the steps that had brought him to this point. Each one, while not huge, had been important. First was the simple act of buying books. He remembered how empty he still felt after BJ's death. A year later that emptiness had led him to that bookstore in Wichita. Surely there must be something more that the world had to offer. Writers who had been down this path must have something helpful to say. He'd been browsing, looking for something, anything, when the clerk came over to him.

* * *

"Can I help you sir?" She asked.

He fumbled for words. "Oh, I'm just browsing." How could he tell her he was searching for some deeper way to understand life, death, or even himself? Part of him wanted her to just go away and leave him alone until he could escape, but he felt so uptight that he couldn't exit gracefully or tell her to leave him alone.

Perhaps sensing his conflict, she didn't leave his side. "If you could give me some idea of what you are looking for, I might be able to help you find something."

Now to risk it, he said, "I wish you could. You see, my wife died of cancer thirteen months ago and . . . ." He left it hanging in midair, at a loss for words. Thank goodness she didn't rush in with an armload of books about living with your loss or spiritual platitudes. Instead she just stood there, waited quietly, pretending not to notice that his eyes had welled up with tears ready to spill down his cheeks. Eventually he said, "I'm not even sure what I'm looking for. I know she's gone, but somehow I sense that there just has to be something more." He stopped again and couldn't go on.

After a brief silence she said, "Come with me," and led him over to a section marked 'SPIRITUAL,' where she picked up a book called *Many Lives, Many Masters* by Brian Weiss, M.D. "This might help," she offered. She hesitated a bit, then picked up another book, also by Dr. Weiss, *Through Time Into Healing,* and handed it to him. With both books in his hands, he looked at the colorful covers, thinking she was finished, but she patiently stood there while he looked at the backs and flaps of the books, intrigued by what he read. Then a little farther along the shelf she picked up another book entitled *Journey of Souls* by Michael Newton, Ph.D. "This might be of use too," she said with a smile, and walked back to her station at the cash register.

Brian stood there for a while longer, browsing through the books she'd selected, looking at the table of contents, chapter headings, and the promo blurbs on the back. The picture of Weiss showed a man who looked distinguished, yet humble and kind. And now that he didn't need to hurry to escape the store, he browsed further and came upon the shelf marked 'UFO,' a subject that had always intrigued him. Several titles looked interesting. He picked up and glanced through *The Day After Roswell* by Col. Phillip Corso, and decided to take it along, just for fun. As he started to walk away he added a small paperback to his pile, *A Mysterious Valley.*

Then he did feel the need to escape. . . with five books in hand, he almost felt embarrassed. But the woman just smiled when he went to pay for them, saying simply, "I hope you enjoy them and find what you are looking for."

"I've not bought this many books at once since college," Brian replied. Somehow, deep inside, he felt a nibbling of excitement. ...and hope too. . . perhaps even a little fear, almost like beginning a new adventure. Little did he know then how true that would be in the not too distant future.

When he arrived home that evening after dinner, he picked up the books, began browsing, and quickly got hooked. He read with fascination Dr. Weiss's experiences with the woman patient who had opened his eyes to a far greater spiritual world of past lives and reincarnation. He wished that he and BJ could have read about this before she died. It would not have altered her death, but it surely might have given them a different way of looking at it. When Weiss related the story of how the spirit of his son, who had died as a very young child, spoke to him and offered him comfort, Brian's own heart felt fuller. What an amazing story!

In the days that followed, Brian became aware of something shifting, down deep inside him. It felt as momentous as if he'd been suddenly transported from McPherson to an orbiting space shuttle, able to look down at the earth and out at the universe, a shift in point of view that transported him physically, emotionally, and spiritually. He noticed changes in his grief process too. Though he still missed BJ, he no longer had fantasies about somehow mystically being able to connect with her or bring her back. Somehow he felt more hopeful about life and the future, knowing that her spirit was surely alive and well, though she certainly had left behind the body that he knew.

After reading Newton's *Journey of Souls,* about life between lives, he became even more convinced there was something more to life than he had previously believed. Wow! He could scarcely believe that he had lived so long with such a limited view of the human spirit. He found the books so fascinating, he sometimes read until one or two a.m. Now he began to see the life of one's spirit, the self, as something so much greater than he had previously imagined. Maybe he and BJ had been together in other lives before this one, or might be again sometime in the future. Whether that ever occurred, somehow believing that her spiritual journey continued was extraordinarily comforting. And with that consolation and knowledge, he began to look outside himself and feel freer to get on with his life.

But what did that mean, to get on with his life? In a way, he considered himself very lucky. He had known and loved a marvelous woman and had a wonderful family. He looked forward to having many years of relating with Jackie and Jenny as they matured into adults. He had a business which should continue to support him well into the future. In a small town like this, it probably wouldn't grow much more, but unless things changed drastically, people would continue to need cars to drive. He felt fortunate to be able to make a living providing them. With Bob to manage the company, he didn't have to worry about it right now.

So what was he to do with himself now? How should he get on with his life? Brian knew that he wanted to travel. His girls had been saying for some time, "Dad, you ought to at least take a vacation." He'd not gone anywhere since BJ's death. When he finally said he would, he did it more for them than for himself, but now he really looked forward to it. Recently, one of his older customers traded in a little used Land Rover in exchange for a new Toyota Camry. Besides being a rugged car, it was well appointed, a luxury Rover, if you will. That spawned an idea.

Why not take that car and head out . . . see where it took him? He asked Bob to have the shop go through it and put everything in top shape, ready for travel. Was this an unrealistic fantasy, to just hit the road and follow his intuition? Maybe, but it sure appealed to him.

For a couple of weeks, making plans for the trip kept him engaged. He put together camping and fishing gear, with both summer and winter clothes, so that he could be self-sufficient and flexible in how and where to spend his time. One of the seats in the Rover folded down so that he could even lay out his sleeping bag and sleep in the car if he wanted. With his lap-top computer, he could keep in touch with the girls at school via E-mail, and with Bob at the business. When he discussed the idea of this trip with them, they were all very encouraging. He knew BJ would be as close to him as she was here at home, no matter where he went. When he began packing the car, his new books occupied an important spot. So where to go? The West appealed to him.

Early one morning, three weeks later, he started out. Wisps of cloud from last night's spring shower still clung tenaciously to the low hill tops, as if reluctant to let go of the prairie's sensuous touch. With the windows rolled down, he inhaled a deep breath of that magical fragrance that follows a spring rain, while his ears caught snatches of meadowlark songs, launched from their perches on the roadside fence posts. He found it fun to really observe sights he tended not to even notice most of the time . . . the spring green of the wheat fields, new calves nursing at their momma's sides, trees breaking out in leaves. Ah! New life emerged all about him, and he was on vacation!

* * *

As Brian approached the Blanding airport, images of his trip flashed through his mind, crossing Kansas and on to Denver, where he'd stopped to explore a bit, and bought more books. Then on across Colorado: South Park; pausing in the little town of Crestone, where he'd had that past life regression; poking his way through the mountains, where winter still reigned, to Grand Junction; then on to Moab, Utah. There he'd rented a bicycle to ride amidst the beauty of the bluffs around Moab and Arches National Park. But he'd begun to feel restless among all the tourists and longed for solitude. When he told the host at the Moab Visitor Center that he wanted to explore ancient Anasazi ruins, she advised him to go south to Blanding, where he would find fewer people and many more ruins. He looked forward to visiting again the area around Blanding, where he had been on an anthropology field trip one summer in college. Now here he was, and he'd found something totally unexpected. A woman he liked. What was he going to do about that?

28

Two Weeks Later

Sally watched Brian drive away again. They'd had, what, five dates by now? Already Sally found herself starting to feel very close to this man and it scared her. Somehow, here in Blanding, that had never been an issue. It wasn't that no nice men lived around here. She'd met several, some single and attractive. However, Sally felt pretty certain that she didn't want to join the Mormon faith. And to link up with almost any man in this community meant that she would have to become Mormon. So here's Brian, single and not Mormon, and she felt attracted to him.

Part of her said she didn't dare fall in love with him. She still doubted her fitness to be in a relationship, doubted whether she could ever be sexual again with a man. She remembered the impact her 'dreams' had had on her relationship with George. They had destroyed it. Scared they might again, she decided she'd been lucky to have not had to deal with those 'dreams' for a long, long time. But now she would have to face up to them. If she told Brian she couldn't see him anymore, he'd want to know why. Did she dare tell him about her abductions in the past. She scarcely allowed herself to think about them anymore. Sometimes she still had a hard time believing they were actual experiences instead of dreams. What should she do? Sally told herself that maybe all her abduction stuff was in the past. Maybe the ET's had forgotten about her. After all, it had been a long time since it last happened. Maybe, it would no longer affect her. Maybe they were over. At least that's what she hoped.

Sally had watched her hugs with Brian become longer and more intimate. And their kisses, tentative at first, grew more passionate with each succeeding date. It seemed as if their shared hunger for love and intimacy, which she knew she had long denied, and probably Brian had too, now recognized the opportunity to grow into fiery passion. Their love and desire seemed mutual, which made it all the more scary!

29

    Meanwhile, second thoughts pestered Brian too. What a surprise to realize that he was falling in love with Sally. After BJ died, he'd doubted he would ever be able to love anyone else like he loved BJ. He didn't doubt the special and beautiful relationship he'd had with BJ. They had many years together and raised two lovely daughters. Nothing would ever change that. If he let himself love Sally, what did that mean about his love for BJ? Maybe he could think of his love for BJ as an affirmation of what might be possible again. How confusing!
    Then he thought, maybe it's too soon. Maybe he wasn't ready. Yet he knew he wanted to see Sally again, to hold her, even wanted make love with her. His arousal during their kisses had caught him by surprise. He'd not experienced that since before BJ died. But how great to feel turned on, alive again, and wanting someone. Uh oh! What if he let himself fall in love with her and she didn't want anything more to do with him? Then he remembered how she'd returned his hugs and kisses. What a gamble! He'd never imagined that starting to date again at his age would bring so much anxiety or fear.
    That's as far as he could let himself think for the moment. Tomorrow they planned to hike out into the canyons. He intended to show her the canyon where Joe had grown up. He wondered whether to tell her about the eerie feelings and deja vue he'd had out there, and about his belief that maybe he had actually lived there himself long ago. He had been pleased with the sense of connection he'd felt with Joe ever since he had related what he really thought it meant. Joe had at first shown surprise, but when Brian described what each room had been used for, Joe had said it matched the stories he remembered his Great Grandmother telling, who had lived there herself. What a small world this is, Brian mused ... the synchronicity of his possibly having lived a life in the same place as Joe, and then meeting Joe here in the year 2001. Almost too much to believe, and yet it really felt quite wonderful to acknowledge such a personal and spiritual connection with someone. Perhaps that's the reason Joe had decided to invite him to fly his Cub. Whatever the reason, he was surely grateful for the opportunity.
    And now he had to decide whether to share any of this with Sally, though he knew it was certainly part of the reason he'd invited her to go. He worried she'd might think him a nut for believing in this stuff,

especially for thinking that he'd been Joe's great-grandfather in a previous lifetime. Wow! What an adventure! But he remembered how real that stone slab had felt on his chest in the regression. And then to see what looked like that very rock there where it had fallen from the overhang!

The next morning Brian appeared at Sally's house at 7:30 as planned. Sally came to the door at his knock and invited him in. "I made us a picnic lunch," she said cheerfully.
"Great idea," Brian responded.
"I thought we might get hungry before we get back to town. Would you grab my backpack and the thermos of coffee there by the door? I'll get the sandwiches and the other goodies from the kitchen. Otherwise, I'm all ready."
"Sure thing," Bryan said as he waited by the door, "You might want to bring your jacket as well. It's still a little cool these days."
"Good thought," Sally returned. "It's so warm here in town, I sometimes forget that it's usually much cooler out in the canyons."
Driving out Elk Mountain Road, the brisk morning air carried in the rich scent of the cedars which lined the road. They inhaled it in silence. Brian's excitement continued to grow stronger, filling him with anticipation for the adventure of the day. He noticed that neither of them needed constant chatter between them to feel connected. An occasional glance and smile sufficed, while each remained absorbed in their own thoughts. Brian slowed the Rover as he neared the turn off to the canyon where Joe had lived as a boy. The road wove its way up the canyon through tamarisk and cedars, back and forth across the small creek. Eventually the Jeep track faded out completely and they had to stop and park beneath an old cottonwood tree.
"We have to walk from here" Bryan said. "It's not too far, only about half a mile."
They loaded their gear, food, and water bottles in their backpacks and soon set out on their way. They saw only a few animal tracks on the trail. In fact, Brian doubted if anyone had been along the trail since his last visit here. He saw one of his own tracks in the mud by the stream, but nothing more. The trail followed what had once been the crude road that led to the small collection of hogans that had been Joe's home village. As it drew them deeper into the canyon, the walls of the canyon rose and narrowed. The stream near their path flowed more strongly here than at the canyon's mouth and looked beautifully clear. When they crossed the stream they saw the tracks of deer and raccoons imprinted in the mud. Brian pointed out where a coyote had walked the trail for quite

a distance.

Sally commented, "I feel such a wonderful sense of isolation and unspoiled privacy here. I've never been out here before."

"Really beautiful, isn't it?"

As they reached the point where the canyon broadened out into the village site, the sun warmed their backs, though the air felt brisk. Not much remained of the hogans. The dirt that had covered the roofs had long ago fallen in, while the soil that had banked the log walls for insulation now formed donut shapes on the ground. The entire setting felt very peaceful and quiet.

When they reached the center of the group of mounds, Brian watched as Sally looked around, absorbing the scene. After a few moments, she said, "I feel a tingle of excitement, as if something magical might happen at any moment. And yet I feel a little sad to think that this used to be such a vibrant place where people lived, and kids played and laughed. Now it is just a place of memories and ghosts."

Brian liked her sensitivity. "Yeah, and though it was a small village, it was home to Joe and his whole clan. The gardens where they grew their food are over there to the east," he pointed to a clearing, now overgrown with sage brush. After a moment of silence, he continued, "Let's head on up the path and see the spring that comes up at the west end of this canyon."

A short walk brought them to the base of the cliff, where the spring rose from the ground in a beautiful deep pool, its center an intense blue-green, fading to very light green at the edges, like a huge morning glory blossom. They saw the stones laid long ago at the pool's edge to make dipping water from the spring more convenient. Walking downstream a short way, they found where the stream flowed into another pool, enclosed in a kind of grotto, high banks sheltering it from the wind.

"Joe told me this is the pool where he used to take a bath and where they washed their clothes." Brian stuck his hand into the pool. Shaking the water from his hand, he remarked, "Brrr, that's cold! I can't imagine getting into that in the spring or fall, let alone winter. Maybe they took water into their hogans and heated it. I'll have to ask him about that sometime."

Sally bent and splashed her hand in the water too, then said with a chuckle, "I'm not sure I would want to get into that water even in the summertime. Though I suppose you could call it refreshing."

"Let's cross the stream here and head over north to the canyon wall. There something else I want to show you," Bryan said eagerly. He led, stepping on the stones in the middle of the slow flowing stream just above the pool. Sally followed behind. Wending their way through the willows, they approached a small fold in the canyon wall. Brian walked up a barely discernible path to a ledge not visible from the canyon floor. There they saw the remains of old dwellings made of rock, mud, and small logs.

"Are these Anasazi ruins?" Sally asked with wonder in her voice.

"I'm not sure," Brian replied. "Joe told me his great grandparents made their home here back in the 1800's. Though Utes were mostly tipi and hogan dwellers, occasionally a few lived in cliff dwellings like the old Anasazi. After all, it made a very energy efficient type of dwelling. They knew about solar energy long before it became popular with the white man. This little pocket in the cliff is protected from the wind and collects the sun most all day long in the wintertime, so would be quite cozy. In the summertime, the overhang shades it from the sun most of the day, as you can see, so it stays cool. It's close to the water, protected from rain storms and not too hard to get to. An ideal place."

"Look at that huge slab of rock that must have fallen off the overhang of the cave," Sally pointed in awe. "It looks like it crushed a lot of their living space. I hope nobody was under it when it fell."

"Well, actually there was," Brian said cautiously. "Joe told me his great grandfather died when that came down in a small earthquake. It came so fast he didn't have a chance to escape. It happened at night when he least expected anything. He only lived for a few minutes after it fell. It literally crushed the life out of him. They had to bring a long heavy pole from the canyon floor to pry the rock up enough to drag him out. By the time they did, he had died. At only forty-two, it was quite a tragedy for the family. After he died the family moved down to the canyon floor and never returned. They have strong superstitions about staying around any place where spirits might still be present."

"How sad!" Sally said. "Joe must have told you all about it, huh?"

"No, actually he's said very little about it."

"Then how do you know what happened? Did you just make up that story?

"No, I didn't."

"Then how do you know?" Sally asked again, sounding puzzled.

"Because I was here," Brian said quietly, and after a long pause. "I think I am the one who died under that stone."

Sally stared at him, comprehension slow to come. When the awareness of what Brian was really saying sank in, Sally stared even harder, eyes wide. "I hope you don't mean what I think you mean by that," Sally whispered.

"Yes, I do," Brian said quietly, almost reverently. "I guess I should tell you the whole story, eh?"

"Yes. I think you'd better," Sally said firmly.

"How about you pour a cup of coffee from your thermos while I tell you about it. This is going to take a while." Brian seated himself on a rock and motioned to Sally to sit nearby.

"Have you ever read anything about reincarnation or past life regressions?"

Sally shook her head, "Not really, though I have seen some of those wild claims in the grocery store rags. But I never really believed any of that stuff." She handed him the cup.

"That's the way it used to be for me as well," Brian said. He paused for a sip of coffee, then proceeded to tell her about the Weiss books, and then about his past life regression in Crestone, Colorado. "When the scene opened and I saw myself as an Indian sitting under a cave overhang, I assumed that I had gone back to an Anasazi life hundreds of years ago. Sally, it seemed so real, almost as real as it is to me right now. I was sitting here by the fire one night, felt the ground shake, and then heard this sharp crack above my head. Almost before I could look up, that rock fell and crushed me. I only had a few moments of consciousness before I died and left my body. I hung around long enough to see them pull my body out, watching from above.

You can imagine the shock I felt when I walked into this canyon and started recognizing it, and then saw this ledge, this place that had been my home. I almost stopped breathing when I saw that big slab of rock. I think it was the one that killed me in that lifetime."

Brian watched Sally, who remained silent, obviously unsure what to say. Brian looked at her, then said, "I know you probably think I'm nuts. I surely would if someone had just told me such a wild story and acted like they believed it. But I swear to God, I am telling the truth, though I can hardly believe it myself. At first, after the regression, I regarded it as something I could either take or leave, thinking it was Anasazi, even though it felt so very real, that is, until I came out here recently. Then I really had to decide whether I believed it or not. I asked Joe if he knew anything about the cave-in up here on this cliff. He said in an offhand way that his great-grandfather had died when that slab came down in the mid-1800s. That's all he said. I eventually told him about my experience here, even telling him about who lived here and the use of each room. He found it hard to believe at first, but confirmed what I said about the people and rooms, based on the stories he'd heard. So there it is. The only other explanation is that I somehow made a psychic connection with that whole scenario, enough to see and feel it in detail. And even that is pretty weird."

Brian watched intently as Sally sat quietly, not speaking. Finally she said, "That is some story, all right. Kinda of makes you rethink what life is all about, doesn't it?"

"It sure does," Brian returned. "I debated telling you about this, or even bringing you here. I was afraid that you would think I was crazy." He paused, waiting for some response. When none came, he continued, "But I decided to take a risk. It's part of who I am and part of what I have come to believe about life. Sally, I want you to know me. If we are to be anything more than just friends, I don't want to have any secrets between us, so I decided not to hide this from you. I hope that you can still accept me, whether you believe it or not."

Sally gave a little shiver and said, "Let's head back to the spring and have our lunch." Her mind wandered to her own secrets. Maybe it would be safe to tell Brian after all.

30

The next morning, when Brian woke and looked out the window, he saw one of those rare days in the desert Southwest. Dark gray clouds hung so low that they brushed the tops of trees, and it looked as if it might rain any minute. After yesterday with Sally, he felt pretty low anyway. The weather only added to his dismal mood. Sally had remained quiet throughout the entire trip back to town. His attempts to engage her in conversation had been fruitless. He kicked himself for having shown her the ruins, and especially for having told her about his past life experience. Maybe it was too much for her. When he tried to engage her thoughts, after a long period of silence, she had merely said that it was a lot to take in all at once, a lot to think about. After that, they had mostly made small talk, both avoiding their real thoughts and feelings.

Not yet hungry for breakfast, Brian decided to head out to the airport to talk to Joe. Maybe that would cheer him up. At least he hoped so. When he arrived at the airport, Joe took one look at him and said, "You look like you've lost your best friend, or else this cloud deck hanging over our heads is about to dump on you."

"You're more on target than you realize," Brian responded wearily. "Yesterday, Sally and I went hiking out in the canyons. I took her out to your old village site, and then up to the cliff ruin. Then I told her the story of my past life regression and that I believed that I died there in another lifetime. I guess it was more than she could handle. She stayed pretty quiet all the way back to town and we didn't see or talk to each other last night either."

"Well, I can see where that would be a pretty big bite to swallow," Joe said. "You and I haven't talked about it that much since you told me about it. I've been wondering when you would bring it up again."

"Yeah, I 'spose I should have talked it over with you before taking her out there. But dammit, Joe, it was so real, I can't deny it! Otherwise I wouldn't have thought much about it. I first assumed that I lived somewhere back in Anasazi times. But when you told me the story of how your great-grandfather died under just such a rock fall, it was too much for just coincidence. And when you confirmed my impressions about the people who lived there, it wrapped it tight for me."

Joe nodded. "When you first mentioned it to me, I have to admit that I found it a bit of a stretch, but those last pieces were confirming for me as well. I also have to admit that ever since you walked in here, I've felt pretty good about you. I don't usually take to someone so quickly."

"And I've been at ease with you too, Joe," Brian said. "When you offered to teach me to fly the Cub, having heard from others around here that you never let anyone fly it . . . well, let's just say I was pretty amazed. I'm very, very grateful that you have taught me how to fly it. I will do my best to take very good care of it. I also want to say that while many folks around town have been friendly, I still feel a little like a stranger, except with you and with Sally. Of course, everyone knows that I'm not Mormon."

"Neither am I," Joe said.

"Yeah, but you grew up here, and people know that."

"True. And you and I have our connection around airplanes and flying. Gives us a lot in common."

"Thanks, Joe," Brian said.

"And as far as Sally is concerned, why don't you cut her some slack, give her a little time to get used to this idea. I heard that you and she had been seeing each other. I hope you realize that you're the first man she's dated since she came here eight years ago. I'll bet she's not pulled back from you as far as you might think."

"I didn't realize that, and I hope you're right," Brian sighed. A long silence followed, and then Brian looked up from where he leaned on the counter and saw once again the picture of Joe with the P-47. Glancing out the window, Brian said, "Obviously, I'm not going to be doing any flying today. If you have time, I'd love to hear more of your story, more about your flying in World War II."

"That's kind of a long story," Joe said. "You sure you want to hear about all that?"

"I've got nothing else to do today. And besides, I need to get my head out of my own gut."

* * *

Brian's request took Joe back almost 60 years in time, to shortly after Pearl Harbor. He'd been only about 20, or maybe 22, at the time that he'd enlisted, not an easy time for anyone, with the nation at war in both Europe and the Pacific. He described himself as one of millions of young men who had to grow up too fast. Telling his story to Brian brought relief as he re-visited old memories and old grief, from his training to the death of Amy, and to his combat experience over Europe. Exposing them to the light of day somehow brought healing. When he finished, he looked at Brian again and sighed.

* * *

Deeply moved by Joe's experiences, Brian scarcely knew what to say. "Thanks for sharing that, Joe. I know that even with your telling it now, more than 50 years after it happened, I can't fully comprehend what it was like. I've been lucky, I guess, to not have to go to war. But I am grateful for what you and so many others gave for people like me. I'm glad that you survived, uninjured in your body. But I know that it must have taken its toll on you emotionally. All, I can say is, thanks, Joe." Even with hearing about Joe's experiences during World War II, Brian still found it hard to reconcile this man, who had the appearance and vigor of someone in his 50's or 60's, with the years he must be wearing. He must be in his 80's by now. Perhaps his Indian genes made him look so young.

"Thanks for listening. I don't think I've ever told anyone the whole story."

31

Since Joe began teaching him to fly the Cub, Brian had felt their friendship grow stronger and deeper, perhaps taking on a father-son aspect along the way. Brian's own dad had died while he was still in college and he'd long missed the camaraderie they used to have. Perhaps unconsciously he'd recreated some of that with Joe.

One morning, after the regulars who gathered every morning at the airport for coffee had wandered off, Brian noticed Joe, elbows on the counter, looking at him intensely. Returning his look, Brian said aloud, "Yes?"

"I've been thinking. You're doing pretty well with the Cub. Now I wonder if you would like to really learn to fly?"

Brian's eyes opened wide in curiosity. What on earth did he mean? Joe had first asked that same question weeks ago. He'd known how to fly back then, but nothing like he knew now after flying the Cub. That time he'd understood Joe to be asking if he wanted to expand his skill by learning to fly the Cub and get tail wheel certified. Now he had no idea what he meant.

"Hey, Joe, we've been through that once already. Remember? You asked me that before we began flying the Cub. Is there something I've missed?" Brian paused for a moment. "I thought I was doing OK in the Cub. In fact you just said so yourself. What are you talking about now? You don't have any other airplanes around here that I'm not checked out in."

"Well, never mind." Joe turned to go back into the hangar-shop.

He must have been expecting a different response. "No, wait a minute. I want to know what you're talking about."

"Well, if you do, be here at five o'clock tomorrow morning." The door into the hangar banged shut behind him, bringing the conversation to an abrupt close.

Brian knew it would be a waste of time to pursue him to try to find out more. He'd learned that if Joe had something to say, he would say it in his own good time. Still puzzled, he went on out to the Cub and went flying. But the whole time he was in the air, Joe's comment and challenge continued to nag at him. So when he pushed the Cub back into the hangar, he said simply, "See you at five."

Pilots often refer to the very early morning hours as 'O-Dark-

Thirty,' meaning thirty minutes before daylight. This gives latitude for not having specific times for the changing onset time of sunrise through various seasons. In the summer, with its long days, it could be quite early indeed. When Brian arrived at the airport a few minutes before five, he found it still pretty dark. O-Dark-Thirty, for sure. A few wisps of ground fog, unusual for this desert country, clung to the runway in the still morning air, lending a magical, mysterious quality to the scene. Sure enough, there sat Joe's old four wheel drive pickup, parked by the gate, with not another vehicle or person in sight this early on a Sunday morning. On the way to the gate, Brian touched the hood. Its warmth indicated Joe had only recently pulled it out of the hangar where it lived. He walked on inside to the welcoming aroma of freshly made coffee and heard Joe say, "Coffee's ready."

    Brian helped himself to a large Styrofoam cup, shook in a little creamer, then filled it with coffee. When he picked up the pot, a few drops fell from the reservoir and sizzled into vapor on the hot plate beneath, a sign the coffee maker had only just finished its cycle. He paused for a moment with the cup beneath his nose and savored the fragrance, knowing that it would still be too hot to drink. He waited patiently. Soon Joe emerged from the little office he called The Dungeon, a title that reflected his less than enthusiastic attitude toward paperwork, though he kept it neat and orderly. Grabbing his key ring, he muttered, "Let's go" and headed for the door.

    Brian followed and climbed into Joe's pickup. The smooth sound of the engine belied its age, a tribute to the meticulous maintenance Joe provided this venerable, but reliable vehicle. They headed south down Highway 163 from the airport, where they shortly turned west on the little jog that continued on west on State Route 95, out toward the canyons. They rolled down past Butler Wash, a small stream bed that backs north into a canyon where Anasazi once lived long ago. The road descended on southwest, deeper down the valley until it bent back to the west to begin its climb up Comb Ridge, a miles-long north-south ridge of upthrust of rock, the remains of an ancient seabed. The enormous deep man made cut in the ridge that permitted the highway to cross this immense escarpment of rock amazed Brian. It made short work of the long, arduous trails that the ancients had to traverse to make this same journey. After coming through the cut, which felt like coming out of a tunnel, the highway turned north along the ridge to ease its descent down the steep incline to the valley below. By now, the dawning day began to light the vast north-south valley. Joe killed the lights, making the ride feel more mysterious. Not a word had yet been spoken by either, though questions raced through Brian's mind. Where on earth were they going?

What does coming out to the canyons have to do with really learning to fly?

On reaching the valley floor, just after the highway bent back to the west, they turned off to the north on a dirt jeep trail and wound their way along the dry stream bed through scrub brush, tamarisk, and old cottonwoods for a few miles, until they came to where a canyon opened to the west. They rumbled across the Bureau of Land Management cattle-guard that protected its mouth, Joe mumbled, "Arch Canyon." From there the jeep track rapidly deteriorated and Joe shifted into four wheel drive and on down to low. They slowly wove their way through small trees and brushes, fording the little stream several times as they made their way westward up the canyon. After a while, the truck climbed up onto a broad expanse of slick rock, characteristic of this area, and Joe abruptly turned left, heading south toward what appeared to be a blank rock wall broken only by a small bunch of willows.

As they approached the wall, Brian shouted, "Look out!" Just before what looked like an inevitable crash, Joe made another quick turn to the right, brushed past some willows, and plunged into the unseen mouth of a small side canyon. Here the narrow track followed a dry stream bed and required careful negotiation of the twists and turns to avoid scraping the sides of the pickup on the rocks. Approaching what appeared to be a dead end, Joe made a hard left turn to follow the narrow canyon once again. Two minutes later another switchback led them back southwest shortly to a natural bowl, a small pocket canyon about two hundred feet in diameter. Here Joe stopped, killed the engine, and they sat quietly, facing a solid wall of small cedars and brush at the threshold of the canyon opening. Only the ticking of the engine and exhaust pipes releasing their heat interrupted the morning stillness. The silvery trill of canyon wrens echoed off the canyon walls to welcome the oncoming dawn.

"Well, here we are," Joe finally said, and quietly opened his door and climbed out of the pickup. Brian's mind had been in overdrive the last half hour, with questions stumbling over one another in their haste to make sense of what is happening, all to no avail. Beautiful as it is, what on earth does this godforsaken spot have to do with flying? No amount of imagination could create a landing strip here in this small bowl, even for Joe's amazing skills with the Cub. Only a helicopter could make it in and out, but why here? He didn't think Joe had a helicopter. Nonplused, yet intrigued, he could only await Joe's lead and follow along.

Pushing their way through the cedars, they entered the open bowl, its flat bottom made of trackless slick rock. Far to one side, Brian heard a trickle of water as it seeped from a tiny spring in the wall and crawled along the perimeter of the bowl, to disappear into the sand near where they had entered. Joe strode over to the southeast side of the canyon bowl to where some dead brush and small trees had apparently fallen against the wall.

Brian stood there, astonished, for as Joe removed the brush, he saw what looked like a set of sliding hangar doors, artfully painted to look like the wall itself, a masterpiece of camouflage. Extracting a key from the many on his key ring, Joe opened the padlock and slid the hangar doors back to reveal a large dark cave. Even in the early morning light, deep within this canyon bowl, Brian saw that it contained something.

Joe's quiet words, "Come on!" finally got Brian moving from where his feet had almost taken root. Moving toward the mouth of the cave, he saw a large rounded form that, in the dim light, appeared at first to be a part of the cave. Moving closer, it materialized into a separate object entirely. His mind had not yet let him fully grasp what he observed. He was seeing it but not seeing it. His brain struggled to process the information coming from his eyes, trying to sort through his lifetime database of visual images, searching for a match. It paused momentarily from time to time, as if a match had been found, then rushed on, searching . . . coming back again and again to the same place, the same match of identification. All this in the space of a few seconds that felt much, much longer. UFO? Flying saucer? Space ship? It can't be! But it is! No! Yes, it is! Still he stood there, truly stunned and speechless! His feelings totally escaped him for the moment as he tried to take in this incredible sight.

"What is it, Joe?" He finally asked. The first of a whole series of questions that tumbled around in his mind. Yeah, what is it? Where did it come from? How did it get here? What is it doing here? How do you know about it? Is it yours? Why have you kept it secret? Did you make the hangar doors? How did you do that? What's this got to do with really learning to fly? On and on his mind rushed.

Joe ignored Brian's first question, as if to say, can't you see what it is? Instead he asked calmly, "Do you want to learn to fly it?"

"Whoa now! Let's just slow down there a minute, pardner." Brian's voice fell into a pseudo western drawl. "You mean you know how to fly this thing?"

Joe merely nodded his head in assent. That started another whole cascade of questions. Fly this . . . this . . . thing? Brian had always wanted to believe in flying saucers, and sort of did. Most pilots do. But to be here and see it 'in the flesh' was almost more than he could handle, and then . . . to think about flying it! Time almost stood still while he tried to take in this new information. Unaware he had stopped breathing for a moment, his body finally forced him to take a deep breath.

Then his mind began to work again. He first became curious, then excited. Underneath the craft he saw landing gear, four equally spaced legs about two feet long, extending to the ground at a slight angle, with a dinner-plate sized pod on the bottom of each to support the weight of the craft. In a way, it really did resemble an upside down saucer. No wonder those first observers long ago had called them flying saucers. He cautiously reached out to touch its smooth rounded rim and felt an electric tingle that made him jerk his hand back in surprise. It was only a very mild shock, much less than an electric fence gives off. Once again he reached out to touch it, and ignoring the tingle, felt the soft, almost velvety surface, very pleasurable to the touch. He walked around it, examining it carefully. It appeared to be about forty feet in diameter and maybe eight or ten feet high at the thickest part, counting the legs. When he reached the opposite side, near the back of the cave, he became aware of a faint hum coming from the saucer. Moving back around to the starting point, he realized he saw no doors or windows. Just a smooth, seamless outer skin. The words 'aerodynamically perfect' floated into his mind and just kept repeating themselves, as he marveled again and again at the sight.

Joe, in no hurry, eventually came over near to where Brian stood. He reached out and touched the rim of the craft, and as if by magic, a two foot wide section of the skin parted, with the bottom part descending to the ground to reveal two steps, while the upper portion rose to form a doorway into the craft.

"Let's go for a ride," Joe said casually, as if it were an everyday event. Brian couldn't think of anything to say just yet, so just nodded his head, though for him it was anything but an everyday event.

To Brian, stepping into the craft felt like entering a contemporary executive jet or twin engine prop plane. Joe went first, ducking his head to move into the dimly lit interior. Brian followed and found himself in a cockpit or cabin different from anything he had ever seen before. Two side by side seats faced a blank forward sloping ceiling and an inclined control panel, blank except for a few buttons. Joe sat in the left one and nodded his head for Brian to take the other, from where he watched Joe begin touching buttons and switches, and heard as well as felt, the craft start to power up, whatever that meant. A slightly louder humming sound now replaced the faint one he had detected earlier. Joe pointed to a headset nearby as he put one on himself.

The headset looked a different from the standard aircraft headset familiar to Brian. Those had cushioned ear covers that contained tiny speakers, with a band going over the top and a microphone attached to facilitate radio communications within the cabin and with outside sources. He used those all the time in the Cub and the Cessna 172, to make it easier to talk over the engine sound. This headset had the familiar set of ear covers and microphone, but also had a wide band that encircled the head, much like the rim of a cap. Putting it on, he found it comfortable. Elastic in the headband allowed it to adjust to his head size.

Joe continued with the startup procedure and soon Brian heard Joe's voice in his headset.

"Comfortable?" he asked.

"Yeah, I guess so."

Then a strange thing happened. Brian heard Joe's voice, only it was not his voice, at least it didn't sound exactly like it. The inflections and words were like his, but it sounded different. Then he suddenly realized that he didn't actually hear Joe's voice at all, but now received his thoughts in his head. What on earth is going on now, he wondered?

Instantly, almost before he had finished the thought, he 'heard' back, *"These headsets enable telepathic communication. It is much quicker than speaking aloud. We'll only use the mikes for communication with other planes if we need it, though I doubt that we will today. Not much traffic out here this time of day. Besides, no one would believe us anyway. But we'll monitor other aircraft frequencies just to be safe. Now here is another little surprise."*

Joe pressed another spot on the panel and what had appeared to be a blank sloping wall in front of them became transparent and they looked out through the 'windshield' at the inside of the cave wall in front of them. He noticed Joe's hand on a small shaped joy stick and then in a moment, felt the craft lift slightly, rock a little bit as the landing gear retracted, and begin to slide out of the cave into daylight. Once outside in the pocket canyon, they began rising, slowly at first and then rapidly, accelerating as they went, until they shot straight up into the atmosphere, thousands of feet per minute. Moments later Joe transitioned into horizontal flight and leveled off. Situated on the windshield was the Heads-Up-Display representation of instruments, providing continuous data about their flight. Brian gulped when he saw an altimeter showing them at 50,000 feet.

"Wow! That's incredible!" he said aloud. Sitting in the center of a round craft, he couldn't look out the window like he did in the Cub to look at the ground below, and wished he could see the ground. He'd forgotten that Joe could understand every thought and saw him reach out with his left hand, touch a button, and instantly he could look down through part of the floor on his right at the earth passing below at a very rapid rate. Since they'd headed west, away from the early morning sun, the earth grew darker below them as they flew, except for the lights of the cities they passed over. They were so high that he had few of the usual clues of speed from passage over the ground, but still it seemed to be going by quickly.

"*How fast are we going?*" Brian queried.

"*Oh, we're just loafing along about 3000 miles per hour,*" Joe responded.

"*Oh.*" All Brian could think to say, having never gone that fast in his life.

With that Joe bent the little joy stick back and Brian felt a momentary gravity change as they zoomed upward, though there was very little of the usual G-forces he experienced in airplanes.

"*Oh, my God! Here we are going higher than 50,000 feet and we don't have any oxygen on!*" He started looking around frantically for something like an oxygen mask.

"*Sorry, I forgot to brief you on that. This thing has an oxygen system that responds automatically to what our bodies need, no matter how high we go. Nothing to worry about, Brian. Just relax and enjoy the ride.*"

Brian looked out the windshield and saw the sky begin to get dark. Below, he could even see the curvature of the earth, and then suddenly realized how high they must be. They were going into the stratosphere . . . and beyond! He was glad he had strapped himself in with the seat belt, so he wouldn't start floating all over the cabin.

Again, he heard in his head, "*I set the gravity at one, so we'll continuously experience the same gravity we have on earth. Makes it easier that way.*"

"*Oh.*"

"*Another part of the briefing I forgot.*" And Brian actually heard a little chuckle to his left.

"*Remember the pre-flight checklist in our planes, where it says to brief the passengers on emergency procedures, etc.? Well, I just sorta forgot that this morning. You see, you are my first passenger in this thing, so you'll have to excuse me.*"

"*Okay. So where are we now?*"

"*Oh, somewhere over the Pacific Ocean.*"

"*And those lights that we saw a few minutes ago?*"

"*Los Angeles.*"

It took a few moments of silence to take that in. "*And how fast are we going now?*"

"*About 30,000 miles per hour.*"

"*Oh.*"

"*Want to fly it?*"

"*Well, not just yet.*" Brian felt too bewildered to know what else to say.

"*Think of this like your first ride in an airplane. Just relax and enjoy the scenery.*"

"*Okay.*" Still in a state of shock and disbelief, what else could he do? Though not totally scared with Joe in charge, he did feel more than just a little uneasy. He always used to pride himself on maintaining situational awareness. That would really be a challenge here.

"*How do you find home again?*" He asked mentally.

"*Well, we just point it back toward home. It has a system that operates somewhat like the GPS in my planes. Only here, we are actually so close to the orbit level of the GPS satellites, they can't help us much. I'll explain it to you later. We don't have to actually DO anything, just image our home port, that canyon and cave, and it will take us there. Join with me. Think about that place, and keep your focus on it, not anywhere else.*"

Brian held an image of that place firmly in his mind, clearly focusing on that bowl shaped canyon. He didn't want to throw the system off. After a while, he felt a change in the craft's momentum and noticed they had started a descent. In just a short time, he saw the features of the earth rapidly growing larger as they descended. A few minutes later he noticed they were no longer going forward, but were hovering and dropping the last 1000 feet or so into the canyon. Joe stopped the descent a couple of feet above the slick rock floor of the canyon, just like landing the Cub, and then slowly moved sideways into the cave. Brian heard the landing gear extend, and with a very gentle thump, knew they had landed inside the cave. Joe completed the shutdown of the systems of the craft and signaled its completion by removing his headset. He motioned for Brian to do the same.

Brian sat there, wordless. Joe patiently gave him time to absorb what he'd just experienced. Brian supposed that if he were some hotshot military fighter pilot or space jockey, he would be thrilled to death. Instead, he only sat there in dumb wonder at what he'd just gone through. No longer hooked up mentally, a million questions flew through his brain, not one of which escaped into words. He continued to just sit there, bewildered.

"Take your time, Brian. I'll be outside." Joe said quietly, and rose from his seat and stepped out through the now open doorway. In the silence, Brian just sat, looking around, the windshield once again opaque, like the inclined panel beneath it, which had so recently been lit up. Finally he gave a little sigh and got up to exit the craft. Stepping out, he found Joe sitting on a rock ledge near the cave entrance, contemplating the sky and listening to the birds. He walked over and sat down beside him with a sigh.

"I know how you feel, Brian, though it has been a long time since my first exposure. I was on my vision quest, only 17, when they picked me up and taught me how to fly one of these things. At the time, I knew nothing of flying. I had seen an old Travel Aire biplane once as a kid, but that was it. I felt totally terrified. I'll tell you more about it sometime."

As if he'd done all the explaining needed, Joe fell silent. Brian just shook his head in wonder. He turned to see the saucer, sitting there on its landing pods, just like an airplane in a hangar back at the field. And again, he shook his head. Belief and doubt battled for supremacy inside his mind regarding what his eyes beheld. His conscious self stood on the sidelines, waiting for the conclusion of the conflict.

"Guess I should ask the question again now, eh?" Joe said.

Brian shot him a look of surprise, wondering what now.

"So, do you want to really learn to fly?"

"Not sure I even know how to answer you, Joe," finally finding his voice. "Why me?" As Brian waited for Joe's response, he wrestled with so many things in his mind. While he'd always sort of believed in such things as flying saucers and extraterrestrials, this was up close and personal. Did it come from that ultra-secret military base at Area 51 in Nevada, or from aliens? Before Joe could answer his first question, Brian asked, "Where does this thing come from?"

Joe just silently lifted his forefinger and pointed upward.

"I sort of thought so," was all Brian could think to say at the moment, his mind still trying to take it all in, sort out the implications, and make sense of it.

"Here, give me a hand with the hangar doors." Joe stood and moved to close the doors. They slid easily on well lubricated rollers on the track above their heads. When they were closed and locked, Joe rearranged the brush to its former position, disguising the already well camouflaged doors, then turned and led Brian back through the cedars to the pickup.

Before starting up, Joe turned to Brian and after a moment of looking into his face, said, "There's just one thing about all this, Brian. You have to keep this totally to yourself. Not one word to anyone else. I am sure you understand that, but I just need to make it clear now. Okay?"

"Yeah. No problem." He wouldn't dare tell anyone else about this. They'd think he was nuts!

Like the ride out, silence reigned on the ride back to town, broken only by the rattle of the old pickup over the rocks on the canyon jeep track before they got to the highway. Except in Brian's mind! On the way out his curiosity framed many questions, but now all sorts of thoughts clamored for air time. As they flickered through his mind, Brian began to understand more of Joe's strategy, first testing him by teaching him to fly the Cub, and now this, though he came no closer to understanding why Joe had picked him for this . . . what should he call it? This experience? And what an experience! What does he have in mind? Where was he going with this?

When they got back to the airport, Joe pulled up and parked in his usual space. Brian's Rover sat next to it.

"How about a cup of coffee?" Joe asked.

"Sounds good to me," Brian replied. And how bizarre, he thought. Here it is, not even midmorning and they'd been up to the edge of space, out over the Pacific Ocean and back again! Just a little morning flight around the neighborhood, and now back for cup of coffee! Sitting in the airport lounge, Brian felt grateful for the warmth of the coffee that seeped through the styrofoam cup in his hand, which trembled slightly, a reminder of earthbound reality. Finally, after they finished their coffee, Joe said, "Come on, let's go fly the Cub," and headed through the door to the hangar.

They pushed the Cub out, climbed in, and cranked up. Taxiing out to the run-up area near the end of the runway, he heard Joe's voice in the headset. "Your airplane," indicating he wanted Brian fly the takeoff. He realized he had to start paying attention, to being present versus being somewhere off in his head. Fly the plane, Brian reminded himself. After the run-up checks, he taxied out onto the runway, advanced the throttle to accelerate the plane down the runway, then lifted off into the familiar air. He saw Mt. Abajo to the north and way to the southwest, could just make out the monoliths of Monument Valley down in Arizona. Even after that incredible flight in the saucer, he was not bored with this wonderful plane and the beautiful scenery. He realized Joe's wisdom, getting him into the Cub again right away. He felt calm and confident, not even thinking as he flew along, intuitively directing the Cub. He decided to head out toward Arch Canyon, to see what the saucer's hiding place looked like from the air. Crossing over the Comb Ridge, he felt the lift of the westerly flow of air that pushed them up abruptly as they crossed from east to west. He angled northwest up Arch Canyon, looking for the site. He finally saw the slick rock area, but couldn't to find the little pocket canyon that hid the saucer. He knew that Joe was well aware of his intentions. Finally Joe said, "Here, I'll show you," and threw the Cub into a steep bank, headed south, and then put it into a tight circle. "Look down." At last Brian could just make out the depression that hid the hangar for the saucer, but it appeared as unobtrusive from the air as it did from the ground. No one would ever suspect what lay in that little bowl canyon. Satisfied, he took the stick again and headed back toward town.

Grateful for his familiarity with the Cub, he entered the pattern and brought it around into a smooth three point landing, touching all three wheels simultaneously with barely a chirp. Taxiing back to the hangar, Brian once again felt back in his body, reoriented to what was real. Pushing the Cub back into the hangar, he looked at Joe and said, "Thanks Joe. Guess I have a lot to think about."

Joe gave him a look of understanding and said, "We'll talk tomorrow."

32

    Driving back to town, reflecting on the enormity of what he had just been through, Brian knew that his life would . . . could . . . never be the same. He thought back to that simple idea he'd had before leaving McPherson, that there must be something more to life. Well, now he had found something more! More than he ever imagined! And similar to when BJ died, he kept asking himself over and over, why? Why has Joe selected me for this . . . this dubious honor, if that is what it is? Maybe it is more of a burden than an honor. What does he have in mind for me? Obviously he is offering to teach me to fly the thing. But why?
    Upon further reflection, he realized that Joe had probably been grooming him for this step for some time. Flying the Cub was just his primary training, in effect. If he didn't wash out there, then he became eligible for the next big step, flying the saucer, the UFO. Calling it a UFO, however, no longer fit. It certainly was no longer unidentified! Brian's mind roamed over the innumerable images and sensations: the cool morning air and bird songs of the little canyon, the feel of the surface of the craft, the acceleration, and the view from space. All in just a little flight around the neighborhood. And now Joe wanted him to learn to fly it!
    Brian drove through town for a late breakfast at Kenny's, his favorite restaurant on the northeast edge of town, a plain and simple place, where many of the locals came to eat. The food was good and the atmosphere friendly, always a good sign. The lady who waited on him actually owned it and her son was the cook.
    "What'll it be today, Brian?" She automatically set a white mug in front of him and poured coffee.
    "Give me a short stack with a couple of eggs on the side," Brian said, as he picked up the morning Denver Post that someone had left on the table by the door. Day-old news by the time it got here to Blanding, he still liked to read about what people were doing in the rest of the world. Plus, he wanted to get his mind off the morning experience for a little while, to NOT think about IT. But that only worked for about two minutes. Relentlessly, his mind jumped back to his new 'first flight' with all its implications, and on to the burning question, why me? Then another question suddenly slipped in to disturb him. Who or what is Joe anyway? He was now no longer just the local airport operator, pilot,

instructor, and mechanic. Seeing him fly that craft into near space, like an experienced astronaut, certainly turned his whole perception of Joe on its ear! And he'd said they taught him to fly it when only seventeen. Questions came easily. Answers were elusive.

Later, back in his apartment, Brian picked up Corso's book, <u>The Day After Roswell</u>, to read more about the whole UFO phenomena. While he had believed most of what he'd read about the famous UFO crash there in 1947, he now no longer needed to question any of it. Hell, he'd not only seen one, he'd flown in one! Of course, no one would ever believe it. How would he tell Sally? She wouldn't believe it either. And what about his kids? Oops! Can't tell anyone. Joe made him promise to keep it a secret. This would be a challenge, to just keep his mouth shut about it all.

And what if he did accept Joe's invitation to learn to fly that thing? He realized that this was not just another aircraft, like the Cub. Flying the Cub took him to a whole other level of flying skill. He had become a better pilot, thanks to Joe's patient instruction, his own diligence, and the capabilities of the Cub. But this was more, so much more, literally an entirely different universe of flight. Could he do it? Joe must think so. But why? What does Joe expect? There must be more to this picture than he saw so far. He figured Joe knew him well enough by now to know that he was likely to go for it, or he never would have suggested it. He said we'll talk tomorrow. Tomorrow seemed like a long time to wait.

The day turned into one of the longest of his life, longer even than either the day of BJ's death or her funeral. Brian felt restless, jazzed up, yet tired and a little groggy. Not only had it been early for him to get up to be at the airport by five a.m., but the tension he'd felt throughout the event had left him physically drained. Several times he laid down to try to take a nap, but his mind started zipping around at light speed and wouldn't let him relax enough to sleep. He just lay there, staring at the ceiling.

Finally, come nightfall, with only a snack for supper, Brian fell into a restless sleep, but wakened early the next morning. After a simple breakfast of cereal and coffee, he headed out to the airport. There the airport coffee-clubbers sat telling the latest jokes, discussing local and world events, and pronouncing their wisdom on how to save or run the world. Eventually, they drifted off with the usual announcement, "Well, gotta go to work," though most of them were retired and didn't work anymore. Brian went out into the hangar, picked up a rag, and started to wipe down the Cub, though scarcely a speck of dust marred its surface. Joe came through from the office, looked at him expectantly and sat down on a stool near the plane, and waited.

"Joe, you know I have a million questions, don't you?" Brian said, still wiping the Cub.

"Yep, I imagine so."

"I don't even know where to begin. I can hardly believe what happened yesterday is real, yet I know it is."

"Yep." With a bit of a smile.

"Before I even get into questions about that . . . that thing, my big question is, why me?"

"I think you'll make a good pilot for it."

"Oh, come on now Joe, there's gotta be more reason than that. You've had other people around here over the years who are good pilots. Probably better than me. So why me? And why me now? Who are you anyway? How did you get that thing? Where does it come from?"

"That's a lot of questions, Brian. Any one you are especially interested in?"

"Yeah! Why me?"

"Well, I've been looking for you for some time, or at least for someone like you."

Brian just stood there, looking at Joe, trying to take in what he had just heard. Finally, after a long silence, he said: "Well, thanks for the complement. I guess that gets me to my next question. Who are you, anyway? You must have a helluva story to tell."

"I guess I do owe you an explanation. But let me warn you. It's a long story, and as you know I'm not much of a talker, so it may take a while. I'll try to make it as short as I can. I'm not sure just where to start. It actually goes back to long before my birth. You see, the Star People have been visiting here for a long time. Sometimes they just came to watch and see what humans were doing. Other times they chose to interact with humans. There's records of this, even way back in the Bible, if you read it with that possibility in mind. Well, they've visited my family for at least three generations that I know of, mostly just looking, checking us out, doing some physical examinations and such, even took eggs from my grandmother and great-grandmother. But with my mother they went further. They picked her up several times while she was growing up. They would usually wipe out any memory of it, so's it wouldn't upset her. Then about a month before she married my dad, they made her pregnant again with me, mixing their genetic material with hers, as they put it. She thinks they may have done it one other time before that too, but early on that time, they came and took that baby out of her, long before it was big enough to be born. I'm not sure whether they had sex with her or just did an artificial insemination for these pregnancies. Anyway, for some reason, the second time they left it and as a result, I was born. I grew up in our little village like the other kids there, except I always looked and felt a little different from the rest. I went to school at the old mission school that used to be out northwest of town.

Then when I turned seventeen, like most boys, I went on a vision quest. Of course I knew nothing about all this stuff then. But one night a mysterious floating ball, sort of a mini-UFO, led me up to the top of the mesa near where I'd camped, and I found a saucer sitting there with the door open. I was pretty curious, so I went inside. The minute I got inside, the hatch door closed on me, and I saw one of the small grey beings. No doubt you've heard about them. I can tell you that really spooked me. About that time it took off with me in it. They had it there, waiting for me that night, like they knew where and when I'd be there, n'such. They kept me about three weeks. When I didn't return to the village by the time I was expected, my family started looking for me and eventually found my camp. They all figured I'd fallen off a cliff or got killed by a mountain lion or bear or something. But I hadn't.

While I was up there . . . oh, I forgot to say where they took me. At first I didn't know for sure where I was. It scared me so bad, I passed out on the way there, or maybe they put something in the air to knock me out. I woke up in this strange place, still scared as I could be. There were several different kinds of beings there. Gradually I got used to it. They taught me about my 'other' ancestors, the ones from space. So I guess I am part Indian and part them. Turns out, they took me to this giant Mothership, parked in a stationary orbit over the earth. Then one day they took me to the hangar bay, showed me some of their saucer craft, and offered to teach me how to fly one of them."

"Wow!" Was all that Brian could think to say. Even with Joe's simple telling, the story sounded so amazing that Brian could scarcely believe it. But then, when he flashed back to the ride yesterday, how could he not believe it?

"Back then nobody knew anything about such things except in Buck Rogers science fiction, and the Mothership was so high over earth that it couldn't be seen anyway. So, they taught me to fly one that they called the Explorer craft. Pretty exciting stuff for a seventeen-year old kid. I'd only seen an airplane a couple of times in my life, starting with that old Travel Aire biplane that flew over town once and landed in a pasture south of town, not too far from our runway out here. When they finally brought me back, everyone thought I was a ghost. You know how spooky we Indians are about ghosts of the dead. But it didn't take'em long to figure out I wasn't dead or a ghost, so they welcomed me back home."

"How did you explain where you'd been for three weeks?"

"I just said I'd gotten lost in the canyons. It's happened before. I did pretty well at finding food by that age, so they didn't think too much of it. Only later, after I told my mother what really happened, did she tell me the story of her own childhood contacts, how she'd been picked up by them too. So after that, I never felt like I quite fit in with the other kids. Then a few years later the war came along and I began to see army planes flying over here all the time. I really wanted to fly, so I enlisted in the Army Air Corps, went off to learn to fly airplanes, and ended up in Europe, flying a P-47 like I've told you."

"Yeah, there's that picture of you on the wall over there with one."

"After the war I bought an old surplus BT-13 that I kept tied down here at the airport. Just a dirt and gravel airstrip back then. What a gas hog that thing was. Even at the prices back then, I couldn't afford to buy gas for it very often, though it only cost me a hundred bucks to buy the plane itself. Not long after that, the guy running the airport had a heart attack and couldn't work anymore, so I told the city I could run it. I've been here ever since. A year or so later, the ETs picked me up again to refresh me on flying a new version of the craft. At first, it was quite a stretch for me to go back and forth between the saucer and airplanes.

Then a few years ago, on one of my trips to the Mothership, they offered to provide me with one of the Explorer ships, but first I had to find a safe place to keep it. That took some doing. I finally found that little box canyon where we went yesterday. It was about the right size. Took me a while, with lots of trips, but I finally hauled enough stuff out there to make and hang a set of hangar doors for it. I painted them best I could so's it would look like the rocks there. When I had it all ready, they had me fly it back and park it there. Been there ever since. I fly it every once in a while." And after a pause, Joe looked up at Brian and said, "And that's about it."

"And you've never told anyone else about it?"

"Nope. You're the very first."

"Wow!" And after another long silence: "So why me, Joe? I still don't understand."

"Well, I'm getting up in years now. I'll be eighty-four pretty soon."

"Geez, Joe, you sure don't look it. I wouldn't take you for more than sixty at the most."

"Guess that's due to my genes. Some of us Indians don't show our age much, and maybe it's partly due to the genes from the Star People too. They live a long time. But the human part is beginning to catch up with me. Got a few aches and pains these days. Anyway, they suggested that I find someone to take over flying the saucer when I can't do it anymore."

"But what's the purpose? Why not just take it back when you can't fly it anymore? Why did they give you the saucer in the first place? And why me? I hate to sound like a broken record, but I just don't understand."

"Well, you know how the sheriff's department sometimes calls on me for search and rescue missions out here in the canyons with the Cub."

"Yeah, I have heard stories about some pretty hair-raising rescues you've made."

"It's sort of been like that with the saucer too. I get called on every now and then to help out with some special missions, usually for the government. Sometimes it's to rescue someone in space, or to take out some bad guy. It's usually a night job, so no one sees me, but I don't mind. It's always a challenge, as well as the challenge to keep it all secret. The Explorer has a mild EMP pulse that puts a person to sleep for a while, so I can get them. Then I leave them somewhere safe. The Star People really do want to help us out. I just got recruited to do a special job here on the planet. You've probably never read anything about it. The Air Force likes to keep those things secret, and even they don't know for sure what's going on. I just show up sometimes. I keep a scanner radio to monitor military communications. There's lots more to it, but maybe that will do for now."

"So you want to train me to take over your job, huh?"

"Yep."

"Actually, you've been training me and testing me for a while, haven't you? From what I hear, you've never let anyone else fly your Cub before now. Yet you practically forced it on me!"

Joe just smiled.

"But how can you be sure I'll take you up on your offer? How can you be sure I won't just go out and blab all about your saucer?" After a pause, a wry grin broke Brian's face. "But then, no one would believe me anyway, would they? You've lived here all your life, and I'm just a stranger in town. A crazy stranger, if I started talking about UFO's. You'd just sit here silent and deny it all, wouldn't you, and I'd get ridden out of town on a rail, so's to speak."

"Probably."

"You must have felt pretty sure about me to take me out and show me that thing though, and then take me for a ride in it too. You sure know how to lead a guy on, don't you?"

"Yep. Now my turn for a question. So, do you really want learn to fly it?"

"Joe, I'll swear that question has gone through my mind a thousand times in the last few hours. I didn't sleep much last night for listening to that one, plus a jillion others. Do I want learn to fly that thing? I'm not even sure I know how to answer your question."

"A simple yes or no would do." Joe said.

"I guess I just can't get it through my head as to what your purpose is. You tell me that you are looking for someone to take over for you. But I'm an out-of-town'er. I sure as hell can't take that damn thing back to McPherson. Wouldn't you have to get approval from them up there? They don't know me. Even if you did teach me to fly it, they might not want me to keep on flying it if something happens to you."

Joe just smiled, and said: "Well, I took a little ride last night after you left, and had a conversation with them about you, . . . up there. They were glad to hear you are interested." His hand pointed to the sky. "There is one thing more to think about. They've decided that it's time to begin letting folks here on earth know more about them, another reason they told me to find someone else to fly it too, and to eventually let people begin to see the saucer."

"And what if I say no?"

"Then I guess we go no further. But, you haven't said no, at least not yet. So what do you say?

"Joe, I have a home and business back in McPherson. I have two girls in college. I can't just up and plop down out here. And I can't take over for you. Furthermore, I'm not a mechanic like you are. I could run the business part of this airport, but I'm not a flight instructor like you, nor could I fly the canyon rescues you do. I suppose I could get my instructor's license, but I just don't see how it would work. I've been over it and over it in my mind, and I just don't see it yet."

"Brian, I've learned the hard way that we can only take life one step at a time. I can't see the future either, but I have learned to trust my gut. It saved my life many, many times during the war, as well as here in the canyons. And my gut tells me that somehow it will work out. You have to learn to trust your gut too. Then there is you and Sally. Bet you don't have that figured out yet either," he said with a grin.

"Boy, you sure have that right!"

"But is that stopping you cold?"

"No, but my feet are pretty chilly and it's sure giving me a lot questions."

"So what does your gut tell you about this one, Brian?"

"Well, my gut is all tied up in a knot over this. So, I guess it's telling me to be cautious. But a little voice inside my head is saying go for it. What pilot would want to pass up such an opportunity? Most would give their right arm to be able to fly such a craft. But I want you to know that I am more than a little scared and uncertain about this whole thing."

"So?"

"You're not going to let me off the hook, are you?"

"Nope, not if I can help it."

For a while, Brian just stood there, looking at Joe, who returned his gaze with equal calm, not blinking an eye. Finally, he opened his mouth and said softly: "Yes."

33

"As I recall, you are not instrument rated," Joe continued the conversation where he'd left off, as if oblivious to the momentous decision Brian had just made, one that would change his life completely.

"That's right." Brian said.

"It would be handy if you were, but not absolutely essential. We can go ahead anyway."

"Do you have something I can study to get ready, like I did with the Cub?"

"I'd give you a manual to study if I could, but there isn't one, and I can't teach you the way they did me."

"Oh? How was that?"

"It was pretty bizarre. One of the little gray ones on the Mothership, designated an Information Keeper, would come over to me, get right in my face, stare into my eyes. Telepathically, it gave me all the information you would expect to be in a manual. The handy thing about that was that I didn't have to really study it to know it. It just stuck, and it's all still there, after all these years. I felt as if I had been given an audio visual on-line ground school course, going through each layer of the craft, beginning with the outer skin, looking at all structures, the electrical and computer systems, the instrumentation systems, and even the power plant. It only took a few hours. We had to do it in several sessions, as I couldn't take it all in at once. What I can do with you will take longer, because there really is no manual. But I have a pretty good substitute. The information is all stored in the on-board computer, which we can use for you to learn about the craft. Meanwhile, I can teach you to fly it and give you a pretty good understanding of how it all works. You up for that?"

"I think so," Brian said hesitantly.

"When can you start?" Joe asked.

"Whenever you want, I guess. I don't have anything that I have to be doing right now, though of course, there is Sally. What'll I tell her?"

"For the moment, nothing. Maybe we can figure out something else later. Since it might not be the smartest thing to start flying it around here in broad daylight yet, I think it's best that we start our training at night. We'll go up pretty high, so it won't make much difference whether it's day or night to us. How about coming back here around sundown this evening and we'll go out and get started."

"I'd planned to meet Sally tonight, but I guess I can tell her that you and I are going to do some night flying, which is fairly accurate I guess."

"You might say that. See you tonight." Joe grinned and turned to go back to the office, leaving Brian standing there wondering what he was getting himself into. Later, he felt disappointed and a little guilty when he told Sally that he would have to change their evening plans. He gave her the explanation that he and Joe planned to do some night training.

As evening approached, a mixture of excitement and anxiety at what lay ahead filled Brian. Nerves squeezed his gut so tight that he couldn't eat. When he drove up to the airport office, he found Joe waiting for him. Without a word they climbed into his old pickup. Their conversation on the journey out to the bowl canyon was limited to comments on the weather. Dusk approached as they arrived at the canyon, and by the time they opened the cave hangar, darkness had closed down around them.

Joe led the way into the cave, touching the rim to open the door of the saucer. "Right now, this is programmed to accept only my touch to open the door. Later on I will program it to identify and accept your energy pattern as well. Step on in and take the left seat, since you are used to flying from the left, though you can fly it just as easily from either seat. Put on your headset and we'll get started."

Joe powered up the craft and shortly floated it out into the open. Then he set it down again. "Before we actually start flying, it's necessary that you go through a little physical adjustment. And before that, I want to transfer at least some of the information to you. As I told you, the computer memory on board contains all the information necessary to understand and fly the craft. Your headset, which enables telepathic communication as you already know, will also serve to transmit the necessary information. I won't give all of it to you at once, Brian. It would be overwhelming, and give you a bad headache. Let me know when you've absorbed as much as you think you can handle. Are you ready?"

Brian nodded, touching his headset for assurance.

"Here goes." And Joe pressed some buttons on the instrument panel.

Immediately Brian found himself mentally seeing the control systems of the craft as if he were actually inside it, not just seeing drawings or pictorial representations, but the actual control systems themselves. He closed his eyes to eliminate the distraction of looking at things in the cabin. He saw how each component linked to the controls at his seat and to the instrument panel. After a thorough review of all the flight systems, Brian sensed overload approaching and held up his hand to signal Joe to that effect. Joe pressed a button, or rather an illuminated spot on the instrument panel, and the images stopped.

"Very good!" Joe said. "Now there's just a couple of other things that we have to do before we fly. The first is to adjust the controls to your touch. So, place your hands on the hand prints on the arms of your seat, which are the primary controls. They will adjust themselves to your hands and your touch, so don't be alarmed." Brian felt the surface of the arms of his seat become almost viscous as the material softened and then reformed itself to fit closely around his fingers. Though an astonishing experience, it didn't frighten him.

"This next step is a little trickier," Joe said, "but totally safe. You're going to experience a little vibration as your body is conditioned to be able to safely handle phase change in flight, where we go from visible to invisible. Don't be alarmed, and under no circumstances break contact with the arms of your seat. To do so would be painful. Just relax and hang on for the ride. It won't take long. Okay?"

With that warning, Joe activated a control on the panel and Brian felt vibration begin in his seat and arm rests, which then moved into his body. Slow at first and not alarming, the intensity and frequency of the vibration increased, until Brian did feel alarmed, and then really scared. In fact, it was all he could do to hang on, to not jump out of the seat and run. The vibration didn't actually hurt, but made him uncomfortable and very frightened. Nothing in his life experience had prepared him for it. Eventually, as the vibration increased, it became so intense that Brian heard a high-pitched sound in his head that was so acute it became painful. Just when he thought he could take no more and about cried out to stop it, it ended as suddenly as it began. Sweat poured off his face and body, soaking his clothes.

"Well done. That wasn't so bad now, was it?"

"Well, I survived it." Brian said with a sigh of relief. "Just a little vibration, huh? What's all this stuff about phase change?"

"Oh, that's when we become invisible to radar and to human eyes. Shall we go fly now?" Joe nonchalantly answered

"I guess so." Brian said, his voice shaky. "But give me a moment to recover first."

After Brian had calmed down, Joe proceeded to instruct him on how to activate and use the antigravity system to enable the craft to rise. "Remember all the times in the Cub when I told you to become one with the airplane? Now you will see that start to pay off, big-time, because that's how you fly this ship. But to help you make the transition from flying airplanes to this ship, I've installed a temporary joystick that you can use. So strap in and we'll be off."

Brian did as instructed and began his first lesson in this flying saucer. Lifting off, they rose straight up into the sky. Brian saw, below in the distance, the lights from a car on the highway, and off to the east, the lights of the town. Those soon receded to near invisibility as they rapidly moved higher. An excellent instructor, not only in the Cub, but here too, Brian knew he was in competent hands and followed Joe's guidance carefully. Before long, he felt the first glimmer of understanding how to manipulate and fly this craft. Later, when they returned to the little box canyon, Brian had a big smile on his face and a feeling of excitement.

In the days and nights that followed, Brian and Joe spent many hours together in the craft. Each session was preceded by an information transfer, until Brian had completed the process, surprised at how his mind retained so much. Not long after, Joe had Brian do the piloting, making only occasional minor corrections. And then one night after returning from a flight, Joe stepped out and told Brian take her around by himself now, just as he would if he were soloing a student in the Cub or the Cessna. Brian proceeded to do just that, letting the craft rise slowly at first, then zipped upward out of sight into the night sky.

A short time later, Brian saw Joe watching as he returned, and carefully lowered the saucer back to the floor of the box canyon, then guided it gently into the cave, as carefully as he would push the Cub back into the hangar at the airport. When Brian stepped from the craft, the grin that creased his face would last for many hours. He wished he could rush home and tell Sally what he had just accomplished. But he had to be satisfied with a brief murmured congratulation from Joe as they put the lock back on the doors.

34

Early July, 2001

After dating for almost two months, Brian realized that he had fallen deeply in love with Sally, though he'd not brought himself to tell her yet. Like many others who have been widowed or divorced, he hesitated to make commitments a second time around. He felt uneasy about the secrecy around flying the saucer and found it increasingly hard to avoid her questions about his activities, especially his absences for night training. To pretend that he was just flying the Cub or the Cessna seemed deceptive. Besides, flying the Explorer craft was such a momentous experience that it affected his personality. He noticed a new sense of confidence in himself, and a renewed excitement about life. He increasingly wanted to share more of himself and his activities with Sally, keeping no secrets from her. But how on earth could he tell her about flying the saucer? He wanted to show it to her. Of course in order to do either one, he needed Joe's permission. He hesitated to ask, for he doubted that Joe would permit him to do it.

When he brought the subject up, Joe expressed reluctance. "Remember how I said this had to be secret? If you start telling other people, then pretty soon it's no longer secret. Can you imagine how media people would climb all over each other to get a look at the craft, to say nothing about the government? They'd like nothing better than to get their hands on it, you can be sure. Once that happened, it would be all over. They'd find some excuse to take it out of here in a flash." Joe paused, then, "I just remembered the Star Council telling me that they wanted us to begin exposing it to the public. But I don't think that meant hands on . . . just more night sightings in the sky."

"Joe, when you talked me into this, you asked if I had my relationship with Sally all figured out. And of course, I didn't. But now, I'm beginning to see where it's going and I like it. I really love her and hope we can make it permanent someday. But there's something in her background that makes her hold back. I'm not sure what it is, but it's something mighty powerful. She's hinted that something happened to her in the past that might cause me to not love her, but she's not told me about it yet. I can't imagine anything that terrible, but there is certainly a reserve about her. Anyway, I just don't feel right keeping secrets from her. It's getting in the way of our relationship, and it's getting harder and harder to explain my night flying as training. Understandably, it doesn't make much sense to her. You said that sometimes we have to play this one step at a time, so I'm asking you to give this serious thought. Maybe even contact the folks upstairs if you need to."

"Okay, Brian. Let me think this over a bit and I'll get back to you."

"Good enough."

For two days, Brian flew neither the Cub nor the saucer. Then to his great relief, Joe called to say that it was okay to show the saucer to Sally. He said he had checked it out upstairs.

That Friday evening after dinner, as they said goodnight, Brian said, "Sally, how about taking a little field trip with me?"

"What did you have in mind?" Sally responded.

"Oh, just a trip out into the canyons," Brian returned vaguely.

"Well, we've been hiking in the canyons a lot lately," Sally said. "What is so unusual about this time?"

"I have a surprise for you. I want to take you to a very special place and show you something," Brian said. "Can you go tomorrow morning?"

"Yes, I think so. But what is the surprise? Have you discovered a new Anasazi site or something?"

"If I told you, it wouldn't be a surprise now would it? I'll pick you up at 7 AM," Brian said. "Okay?"

"Sure, I guess so. I'll be ready at seven, but I gotta tell you, I don't much like surprises."

The next morning, Brian arrived as promised at Sally's door at 7 AM, excited about what the day would hold and happy to think about what a wonderful surprise it would be. He shrugged off the momentary concern that it could be a repeat of their trip to Joe's old village site and might disturb her. After loading their gear into the Rover, Brian followed the now familiar route to the pocket canyon.

"Where are you going?" Sally asked, when they turned off the highway toward Arch Canyon. By now she was certain that he had discovered a new set of ruins, but she grew uneasy with his continued his refusal to tell her. She had never liked surprises, hated them in fact, especially since most of the surprises in her life had been so devastating.

"You'll see."

"Are you crazy?" Sally demanded, when he turned off the trail toward what looked like a blank wall. "There's nothing out here." She could not see the entrance to the canyon and thus it looked to her as if he intended to drive right into the canyon wall.

"Lookout!" Sally cried out.

But Brian expertly steered his Land Rover through the willows into the narrow opening in the canyon wall and followed the small creek bed on its twisting journey to the pocket canyon. He stopped the car in front of the screen of cedar trees. Climbing out, he turned to Sally and said, "We're here. Come on, let's go!"

"Go where?" Sally answered, wanting to trust this man she had come to love, but unsure what awaited her.

"Our destination is just through these trees," Brian said.

"Okay, if you say so," Sally said.

Brian led the way through the cedars and into the circular opening of the pocket canyon. Sally still didn't see anything worthy of interest and felt disappointed to not see an Anasazi cave site with ruins.

"So what's the big deal?" She asked.

Sally watched Brian walk over to the canyon wall and start removing some brush that lay piled against the wall. Only then did she notice the large sliding doors, painted to look like the canyon wall. Puzzled now at seeing doors like those she'd seen on the airplane hangars at the airport, she wondered what on earth they were doing here in this canyon. Soon Brian had the brush removed and unlocked the padlock securing the doors. Sally's curiosity grew as she stepped closer, eager to see what waited behind the doors. Brian slid the doors all the way open and entered the cave, its interior still obscured in the early morning shadows.

"Come on in, Sally," Brian said, sweeping his arm in front of him. "This is the surprise!"

Sally moved cautiously into the cave, giving her eyes time to adjust from the bright light outside to the dim light within, which prevented her from immediately seeing what the cave held. But then the enormity of what her eyes beheld struck. She scarcely dared to believe it. She froze in her tracks, speechless. Then she opened her mouth in a blood-curdling scream that seemed endless, the sound echoing off the canyon walls. Her mind raced, flooded with images and memories from the past, from her childhood and adult life. It must be happening all over again! A saucer, just like she'd seen so many times before, in her dreams, she'd thought. Was this real? A dream? The day had started out so nicely with Brian. But now fear and doubt took over. Who was he really? Was he an alien in disguise? Here she was, way out in the middle of nowhere with him, and he was coming toward her, reaching for her. Terror filled her throat, choking her until she screamed again in panic, "DON'T TOUCH ME!"

* * *

Totally taken by surprise at the intense reaction from the woman that he thought he knew so well, all Brian could think to do was to reach out to try to calm her. Her eyes were wide as she turned and ran from the cave. He followed her out into the open area of the pocket canyon. When he drew closer to her, she again looked at him with blind terror and screamed, "Get away from me!" and ran back toward the car. Bewildered, Brian followed slowly and cautiously. This time he began talking to her from several yards away, hoping to calm her fears. He could see from the look of her eyes that she must still be terribly frightened.

"Sally, it's only me, Brian. Nothing is going to hurt you. You're OK. It's just me. I don't know what just happened, but it's OK now. You're OK." Brian kept talking in a calm voice as he eased closer to Sally, who stood near the car. "Look at me, Sally. It's just me, Brian. Can you see me? Can you tell me what just happened? It's OK now. You're OK now. You're safe now."

He watched Sally tremble so violently that she had to lean against the car for support. Brian was afraid that she would pass out and fall, but he didn't dare move close enough to catch her if she did. Still utterly mystified, he kept on talking calmly to her, hoping to bring her back from whatever terror still gripped her. Seeing the saucer must have triggered something in her. Finally she looked up at him and said in a voice so filled with fear that only a hoarse whisper emerged, "Who are you, anyway?"

"I'm Brian, the person you know. I won't hurt you."

"But . . . but who are you? Are you one of them?" Sally asked again, with desperation in her voice, and eyes filled with tears.

"Sally, you know me. I'm just Brian. I'm the guy you've been seeing for the last two months. I'm not one of them, if you mean the ETs."

"But what about that . . . that thing in there? Where did you get that thing? Where did you come from?"

"Sally, I came from Kansas. You know that. I didn't come from outer space, if that's what you mean. And I didn't get that thing. It's Joe's. Joe has been teaching me to fly it. What's the matter Sally? What's this all about?" Brian said. "I'm sorry. I thought you'd be excited to see it."

Sally continued to stare at him apprehensively. After a time she said, "There's a lot you don't know about me, Brian. There's stuff that's happened to me all my life, stuff I've tried to forget, stuff I've tried to pretend didn't happen, but knew underneath really did. I thought I got away from it all when I came out here to Blanding."

"Surely it can't be that bad, Sally. Can you tell me what happened?" Brian said softly, wondering if she might have been molested or raped or something else equally traumatic. Perhaps this was what had kept her so reserved.

"If I tell you, you won't want anything to do with me," Sally countered.

"Nothing can be that bad, Sally."

"But you don't know me. You don't know what's happened to me. I'm not normal." She paused a long time. "I'm afraid to tell you."

"Here, Sally, take my hand. No one is going to hurt you." Brian reached out his hand to her. He hoped she would let him come closer, but Sally instead backed away again, fear radiating from her eyes and body.

Not wanting to frighten her more, Brian slowly slid down to the ground, his back against one of the cedars nearby. She reminded him of a frightened animal, like the dog he had as a boy, who got caught in a trap set for coyotes. He remembered the dog's eyes, with the whites showing all around, revealing its pain and the fear. The scars on his hand, where his dog had bitten him when he tried to open the trap, served as reminders of how potent its fear had been. "I'm not going to hurt you, Sally. Just tell me what's going on, when you're ready."

Sally backed away more, reaching out behind her until she felt the fender of the car and slid down to the ground and sat, hugging her knees. She dropped her head between her knees and began to cry, quietly at first, then escalated to great heaving sobs. Brian felt torn between wanting to comfort her, but fearful that if he went closer, he would drive her further away, further into her terror. With great anguish, he restrained himself and just waited. After what seemed an eternity, Sally finally looked up at him, eyes and face wet with tears, still trembling slightly. "I don't know whether I can trust you, Brian. First you told me that wild story at Joe's old village and now this. I told you I've never liked surprises."

Brian heard a hint of anger in her voice, but remained silent, deciding to give her time. Nothing he could say at this moment would create trust. She would have to come to it herself when she was ready.

"I want to trust you," Sally continued, looking down at the ground for a long pause. Then she looked up at the sky before speaking, "Oh, this is so crazy! Here we are sitting out here with not another soul around within miles and I'm freaking out! I'm sorry, Brian, but seeing that . . . that thing in there was NOT what I expected when you said you had a surprise for me, and were so excited and mysterious. I thought maybe you had discovered a new Anasazi site. I'm sorry I freaked out. I just couldn't help it."

With great difficulty, Brian quietly waited through another long pause before she continued, "I don't even know where to begin. It goes way back to my childhood. The first time I was only nine years old . . . when they came and got me, and took me . . . up there, " Sally pointed upwards with her hand, "In one of those things, a saucer just like that one back there. I was so scared. They tried to convince me, or I convinced myself that it was all just a bad dream. That's what my Mom and Dad said too, when I was so terrified. But then it happened again when I turned sixteen, only that time they hurt me inside and I was bleeding afterwards. Part of me knew that it was real, but another part of me wanted to believe that I'd dreamed it, that it didn't actually happen. But it did happen . . . again and again. It went on for years. It ruined my marriage because I usually couldn't be sexual with George afterwards. I kept denying it by calling it dreams -- bad dreams." Looking up at Brian, she continued, "It's even made me scared of getting close to you, because I wasn't sure I could ever be sexual again, though you are the first man I've been remotely interested in since my divorce."

Sally looked down at the ground again for a long time. "Seeing that thing back there brought it all back, all the terror I had as a little girl that I'd just stuffed. It's just like the one they used to come get me. Something in me snapped. Seeing it . . . seeing it there in the cave means I can no longer pretend that any of it was just dreams. It all must have really happened." She fell silent.

Finally, Brian said, "Sally, I'm terribly sorry about whatever happened to you. And I'm sorry that bringing you out here brought it all up again. All I want to do is just take you in my arms and comfort you. I'd like to come over there and hold you, if you'll let me, and help you know you are safe now," Brian said compassionately.

"But that's just it, Brian. I'm not safe. Not now. NOT EVER!" Sally cried out loudly, with fear and anger in her voice, sobbing again. "Don't you see? They can come get me anytime they want. I can never run far enough away, never escape! They can find me no matter where I go. It wouldn't matter whether you are there or not. They can take me. They used to take me even with George sleeping right beside me. If he'd start to wake up, they'd make him go unconscious so that he never knew about it and never believed me. He thought I made it up to avoid him," she paused, "or that I was crazy."

"I believe you, Sally. I believe you," Brian said softly. "I never would have believed that saucer was real either, if Joe hadn't introduced me to it. The first time he took me for a ride, trust me, it scared me plenty. I couldn't believe it was really happening. I thought I must be having a dream, but I wasn't. Oh, I've heard of UFOs all my life and sort of thought that they existed, but I never really expected to see one, or if I did, that it would only be lights or something in the night sky. But to see it, to touch it, and even to ride in it, was more than I could handle at first. And then . . . Joe wanted me to learn fly it!" Brian's voice trailed off into silence as he looked away into the distance.

"When I saw you with that thing in there, Brian, I thought you really must be one of them, that your Brian identity was only a disguise, and they were after me again. That's why I asked who you are! They never really cared about how I felt or what it did to me." She started crying again.

After the tears finally subsided, she said, "But then who the hell is Joe if he's the one who's been flying this thing? What's he doing with it here? How did it get here? God, Brian, what does it all mean? I just can't believe it. Why does he want you to fly it? What's that all about?"

"It is pretty incredible I have to admit. I can still hardly believe it myself." Brian looked up at the clear blue sky and watched a lone vulture circling far above, searching for something on which to feed. He was uncertain how much he could tell Sally at this point without violating the confidence Joe had entrusted in him. He decided to stick with the known facts at this point.

"You know that Joe grew up here, out in the canyons northwest of town, where we went to visit that day. Remember? You may or may not know that Joe was a fighter pilot during World War II."

"Really? I didn't know that. All I knew was that he ran the airport. He's been there for as long as most people around here can remember," Sally said.

"Actually, he enlisted in the Army Air Corps and eventually flew P-47s in Europe during the war. After the war he worked for a while doing maintenance for Trans World Airlines, then went back to school at the University of Colorado for a degree in business, but wound up coming back to Blanding where his roots are. I think he's been here ever since. But the story of this thing goes back even further, apparently to when he was a teenager. They picked him up when he was on his vision quest and kept him for three or four weeks. His family figured that he had died somewhere in the canyons. Actually they kept him on board a huge UFO in a stationary orbit, what he called the Mothership, all during that time. I don't know enough to tell you the whole story at this time, Sally. I would rather that he tell you himself. I think that's the logical next step, if you are open to it."

Sally hesitated before speaking, "I guess so."

"And some time, Sally I want to hear more of your story, as well as tell you more of my experience with flying the saucer. It really has been quite an adventure. It's far more than I ever imagined I might experience. I brought you out here because I felt like I've been hiding an important part of my life from you. All the night flight training I've been doing was in this saucer, which they call an Explorer craft. We had to do it at night in order to keep it secret. I didn't want to go further with you without letting you know who I really am, what's going on in my life, and where I've been going on those nights when I'm out flying. I didn't like keeping such a big secret from you. It just didn't feel right. I hope that you can believe me."

"I do believe you. And maybe sometime I can tell you more, Brian, about what happened to me, but not now. I just want to go home. Is that okay?"

"Of course," Brian said, "but first I have to go close the cave, or the hangar."

"Okay, but I think I'll stay here by the car."

"It will only take me a few minutes to button everything up. I'll be back as quickly as possible. Don't go wandering off now. Okay?"

Sally nodded, and Brian disappeared through the trees. When he returned he found Sally sitting in the car, staring vacantly into space. He suspected that she was immersed in her memories, the experiences that had so traumatized her earlier in her life. He reached out to touch her hand to comfort her, which she allowed, but gave no other response. Then he inserted the key, started the engine, and turned the car around to leave the canyon, relieved that this episode was over. Little had he imagined that it would turn out this way. What he had thought would be an exciting adventure turned out to be more than he had bargained for. They made the trip back to town in silence, each lost in their own thoughts. Brian wondered, where do we go from here? We've opened up a can of worms that we can't just ignore. He hoped that Sally would trust him enough to tell him what happened to her, to let him be with her, but he didn't dare push her on it.

When they reached her house in town, Brian pulled into the driveway behind her pickup. Sally got out immediately and headed for her front door. Brian started to get out too, but stopped when Sally said, "I'll talk to you later," and disappeared into the house.

35

    Home now, Sally just wanted to be alone, and yet she felt afraid. Her mind flooded with memories of all that had happened to her as a child and as a young woman. She sat in her kitchen, elbows on the table, head in her hands, exhausted and drained, unable to keep the feelings of terror from periodically welling up inside her, feelings that she had kept in check for so many years. While she had tried to believe her experiences were just bad dreams, she'd always teetered on the edge of knowing that they were real events, not dreams at all. Seeing the saucer had shattered what remained of her denial, leaving her defenseless against the images and feelings that invaded her. She recalled again the powerless feelings that had colored her childhood and adolescence and filled her with fear and shame. Over her adult years she had finally come to feel better about herself. Living here in Blanding, so far from her roots in Ohio, she'd almost come to believe that it had all been a bad dream, now behind her, for they had not come for her during her entire time here in Blanding. But now, after seeing the saucer, she felt robbed of that illusion of safety. What would happen now? What could she do now? What did it all mean? She knew that she would have to face up to her earlier experiences. They now stared her right in her face.

    And what about Brian? She had no question that she enjoyed their companionship and their intimacy. She knew she was falling in love with him, but now she wanted to run away from him. At the same time, she wanted his comfort. She believed he had fallen in love with her too. She didn't want to stop what was happening between them, but she had deep doubts about whether she could move forward with their relationship. Afraid she was not normal, she doubted whether she could ever be sexual with Brian and felt afraid to try. What if they started to make love and she froze, like she had so often with George? What if she started screaming at him and told him to not touch her, to go away? She didn't want to hurt him, didn't want to drive him away. To settle her churning stomach, she poured herself a glass of milk and warmed it in the microwave. After a while, her thoughts just went around in circles, playing the same track over and over, leaving her increasingly exhausted, until finally she went to her bedroom, slipped off her shoes, crawled into bed fully dressed, and fell into a restless slumber.

The ring of the telephone next to her bed shattered her sleep. When she reached for the phone she noticed that it was already getting dark outside. Surprised that she had slept so many hours, she groggily said, "Hello."

Brian's familiar voice reached across the line, "How are you doing?"

"I've been asleep all day. The phone just woke me up."

"I'm sorry I woke you. If I'd known I wouldn't have called."

"No, it's okay. I needed to wake up. Otherwise I would wake up later and be awake all night."

"I'd like to come over and see you," Brian said.

"I'm not sure, Brian. Part of me wants to see you, but then I'd have to talk about what happened out there and I'm not sure I'm ready for that."

"We don't have to talk about it until you're ready, Sally," Brian offered.

"You might not have to, but I sure would," Sally retorted defensively. Then after a pause, "But I guess I have to talk about it sometime. Maybe now is as good a time as any."

"Can I bring you something to eat?" Brian asked.

"I don't think I can eat anything just yet. Why don't you get something for yourself if you've not eaten, and maybe I'll warm up a can of soup later."

"Okay, I'll see you in a little bit."

Before Brian rang the doorbell a few minutes later, Sally managed to splash some cold water on her face and run a brush over her tangled hair. She made her way to the front door in the now dimming twilight, but left the hall light off. When Brian entered, he reached out to give her a hug, but she turned away, reluctant to let him touch her, though she chided herself for that too. She walked into the small living room and sat down in the easy chair, leaving Brian to sit on the couch by himself, the same couch where they had snuggled many times in the past few weeks, her action a declaration of the space that she needed just now.

"I don't quite know where to begin, Brian," Sally said. "It is not a very pretty story, nor a fun one to recall. I'm trying not to be a mad at you for taking me out there to see that thing. I'm trying to see it to as an opportunity to heal what has been the most painful part of my life, worse even than my divorce. It has essentially dominated and controlled my life from the time I was young girl."

"You don't have to talk about it right now if you don't want to," Brian said.

"I know. And I really don't want to talk about it, but I have to. I've been afraid to tell you because I didn't think you could handle something so bizarre, and feared you wouldn't believe me." She hesitated. "Ha! That's a good one, with what you've been doing! It's been hidden too long. So I might as well tell you about it." Sally knew her voice carried a tinge of anger, but she continued and began to tell Brian her story in more detail than she'd offered out in the canyon.

The chronicle tumbled out, beginning with the events of her childhood: the first abduction when she was nine, then again at sixteen, on into her adult life, and during her marriage. Sally wavered at times, struggling to make sense of the kaleidoscope of the images, feelings, and memories tumbling through her mind. She noticed with surprise that, as she talked and let herself believe that it all really happened, new images and memories emerged that she had never recalled before. It still seemed crazy to her. The idea that she had been abducted by creatures in the UFOs, taken out of her bedroom window, right through it in fact, then taken aboard a space ship and examined, first as a child, then as a teen, and then had eggs harvested for whatever purpose they had in mind. It was almost more than she could allow into her consciousness.

***

Brian sat spellbound by the story, incredulous, and yet totally believing her. It matched so well the story Joe had related about what happened to his mother, Little Moon. The terror he had seen in Sally's face earlier that day out in the canyon, followed by the silent zombie-like countenance that accompanied him back to town, certainly gave credence to the truth of what she said. He wanted to reach out to this woman whom he loved, to try to console her, to lessen the pain she was experiencing. He wanted to take her into his arms and hold her, comfort her, yet sensed that he must wait. He saw the reserve in her face, the stiffness in her body that said she was not ready for his touch, and probably not his words either.

***

When Sally finished telling her story, silence settled between them and her fear began to escalate again. She convinced herself that Brian's silence meant that he felt repulsed by her, confirming her belief that she'd forever be damaged goods. How could any man want to touch her or love her, once they knew what she really was? She remembered the old saying that while guilt is only skin deep, shame goes clear to the bone. She definitely felt shame. She almost regretted telling her secret, yet knew it was the right thing. Nothing else would have explained her behavior in the canyon. She felt her heart closing the door of hope that had begun to open with Brian. Hopelessness clouded her face, and she steeled herself against what he might say next, certain that he would walk away, go back to Kansas, and never want anything more to do with her. Still she sat, wordless, waiting, while her body slumped deeper into the chair, the tension draining away. She felt her tears just under the surface, her throat cramping in painful constriction. She silently begged him to say something . . . anything.

36

Finally, after a long silence, Brian spoke softly, "I love you, Sally."

"What?" Sally said loudly, not sure she'd not heard him correctly.

"I said, I love you," Brian replied, surprised at how easily the words slipped out, as if it were the most natural thing in the world. Silence hung heavily between them for a few more moments.

"How can you say you love me after what I've just told you? Knowing that they did things to me, sexual things, maybe even made babies from me?"

"Sally, that doesn't change who you are to me. You are still the same person I met not so long ago, the same sensitive, caring, wonderful teacher, the same woman who's gone flying and hiking with me. If anything, knowing the terrible fears you've been living with for so long, makes me admire and love you even more. To go through all that takes incredible courage and strength."

* * *

Sally sat still, as if not fully understanding what Brian had just said. She had not yet dared let herself say those three little words to Brian, scarcely even let herself know she felt that way. How can a person want something so much and yet be so scared of it? All her life, she had felt like there was something defective about her. When George turned to another woman, it confirmed that damning self-judgment. When she met Brian and felt a spark of interest deep inside, she found it hard to acknowledge the change. When it became apparent that he was interested in her too, the faintest glimmers of hope began to whisper in her long closed heart. Now he'd proclaimed his love for her, in spite of all she had told him. Dared she let herself love him? Could she ever make love with him? She blushed as she remembered the surges in her body that occurred more and more when they held each other or kissed. She decided to be honest with him.

"I'm scared, Brian."

"I won't hurt you, Sally." Brian said evenly and calmly. "I'm sorry that the saucer scared you so badly. Had I known, I wouldn't have taken you out there."

"It's not that. It's probably a good thing that I went. God, how I must have scared you when I freaked out like that. I didn't know I had that much emotion in me. You must have thought I'd gone totally bonkers."

"I don't think I've ever seen such a look of terror on a person's face as you had on yours this morning. I couldn't imagine what was going on."

"I'm sure not. But what I meant just now when I said I was scared, is not so much about the saucer and . . . them, but about us. I'm scared when I hear you say that you love me . . . even though I am weird and not normal. I think I'm scared to admit that I'm beginning to love you too. After George, I mostly gave up hope of ever having a decent relationship again. I'm not even sure now that I am fit for a relationship, fit for someone to love, though I know deep in my heart that's what I want."

The longer she talked the more Sally felt her reserve melting away, crumbling the walls she'd put up for so long to protect herself. Looking at Brian across the room on the couch, she longed for his touch, longed to be held, yes, longed to feel safe again. Yet she couldn't quite bring herself to get out of her chair and go over to him. Then a little giggle slipped out, as she suddenly recognized that what she really wanted -- to take him by the hand and lead him to her bedroom. The look of anxious concern on his face would certainly change if she did that. She knew she didn't want him to feel sorry for her. God, why is it so hard to let love in?

Noticing the change, Brian said, "What's so funny?"

"Oh, just a crazy thought I had!" Sally smiled.

"I'll listen. It must be good to create such a change so quickly." The creases of concern on his forehead softened with the beginnings of a smile that now crept onto his face. Sally only smiled some more and looked down shyly, but didn't speak.

"Is it too crazy to share?" Brian asked playfully.

"Maybe."

"I promise I won't laugh or judge you."

Sally, rather than replying verbally, got up and started to the kitchen. Over her shoulder, she asked, "Did you get any supper?"

"No, not yet."

"How about some soup or a sandwich?"

"That sounds good, but I'm still interested in that funny thought," Brian said as he followed her to the kitchen. He came up behind her and put his hands on her waist, and when she did not resist, slid his arms around her, and held her to him. Sally slowly rotated her body in his grasp until she faced him, looking up at him. "Kiss me," she whispered. "Kiss me," and lifted her face to him.

Relieved, Brian bent to her and touched her lips with his as gently as a butterfly landing on a flower. On feeling her eager response, his pressure increased into a passionate kiss and embrace. When she wrapped her arms around him, pulling him to her, he responded in kind. Her breasts pressed against his chest and her pelvis against his. Brian let go of his anxiety. He felt her cling even tighter to him, her lips hungry on his. Finally, they each leaned back, pulling in a deep breath.

"Wow!" Brian exclaimed.

"Yeah, wow!" Sally said, a little breathless. But neither of them lessened their grip. As she leaned forward for another kiss, her tongue danced out playfully to touch his lips, which opened slightly in response. Soon their tongues met as well, exploring hesitantly at first, while igniting a deeper fire within.

* * *

Brian found it hard to believe the change in Sally, from the frightened woman, rigid with terror, not wanting to be touched, sitting across the room from him for safety, to the warm, passionate woman in his arms now. Not that he felt disappointed, for he'd longed for this kind of embrace. Yet he feared to press ahead, the afraid that she would suddenly pull back in fear. He also felt a little shy and embarrassed about the swelling in his crotch, afraid that Sally would notice. He pulled his hips back so that she wouldn't notice, for he knew he could not stop his body's response.

* * *

But Sally had noticed, and instead of pulling back herself, she pulled him toward her, pressing herself against him, happy with his response to her. Sally sensed stirrings deep within her own body. A warmth spread down through her abdomen and even lower. How long since she had felt that? Her breasts tingled, reaching out for Brian as eagerly as her arms. She began to tremble with the energy that surged through her body. At last she pulled back far enough to look into Brian's eyes in the dim twilight coming in through the kitchen windows. The semidarkness increased her sense of safety and intimacy, though she felt almost as jittery as she had as a teenager.

"Whew!" She managed to say, as she slipped out of the embrace and turned toward the stove.

"I don't know if your thought is hot enough to cook soup, but it sure is warm so far," Brian said playfully, letting out a big breath, his erection now obvious to both of them. "Was it that hot?"

Sally stepped away and looked back at him and said simply, after a pause, "Hotter!"

"I didn't think it could get much hotter!" Brian paused, then teased. "So, are you going to tell me?"

"Do you still want that soup now?" Sally teased back. "I've heard that the way to a man's heart is through his stomach."

"I doubt if I could eat just now. I suspect it wouldn't digest very well. Other things seem to be more pressing at the moment." Brian responded, then with a grin, said: "I'm still waiting for that thought."

Sally looked shyly at him for a moment, then took his hand and started leading him back through the living room toward the bedroom. "I don't want soup now either."

* * *

At first Brian wanted to throw caution to the winds and eagerly follow Sally's lead. But then a small voice of prudence sounded within, both for himself and for Sally. On the one hand, it felt so natural to plunge ahead spontaneously and make love with Sally. He had fantasized about it often enough in the last few weeks, in fact, ever since shortly after he'd met her.

When BJ died, he had wondered if he could ever be with another woman, ever even want to make love with someone else. At the time he'd doubted it. He fleetingly remembered the last time he and BJ made love. She was already pretty sick and very thin, making it painful for her. Afterward he'd felt guilty, though she had wanted it too, each of them sensing that it might be their last time, as indeed it had been.

Now Sally, who less than an hour ago had been too frightened to even let him sit beside her, who told him that she was afraid of falling in love, and worried if she could be sexual with him, drew him toward the bedroom. While he didn't doubt the genuineness of their kisses, he wondered if it was too soon. Was she trying to prove something to herself? Would she regret it later? Yet he didn't want to push her away, nor have her think he didn't want her.

"Sally, wait a minute." Brian spoke hesitantly, as he put his arm around her and stopped her movement across the living room toward the bedroom. "If you are leading where I think you are, there's nothing in the world I would like more than to make love with you right now. But I'm wondering whether we're ready for that step yet. Not that long ago this evening, you couldn't even let me touch you." Then pulling her to him, he turned her so that he could look into her face, seeing what he thought was a mixture of fear and excitement.

Tears welled up in her eyes as she spoke, her voice trembling, "I am scared, Brian. I felt so excited that I even wanted to make love, I thought that if I let the moment pass, I might not ever feel it again, like I was testing myself. Maybe that's not fair to either one of us." She let him fold her in close to him, leaning her head on his shoulder, tears streaming down her face now. Shuddering at first, sobs followed as she let go of the tension she'd been holding inside. She clung to him. Brian continued to just hold her close as she sobbed, relieved that she could let herself cry with him. He felt some of the insulation he'd held around his own heart melt as well, and moved ever closer to this wonderful woman in his arms. Though he had missed a vital sex life, he knew that he missed even more an intimate bonding with a woman.

Brian knew now for certain what he had dimly understood for some time. Though an independent person, he also needed a woman in his life in order to feel whole. The give and take of marriage had honed him, made him more aware of himself, less able to deny his weak spots. It made him a better man, a more human man. BJ had always called out the best in him, unsatisfied with anything less. He sensed a similar possibility with Sally. He acknowledged that he needed love . . . the opportunity to both give it and to receive it. He felt humbled to recognize how much he had closed off his heart in order to live with the pain of his loss. Now he sensed his heart opening to this woman in his arms. "I love you, Sally. I need you in my life. I want you in my life." And after a pause, "God it feels good to say that, to admit that. I feel like I have come back to myself again. Thank you for being here, for letting me into your life. And I do want to make love with you, to touch your body, to give you pleasure, and I trust that we will find plenty of opportunities when the time is right."

* * *

Sally looked up into Brian's face, surprised to see his eyes starting to spill tears and yet relieved that he'd had the wisdom to call a halt to her headlong rush to avoid her fear. Now she took comfort in knowing that her body would respond with powerful sexual urges. Perhaps more would come soon. Maybe she wasn't so damaged. Maybe . . . just maybe, she wasn't abnormal after all. She hardly knew what to say, and spontaneously found herself hugging Brian again, her head on his chest, when she noticed how wet her tears had made his shirt. Finally she said, "I've totally soaked your shirt. I'm sorry."

"I'm not. My shirt will dry, but I'm not sure my heart ever will, you've soaked your way in too deep," Brian replied with a grin. "I feel closer to you now than ever." And after a long pause, "I don't even know what to say . . . and that's unusual."

"I'm mostly out of words myself," Sally returned. "Maybe we don't need lots of words just now. I just know it feels incredibly good to be here with you right now. Thanks for . . . everything, Brian. You are a wonderful man. And . . . I love you too." She gave a little involuntary shiver and hugged him tighter. "I'm not sure what this all means, or where it will lead, but I like it. Thanks!"

37

Staring out the window, Sally watched Brian drive away from her house. The knot in her stomach tightened until she found it hard to breathe. She wrapped her arms around herself in a feeble attempt to comfort the ache in her heart. Doubts attacked her like a pack of hungry wolves. God, how could she be so impulsive? Sally, the ice queen, the one who usually held back from anything physical! How confusing. He said he loved her, but will he still think that later when he gets back to his apartment? And what will he think about the way she totally freaked out this morning? That she's a basket case? And yeah, though she hated to admit it, it had been too soon for them to sleep together. But damn it, she surely liked having him put his arms around her. She liked being held and kissed! She hadn't realized how lonely she'd been, how hungry she was sexually. God, how long had it been? More than 10 years?

Immediately, her mind jumped years ahead, pursued by fear, unable to stay with only the present moment. If we get married, where would we live? Here in Blanding? Back in McPherson, living with the ghost of BJ all over town? What would I do there? I could probably get a job teaching, but if we stayed here, what would Brian do? I need to know more about possibilities of the future before I jump into marriage, not that he's asked me. And I've always been the one to be so cool and calculating!

The way her body felt right now only added to her confusion. What a delight to have felt so aroused! She'd forgotten what it felt like to really want someone with her whole body. Such a surprise to feel that rush of warmth squirm its way down into her very core, and now be left with an unsatisfied ache down there. She thought with irony, unfulfilled love! But that part doesn't have to try to sleep tonight.

* * *

Confusion reigned in Brian's mind as he drove away. As mind-boggling as flying the saucer had been for him at first, the story that Sally told him tonight sounded equally amazing and more disturbing. It left him with many more questions than answers. What was he doing here in Blanding anyway? Did he and Sally have any future together? He wanted to think so. Would she go back to McPherson with him? Did he want to go back? In learning to fly the saucer, who had he become? What did he want to do with his life from now on? And who were the beings who took her? What did they want with her? It sounded so much like what happened to Joe's mom.

Was he ready for all these changes? It felt so wonderful to have a woman in his arms again and to feel so turned on. Yet he realized that some part of him had not completely let go of BJ. Stopping their rush to the bedroom hadn't been entirely to protect Sally. It had served him too. What must Sally be thinking right now? After all, he had rejected her advances. No one, woman or man, likes to be rejected. Would she turn away from him now? He hoped not. He could almost feel her in his arms at this moment. The ache in his groin reminded him of that potent reality. He glanced at his left hand on the steering wheel. It had never seemed quite right to remove his wedding band, but he realized that in order to move ahead in his relationship with Sally, he needed to put closure to the memories of BJ.

Back at his apartment, Brian took a good long look at himself in his dresser mirror, then let his eyes fall to his ring finger. Was he really ready to take off the ring? A sudden flood of tears washed his eyes and cheeks as images of BJ filled his mind. Would his grief never end? He hadn't cried in a long time. How could he be falling in love with Sally and at the same time stand here crying for BJ?

He started to pull the ring off, but it stuck on the knuckle of his finger. Maybe the ring personified his reluctance to let go, symbolic of the confusion in his heart. The ring hadn't been off his hand in so many years that it would not slip off easily. Yet he knew he must remove it, with all it meant, in order to move on in his life. He and BJ had discussed it several times. Early in their marriage, they had agreed that if either one of them should die, the other should feel free to move on and find another person to love, that doing so meant no disrespect or lack of valuing what they had together. With a final tug, he worked it over the knuckle of his finger, and held it tenderly and carefully in the palm of his hand, his mind paging through memories from the past. He placed it in the jewelry pocket in the corner of his dop kit where it would be safe, then climbed into bed, conscious of the deep empty place in his heart that wanted filling. He knew it related to both Sally and BJ. He shook his head at the ironies that life now presented him and wondered what would come next.

When Brian arrived at the airport the next morning, Joe had coffee ready as usual and asked, "How'd it go with Sally yesterday?"

"Don't waste any time do you?" Brian came right back.

"Not usually," Joe said with a smile, and after waiting a bit, "Well?"

"Turned out to be a real can of worms. I expected Sally to be surprised, perhaps even a little shocked. But I got much more than I ever expected. I'd kept it as this big surprise, wouldn't tell her where we were going or what I wanted to show her. And boy, was it ever a surprise! For me. When I opened the hangar doors out there and invited her in, as soon as she got close enough to really see the saucer, she started screaming with the most terrified animal sound I've ever heard in my entire life, Joe. She ran back to the car and when I tried to approach her, she was terrified, even of me. She wanted to know who I was. I guess she thought for a while I was an alien in a human disguise. I didn't find out until last night the source of all that, when she finally told me about her childhood experiences of being abducted and taken to some giant spaceship. Those began when she was only nine years old and went on for many, many years. For much of that time, she tried to divert the trauma by thinking they were just bad dreams, but underneath she no doubt knew it was real. However, her husband never believed her, never believed that they actually took her from the bedroom. I guess all of that trauma and terror interfered with their sex life and contributed to the breakup of their marriage."

"Seeing the saucer out there apparently brought it all back. She couldn't deny its reality any longer. The terror welled up and took over. She must have screamed for 10 minutes, Joe, like an animal. I've never heard anything like it before. I felt so sorry for her, but I couldn't even get close enough to try to comfort her. She wouldn't trust me not to hurt her. She kept asking, over and over, 'Who are you?'"

"I kinda wondered what would happen," Joe said. "I didn't think it would be easy for her."

"What you mean?" Brian asked, suddenly alert.

"Well, when I asked them if it was okay to show her the saucer, they actually seemed quite happy. They said she'd been on board the Mothership several times, but that it had been so upsetting for her, they'd blocked her memory of those events and tried to instill the idea that the experiences were just dreams."

"They told you that!" Brian said. "And you didn't tell me!" his voice rising.

"It didn't seem necessary," Joe responded. "I had no way of knowing what would happen when you took her out there."

Angry now, he said, "Well, you might have given me a heads up."

"Would you have been any more prepared for her reaction?"

"Probably not." He reluctantly admitted. "I think I had my own fantasy about what it would be like for her. Guess I struck out there. Anyway, she finally got calmed down late last night. She finally trusted me enough to let me hold her and give her some comfort. For a while there, I was pretty worried about her. I don't think I'll get her out there again anytime soon."

"Yeah, it would probably be better to let her calm down before you try that. Thanks for letting me know what happened, though. You just never know what a person's reaction is going to be. Hang in there with her, Brian. She's a good woman. You both deserve someone like each other."

"Thanks, Joe."

38

Sally continued to date Brian, but kept their relationship casual enough to feel safe. As summer moved on, daytime temperatures rose. They preferred morning hikes in the canyons while it was cool, sometimes exploring ancient Anasazi ruins after getting guidance from locals who knew the canyon country well, including Joe. Their friendship deepened and their love for one another grew as they came to know each other better. The fact that neither one of them had been particularly looking for a new partner made it seem all the more a gift to have found each other. Sometimes they spoke of the day that Brian had shown her the saucer and laughed over the turmoil it had caused for them both. Sally made it clear she did not want to go back there any time soon. Though they both knew they were moving closer together, getting clearer on what they wanted, neither cared to rush it. They didn't want to rush into bed either, knowing that too would come when they were ready. Sally was grateful to not feel pressured.

As well as being great weather for hiking, summer brought good weather for flying, especially in the mornings. With school out, Sally went flying with Brian in the Cub several times and enjoyed it more each time. They usually went back to town to have breakfast together after their morning flights, sometimes at a restaurant and sometimes at one of their places. After one such flight, they both felt flushed with excitement over the beauty they had just seen, bringing a wonderful feeling of closeness. They had ridden out to the airport together in Sally's pickup, and as they climbed in to return to town, she looked over at Brian and said mischievously, "Your place or mine?"

Brian glanced at her, surprised at the playful sound in her voice. He wasn't sure whether she had just invited him to breakfast or whether her invitation meant much more. He suspected, even hoped, that she intended more. So he simply said, "I'm riding shotgun. I'll go where you go."

Silence ruled on the way back to town. Sally debated in her mind whether to go to her house or to his apartment. She knew well that in a town this size, secrets had very short lives. Her friends had already been teasing her about her developing relationship with Brian. Even as they teased, they also encouraged her, as if having a single woman like her around made their world slightly out of balance. In the past, their efforts to play matchmaker had been stunningly unsuccessful. She just didn't seem interested. Now, here she had found someone all by herself and they were happy for her, especially her best friend, Helen. Though she knew that tongues probably wagged behind closed doors whenever she and Brian spent any time together, either at her house or his apartment, no one had said anything beyond the subtle teasing. Somehow she knew it would be okay. So what did she want? Would she rather go to her house, or Brian's place?

Suddenly, she knew, and drove straight to her house. She decided she didn't care what others thought. She didn't want to live her life worrying about what other people imagined. They got out of her Toyota, still silent, and walked into her house. Once inside, Sally turned to Brian and reached for him. Their embrace was neither hurried nor forced. They melted the space between them, until every contour of their bodies matched. She heard Brian inhale deeply. Maybe he was taking in the orange blossom fragrance of her hair, from her shampoo. Meanwhile she drank in both the feel and subtle aroma of the man in her arms. Still in no hurry, she lifted her face for a kiss. Time seemed to disappear as they held their embrace, their deep kiss, which pulled them deeper and deeper into each other's heart. She didn't need the playful banter that had characterized the first time they had approached this moment earlier in the summer and neither did he. They both knew where they were headed and both felt ready.

When Brian's hands came up to cup her breasts, her body seemed to draw the warmth from them and shoot it right down into her belly, triggering a sudden sharp intake of breath. In response, she pressed her hips more tightly against him. With her lips still firmly connected to his, Sally began to slowly unbutton his shirt, and felt him respond by reaching for her buttons as well. His hands slid under her open blouse and around behind her back, clasping her to him again. Minutes felt like seconds, as the pressure of their kisses increased, became more demanding. Then she felt her blouse eased off her shoulders and down her arms. Sally's excitement grew as Brian's gentle hands caressed her body. When he fumbled for the clasp on the back of her bra, she whispered, "Need any help?" Without a word, he broke their kiss, gently turned her around, unhooked her bra, cast it off, and then slid his hands around from behind to hold her breasts in his palms. He gently caressed and kneaded them, then softly rolled her nipples between his fingertips, while kissing the back of her neck, sending shivers through her body. Sally drew in a sudden deep breath, surprised at the power of her rising need and passion.

Where they had been in no hurry whatsoever, now they began to move more quickly. Sally turned around until she once again faced him. She pulled his shirt off and first teased him by brushing her firm nipples across the bare skin of his chest, then pressed her breasts firmly against him. With a sharp intake of breath and a slight groan, Brian pulled her tightly to him, his lips reaching hungrily for hers. Then he paused and leaned back, looking at her face and body, "You are so beautiful, Sally! So beautiful!" And again he drew her to him. Locked in an embrace, Sally's tongue danced out to touch his lips inside their kiss. Brian reached for her buttocks and pulled her tighter against him. Sally slid her hands down his back to match him. Lips still locked, she felt him pull back until his fingers could reach between them to undo the button and zipper of her jeans. As he pulled them down, she wiggled her hips to ease their passage. Barefoot, she stepped out of them, kicking them a little when one pant leg caught momentarily on her left heel. Hands trembling, she slid his zipper down and reached in through his boxers to grasp his erection, amazed at her boldness and courage. Pleased when she heard him gasp, even in the midst of their lips being firmly locked together, she felt a rush of warm moisture slip from inside her. Breathless and with her heart beating rapidly, she whispered, "I want you . . . now!" She unfastened his belt, undid the button at his waist, and pushed his pants down as far as she could reach without breaking their embrace, finishing the job with her big toe. Finally, stopping their kiss, she pulled him toward the bedroom.

There, she flipped the covers down, threw herself onto the bed, slid over, and pulled him down beside her. Laying side by side, holding each other tightly, they sorted out where their arms and legs should go. Then, Brian kissed his way slowly down her body, first nuzzling her neck, then using his tongue to tantalize his way toward her breasts. Breathless now, her soft moans and humming sounds signaled her pleasure more than words ever could. When Brian's tongue reached her nipple, Sally let out a cry and spontaneously pulled his head tight against her, so that his warm mouth engulfed her breast. She hadn't realized how much her body needed to be touched, loved. His spontaneous sucking further aroused her, augmented by his hand, which slipped slowly down her belly, inside the waistband of her panties, and on down to slide across her wet hair. When his small gentle finger movements parted her lips enough to bring fire to her pelvis, she arched her hips up toward him. Her panties and his shorts soon landed in a wad at the foot of the bed.

Sally reached down to touch him, not surprised to find a wetness that matched her own. As Brian's mouth went from first one breast to the other, kissing, sucking, then blowing cool air on her wet nipples, making them harder and more erect, her desire rocketed higher than she could ever remember. His fingertip continued to circle her button, driving her higher and higher, ready to explode. Finally, unable to control the energy a moment longer, she surrendered to it, letting out a great shriek as her orgasm spasmed through her body, carrying a tingle all the way to her toes.

"I hope I didn't ruin your ears forever," her first words when she was able to speak. He shook his head and accepted her unspoken invitation as she opened her legs to welcome him in. Their thrusting movements rapidly carried him over the top too, accompanied by ecstatic cries of joy. For her it was a kind of deep pleasure at being able to give to him, different from her own of a few moments before.

Out of breath, their faces glistening with sweat, their smiles expressed the exaltation they both felt. Now lying side-by-side, Brian pulled Sally close to him once again, and heard her begin to cry softly.

"Are you okay?" Brian asked gently.

"Oh yes! More okay than I've been for a long time."

"Me too. Me too."

Holding each other, the warmth of their embrace began to fill the deep hunger of their hearts. Neither would have been ready to admit the extent of that hunger and emptiness, but both felt grateful for the nurture they were experiencing. Words seemed unnecessary. The beauty and delight of skin on skin sufficed, as if their skin itself hungered for touch, for wholeness. Only time and more touching would fill that emptiness.

After a while, Brian heard Sally chuckle, "Now I am hungry, but not for you! Could I fix us some breakfast?"

"Yes! Now that you mention it, I'm hungry too, though I'd not noticed it until you brought it up."

Slipping out of bed, Sally felt a little shy at being naked in front of Brian, even after their intimacy. She dug out her panties from the bottom of the bed, and tossed Brian his shorts.

"I guess we get to follow the trail to find the rest of our clothes," Sally commented dryly.

"Yeah, they're somewhere back there in time and space," Brian said, as he followed her from the bedroom. As they retrieved their clothes, she enjoyed the smile of obvious pleasure on his face as he watched her get dressed. She momentarily wondered if he was comparing her to his wife, then decided it didn't matter. She too enjoyed watching him go through those everyday movements of putting on his clothes. Dressed, they headed for the kitchen, sated, yet hungry.

39

July 16, 2001

"Joe, I can't believe what you're telling me!" Brian said, incredulously. "After all the effort that we've put into keeping this thing secret, you're now saying we're supposed to take it out in the open and show the whole world. What on earth is going on? It just doesn't make any sense to me."

"Well, I have to admit I was surprised myself." Joe replied. "But that's the new assignment we're being given."

"Is that all they told you?" Brian asked. "Didn't they give any suggestions as to how we're supposed to reveal this thing? You know the instant this thing shows up in public, the military is going to be all over it and probably is gonna have us locked up so tight we won't see the light of day for a long time. They're not going to want to let the public see this or learn about it. How do your friends expect us to get by that obstacle?"

"I don't know. Nevertheless, the Star People want the public to know about it. They're changing their strategy I guess. Up until now, they have kept their craft secret from public view. Most of the activity has been at night. Maybe they're getting ready to move into a new phase of interaction with us and want people to know. I read a survey the other day that said over sixty percent of Americans believe in UFOs and believe that there are Star People out there who want to interact with us. That's about as good a percentage as we'll ever get, I think. I've long thought that the time had come to let this thing go public. I've wished for many years to be able to really share what I do and what I have."

"So maybe our challenge is to think of a way that we can safely show this to the public. Perhaps if we start flying around in the daytime where people can see it, and fly it slow enough that people could really identify it, maybe they wouldn't be so scared and begin to accept it."

"Yeah, maybe." Joe appeared deep in thought, but sounded doubtful.

A long silence ensued, with each man lost in his own thoughts. Then Brian smiled, and followed up with a hearty chuckle.

"What?" Joe asked, looking up.

"This is probably totally nuts!" Brian exclaimed.

"Well then, don't keep me in suspense," Joe said.

"You've heard of the big EAA air show at Oshkosh haven't you?" Brian asked.

"You mean that experimental thing?"

"Yeah, the Experimental Aircraft Association fly-in is held every summer in Oshkosh, Wisconsin. It's the biggest aviation event in the world, with close to a million people attending. Ten to twelve thousand airplanes fly in there for the show, everything from Jennies to jets, including some of the latest military hardware. Now, wouldn't it be a kick for us to show up there with the saucer? That would knock the socks off everybody for sure. It also might be the safest place in the world for us to show this thing. We could announce ourselves to air traffic control as an experimental, which in a sense we are. There sure aren't any other airplanes around like us."

"I've read about that fly-in for years," Joe said. "I've always wanted to go, but somehow just never got away. Have you been there?"

"Oh yes! Several times. It really is quite an event. If you like airplanes, that's the place to go. There are more airplanes there than you'll ever see all at once anywhere else in your entire life! There are Experimentals, homebuilts, antiques, and usually lots of World War II planes including your old favorites, the Stearman, the T-6, the P-47, and lots of P-51s, as well as a B-17 or two, the B-24 and many others. And of course there are thousands of the spam cans too, the Cessnas and Pipers."

"It would be nice to see some of those old planes again." Brian heard the wistful note in Joe's voice.

"Though there are usually a few current military planes there, they're mostly National Guard, and I don't think those guys would give us a lot of hassles. Plus, with our speed we could fly in and out in a day. That would make maintaining security easier for us, not having to be there overnight. We would want to take some stakes and a rope to make a security perimeter around the craft, but we wouldn't have to reveal what's inside the cockpit. If we keep it closed, nobody could even see in, let alone get into it. And if we only stayed there one day, one of us could be on guard at all times."

"Well, that's certainly about as public a venue as we could ever find. If thousands of people saw it, took pictures of it, it would be pretty hard for the government to pretend it doesn't exist. Plus, it's not a military airplane, it's ours," Joe said, thoughtfully.

"I'm having fun just thinking about it!" Brian exclaimed. "If we register it as experimental or home built, we're not restricted and can park anywhere on the field we want, and I know just the place to park it."

"Oh? Where would that be?" Joe asked.

"Well, if we want people to see it, we might as well put it where everyone will see it. I think the best place would be close to the central display area for the air show. We could slip into the antique area, where you essentially park yourself. Experimentals are allowed there too. And there usually is extra space there, which would give us room to set up a perimeter rope around the saucer. And it would make it easier for us to visit other things, one at a time, if we wanted to. The tent where the WASP ladies hang out is usually not far away either. You might even find someone there you know. Didn't you say that you met some them at your training base?"

"Yeah, but I don't know about that," Joe protested, suddenly sounding alarmed at the idea of visiting some of those dark closets which had been sealed for such a long, long time.

Brian wondered if he was thinking of his girlfriend who'd been trapped and died in the crash and subsequent fire in her airplane, or the men he flew with who never returned from their missions in World War II. He saw Joe give an involuntary shudder, as if to shake off those memories. After a long silence, in which Brian observed Joe apparently disappear into the far reaches of his mind, he finally asked, "Where did you go there, pardner?"

"Just some old memories, I guess," Joe admitted.

"I have time to listen," Brian said gently. "I expect there's quite a lot of heavy-duty stuff from those days."

"Yep, sure is," Joe said, getting up to indicate that it was a closed subject for now.

A silence descended over them like a heavy mantel, holding them close together, yet keeping them separate. Brian returned to the idea of flying into Oshkosh. How would they do it? Would they fly the entry track like everyone else coming from the west, flying at the required altitude and speed until being vectored by the air traffic controllers into the trail of planes that went over the small town of Ripon, Wisconsin, all the way to the runways of the Oshkosh field? If they suddenly showed up in that pattern, would it freak out the other pilots?

Another possibility would be to join in with the helicopters and ultra-lights who typically a circular pattern in the early morning from the ultralight field. But it might be harder to co-ordinate their arrival with all the flying activities there. He could see that they had a few problems to resolve if they decided to carry out his wild idea, but it would be fun to plan such a flight. Brian chuckled to himself once again as he thought about the stir they would create. Little did he know how much of one it would become.

"What do you think Joe?"

"I'll give it some serious thought. Maybe even check with the folks upstairs," Joe replied.

"I think it would be a real hoot, to say the least," Brian said.

"I've never been there, so for me it's unknown territory and feels pretty risky. On the other hand, it seems like the military would be less likely to try anything there. And even if they did, we can certainly outrun them if they give chase. We could disappear off their radar screens by slipping dimensions."

"I have a videotape of last year's air show at home, Joe. I'll bring it out for you to see. That would give you a better idea of the event, and perhaps even a picture of the site I'm talking about. I can of course picture in my mind exactly where I'd like to park the saucer, just southeast of the Theater in the Woods where they hold the evening programs, in the northeast corner of the Vintage parking area. To get in there, we would have to fly in over the runway, just like all the other planes, and then hover taxi all the way up to our parking place. Also, when you arrive at the show in a plane, according to the NOTAM (Notice to Airmen) you are supposed to display a large card or sign in your window to let the ground controllers know where you want to park. But since no one can see a window on the saucer, can we open the hatch before parking, so that I could reach out and tape a card to the side of the saucer?"

"Yeah, maybe, though we don't usually open it until the landing pods are down and secure. Would it work to just call out our intentions for parking. There is a small speaker embedded in the bottom of the saucer for just such external communications"

"Yeah, that would work. And if we went early in the morning, before the crowds gather, there would be less likelihood of disturbing so many people. We can just pretend that we are another experimental airplane. We'll have to figure out our story to explain to people about our ship. If we put up a rope perimeter around it, most people will respect that and keep their distance. You can be sure it will be an attention getter. The aircraft registration shack for Experimentals is right nearby, so that will be handy too. I'll bring that video out tomorrow, Joe, so you can see it."

"Good enough," Joe said, and headed back into the hangar. "Guess I better get back to work."

The next day, after watching the video together, Brian explained the approach procedure to Joe. He had down-loaded a copy of the NOTAM (Notice to Air Men), the pre-flight briefing from the FAA explaining arrival procedures for all pilots who fly into Oshkosh for the air show. It was a little over 1000 miles from Blanding to Oshkosh. So to arrive around 7:00 a.m. Central Daylight Time in OSH, when the field officially opened to air traffic, they would need to depart by 5:30 a.m. MDT from Blanding, to accommodate the time change. After takeoff, that would allow about 20 min flying time at 3000 mph, plus the approach time to arrive by 7:00 a.m. Brian considered flying the war bird approach out over Lake Winnebago east of the field, which is reserved for the faster WW II aircraft and jets. They certainly qualified for that, but he thought it would be more fun to fly the regular plane approach, since the saucer had no problem flying at the slower airspeeds.

Brian and Joe discussed various options for how to explain the Explorer to the public, how they would answer all the questions bound to come, and especially how to handle any questions they might get from the military or government officials. They decided the best approach was to give out minimal information, keeping it simple and straightforward. Perhaps the best way to go would be to describe it as still in development, and therefore they were not at liberty to disclose much information. They hoped it would be enough.

July 26, 2001, 6:45 a.m. CDT

Approaching Oshkosh, still communicating telepathically, Brian said, *"We are just passing over the Mississippi river now, Joe, passing through 10,000 ft., and down to 500 mph. I think we better get down a little closer to our approach altitude and speed. We'll be coming up on Green Lake and Ripon soon, where we'll need to slow down a lot more. I think our approach into Oshkosh will be easier for us if we go with the slightly faster traffic at 2300 ft. altitude and 135 knots airspeed. We'll probably cause fewer disturbances at that level as well. Automatic Terminal Information Service says that the wind is calm, so we should be able to request entry on runway 36 (landing to the north). That will make it easier for us to get to where we want to park."*

"Brian, why don't you fly this approach and landing, since you've been in here before and are more familiar with it than I am. I'll be your backup and watch out for other traffic."

"Okay. You can't have too many eyes out on this approach, though getting here this early should make it a lot easier. Even so, we can expect lots of traffic. The air show opened yesterday, so lots of the planes will already be there, but more will be coming every day."

"We're coming up on Green Lake now," Joe said, comparing the sectional map to what he saw on the ground.

Switching to audible voice, Brian said aloud, "Tune in Fisk Approach on 120.7. Don't be surprised when the controller sounds more like an auctioneer at the local sale barn than a flight controller. He is usually busier than the proverbial one-armed paper hanger, though maybe it won't be so bad this early in the morning. Also, instead of responding verbally, we're supposed to rock our wings to acknowledge his directions. I guess we can rock the saucer side to side, huh? And since we can slow down to whatever speed we want without stalling out, this approach will be better for us."

Brian continued, "Okay, we're coming up on the little town of Ripon now and we're right on target at 2300 MSL (Mean Sea Level) and 135 knots. I'll be following those railroad tracks down there right through town and on toward Oshkosh. It's going to be fun to see what the controllers do when they see us."

"Yeah, I hope nobody goes berserk. I still feel uneasy about this. I hope you know what you're doing."

Brian replied, "Flying into Oshkosh for the air show is probably one of the most demanding pieces of flying anyone can ever do."

"Yeah, I can already see about five airplanes lined up ahead of us. Looks like there's only one other one at our altitude though. The others are below us at 1800," Joe said. "I'm glad we're not down there in that line-up."

"Okay Joe, see that flashing strobe up ahead on the left? It's just north of the little village of Fisk, so they call it Fisk Approach. They put a small trailer out there with a bunch of controllers armed with binoculars and a radio," Brian said. Indeed they could hear the controller calling out to the various airplanes, reminding them to stay in trail, no over-under, no side-by-side, and to rock their wings to acknowledge his directions.

Then they heard the controller exclaim, "Oh My God! I can't believe it. What in the hell is that? Must be some new type of experimental." Then they heard, "Uh, saucer, are you in line for Oshkosh? If so rock your...uh... saucer." And Brian dutifully rocked the saucer side to side. "Good rocking there, saucer. Thank you! Are you taking the high road at 2300?" And once again Brian rocked the saucer. "Okay, turn right onto a heading of nine zero. Follow that Lancair ahead of you. Expect 36 left. Listen for the Oshkosh tower on 126.6." Brian turned the saucer to the east, following the blue and white Lancair IV ahead.

"Well, we made it past that one. Let's see what the next one does," Brian chuckled as he tuned the radio to the tower frequency. Then as they approached the runway and made a left turn into their final approach, still following the Lancair, they heard the tower give the Lancair clearance to land. Then they heard the controller say, "Uh oh!

What's this? Uh... saucer, uh... just follow that Lancair in, I guess. Are you War Bird or experimental?" Brian didn't know what to say. Normally you're not supposed to respond back to the controller, in order to keep radio chatter to a minimum. But since the last was a direct question Brian decided to respond and said, "Experimental."

"Okay, cleared to land. Watch out for other aircraft ahead of you. Turn off at the first taxiway if you're able."

Brian rocked the saucer in response and came in over the runway, slowing dramatically as he descended to just 3 feet above the runway. Then, remaining airborne, he turned left off the runway on the first taxiway as directed. He knew they would create a stir by coming into Oshkosh this way, even this early in the morning. By virtue of the fact that they had no wheels rolling on the taxiway, and the only sound they made was a low hum, he knew it must be mind-boggling to the ground flag-man. The man's eyes grew big as saucers in his astonishment. But after a moment, he recovered and waved them on to follow the line of planes down the taxiway. Now came the tricky part, informing the ground people where he wanted to park. Joe switched on his microphone so that he could be heard on a speaker outside the craft and said to the next flag-man, "Vintage parking." Once again, there was a dumbfounded look on the guy's face, but he directed them to turn left and follow a man on a motor scooter, west across a wide lane of grass, past a row of airplanes which included a DC-3, and then across the road into the Vintage Aircraft parking area. Both Joe and Brian found it interesting to watch the reactions of the people already out and about on the field. Most responded with open mouthed staring and then moved to get out of the way. The voice of the man on the scooter was louder than their hum. At 40 feet in diameter, the saucer didn't take up any more space most of the other aircraft, but it was certainly very different in appearance, almost flat on the bottom and like an upside down saucer on top. The flag man directed them to park at the east end of the front row of Stearmans and other vintage planes that faced the Theater in the Woods. When they reached the spot, the flag-man hopped off his scooter and crossed his arms over his head in the well-known signal to shut down the engine. Still hovering, Brian extended the landing gear, gently touched the earth, and continued the shutdown procedure.

Taking off his headset, Brian remarked with a smile, "Well, here we are Joe! I guess we better get ready. I'll bet we'll be the star of the show today. I'm sure glad it's early in the morning. It's only 7:15 here, and the longest part of our trip was driving out to the canyon from town."

Joe just sat there in his seat, unsure if he was really ready for this much exposure, though he did feel excited. Once again, he wondered what he would say or do if he saw someone he knew from his WW II days. And how would they answer all questions he knew were going to be flooding them from the moment they stepped out of the craft? He questioned Markel's wisdom, who had directed him to reveal the craft and had approved this trip. Maybe they shouldn't have chosen quite such a public place to do it. Oh well, too late now! Best get on with it. By this time, Brian had opened the door and climbed out of the craft, carrying the hammer, the stakes, and the yellow nylon rope, which he intended to erect around the craft to keep people from touching it. Brian wore a pleased grin on his face as he proceeded to pound in three-foot high stakes in a circle around the craft, giving an extra six feet of space all the way around. He didn't really look forward to all the questions, but knew that's what they had come for. Joe followed him around with the rope, and in a very short time they had established their perimeter. Not that it wouldn't be easy for anyone to step over the rope, but he knew people generally respected such things here. Brian then stepped over to the craft, put the hammer away, pulled out a couple of lawn chairs, and closed the door, leaving no visible indication of either door or windows. The exterior of the saucer appeared seamless. Only the four plates and the legs of the landing gear broke the smooth exterior.

"I'll go register us, Joe," Brian said, setting up the chairs outside the rope and pointing to the small pilot registration shack nearby.

When he walked up to the window, he heard excited chatter inside and spoke to the lady sitting at the window, who had obviously seen them taxi in. "I want to register my aircraft."

"Okay, just fill out this form," the lady said nervously.

Maybe she expected him to look like an alien. Oh well. Brain realized he had a problem now. They didn't have the regulation N number the FAA requires, so he decided to make up one and selected 726JB, the date and his and Joe's first initials. If an FAA official challenged them about it, they would be gone before anything could be done. When it came to the place for his address, he didn't want to write in Blanding, so he wrote down Kansas, with no street address or phone number. That part was true. He did come from Kansas. He decided it would be better to not even mention Joe. For type of aircraft, he wrote: Experimental Hovercraft. He paid the fee for a one-day admission for each of them and received wrist bands that would allow them to move freely about the field.

After receiving the prop card, normally hung on the propeller to provide information to the public about the craft, he asked for some tape to attach it to the saucer, since he didn't have any propeller to hang it on. Then he strolled back to the saucer and filled out the card. Probably the most important part of the card was the area where it said, "Look But Please Do Not Touch This Aircraft." He hoped people would comply. As for the rest of the information, Brian wanted to keep it minimal. For the aircraft name, he wrote down Explorer 1. He didn't think it would be particularly useful to fill in the rest of the data, so he left it all blank. He taped it on the side of the saucer, and turning to Joe said, "You ready for this?"

"I hope so," Joe said, still feeling uneasy. "I hope the story we rehearsed will do the job. We already have quite a crowd gathering."

Most just stood, pointing, and looking in stunned awe. Circular aircraft had appeared at Oshkosh in the past, but they'd had an obvious engine, propeller, and control surfaces and were fairly crude. Anyone could easily see that this was something entirely different. Those with cameras had already started taking pictures. Some with video cameras walked all around the craft, recording as they went. Brian figured that by nightfall, pictures of the craft would probably be in most every newspaper in the country and on the major TV network news programs as well. Some from the crowd were already coming up to them with questions. One little boy, holding his dad's hand at the very front of the crowd, seemed unafraid of them, and asked, "Hey mister! How do you see out? I don't see any windows."

Joe gave Brian a nod, indicating he was to take this one. So Brian answered, "Good question. There are windows there, but they're a little smoky, so you can't see them very well."

"Well, where's the motor?" the boy continued.

"It's inside. You just can't see it. But thank you for asking."

Thus began the first of what they knew would be thousands of questions put to them during the day. It eventually became more exhausting than they had imagined, yet exciting in a way. And it really was doing what they had intended, exposing the craft to the public. He hoped that they would be able to do justice to the craft and to its creators. At one point he looked up and saw three guys in desert camouflage uniforms standing in the back of the crowd. As they worked their way toward the front, Brian found himself feeling nervous. He knew that there really wasn't anything they could do to them, but he worried nevertheless. When the three men reached the front, one of them asked in a brusque manner, "Are you guys really civilians?"

"Yes," Brian said, almost adding the common response of "sir." He was glad he didn't.

"Can you tell me about your power plant?"

"I'm sorry. I can't give you any details. You see, the ship is still in development, so we're not allowed to divulge any of the performance or equipment specs just yet," Brian said cautiously.

And so it went throughout the morning. An exciting moment came when the man who founded the EAA came by with his son, the current president, to greet and welcome them. Interesting also, was the pair of older men who came by, and after spending some time observing the craft, worked their way close enough to where they could speak to Brian and Joe. With a peculiar smile on his face, one of them said, " Finally got one of them out in the open here, huh?"

This time Joe responded. "That we did. Seems like I ought to recognize you guys, like I've seen your faces somewhere, but I don't think I have ever met you." They proceeded to introduce themselves as former astronauts. Then the other one spoke, "Now maybe they'll believe us, when we tell them that we saw these things out there."

"So you've seen'em before?" Joe asked.

"Of course! And up this close too, though out in space. Mostly no one believed us, so we learned to keep our mouth shut about them. That's the way NASA and the Air Force wanted it, anyway. Now maybe we can talk about it openly. Someday I'd be happy to tell you a story or two about our experiences up there. They can't hide it anymore."

"I'd be more than glad to listen," Joe said. And then after a few moments of silence, during which he looked at them very carefully, he made a decision to trust them and pulled out his wallet to extract a well-worn business card which contained only his name and telephone number. He handed it to them. "Now, this is just for you personally, not for any of the brass. You copy?"

"I read you loud and clear," the man said, and with that he and his friend faded back into the crowd.

"Can you handle it here for a bit, Brian?" Joe asked. "I need to get away for a few minutes, get a bite to eat and take a break."

"Sure thing. Take your time," Brian replied.

With that, Joe walked away to the food concession tent on the other side of the drainage ditch and bought a sandwich and a soda. Already feeling overwhelmed with the crowd they had faced all morning, Joe slipped out and sat down under a tree to eat, enjoying the peace and quiet as much as his food. Afterwards, he walked over to the line of porta-pottys nearby to relieve himself. Not far away, he saw a white tent with a big sign spelling out WASP. On a whim, he walked over and peered in. He saw several white-haired ladies in blue skirts and crisp white blouses, with a name tag plus a wings insignia on the left breast. Each wore a deep blue scarf knotted around the neck which bore the name "Women's Army Service Pilots" printed in multiple rows on it. When one of them in the back with a group of visitors, turned in his direction,

Joe felt a chill of recognition. Was that Donna? The tall one who had been there when he first met Amy? He found it hard to reconcile this elderly woman with the girl he had known so many years ago. Surely not. And even if it was, he wasn't sure he wanted to speak to her. Nevertheless, trembling inside, Joe turned and took a couple of steps in her direction. Tentatively, he spoke, "Donna?"

She turned in his direction upon hearing her name spoken. Curiosity filled her eyes as she turned to look his way. Then, slowly but surely, recognition dawned on her face, and she smiled. "Joe? Joe Star?" Joe nodded. "After all these years, I can't believe it!" She stepped over to him and gave him a long hug. With tears streaming down her face, she said, "I can't believe it's you, Joe!"

Joe's heart was so full at the moment that he couldn't say a word and his eyes filled with tears as well. When he finally regained a little composure, he said, "I never in the world imagined I'd see you here. What about Betty? Did she survive the war?"

"Yes, but unfortunately she died a couple of years ago. I went to her funeral down in Goshen, Indiana. After we all left Randolph, I never heard another word about you. I didn't know whether you survived or not. Did you fly the P-47 in combat?"

"Yeah, my unit went to England and flew out of Duxford. We lost a lot of guys over there, but I was lucky enough to make it back."

"After Amy died, I never knew what happened to you. I never even got a chance to say goodbye to you. Where are you located now?" Donna asked.

"I run the airport out in a little town called Blanding, Utah. I've been there ever since a few years after the war. I tried to get a job flying with the airlines, but couldn't. So I took a college degree in Business and got certified as an A & P. What about you?" Joe asked, his voice soft.

"Well I'll be! It sure is a small world. I'm just up the road from you. I live in Moab. After the war, I went back home to Salt Lake City and became a nurse, but about 10 years ago I retired and moved to Moab. I like the small town atmosphere. I'm surprised we've never run into each other. Did you fly up here?" Donna queried.

"Yeah, I came with a friend in an experimental we brought up," Joe returned.

"How long are you here for?"

"Just today. We're going to head back after air show today."

"That's too bad, I'd like to chat with you some more. But as you can see, I'm busy at the moment with this group. Here, let me give you my card with my phone number. Give me a call when you get back home, okay? I'd love to get together and talk over old times, if it's not too painful for you. I know you took it hard when Amy died."

"Thanks, Donna. I will call," Joe said. "It's been a long time since those days with Amy. It's nice to see you again." He turned, and with a wave of his hand, walked out of the tent, grateful for the breeze out of the north to cool down his inner flush of heat.

Looking east now, out toward the north-south runway, he heard the familiar sounds of Merlin engines in several P-51s, and the throaty roar of the big round engine in two P-47's as they taxied down to the south end of the runway for a northbound takeoff to begin the afternoon air show. Joe had not expected to hear the sounds of the 51s or his own plane, more than 50 years after he'd last flown one. He found it hard to believe there were so many of them still flying.

He choked up as he remembered his own flying days and the faces of his buddies who never made it back from their missions. He was glad that he didn't have to speak to anyone just then, for he doubted if he could have made a sound. He was just another old man in the crowd, alone -- which was just the way he wanted it.

Shortly, the fighters came roaring off the runway in a formation take off, pulling up their landing gear as they flashed past him a few feet off the ground. The earth under his feet shook with the sound of the engines, and suddenly Joe felt like he was in another place, another time, seeing himself at the controls of one of those magnificent planes, almost as if he himself pulled back on the stick and rocketed into the sky. He had seen such a display on the videotape that Brian had shared with him, but it was nothing like being here in person and seeing, hearing, and feeling those planes that he had both loved and hated. Loved, because he loved flying them. And hated because they took the lives of so many of his friends.

Later, as the afternoon air show got underway, he was deeply moved again, to see waves of World War II airplanes fly overhead in formation, one echelon after another. And not long after, he shook with fear and trembling, transported back in time, when the fighters flew low passes over the field and pyro-technicians set off ground explosions to simulate the sights and sounds of strafing runs and bombs. He didn't want to look, yet couldn't tear his eyes away from the scene either. Seeing the flames and black smoke roiling from the ground took him back to when he flew through similar clouds of smoke and debris from explosions on trains, convoys, or buildings ignited by his bombs or the hammering of his eight 50 caliber guns. He thought he had totally forgotten those days, those times, and those feelings. Feelings of power, of elation, . . . and terror. Always the terror! It had never left him, and still felt locked in his muscles. Even today, it gripped him in its icy clasp. At last he did turn away and headed back to the saucer. With the air show on, the crowd around the saucer shrank a bit, though it never completely dissipated. He wondered how they would get out at the end of the day.

Arriving back at the saucer, Joe said, "Sorry to be gone so long. I ran into someone I once knew. And then when the fighters took off, I guess I just got distracted. It brought back a lot of memories."

"I figured as much," Brian said. "Not to worry, but I could use a break about now. Can you take over for while? I've been fairly close mouthed about the saucer, in terms of its capabilities and equipment. I've just been saying it's still under development by a private company and we're not allowed to disclose any technical information. That seems to satisfy all but the most persistent who go away frustrated. When I'm asked how high or how fast it goes, I just respond vaguely very high and very fast. I didn't know how much you'd been authorized to say about it, and I sure didn't want to overexpose us. As it is, there have been thousands of pictures taken today. Even the network news teams here for the show stopped by and shot some footage. They wanted to interview me, but I said no. I hate to think what will happen when our faces appear on the news tonight or tomorrow. I did tell Sally we were coming here, but my girls don't know. So if they happen to see it, it will be quite a shock. Since anyone back in Blanding who sees it is going to recognize us, it's probably going to make it challenging for us back there after this. I hadn't thought about that aspect. What are we going to tell them, Joe? I guess I got too caught up in the excitement of coming here to think it all through. I hope you have an idea for how to deal with it back home."

With that, he strode away for a rest break, some food, and the treat of an ice cream cone, which he knew was available up the line a little way. He remembered how the kids in the booths made extra tall cones of soft serve ice cream, a welcome respite on a hot July afternoon. While he ate, he reflected on all the questions coming from people he had faced so far today. He knew that his life would never be the same again, probably never be as private.

40

    As he watched Brian leave, Joe wished that he could walk away too, already tired of the crowd of people. It seemed like the circle of people around the saucer had never been less than three or four deep all day long. Now that the aerobatic part of the air show had begun, there were fewer people, but they still pressed him with many questions. Actually, it was mostly the same few questions over and over. How does it fly? How fast does it go? How high does it go? What is the power source? Can I look into the cockpit? What's it made of? Did you fly it here? Are you from space? Where are you from? Did you build it? Is it military? Maybe they should've made up of question-and-answer sheet that they could just hand out.

    One time during the afternoon, when Joe paused for a drink of water, he looked up and saw an old man tottering his way on a cane. He stood on the outer perimeter of the circle, just as many others had done. After a long period of intently looking at the saucer and staring at Joe, he moved toward the rope, the crowd politely parting to make way for him. He waved his cane, signaling Joe to come over to him. Bent and stooped, he rested his weight on the cane. His face was shaded by a large-cap, while sunglasses obscured his eyes and part of his face, but not the small, neat, well-trimmed white mustache that adorned his upper lip. Short pants revealed the painful arthritic knees that supported his slight frame. Finally, in a voice that was more a croak than a normal voice tone, he asked, "This yours?"

    Joe, in an equally circumscribed manner said, "Yep." As he spoke, he felt a vague recognition of the voice and the man, but couldn't quite place him. He wasn't sure whether this was someone he had known a long time ago, or whether he was just a type that he might have known sometime.

    Then the man said, "Looks like you finally learned to fly, eh?" Joe looked puzzled. After a pause, the old man continued, "Don't recognize me, do you? Not that I can blame you. I'm not much more than a shadow of what I used to be, and you haven't seen me in almost 60 years. The name's Will. Now do you remember?"

    "Will? Killer Will?" Joe asked incredulously, reaching out to shake Will's hand. "I can't believe it. After all these years!"

    "Yep. I'm still hobbling around on these pins," he said gruffly.

"And here you are with this thing, parked right next to those Stearmans, which, by the way, look a helluva lot better than the ones we flew. Hell, they look brand-new, rather than all beat up like the ones you guys flew."

"Yeah, I've been looking at them all day, wishing I could get in and fly one, just for old-time sake. And like you say, they look in a lot better shape than the ones I flew when you were teaching me to fly. God, how great it is to see you again, Will. You'll never know how many times I thanked you for how well you taught me to fly. And even now, flying this thing, I sometimes hear your voice in my head, as if through the Gosport, reminding me to fly the airplane. You were a good instructor, Will."

"Thanks. I've been wondering what they'd do if we were to just climb in and take off in one of those Stearmans. On the other hand, the shape I'm in, I doubt if I could even get into it, let alone fly the damn thing. I haven't flown in many years. But I come up here every year. I wouldn't miss it for the world. Kind of helps me stay alive, just being around all these airplanes. And there's always something new to see, like your ship here. I never in my life thought I'd ever see one of these, though I've always wanted to. They give you any hassle about coming in here?"

"No, we just got in line this morning and flew on in, as if we had every right, though we dropped a few jaws on the way. Getting out of here may be a problem though. I'm keeping my eyes out just in case somebody tries to get in our way, or wants to try to confiscate it."

"Yeah, I can imagine there'd be a bunch of people would like to get their hands on this baby. It's a real beaut. I won't even ask where you got it. They show any interest today?" Will asked.

"There were three guys that came by and tried to throw their weight around a little. But I just pretty much ignored them. I wouldn't be surprised to see them back later," Joe admitted. "I'm beginning to have my doubts about being able to taxi out after the air show like we taxied in. I'm afraid someone may try to stop us."

"If what you have here is what I think it is, Joe, don't let them get their hands on it, or you'll never see it again. Don't let them get their hands on you either, or you might spend the rest your days locked up," Will said. "Well, I guess I'd better be getting on. Good to see you Joe. Glad you made it through the war. What did you fly?"

"I flew P-47's out of Duxford, England with the 78th Fighter Squadron."

"So you saw your share, didn't you?"

"I sure did. More than I ever wanted. By the way Will, I didn't lie to you, way back on that first Stearman flight, when I told you I'd never been in a plane before, but I had already been taught to fly one of these . . . when I was seventeen years old."

"I'm not surprised. I did wonder, but if you'd told me about it then, I wouldn't have believed you anyway, so it's just as well you didn't. We didn't even know about these then. Well, take care of yourself, Joe," Will threw over his shoulder as he shuffled off.

Unexpectedly, Joe felt tears in his eyes as he watched the old man move away. He thought about how life is such a great circle. Here in just one day, he had met two people out of his past that he had never expected to see again. It brought back a part of his life that he had laid to rest long ago. It also reminded him of the pain and loss that had caused him to remain so alone all of his life. He could never get that back again. All those young lives, lost forever. And Amy! He still missed her. He couldn't imagine her being old like Donna. In his mind she remained forever young and vital.

When Joe spotted Brian coming through the trees north of him, he slipped away from the crowd circling the saucer, and with a nod, signaled Brian to join him some distance away. When they were alone together, Joe asked, "You got any ideas about how we'll get out of here safely? I have an uneasy feeling that we are going to get hassled, or that someone may try to stop us. I'll bet there's more than one bunch that would like get their hands on this thing. And if they can stop us from leaving . . . well, I'm afraid we might have a problem. What if they won't let us taxi out the same way we taxied in?"

"I've been thinking about that too," Brian admitted. "At the end of the air show when they open the field again to traffic, there usually is a huge crowd of planes trying to get in line for takeoff. I really don't want to get caught up in that. On the other hand if we wait until much later, we may be more at risk for someone trying to stop us. Maybe one of us should get on board and stay there until the air show ends, which will be pretty soon anyway, get the ship cranked up and ready to go. There won't be any air traffic straight up. That way, if someone tries to hassle us or stop us, we can get the ship away, even if one of us gets left here. Or maybe the other one could hop in at last-minute even if we leave our rope and stakes. We could just go straight up like we do in the canyon, without putting anyone around us at risk. If necessary, we can go into phase change and become invisible immediately, though I'd rather not reveal that capability."

"Sounds like a good idea to me," Joe said, "you want me to get on board, or you want to?"

"I think you should, Joe. You're the most familiar with the craft, and I'm probably the one the most comfortable with the crowds. That okay with you?"

"Let's do it," Joe said, and started walking back to the craft. Once back, when one of Sean Tucker's famous sideways fly-bys distracted the crowd, Joe opened the hatch and slipped in, closing it rapidly behind him. Few people even noticed him. Fewer still noticed the slight humming sound which followed as Joe powered up the craft. The noise of the aerobatic planes in the show more than adequately covered it.

When the air show came to an end, people began streaming from the flight line toward the gates, carrying lawn chairs and umbrellas. Many spotted the saucer for the first time and crowded around with cameras and the usual spate of questions. Though tired, Brian remained courteous. However, he felt an instant sense of alarm when a man came up and announced he was with the FAA.

"Interesting ship you have here. I noticed it earlier today and I checked on the N number you have there. We don't find that in the database. I'm afraid that creates a problem for us, or rather for you. We can't legally let up fly that out of here. You couldn't legally fly it in here, for that matter. Can I see your certificates of airworthiness and registration?"

Brian's sense of alarm shot way up, particularly when he looked around the circle and noticed several men wearing sports coats, moving to encircle the craft. Unusual clothing for this crowd, and which probably concealed weapons. Now he knew they were in big trouble. They would have to implement their emergency plan. He asked, "May I see your identification?"

"You don't need that. Take my word for it, I'm with the government," he said, as if giving an order.

Really alarmed, Brian now felt certain that the guy was not FAA, but no doubt was from some arm of the government, probably the military. "I'll have to go inside to get it," Brian said in a submissive voice. He knew that Joe would be watching him and gave the signal for Joe to open the door. Turning toward the craft as the door opened, Brian stepped in and yelled, "Close it!" And then, "Let's Go!"

When the saucer door snapped shut and the government man realized what was about to happen, he drew his pistol and yelled, "Stand back, everyone!" Immediately, several men from the crowd converged on the saucer with drawn weapons. Gasps of alarm rose from the crowd! People began to fall back, frightened by this new development. Those still close-in saw the saucer rise a few inches, heard a little 'thup' as the landing gear retracted and the saucer continued to rise rapidly. In only a few seconds more the saucer was far above the heads of the crowd and shooting straight up. The man in charge yelled, " Stop them!" One of his group fired his pistol at the saucer, but in his excitement, his aim was far amiss. In just a couple seconds more, the saucer had disappeared from sight. All that remained was the prop card that fluttered down some distance away, unseen by the aggressors. An old man picked it up, looked at it, tucked it under his armpit, and silently hobbled away on his cane, smiling.

"Damn!" Exploded loudly from the mouth of the government man. The cheers which erupted from the crowd at the escape of the saucer drew frowns from the would-be captors. It surprised no one to see the authorities try to confiscate the saucer. Many, who had experienced Brian and Joe's courteous attitude throughout the day, had worried about this very thing and were glad to see them get away. A few moved in close to where they could see the round circles still pressed into the grass by the landing gear of the saucer. One older man began to take down the rope from the stakes surrounding the now empty circle. One of the armed men came over and grabbed him roughly by the arm, asking, "Are you with them?"

"Nope, I just figured they weren't coming back and wouldn't be needing this anymore. I thought I would get it out of the way. That okay with you?" He asked somewhat defiantly.

"Yeah, I guess so. Hey, don't I know you?"

"I seriously doubt it, unless you were part of the astronaut program in NASA, which I also doubt very much. Who are you, anyway?" The man demanded.

"You don't need to know," the other said, and walked away, shoving his pistol in the shoulder holster under his jacket.

On board the saucer, Brian took his seat and tried to calm his racing heart. "That was close! Let's just go home," he said, as the late afternoon sun beckoned them westward.

41

September 11, 2001, 7:00 a.m. MDT

Brian pushed the Cub from the hangar in preparation for an early morning flight. He went into the office to make a final weather check before takeoff. When the telephone rang, Joe was up to his elbows in an engine in the shop, so Brian answered the phone.

"Hello, Blanding airport."

"Brian, something awful has just happened. You've got to turn on the TV. An airliner has just crashed into the World Trade Center in New York City!" The anguish in Sally's voice was palpable. Stunned, for a moment, Brian could not move. He couldn't quite believe what Sally said. It sounded too incredible. But he stepped across the room and turned on the television kept there for pilots to watch the Weather Channel. He turned the channel to CBS, thinking that if someone had made an erroneous or false report, Dan Rather would be reporting it. Moments later, he watched in horror as a second plane flew right into the south tower and exploded out the other side, like a bullet blasting flesh out through a body. He brought the phone receiver to his ear and asked, his voice trembling, "Sally, are you still there?"

"Yes."

"This is so incredible!" Brian said. "I just can't believe it!"

After the second plane hit, the newscasters began describing this as an attack on America, rather than some tragic accident. Pictures started to come in from Washington, D.C. as well, where another plane had just crashed into the Pentagon. He wondered what would be next. It all seemed just too unreal. "Sally, I'll get back to you later. I've gotta go find Joe to get him in here."

Brian went to the door that opened into the hangar shop, pushed it open, and called out to Joe in a strange tone of voice, "Joe, stop what you're doing and come here right now."

"Why, what's going on?" Joe replied, alarmed at Brian's tone.

"It's almost too unreal to describe," Brian said. "Two jetliners have just crashed into the towers of the World Trade Center and one more into the Pentagon, and they're all in flames. Joe came quickly to the lobby and stood shoulder to shoulder with Brian, staring in fascinated horror at the scene unfolding. They watched as the networks played the scenes over and over. They joined all of America, as everything and everyone came to a standstill, watching the terrifying scene taking place in New York City and Washington. And then, after about an hour of watching, their expression echoed so many millions, "Oh, my God!" as the south tower imploded and collapsed in a horrendous cloud of dust and debris, only to be repeated about twenty minutes later, when the north tower collapsed too.

All thought of flying completely left Brian, and it became a moot point not long after, when the FAA closed down the entire US airspace to all aircraft except those of the US Air Force. Only much later in the day did Joe and Brian begin to discuss what, if anything, could have been done to stop it. Could they have used the saucer to intervene? Surely, someone could have done something. Then Joe came up with the idea of using the saucer to fly up behind the airplane and press against the rudder to turn it from its intended target.

Had they been able to be there in time, they might have been able to divert the airplanes. Of course, it would have required knowing about it soon enough to get there. Joe referred to this maneuver, which could be dangerous to the saucer, as 'wagging the tail.' That day burned itself into their memory, as it did for most people around the world, as one of the most unforgettable events and experiences of all human history.

42

October 2001
The Occupied Territories, Israel

Mallah Hassan, a young woman of 32, took a leave of absence from her job as a translator at the UN in New York City to go to Palestine, to the town of Jenin in the occupied territories of the West Bank. Her 80 year old grandmother was confined to her bed, while her nearly blind grandfather required assistance to get around, even to buy food. Kind neighbors and friends, who had long been assisting in their care, were relieved when Mallah arrived to help.

While there, she became acquainted with the horror of the ongoing Intifada. It occupied the minds and hearts, as well as the conversations, of everyone in the village. She felt especially frightened one day when she learned that another suicide bomber had struck in Israel, killing 17 people in a crowded market place and injuring many more, most of them women and children. Even more chilling was the news that the suicide bomber supposedly had been a young man whom she had known as a child. He had grown up next door to her grandparents and had in fact played with her and her twin brother Ali, as children, when they came to visit their grandparent's home.

Two days later, Mallah woke to the sounds of heavy engines outside in their street. The Israeli army had announced their intention to destroy more of the village in retaliation for that bomb attack, since the bomber had come from here. Though they'd been told by the authorities to get out the night before, her grandparents remained inside, along with Mallah, because they had no place to go. Mallah hurriedly dressed in her jeans, T-shirt, and sneakers and rushed out to confront the driver of the bulldozer. Shouting in English, her only language beside the Arabic of her grandparents, "You can't do this! They have no place to go!" She stood defiantly in front of the bulldozer driver, in a desperate attempt to keep the house and her grandparents from being destroyed. The young Israeli dozer driver didn't understand English and dismissed her with a wave of his hand to get out of the way. He climbed back on his machine, throttled up, and rumbled toward the house, ignoring her presence.

Mallah frantically rushed inside to try to get her grandparents out as the bulldozer blade relentlessly advanced right behind her. She screamed as the dozer penetrated and collapsed the front wall of the house, dropping the roof on her and her grandparents. Neighbors stood by in horrified awe. The dozer ground right on through the house, pushing walls and furniture in front of it, until it emerged through the back wall. Then it pivoted, came back through the debris, oblivious to the now silent screams of the dead beneath its tracks, bodies covered by the collapsed roof, their blood obscured by the dust cloud that covered the scene. Then the dozer turned to the right and moved on to the next house in the row of humble mud brick dwellings. If the driver felt any remorse for the deaths he'd just caused, or even knew of them, he gave no sign.

The neighbors stood in stunned silence for only a few moments before they rushed to the pile of rubble and frantically began digging, hoping against hope to find life. They found Grandmother still sitting in the remains of her bed against an outside wall. Lifeless eyes stared out of a face covered in dust, horror, and fear, her heart stilled by the terror she'd just suffered, a blessing perhaps. Now she'd not have to live alone without her husband of 60 years, nor know the trauma her granddaughter sustained. The neighbors found the old man under a pile of debris where both ceiling and a wall had fallen upon him, crushing the breath from his chest. But what of the young woman? Not until they began digging out the crushed pile of stones and mud bricks near the front of the house did they find her. First a bloody foot appeared, its Nike sneaker twisted off, lying nearby. Wailing of the watching women now filled the ears of the men digging with their bare hands in the rubble. Tears washed the dust from their eyes, but their hearts were buried in deep hatred for the monsters that did this inhumane act. As they dug, more and more of her body appeared. They already knew she was dead, her body a lifeless lump of flesh. But when they got to her head and lifted a small slab of the roof covering it, they saw that the tread of the massive bulldozer had passed right over the slab. Beneath it her head lay crushed, flattened into a shapeless mass of blood, bone, brains, and hair, with one eye, forced out of its socket, staring up at them. They tried to be as tender as possible with her body as they continued the gruesome task of extricating it from the rubble, though their own bodies shook with rage and grief.

One day later
Nellis AFB, near Las Vegas, Nevada
Ali Hassan, proud of his piloting skills, eased his huge KC-135 tanker aircraft onto the runway for a smooth landing. As he rolled to a stop, he thought about his life journey. What a long way he had come from his early childhood in the refugee camps of the West Bank. His parents departed for the United States when he was only ten years old,

convinced that he and his twin sister Mallah would have little chance of going anywhere with their lives or of even getting an education back there. Life had been hard when they first arrived in Chicago. Unable to speak English, Ali spent his first year of school learning the language, while dodging the insults of his school mates. He and Mallah felt fortunate to have each other for support. But gradually they felt at home in their community on the south side of Chicago. Their father worked very hard in an auto repair shop to make a living for his family. When the day came for Ali and Mallah to graduate from high school, they brought a great deal of pride to the whole family.

After high school he and Mallah enrolled at the University of Chicago. Both had to work to make ends meet and both lived at home to save money. Though Ali sometimes chafed at having to live at home, he loved his family dearly and was grateful for their close ties. Ali followed a course in aeronautical engineering, a tough challenge, while Mallah went a different direction, pursuing a degree in International Relations, hoping to use her dual language skills and background to eventually make a difference in her former homeland. Their grandparents still lived there, and though they had only been back to visit them a few times, they still felt very close to them. He remembered Mallah's pride the day she came home following her graduation from college and announced that she had landed a job at the United Nations.

Meanwhile, after his own graduation, Ali decided to enlist in the US Air Force. He really wanted to fly and throughout his early training, he consistently made outstanding ratings. When he applied to get into jet fighter training, his commanding officer told him that they had no openings at the time, but that they had an opening to fly heavy aircraft, transports. This became the first in a series of setbacks that Ali suspected was at least partially racially motivated.

Nevertheless, Ali plunged into advanced training with as much vigor and intensity as he could muster, and achieved outstanding ratings again, as he moved from flying twin engine trainers, to the four engine C-130. He loved that airplane. It was such a capable and strong airplane. He trusted it implicitly and really felt at home in it. Then he moved on to train in the jets. That became a thrill too, as he moved up in planes and power. He entertained hopes that he might make it into a bomber squadron, even if it meant flying that old dinosaur, the B-52. But when he finished his multi-engine jet training, there were no openings for bomber pilots. They offered him an assignment to fly tankers, doing aerial refueling for the same fighters and bombers he wanted to fly. Though disappointed, he accepted the assignment. At least he was flying. He addressed himself to that job as well, and soon became known for his skill in handling the big jets for the smooth flight required for his 'little brothers' to come in for a drink.

Much as he liked his job, he somehow never got very close to the men in his crew. Relationships became especially painful after 9-11 when Saudi's flew the airliners into the World Trade Center and the Pentagon. A lot of the guys were more distant with him, distrustful even, though he had never given them any reason to doubt his integrity or his loyalty. It seemed as if all America became suspicious of people of middle-eastern descent.

As Ali taxied the big tanker to its parking place, the controller contacted him on the radio.

"Six Alpha Tango," Ali heard Ground Control calling through his headset.

"Roger, Six Alpha Tango here," Ali responded.

"Your name Hassan?"

Ali grimaced as the controller mispronounced his name by putting the emphasis on the first syllable instead of the last. Finally he said, "That's affirmative."

"Your CO wants to talk to you after you finish your paper work."

"Did he say what about?" Ali asked.

"Negative," the controller came back.

"Must not be anything critical, if he wants me to finish the paper work first."

"Probably," the controller chuckled.

"Six Alpha Tango out," Ali signed off. Still, he wondered what was up. Whenever the Commanding Officer called for you before you left your plane, it usually meant something significant had come up. He couldn't think of any mistakes he'd made recently. As far as he knew, his CO thought he was doing a good job. Oh, well, he thought, he'd do his logs first.

Ali finished typing his flight report on the computer assigned and saved it to the database where they kept the records. Then he made his own hand-written entries into the aircraft log book and his pilot logbook, and signed them off. Next stop would be Colonel Stevens' office. He was certainly curious about what the CO wanted. Though not close, he did have a cordial, professional relationship with the Colonel. Crossing to the building that housed the CO's office, Ali removed his cap as he entered and went down the hall to the office. He approached the desk of the young man serving as secretary.

"I'm Captain Ali Hassan. Colonel Stevens said he wanted to see me."

"Oh yes, Captain Hassan. He said to send you on in when you arrived." Ali walked past the desk, knocked on the door to the Colonel's office, and opened it when he heard the invitation to enter.

"Come on in and have a seat, Ali."

"I got word from Ground Control that you wanted to see me, sir."

"That's right. Fraid I have some bad news for you, son."

Ali stiffened inside, anticipating a reprimanded or some other dire consequence from some unknown infraction. No infraction. It was worse!

"It's about some members of your family, Ali. I received word this afternoon that your sister Mallah and your grandparents have died in an accident in Jenin. I wanted to tell you in person. I've cut leave orders for you to go to your family. I know that you'll want to be with them as soon as possible."

Stunned, Ali sat mute for a few moments, letting this news sink in. It seemed impossible that his twin sister Mallah was dead, though for some unknown reason he had begun feeling uneasy last night. They had always been incredibly close and connected, though still able to be independent of each other and go their own way. And his grandparents too! He'd known that it was risky for them to remain in the occupied territories, where anything could happen, and often did. He first wondered if a bomb had exploded and killed them or if they were in an auto accident. He lifted his eyes to the Colonel's face and asked:

"Was it an auto accident or a bomb?"

"I'm sorry, but I don't know any details. I'm sorry to have to bring you such news, Ali. If I can be of any help to you, let me know. Consider yourself off duty now to take care of whatever you need to do. I've instructed my assistant to get you on the next plane from Vegas to Chicago. Call your father to find out more. He called us here at the base to give us the news."

Ali, his face drained of color or expression, mumbled a brief "Thank you, sir," and turned away, all but blinded by his tears. How was it possible? All dead? Was it really an accident? He knew he had to learn more, but he felt a huge black pit begin to form inside his gut, as fires of anger and grief ignited in his belly.

The next two hours were a turning point for Ali. When he heard what had actually happened, coaxing the details from his dad, he mentally turned a corner onto a totally new and different path from what his life had been up to now. It felt like some enormous pressure inside his head swelled until it reached a bursting point. Ali set his jaw, his face, and his life on one focal point: REVENGE! That primitive raw emotion took over his whole being and personality. He'd never known such rage as burned in his heart and soul now. A part of himself had been forever destroyed with the death of Mallah. A braver or kinder soul had never been. He wanted to go out and do something to retaliate immediately, but his civilized veneer won out and convinced him that agenda would have to wait. Right now his family needed him more. He would have to be strong for them. But he would not forget—ever!

The next few hours and days came and went in a blur: the flight home to Chicago; his father meeting him at O'Hare field. Grief kept the silence between himself and his dad unbroken on their ride into the city to their home. His mother greeted him at the door and fell into his arms, sobbing and wailing. He tried to console her, but to no avail. Neighbors had learned of the tragedy and had lovingly brought food. They had so many details to take care of, once Ali arrived home. Should they bring Mallah home for burial, or bury her in the Territories with her grandparents, who would surely want to be buried in their homeland? In the end they decided to bury them all together there.

Ali and his parents made the long flight together to Israel, and hired a taxi to take them from Tel Aviv to Jenin. There, after the burial ceremonies, Ali went to the site of his grandparents' home and saw firsthand the destruction that had been wrought. He found it hard to even recognize where it had been. All that remained was the concrete slab floor, stained with Mallah's blood. Only a little rubble remained to mark the place where he'd spent so many happy hours as a young boy, both in the home and in the back yard under the shade of the two olive trees. All of that was gone now, bull-dozed away, part of the enormous mountain of rubble that rose a short distance away, like some obscene monument to the sadness, the anger, and the chaos that gripped the region.

He also saw, first hand, the hatred that burned in the hearts of so many around him, especially the young men, and it fueled his own. He heard over and over again from the friends he'd had in childhood, the perceived connection of Israel and the United States. He kept silent about his membership in the US Air Force, but the notion fertilized his growing hatred and vow of revenge.

After spending a few days with his extended family, Ali flew back to Chicago with his father, leaving his mother behind to assist the remaining family members. After two very quiet days at home, his father went back at work to calm his own grief and rage, and Ali decided to return to his base in Nevada. He couldn't just sit and do nothing. He loved his flying, but felt unsure what would come next for him in his life. He knew that he would never again look at his uniform, his country, (was it still his?) or the U.S. Air Force in the same way. Evil had now tainted it, and he could barely hide his contempt as he returned to his job.

Back at Nellis AFB, Ali said very little to his flight crew or his friends about what had happened, though some of the story leaked out and circulated as rumor. They tried to express sympathy for his loss, but he allowed little of it to penetrate. As the weeks went by, he withdrew more and more into himself, until his colleagues began to feel concerned about him. Privately, they thought he was about ready to crack up, if he had not already done so. The tension around him was palpable, though whenever anyone spoke of it to him, he denied it and claimed he was fine. Even his CO, Colonel Stevens, noticed it and called him in one day. After he'd suggested that Ali see the Chaplain, Ali resolved to hide his feelings more carefully. No one must know of his feelings, nor especially of the plan that had begun to form in his mind. And in fact, as he began to work out the details in his mind, he did become more cheerful. Almost his old self, others would later say. How wrong they were.

43

All during the fall, Ali entertained himself with following his favorite sport, football. As the season roared down to a close, good-natured joking among his fellow officers was followed by friendly betting as to who would play the bowl games. Now, the plan that had been silently forming in the back of Ali's mind began to take final shape. Like everyone else, he had been shocked by the 9-11 events, but not long after he returned from Palestine, Ali had begun to entertain the idea of doing something similar. After all, he had access to the greatest flying bomb of all, the KC-135. He carried 25,000 gallons of fuel in addition to his own fuel load. What a fireball that would make! He only had to figure out a way to get rid of his crew, or at least how to get them out of his way. And then... choose his target and time. He wanted to make as big an impact as possible, to make as big a statement as possible.

As the Christmas holidays approached, he played with images of flying his tanker into one of the bowl games. He would far outdo his predecessors who flew into the World Trade Center and the Pentagon. Sometimes, as he thought about it, he would shudder in horror at the havoc he would cause. But his mind, twisted with hatred and the desire for revenge, justified it, just as the military often justified the collateral damage of some of its actions. The United States, through its support of Israel and its policies, had helped killed Mallah. They deserved to suffer as he had these many weeks. But who is the United States? He had considered a lot of ways of trying to exact revenge, all the way from attacking one of the US air bases, to the wild idea of trying to attack Washington, DC, itself. He ruled those out as impractical. He knew he would never get through the cordon of defenses around Washington, especially since 9-11. Attacking an air base would not be very satisfying either. And he knew he could not make an attack on Israel itself. Thus he knew that it would have to be some symbol, some giant symbol of the US and its decadence. He was delighted when his mind latched onto the idea of flying his tanker into one of the New Year's Day football games. He flew training missions not far from the Rose Bowl. What a perfect target!

Now, all he had to do was to see that he got posted for duty on that day. When Christmas time came, a lot of the guys on base sought to go home. As a Muslim, no one thought anything of it when Ali elected to stay on base through the holidays. They accepted his explanation that his family didn't celebrate Christmas. And when the postings came on the board for sign up, he made sure that he entered his name for the training mission scheduled for January 1st. It was all beginning to come together.

When that day came, Ali was glad that his regular crew had gone home for Christmas. He really hadn't looked forward to having his own crew be involved in what he planned. Having strangers on board made it easier for him, at least in his mind. His mission that day was to refuel flights of F-16's and a flight of B-1 bombers, known as 'Boners,' over the bombing range in central Nevada. This would make it a short run to divert to Pasadena, California and the Rose Bowl. The final question lay in whether the mission would go in the morning or in the afternoon. Either way was a winner. If he went in the morning, he would target the Rose Bowl parade. In the afternoon, it would be the stadium itself, which of course, would be the most desirable. It would provide the highest concentration of people and the biggest impact. He knew that afterwards, his belongings would be searched for clues to his seemingly bizarre behavior, so he secretly prepared a letter to leave behind, explaining his actions. He left a clipping from the Chicago Tribune describing Mallah's death with the letter. The horror of her death had made many of the national papers, especially in Chicago, where she had grown up. He really believed that the time had come for someone to stop the course the United States had been taking with Israel. Someone had to stop the travesty happening in his homeland. He felt he had to do his part. This would certainly be one way to get someone to pay attention.

After making this decision and writing his letter, Ali felt more at peace with himself than he had in many, many weeks . . . ever since first hearing of Mallah's death.

44

January 1, 2002
15:30 hrs., MST

Aboard the KC-135, when the co-pilot announced that he had to go to the head, Ali decided the time had come. He threw the plane into some violent maneuvers, chopped the throttle on three of the engines, and announced over the intercom, "Mayday, Mayday! We've got massive control and engine failure." Then after a pause, during which he made some more violent maneuvers on the controls, "Bail out! All bail out! Boomer, (boom operator) come forward and bail out. I'll stay with the plane to give you guys a better chance to get out safely. Go. Go. Go now!" He knew that each crewman carried an ELT (emergency locator transmitter) and two way radios in his flight suit that would enable them to be found and picked up. The co-pilot surprised Ali when he pulled himself back into his seat in the cockpit and snapped his seat belt together. He had heard the announcement from the toilet. On sliding into his seat, he announced, "I'll stay and help you with the plane."

"No! Get out of here while you can. That's an order!"

"I'm not going." He replied. Then as he looked over the controls and saw all four engines spooling back up and functioning perfectly, he said, "Hey, wait a minute. What's going on? There's nothing wrong with this ship. What are you doing?" He turned to look at Ali and found himself staring down the barrel of Ali's 9 mm automatic. "What the hell? You gone crazy? Put that thing down."

"One last chance. Get out of here now!"

"No, man! You're crazy!"

He recoiled as the first slug hit him in the chest, punching him against the side of the cabin. His collapsing movement caused him to take the second bullet in his head, splattering blood and brain matter onto the window and wall. His seat belt held him off the control column, but his death throes continued to throw blood all round, including some on Ali.

Ali heard his mission controller calling from Nellis, saying he had heard the Mayday and asked what problem was. Ali chose not to answer. He pulled a chart from his bag and re-established his course for Pasadena. Finally, in response to the persistent calls, he said, "I am diverting. I ordered the crew to bail out back near Tonopah. You'll find the boomer and the navigator back there. Co-pilot is still with me."

"What's going on? What's happened? Where are you diverting to, Edwards?"

"Pasadena. Think I'll go see the football game. Always did want to see the Rose Bowl."

"Are you crazy? You are ordered to return to base immediately. Do you copy?"

Ali switched off that frequency. He didn't want to listen any more. A few minutes later, he realized he had made a big mistake. On another frequency, he heard the controller call to the pair of F-16's he'd been scheduled to refuel, telling for them to engage in pursuit, giving them his exact location. He'd left his transponder on, revealing his position. He turned it off.

15:45 MST

Brian was flying the Saucer over southwest Utah when he heard Joe calling him on 122.95, the frequency they had agreed on for in-flight communication.

"Brian, you with me on 22.95?" Brian heard in his headset. He recognized Joe's voice, but also remembered their agreement that they would not talk to each other on the radio in the Explorer except in an extreme emergency, and only on this frequency, though anyone hearing them would probably think it normal. Most pilots used 122.75 or 122.85 for in-flight communications between planes, and only used 122.95 occasionally when too much chatter filled the other frequencies. The common air traffic frequency at the Blanding airport was 122.8. What could be happening that caused this, Brian wondered?

"Affirmative," Brian said, deciding to keep his responses short, just in case someone else was monitoring the frequency.

"Say your location and altitude."

For Joe to ask for this information made Brian think this must really be an unusual situation, for this went beyond all the norms they had established. They had worked out a code to give each other a general location, so Brian called out: "Sierra Whiskey Uniform Tango, Angels 250." This located him over southwest Utah at an altitude of 250,000 feet, rather than the 25 thousand feet that Angels 250 would normally indicate, which placed him far above the practical altitude of any aircraft except for space-craft.

"Got a mission for you. Condition double red."

The hair on the back of Brian's neck rose. Double red meant not only an emergency, but a highly critical one.

"If I come in now, can you fly the mission?"

"No, Brian, there isn't time. This one is going down in a hurry! You'll have to handle this yourself. Besides, it is practically in your backyard already. And Brian, you're probably going to have to wag the tail on this one."

Brian shivered when he heard Joe say that. He knew that this meant another suicide aircraft situation and that he had no alternative but to take the mission. He and Joe had discussed possible ways of using the saucer to force the airliners to turn aside, had they been informed of the planes heading for the World Trade Center on 9-11. Joe had used the term 'wagging the tail' to describe how he might fly up behind the plane, push the nose of the saucer against the rudder to force it to one side to turn the plane from its flight path and away from its intended course. Could they have forced the planes down into the Hudson River or farther, out into the ocean? And if they had, would there have been any way they could have saved the passengers? Would that action damage the saucer? Though the skin and structure of the saucer was incredibly tough, would it be tough enough? They weren't sure how well it would work, but it would have been worth a try. This sounded like the take down situation they had discussed.

"Can you give me more information?" Brian asked.

What I've got is limited," Joe said. "All I have is what I picked up off the scanner." Brian remembered the high-powered scanner Joe had in the office, which monitored military frequencies, as well as the civilian ones.

"We've got a KC-135 inbound for The Rose Bowl with a full load of fuel. If he makes it, it'll be worse than 9-11."

"You sure?" Brian asked.

"Affirmative," Joe came back. "This is a big one, Brian."

'Do you have the last known position?"

"Well, from what I heard, it headed for Pasadena from Tonapah, Nevada. He bragged about going to the Rose Bowl. Here's the co-ordinates of the last reported position," and proceeded to read off a list of numbers, which Brian typed into the saucer's computers, along with those for the Rose Bowl. "Better get on over there fast, as he is closing on the target. Good luck, Brian. This one is all yours."

"Roger"

"Also, watch out for company."

"Company?" Brian questioned back, already accelerating through 5,000 mph.

"Yeah. There's a pair of F-16's heading that way too, fully locked and loaded, with orders for a take down. Don't get caught in a cross fire."

"Roger that!"

"Good luck, Brian."

"Roger that too. Sounds like I'm going to need it."

Brian shivered as a wave of fear flashed through his body. What had he let himself in for? Could he really take down an Air Force KC-135? And even if he was brave enough to try, could he actually do it? Would the strategy that he and Joe had discussed work?

He set the controls for the UFO to proceed at the highest speed possible to the position that Joe had given him. He had little doubt that he could get there in time, as he knew that he could fly at much more than 30,000 miles per hour, even in Earth's atmosphere. In an ordinary aircraft, which this was definitely not, he would have been feeling extraordinary acceleration as he flew to his target. As he approached the position, he did feel the saucer slow and descend rapidly, and in a short time he recognized the KC-135 a few miles ahead of him as he closed rapidly in trail of the aircraft. He decided to give the pilot of the plane a chance to abort. He flew over the plane, just above and to the left of the nose, until he could see down into the cockpit. He thought he saw the body of the copilot slumped in his seat, with a splash of red on the windshield beside him. Blood! When the pilot looked up and saw him, the big plane lurched to the right, apparently surprised at seeing the UFO in such close proximity. Now what? Brian decided to try the classic signal to land, so he punched the button to lower his landing gear. He flew in close formation with the 135 for a couple of minutes, but saw no response. He then slid his craft in closer, so that he could look right down into the cockpit of the plane and cycled his gear again. He knew that the pilot could not see him through the skin of the saucer, but Brian could see the pilot, sort of like a one way mirror. Then he saw the pilot give that classic sign, the raised fist with the middle finger extended, and knew that he wasn't going to succeed in convincing this guy to abort his suicidal mission to attack the Rose Bowl, using the plane as a flying gas bomb, just like the attackers on 9-11 did in New York City and Washington, D.C. Now he knew he would have to try to divert the plane. He retracted the gear and allowed the KC-135 to slide ahead of him, then he pulled in directly behind the big plane. The turbulence from the air flowing off the plane bounced him around as he maneuvered toward the tail of the aircraft. He nudged the saucer forward until he was just inches from the huge tail of the plane. Then he accelerated just enough more to put pressure on the rudder with the nose of the saucer, pushing it to the right, forcing the plane into a gentle turn to the north, away from the city. He felt the pilot's attempts to resist and thwart his efforts, first trying to force the rudder back to center, and when that didn't shake Brian off, he used the throttles to apply differential engine power to try to force the plane back on course. But Brian directed the saucer to lock on to the plane, so that, no matter what the pilot tried, the saucer would stay right there against the rudder, the two craft locked together, flying in a wide circle, but with little or no altitude change. Now what?

    Aboard one of the two F-16's, many miles to the rear, Captain David Miller rapidly calculated his options. He had been ordered to intervene with the KC-135, to try to force him to land, and if that failed, to shoot him down, though that would now be an extreme risk too, as the plane was already approaching a densely populated area. If he sent a Sidewinder missile up the pipes of the engines, the tanker would explode in a massive fireball, reigning fiery debris and burning fuel down on the unsuspecting people below and set off all kinds of fires, probably with a great loss of life. Without saying anything, he knew that his wing man felt the same dilemma.

    Just as this thought passed through his mind, his radar began to signal it had picked up a target, forty miles ahead. Already in full afterburner, consuming fuel at an awesome rate and closing fast, their speed exceeded the speed of sound, more than double that of the tanker. Miller decided to first call the pilot on the radio.

"Tanker one, do you read me?"

"Yeah, I read you. Who are you?" Ali responded.

"This is Captain David Miller, with a flight of F-16's out of Nellis. You are ordered to turn and fly to Edwards immediately."

"I'm not going anywhere but straight on to the Rose Bowl. Always did want to see that game."

"I have orders to shoot you out of the sky if you don't comply."

"Fuck you. And fuck the whole US of A!"

"Let me speak to your co-pilot."

"Uh, he's not talking to anybody just now. In fact he won't ever again."

"And why is that?"

"Well, the brains he'd need to do that are plastered all over his window over there."

"What happened?"

"Let's just say he got in the way. He didn't want to bail out or go for a ride with me."

"What about your navigator and boomer?"

"I ordered them to punch out a while back. They're back in the desert somewhere near Tonapah. If you want to shoot somebody, shoot the goddamned UFO that's bugging my ass."

"UFO?"

"Yeah. The bastard came up beside me and dropped his gear to try to get me to go down. Then he swung around behind me and is pushing on my rudder. I'm going around in circles."

David felt sure now the guy had gone absolutely loony tunes. But his radar did show the tanker in a circling pattern indeed. He switched radio channels. "Rip, you copy that?"

"That's affirmative. Guy must be crazy."

"We'll have him in sight shortly and see what the hell is going on. At least he is not getting any closer to the target at the moment."

Just then Miller heard a call from his commanding officer, Colonel Johnson, back at the base. "Miller, what's going on out there? You got him in sight yet?" The Colonel had given the order to try to force him down and if not, shoot him down.

"We're just coming up on him now. I ordered him to land, and he blew me off. He ordered the navigator and boomer to bail out back near Tonopah and has killed his co-pilot. Then he said he had a UFO on his tail, pushing on his rudder, forcing him into a circle."

"A UFO?"

"That's what he said."

"Sounds crazy! Let me know when you've got visual on him."

"Roger that."

Just then Rip called out: "Tallyho! 1:00 O'clock low."

Miller looked, and sure enough, ahead, and below, he saw the sun reflecting off the outline of the KC-135 against the ground clutter below. As they drew closer, he thought the tail did indeed look odd. Closer still, he could make out a circular form at the tail of the tanker, apparently pushing the rudder to the right, forcing the tanker into a circle. My god, he thought to himself, it is a UFO! Was this some super-secret aircraft out of Area 51 at Groom Lake?

Inside the saucer, steely calm came over Brian. He knew that he would have to somehow deflect the elevator of the big tanker as well, to force the plane to descend. Going around in a circle was not going to cut it. But how? First he reduced the pressure on the rudder enough to slide the saucer down to the very bottom of the rudder, to try to simultaneously put pressure on the elevator as well as the rudder. But the saucer was not thick enough to push on both at the same time. He could see the elevator just below him through the bottom viewport. Then it occurred to him that maybe he might be able to move it by lowering the landing gear. He pressed the button to extend the gear and saw the elevator slowly deflect downward when the gear made contact. He felt the pilot fighting him for control, jinking the big plane first one way, then another, but Brian kept the pressure on the elevator and rudder, so that the saucer stuck to the KC-135 like a burr. Slowly but surely, both the plane and the saucer began to move downward in a slow descending spiral, curving toward Mt. Wilson to the northwest of their position.

    Brian knew he would have to time it just right, to disengage in the very last second before the big plane crashed in a huge fireball that would incinerate both the plane, its occupants, and probably himself as well. He didn't think that going into phase change would protect him. He knew that it prevented others from seeing him or getting a radar signature on him, but would it protect him from the blast? He had never put the saucer into any violent maneuvers, changing direction instantly, though Joe had said it was capable of doing just that. That might be the best thing to try. He didn't know if it would work, and he had no time to ask Joe. He reasoned that if it didn't succeed, it would be better for him to die than to have so many thousands of others die a horrible burning death. Thoughts of Sally flashed through his mind, and of his girls, Jackie and Jenny. If he died, probably no one would ever know, except for Joe. He would just disappear. But would Joe know how or where to contact the girls? He would certainly tell Sally. But Brian couldn't remember whether he had told Sally how to contact them. All this flashed through his mind as the two craft, flying as one, made a lazy descending circle in the sky. Then he had a sudden flash recall of the dream he'd had way back in McPherson before BJ's funeral. Here he was in that strange cockpit and he did indeed have something very special he had to do.

    As Miller watched from his F-16, he saw the saucer lower its landing gear, pushing the elevator down, which forced the plane into a descending spiral. He called back to his base: "Colonel, you're not going to believe this. There is a UFO riding the tail of the tanker! He's pushing the rudder to the right and pushing the elevator down with his gear. He's taking it down."

    "You're not shittin' me?"

    "No sir! Must be something out of Area 51!"

    "Well, I'll be damned!" The colonel responded. "See if you can make contact."

    Roger tried first on the standard military air to air frequency. "Saucer, this is F-16 on your six. Do you read?" No answer. He repeated the call

Silence. He then decided to try guard frequency, the emergency frequency for general aviation, 121.5. Switching, he again called out. "Saucer with the tanker, do you read me?"

David was relieved when he heard a voice come back in English, "Affirmative."

"What the hell is going on?"

"I got the call that this guy planned to try to take out the Rose Bowl with his plane and a full load of fuel. So I came to see what I could do. I pulled up close in formation over his cockpit and saw that he'd shot his co-pilot. I dropped my gear to try to get him to turn away, but he gave me the finger, literally. I can't let him kill all those people. I'm gonna put him into the ground, out where it's safe."

"What base you out of . . . Groom Lake?"

"Negative."

"Just who the hell are you?"

"I'm not at liberty to say, sir." The only thing Brian could think to say.

After a moment of silence, David said, "I got orders to shoot this guy down."

"I figured as much, but I don't think that would be too smart just now, since we're over the city already. It would take out too many people. But I think I can force him down this way, away from the city. I've got him descending and heading back toward the mountains. I intend to ride him all the way to the ground."

"Yeah, but it will fry your ass too."

"I'm going to try to cut loose at the last moment, when I'm sure he's going down in a safe place. Give me some space here so I can get the job done."

"OK, but if he gets too close, I'm gonna have to take a shot and it will take you out too!"

"I realize that," Brian said. "I'm gonna be busy here, so I won't be talking to you for a bit."

"Good luck, whoever you are."

Miller then called back to his CO at Nellis. "Colonel, this guy in the saucer seems to be doing the job, diverting him away from the city and into the mountains. Said he's gonna take him down and try to pull up at the last moment. He definitely sounds like one of our guys, but he won't say where he's out of. Must be some sort of super-secret ship."

"You really think he can do it?" Johnson asked.

"Well, he's making good progress as of now. At least he's heading the right way, back out into the boonies toward Mt. Wilson."

"Keep a tight rein on the situation. Remember, shoot if you need to.

You are fully authorized. We'd prefer that this guy not go down in the city, but better that and suffer the collateral than to let him get to the Rose Bowl. If you get low on fuel, you can go into Edwards (AFB)."

Miller shuddered to think of the swath of destruction that would be wrought from an exploding tanker on the city below, but the alternative, that same destruction contained within the confines of the Rose Bowl, would be unthinkable.

"Roger that. We're right on his tail. We can take him out in two seconds."

Brian fought the pilot of the KC-135 to stay on his tail. It reminded him of his first time on an unbroken colt many years ago back in Kansas, where he had all he could do to just stay on the horse, as it bucked and jerked from side to side to try to get him off. By now they had punched through the thin layer of haze high over the Los Angeles basin and he could see a mountain range ahead that looked pretty bare of any habitation, with not much vegetation either. Directly ahead was a mountain with a white observatory on top. He allowed the rudder to come back toward the center, to straighten out the flight path. He reviewed in his mind the exact maneuver he would have to make to release from the 135 and jump into vertical flight, away from the plane, hopefully to avoid the effects of the explosion and crash. Such a move would be impossible in any other craft, but this saucer had the capacity to change directions in an instant, according to Joe. He was grateful that it would also automatically compensate for the G loads, or he would be crushed into a pile of quivering flesh on the floor by such a maneuver.

When they were low and on a direct heading for the mountain with less than three seconds before impact, when Brian thought there was no possibility that the pilot of the KC-135 could pull up in time, Brian initiated the sequence to take him out of harm's way, zooming up and away from the explosion that would immediately follow. When the pilot felt the saucer disengage, he made a desperate attempt to turn and pull up, but plowed into the side of the mountain, creating a massive explosion. Only then did Brian dare look down at the huge fireball from thousands of gallons of fuel that came rolling up from the mountain below and engulfed him.

Back in the F-16, David Miller watched the scenario unfold, relieved, yet hardly believing what he saw. He called out, elated, "Did you see that, Rip? Wow! He did it! And did you see what he did with that saucer? He went straight up, but the fireball caught him, and he's gone now! Out of sight! I've never seen anything fly like that!"

"Copy that," Rip said, as they circled the crash site, staying clear of the smoke and debris to avoid sucking anything into their engines.

"What's the situation there now, Miller?" Colonel Johnson radioed.

"It's all over, Colonel. He did it. I don't know who he is, but he did it. He put the 135 right into the side of a mountain. Then he zoomed straight up, but the fireball caught him and now I don't see him. Not sure whether he made it or not, but I doubt if he survived. I can't believe what his ship could do."

"That's a lucky break for us." Then after a long pause. "I'm not sure how we're gonna write this one up. Who'd believe it? Flying Saucer? I gotta take your word for it, I suppose. I'm just glad that nut is down and out. As of now, you and your wing man are ordered not to say a word about this to anyone. As far as you are concerned, he went down from unknown causes. Got that?"

"Yes, sir."

"You got enough fuel to RTB (Return to Base)?"

"I don't think so, even if we go to economy cruise. This was the guy who was to refuel us."

"OK, refuel at Edwards and report to my office as soon as you get back to base. Both of you! I want a full report of what happened, whether we write it up or not."

"Yes, sir!"

45

    Brian had pre-programmed the craft to zoom up to 10,000 feet and head for home, but when the KC-135 exploded, the pressure wave and concussion caught the saucer. First it jammed Brian down in his seat, then threw his body up with such force that it broke his seat belt and slammed him against the ceiling of the saucer. He'd waited too long before he had punched the button to release the saucer. He blacked out.
    Groggy and disoriented when he regained consciousness, at first nothing looked familiar to Brian. As consciousness returned further, he recognized the cabin floor of Joe's Explorer craft and became aware of a strange movement in the saucer. A wobbling sensation! When he reached up to scratch the tickle on his forehead, his hand came away bloody. Pain lanced through his head. A head wound! Slowly and painfully he crawled back into his seat, but passed out again from the effort. Several minutes later he came to again, still sprawled in his seat. The wobble of the craft felt more intense now. What was going on?
    Slowly but surely, his memory returned. First, the chase, then engaging the KC-135, spiraling down to the ground, and the explosion, when all went black. The saucer must have been damaged in the explosion! At least it was still flying? Better get on the ground soon. He had to first get it slowed down, and then ease it down to the ground safely. He scanned the instrument panel. His heads up display wasn't working, though the panel was still lit up. He tried to punch up the visual display of the ground through the bottom of the craft. Nothing! Next he found his headset on the floor and put it back on, hoping that he could control the craft mentally, the way he usually did. That didn't work either, but he discovered he had limited manual control with the joy stick. Could he get this thing down to the earth safely? The wobble kept getting worse and worse and the saucer became increasingly unstable. How would he ever bring it in to hover for landing? The landing gear was not designed to roll like a plane, for it had no wheels. He manually cycled an override switch to turn off the power to try to slow and descend the craft. He had never learned how to glide this ship with the power off. Time to ask for some help.
    First he got on the radio and tried to make contact with Joe, but heard no response. Then he recalled that he had been talking to the F-16 pilots on the emergency frequency, 121.5, so he decided to try that. He

called out on the radio, "Mayday, Mayday!" hoping that Joe or someone might be listening, but again he heard no response. His radio receiver must not be working. Was the transmitter? He could only hope. The moving map on his panel showed that him over southern Utah, moving east. He had programmed in the coordinates for his home base before the crash, so he assumed he must be somewhere between the crash site in California and Blanding. But how much the explosion had thrown him off course, he couldn't begin to guess. Added now was the unstable nature of the craft.

As Brian descended, the wobbling became more severe. His mind flashed on the emergency procedures he had memorized several months ago and he went to full manual control of the craft. He did his best to slow his descent, but saw, from the speed at which the earth rushed toward him in the front view screen, that he was coming down fast and would crash soon. In the hope that the radio was working, he shouted out again on the emergency frequency, "Mayday, Mayday! I'm going down. I'm in an uncontrolled descent." He called out the GPS coordinates he saw on his panel, then saw that he had descended into a canyon over a river. He made desperate maneuvers to follow the twists and turns of the river to avoid crashing head-on into the canyon walls. Finally, he could hold the craft off the water no longer. He hit the river with a huge splash, felt the saucer shudder as it caromed off a submerged rock in the water, which spun it around and slammed it onto a sand bar. It bounced and skidded up and over it, like a rock skipped on the water, then nosed deep into the dirt and tamarisks of the river bank, half burying itself in the sand and silt. His last visual impression was of dirt and branches flying everywhere in front of him. As his body flew out of his seat, his head hammered the control panel in front of him and he was slammed into unconsciousness. He ended in a crumpled heap on the floor of the saucer.

Eventually Brian clawed his way back to consciousness, accompanied by blinding pain throughout his body. His head hurt. His chest hurt, and he found that no matter how hard he tried, he couldn't get a full breath. He felt on the edge of suffocating. Why? When he tried to open his eyes, he saw nothing. Total darkness. Was he blind? Painfully he moved his left hand to his face, bringing it away all sticky with what he realized must be his own blood. He wiped it away from his eyes as best he could. His head wound was worse than it had been the first time, but at least he wasn't blind like he first feared. Now he could dimly see a small amount of light coming from somewhere behind him. When he attempted to push himself up and away from the panel where he had hit, excruciating pain stabbed through his right wrist. Must be broken. His other hand hurt too, sprained perhaps, but not with the stabbing pain from the right one that brought a scream to his lips. Slowly and very carefully, he pushed himself back from the jammed-in position his body had taken at the front of the saucer cabin. Thank God this was a round cabin. Sharp corners might have been fatal.

But where was the faint light coming from? Even in his dazed condition, Brian instinctively moved toward its source as he tried to wipe more blood from his face and eyes. At least his eyes were not damaged. Lucky this craft wasn't fueled with gasoline. Otherwise he'd be dead for sure.

As Brian slowly and painfully inched his way toward the light, he saw that the door of the saucer had been sprung in the crash and was slightly ajar. Hope! Maybe he could escape after all. He had no way of knowing if his calls for help had been heard. The light came from the sun reflecting off the surface of the water, flowing just beyond and below the edge of the craft, shining up through the crack in the door and onto the ceiling. A wave of relief and hope swept over him.

But when he pushed against the door, it wouldn't budge. He could see that it was jammed in against the earth and tamarisk roots of the river bank into which the saucer had crashed. The saucer was probably more than half buried in the earth. Lucky for him, it was turned so that the door faced toward the river, rather than buried completely in the bank. When he pushed on the door using his good arm and shoulder and his leg for leverage, he was at first encouraged to feel it give a little, enlarging the crack in the doorway to almost six inches. Then it stopped. Amidst a flood of discouragement, intense pain slashed through his body and he faded away into unconsciousness.

When he came to again, only a little light still came through the crack. It was getting dark outside. With a heroic effort, he gathered himself and pushed against the door, but couldn't move it any further. He did discover that he could reach out and touch the dirt, a mixture of sand and silt from the river, deposited long ago in the distant past. Maybe he could dig his way out. He tried digging with the fingers of his left hand, but only managed to scrape a little away before his fingernails broke. To make any progress he'd have to find something to use for a tool. He paused, for just then he thought he heard the sound of an airplane engine. Maybe Joe had come looking for him! But it passed on, leaving only the sound of the water flowing nearby. He was on his own. Looking back into the cabin, he noticed that one arm of the seat had broken off. Maybe it could serve as a tool. He crawled toward it, but the pain became overwhelming and he felt himself slipping into unconsciousness again.

When next he came to, total darkness cloaked the cabin. He must have been out a long time. He felt cold, chilling, and still unable to take in a full breath. His lungs must have partially collapsed from the impact or even be punctured from a broken rib. He had to discipline himself to take small steady breaths and not panic. It gave only small comfort to think that if they had totally collapsed, he would be dead. At least he was alive enough to hurt and to know it. How long he would stay that way was open to question. He knew that he had to get some help soon or he would die. Winter nights would be cold down here in the canyon. Then he remembered the space blanket he and Joe had included in the emergency kit they had placed in the saucer. They had chuckled at the irony of putting a space blanket in a space ship. If he could manage to get it out of the compartment where they had stored it, it would help him conserve body heat, which he must do to have any hope of survival. He felt so cold that already he was losing strength. He crawled to the compartment where they had stored the kit and reached in. It wasn't there! It must have been dislodged in the crash. He felt around on the floor, trying to locate it in the dark.

What a relief when his numb, fumbling fingers touched the package! However, with only one hand functional, he couldn't open the heavy snap holding it closed. With tears on his face, he felt like giving up. Then he remembered Sally and clung to her image to give him strength. He had to keep trying! Finally, he managed to jam the pack between his leg and the floor to hold it so that he could open the flap of the package with one hand. He reached inside and found the space blanket, still in its own little container. Another challenge! Why hadn't they thought to leave it out of its container? They had not considered trying to use the kit if injured. After another long struggle, he managed to extract it, open it, and pull it over his body, a painful ordeal, enduring the intense pain that wracked his entire body, especially his right wrist, his head, and his chest. His head pounded, each beat of his heart another hammer blow. Slowly, his body began to warm itself as the space blanket captured and reflected his body heat. Though grateful for the change, he was exhausted by his efforts, and consciousness once again began to take flight. He surrendered himself to the relief and lay still upon the floor.

Blanding

When Joe first heard Brian's Mayday, his heart leapt in his throat. "Oh, no!" Partway out the door, he heard the second Mayday, and barely heard Brian's effort to call out his GPS coordinates. He quickly reached for a pencil to jot them down, and then went to his sectional map to plot where Brian might have gone down. He located the co-ordinates near the San Juan River, upstream from Lake Powell. Already late in the winter afternoon, he knew he would soon lose daylight. He must start the search as soon as possible. But he also knew that in order to fly a search pattern close to the ground or in the river canyon, especially with night coming on, he needed someone else along as a spotter. He couldn't fly down low and search at the same time. Whom could he trust with knowledge of the saucer? He put in a hurried call to Sally, and prayed that she would be at home.

Sally picked up on the third ring. She immediately caught the rising note of concern in Joe's voice, when he asked her to come to the airport as fast as possible.

"What's happened?" She asked.

"Brian has crashed in the saucer somewhere west of here and we have to go find him. Can you come help me search?"

"I'll be there in five minutes, just as fast as I can drive," Sally said.

"I'll have the Cub out and ready to go," Joe said and slammed the phone onto its cradle.

When Sally arrived, Joe was already in the plane, engine running and ready to go. She hurried over to the Cub, approaching from the rear to avoid the spinning prop, climbed into the back seat and fastened her seat belt as Joe started the Cub moving toward the runway, followed by a short take off run and lift off. When he was only a few feet off the ground, Joe started a shallow turn to the west, keeping the throttle all way forward to accelerate as rapidly as possible. He skimmed the ground as he headed west, using all his power to cover as much territory as he could before dark, which came early here in the middle of winter. Only gradually did he climb to a safer altitude. He passed back the sectional map on which he had marked the approximate location of the GPS coordinates that Brian had called out. It was a particularly rough stretch of canyon along the river. Joe knew that even if they found him, it would be difficult to get down to carry out a rescue. Thirty minutes later, they arrived in the vicinity of the coordinates. Joe ran his first few passes above the rim of the canyons, looking at the tops for any sign of the saucer. No luck. He would have to get down into the canyon, even with darkness approaching.

"Sally, we're going to have to go down low, close to the river. We'll have to depend on your eyes, because I'll have to give all my attention to flying so we don't crash into the canyon walls, especially now that it's getting dark," Joe said. "Hang on." Joe dove the Cub down toward the river. He followed the twisting course of the stream about 50 feet above the water, hoping that they might spot some sign of the crash wreckage. After covering about 5 miles, Joe knew that they had passed the area where the saucer might have crashed. He pulled up, turned, and dove to make the next pass going back upstream, even closer to the water this time. Still, neither he nor Sally saw anything that resembled the saucer or even any wreckage. By now, the sun had dropped well below the horizon, making it so dark in the canyon it was too dangerous to continue their search.

"Sally, it's too dark. We're going to have to quit for tonight and come back in the morning. If he's alive, I hope he can survive the night." Their hearts were terribly heavy as Joe reluctantly pointed the Cub back to Blanding.

Back in the airport office, Joe re-plotted the coordinates he had heard and marked the search area, while Sally hovered anxiously at his side.

"Can you come early?" Joe asked, looking up when he had finished his task.

"I'll be here whenever you say," Sally replied. "I doubt if I'll get any sleep tonight anyway."

46

Daylight had just begun to define the rim of the eastern horizon when Joe pushed the Cub out of the hangar. He had refueled it the night before to be ready to go. When Sally arrived, Joe showed her the map where he had outlined their search area and explained carefully how they would conduct the search. Both were anxious to get going, to be there just as soon as there was enough light for their search.

"I'm hoping that we might catch a reflection of the morning sun off the saucer," Joe explained. "So watch especially for any flash or reflection that you might see. Our search area is basically the same as we covered last night, but I'm hoping that the different angle of the sun will help us. Plus, it will be getting lighter instead of darker, so I can fly closer to the river. Any questions?"

"I guess not," Sally said, her lips trembling and tears filling her eyes. "I just hope we're not too late."

They climbed into the Cub and took off. As he flew southwest, Joe found it encouraging to see the rising sun reflect off windshields of cars they passed over. He hoped it would reflect off the saucer as well. He had flown a lot of rescues in the canyons, but none as critical as the one he faced now. Thirty minutes elapsed by the time they reached their search area in the rugged canyon area eighty air miles southwest of Blanding.

* * *

When pain pulled Brian back to consciousness, he lay waiting in the darkness until the canyon gathered enough light from the sky to define the objects inside his prison. He knew that if he didn't get out soon and get help, he would indeed die. He already felt weak from loss of blood and hypothermia. His pain would only go so far in keeping him conscious. He crawled toward the door, sliding the chair arm along in front of him. Taking as deep a breath as he could, he reached through the opening with it and began to scrape at the earth. As he dug and scraped, more earth fell from above, splashing into the river, exactly what he had hoped. Encouraged, he kept on digging, until no more earth and sand fell. Gathering all his energy, he pressed his shoulder against the door. It moved a little more and then stopped, the opening still not large enough to permit him to escape. But now he could at least reach out and swing his arm up a little beyond the edge of the door and scrape down more dirt to the river below. By repeating this action, scraping, then pushing against the door, he made slow painful progress in enlarging the opening.

When he thought that he had the opening big enough to squeeze through, he remembered the emergency kit which contained food and water. He would need it to survive and was glad he thought of it, for he doubted he would be able to climb back into the saucer to retrieve it. He turned and crawled back to where he had left the packet. He slowly pushed it, with the space blanket, toward the door. On reaching the opening he pushed the packet through where he hoped it wouldn't fall into the river. Then he began to calculate how to lower his body through the opening with the least amount of pain and yet not fall into the swift current that surged nearby.

* * *

Joe and Sally flew their first pass over the search area level with the rim of the canyon, but saw nothing. The rays of the sun were just reaching their location. As they made their second pass, now down in the canyon, Sally suddenly screamed out, "There!" She pointed down and to her right. "I saw a reflection on the right!" Joe immediately hauled the Cub up above the canyon rim and back around in a tight turn to get back down to where she had seen it.

"I can't see it now," Sally said, as they passed over the area a second time. "I think we have to be at just the right angle, like before."

"I'll get down close to the water again," Joe said, as he circled back and dropped down to just a few feet above the water. This time he too watched intently for a telltale flash. Sally yelled, "There!" as she pointed off to the right and up ahead. This time Joe noticed it too. He pulled up and circled just above the spot where they had seen the flash. They now saw a gouge in a sand bar, leading to a swath where the tamarisks had been mashed down. Then they spotted the rim of the saucer protruding from the edge of the river bank! They had found it!

How would they get down there to see if Brian was still alive, Joe wondered, as he circled over the spot. He climbed and saw, not far away, a sand bar along the edge of the river where it made a slow sweeping curve, but he realized with dismay that the sand bar was far too short to land the Cub. He flew both up and downstream, but went more than a mile down river before he found another sand bar more suitable. It was too far away and the terrain was too rough in between to make it feasible for their rescue effort. Somehow he would have to get down on to that sand bar near the crash site. How could he do it?

He remembered reading an article in an aviation magazine about a bunch of crazy bush pilots in Alaska conducting a short landing contest in which they ran part of their landing and takeoff roll on the surface of the water itself. They would come in low and roll the wheels on top of the water, slowing at the last moment as the wheels touched the sand bar. The idea was to use the surface tension of the water as part of their landing strip, trying not to miscalculate and slow too much, sinking the wheels and the plane in the water. He also remembered the picture of one plane standing on its nose in the water where the pilot had misjudged. He had been amazed to see the sequence of photos of a plane rolling its wheels on the river, water spraying out in all directions, and then the following photo showed the plane rolling up on the sand bar. He had never tried it, but it was the only thing he could think of at this time.

"I'm going to try to land, Sally. We've got to get down there and see if Brian is alive."

"I've heard lots of stories of your rescues with the Cub, but that sand bar looks awfully short to me," she said.

"Yeah, it is. So I'm going to have to try to run part of the landing on the water itself. If I time it just right, I'll be able to roll the wheels on the water and then right up on the sand bar, and hopefully stop before I run off the other end. So hang on tight. I'll do my best." Joe hauled the Cub around into a low approach over the river, heading upstream for a landing on the sand bar. He kept his wheels just a few inches above the surface of the water as he approached and very carefully lowered the plane until the wheels just touched the surface of water. As he approached the sand bar, Joe pulled the throttle back. The wheels rolled deeper into the water, throwing sheets of water out to both sides, and just as it appeared they were about to sink too deep, the tires rolled onto the edge of the sand bar beneath the surface of the water and then up on to the dry sand itself. Joe stood on the brakes. The combination of the braking and the soft sand jerked the plane to a halt just short of the other end of the sandbar. Joe cut the engine and let out a sigh of relief.

As Sally climbed out of the Cub on trembling legs, shaking her head in disbelief, she said, "Amazing! Now we've got to get to Brian." Together, she and Joe fought their way through the tangle of tamarisks to where they had seen the rim of the saucer hanging over the edge of the river.

* * *

Faint at first, then louder, Brian heard the sound of an aircraft engine. Were they out looking for him? His heart fell when the sound faded in the distance, then rose anew when he heard the engine again.

This time he could tell that it was circling. They must have found him! But then it faded again, leaving him desolate. Maybe they couldn't see the saucer. The sound returned and swept close by and Brian recognized the sound of the Cub's engine throttled back for a landing. He felt an enormous relief! Help was on the way. Should he go-ahead and crawl out now or wait for help? Waiting seemed the better option.

Not long after, tears of relief flowed down his face when he heard Sally's voice calling, "Brian? Brian? Are you okay?"

He managed to croak, "I'm here!"

Joe and Sally clawed more dirt and roots away from the door, until they could pry it open enough to get Brian out. Brian told them his wrist was broken and he suspected a collapsed lung. All three were in tears as they half-carried him back along the path they'd made through the tamarisk bushes. To Brian, the sight of the yellow cub sitting on the sand bar was the prettiest thing he had ever seen.

"My God, Joe! How did you ever land it in such a short space?" Brian asked, when he saw the length of the sand bar.

"Used the river," Joe said laconically.

"He landed on the water. I couldn't believe it!" Sally exclaimed. "I thought we were goners when the wheels started throwing water out to the sides, and then we just rolled up on the sand bar."

"Unfortunately, we have to take off the same way," Joe said. "But I don't think we can make it with all three of us on board. It really is a little short. Sally, what do you think of staying here while I fly Brian to the hospital?"

"Well, I have to admit I am not too excited about it. But there's really nothing that can happen to me out here. I'm just so relieved that you're alive, Brian."

"There's water and energy bars in that emergency pack back in the saucer. That should help," Brian said, reluctant to leave Sally behind, but given the extent of his injuries, he knew he needed medical help as soon as possible if he hoped to live. He still could scarcely breathe.

"I'll have to fly all the way up to Moab where there's a hospital. So I think it will be noon or later before I can get back for you," Joe suggested. Then he paused, looking at Sally, "There's just one other thing. We may not be the only ones looking for this saucer. If you hear anybody else come along, maybe you would be wise to try to hide in the tamarisk. We know that the military would like get their hands on this craft, especially after seeing what Brian did with the KC-135. If they heard his Mayday and his position, they may come looking. Just be careful."

"I will," Sally responded, "I'll be okay. Just go. Get him to the hospital."

Joe turned the Cub around and pushed it back until the tail wheel sat in the water at one end of the sand bar. Joe and Sally helped Brian over to the plane, into the back seat, and fastened the seat belt.

"It's going to be close, but I think we can make it," Joe said. With that, he climbed into the front seat, closed the doors, and started the engine. He lowered the flaps and held the brakes tight, shoved the throttle forward until the engine roared at its fullest power, the prop blowing loose sand back behind them. When he released the brakes, the Cub gathered speed quickly, and by the time it hit the end of the sand bar, it was almost ready to lift off. After just a few yards of rolling on the surface of the river, the Cub lifted and flew off downstream.

Sally's heart stayed in her throat until she saw the plane detach itself from the water. She watched until it went out of sight around a bend down river, and then pull up out of the canyon, before she turned to her present situation. Though the winter sun provided some heat, the air stayed cold down here by the river, making her glad she had worn her heavy jacket. She returned to the saucer for the emergency kit and the space blanket. She cried at seeing Brian's blood all over them. Retrieving them, she made her way back to the sand bar and thought of Joe's parting words. What if the military did come along? She was not experienced in the wilderness, but maybe she should find a place to hide if she should need it. She gathered the space blanket and the emergency kit and headed for the bank. She climbed up the low bank and into the tamarisk thicket. Then she thought, what if they land? She was still close to the river. So she pushed her way back further into the dense tamarisk bushes, quite a distance away from the river bank. She broke off a few of the fronds to make a soft place to sit and to keep her body off the damp, cold earth while she settled down to wait.

Though she could hear the murmuring sound of the river not far away, she was also impressed with the vast quiet of this place. So peaceful. She wrapped the space blanket around her for additional warmth and then found herself getting drowsy. She had slept so little overnight, worrying about Brian, that sleep soon claimed her.

She came awake to a distant thump, thump sound. A helicopter! Before long, she could make out the black outline of a helicopter coming up the river from the west. Remembering what Joe had said, she crumpled the space blanket into a ball and tucked it under the tamarisk, so it wouldn't reflect the sun. Her blue jeans and dark jacket blended well with the tamarisk as she crouched down to make herself less visible. The helicopter swept by, but then circled back and hovered, first over the sand bar, then upstream to where the saucer was embedded in the bank, and then back to the sand bar, where it landed. After it sat down, two men in black uniforms jumped out and followed the path that Joe and Sally had made up to the saucer. After a few minutes they returned to climb back in the helicopter and took off, heading toward the west.

Sally was relieved to see it go. She didn't want to have to face those guys. Thirsty, she sipped some water from the emergency kit and nibbled on a food bar. About an hour later, Sally heard the sound of another helicopter. This time, the thumping sound seemed heavier, slower in rhythm, and louder, as it came up the river from the west. A huge helicopter hove into view. When it settled on the sand bar, twelve men jumped out, three with automatic rifles who took up guard positions around the chopper. Others with axes and shovels moved up to the site of the saucer. They're going to take the saucer, she thought with alarm, but she knew she was powerless to do anything about it. Then she heard one of the men on guard say, "Hey Sarge. C'mere, take a look of this," pointing to the tracks the Cub left on the sand bar. "Looks like somebody's already been here. A plane?"

"Yeah, looks like a tail dragger. See that little wheel track. The only thing that could get in and out of here like that is a Super Cub, and some super Cub at that! Must've come to rescue the pilot of that saucer, and judging from the blood here," he pointed to drops of blood on the sand, "he must have been injured. Keep your eyes open for anything else you see."

"Okay Sarge. You know, something else is funny here. Look here over by the edge of the sand bar. Looks like the tracks of three people. Close together, too. The one in the middle must have been the one hurt. See? His tracks drag a little."

"Say, you're right. Now I'm no pilot, but I think a Super Cub only has two seats. Besides that, I don't think they could get a Cub off of this short sand bar with three people on board. That means one might still be around here somewhere. You guys better take closer look."

When Sally heard this, she crouched down even closer to the ground. She knew she didn't dare move or they would hear her and find her. It hadn't occurred to her to cover her tracks when she'd made her hiding place in the tamarisk thicket. Now she wished she had. Her fear grew as the two searchers came closer and closer, obviously following her tracks.

Just then, a huge racket erupted a few yards away, as a small deer bounded out of the thicket, spooked by the approaching men. One raised his M-16 rifle and loosed a barrage of shots, dropping the deer. "Got him," he yelled, as he ran over to where the deer lay kicking and struggling in its death throes, its eyes frantic and fearful.

"Now why'd you go and do that?" The other asked.

"Just felt like it," the shooter said.

"What you gonna do with it?"

"Nothin'. Just let it be breakfast for the wolves and the buzzards."

"Why not take it back to the base for some venison steaks. No point in wasting it on the wolves and buzzards."

"Good idea."

Sally heard the shots and this exchange with a growing sense of terror. These guys obviously didn't care about much of anything. She wondered if she would get out of this alive. She didn't dare move. The men came closer and closer. Then one called out, "Come out of there with your hands on your head." Sally didn't move.

"I know you're in there. Come outta there with your hands up." Silence.

Sally heard a hailstorm of bullets crashing into the bushes over her head. Remembering what he had done to the deer, Sally decided to comply. "Don't shoot!" She yelled, and slowly stood up from her hiding place.

"Hands on your head," the one with the rifle said. Then, "Hey, it's a woman!"

The two men stepped forward, grabbed her by the arms, and roughly pulled her out of the thicket. They dragged her back to the sand bar.

"Well, look what we have here," sneered the one called Sarge, as they came up to him. "Who are you?"

When Sally didn't answer, he moved up close and got right in her face, "I said, who are you?" Silence. When Sally didn't answer this time, he slapped her on the side of her head. "I don't like disrespect. When I ask a question, I expect an answer."

By now Sally felt terrified and didn't know what to expect. She was totally at the mercy of these men, but to protect Brian and Joe she decided she'd be better off to say nothing. She glared at the man defiantly. He turned away in disgust, "Cuff her and put her in the chopper." And as an afterthought, "Better blindfold her too. The less she sees the better."

Sally found herself on a small bench in the back of the helicopter, with her hands bound behind her with one of those plastic cable ties used as handcuffs. The men had been rough on her, and her wrists hurt where they were tied together.

After what she guessed to be about an hour, she heard some of the men return and felt a thump as something heavy landed on the floor of the chopper. The pilot started the engines of this big helicopter and she heard the rotor start turning. In a few moments, the helicopter lifted off the ground, flew only a short distance, then hovered. She heard a winch unwind and guessed that they were going to pick up the saucer and haul it off. She heard the winch rewind and felt a little shudder as the helicopter took up the slack, took up the weight of the saucer, and lifted it from its resting place.

"Drop the rope ladder," Sarge ordered. "Let's get everyone on board." The rest of the men climbed back into the helicopter and they flew away.

* * *

When Joe returned to the canyon where he had left Sally, he was dismayed to see the large empty hole where the saucer had been embedded in the bank, his worst fears realized. With the saucer gone, he feared Sally might have suffered the same fate. He flew the same approach and landed on the sand bar as he had before. After shutting down the engine, he sat with the Cub door open, looking down at the sand beneath him. With a heavy heart, he stepped out onto the sand bar to try to read the story of the tracks. Since Sally had not come out of the tamarisks to greet him when he landed, he assumed she was either gone or dead or both. It became obvious what had happened on the sand bar. He saw the deep impressions left by the large helicopter tires, and many footprints around it. If Sally's footprints were among them, they had been trampled out by the others. As he explored further, he saw tracks leading off into the tamarisk bushes, going upstream to where the saucer had been. Some others went directly up the bank inland. Following these carefully, he came to the place where a puddle of blood stained the earth. The hair stood up on the back of his neck. He knelt to the ground, placed his finger tip in the blood, already congealed on top and starting to turn dark purple. They must have arrived not long after he left. The emptiness that gripped him at finding the blood caused a soft moan to escape his lips. He should've taken Sally with him, or the very least, helped her find a safe hiding place. Tears came as he scoured the ground further for clues. A flash of rage obscured some of his grief and he shut his eyes. He opened them to examine the killing site more carefully and now noticed a few hairs on the ground by the blood. Deer hair! Better a deer than Sally. That its death had not come easily was evidenced by the marks on the ground of kicking its death throes.

Relief flooded through him, even with seeing those signs of suffering. Maybe she wasn't dead! Obviously the people that had come for the saucer had killed the deer, though for what reason he couldn't imagine. Joe stood up and followed the tracks deeper into the tamarisk and found where Sally had holed up. There he saw where bullets had slashed through the bushes about three feet off the ground. That must be how they had taken her. He found the emergency kit still there, with the space blanket rolled into a ball and tucked under a root. He noticed that she had consumed some of the water and a food bar. He heaved a sigh of relief when close examination revealed no blood there. He gathered up the remains of the emergency kit and made his way back toward the sand bar, following the tracks of three people side by side, with the one in the middle leaving drag marks. Sally must have resisted, if the intermittent marks where her feet dug into the soft dirt were any indication. At least she had been alive at that point. Going up river to the site of the saucer crash, Joe saw where they had dug out the soil and Tamarack debris from the top of the saucer and also noticed the faint impression from the sling they had slid underneath it to lift it out with the helicopter.

The deep void Joe felt inside reminded him Amy's death so many years ago. But now his grief and anger began to turn into hatred, something that he seldom ever felt. He felt violated! They had stolen from him. They had taken Sally and the craft. Though it looked like she had been alive when they caught her, able to resist, there was no telling what they might have done to her, how they might still violate her, especially if these were the rogue black ops people from Area 51 he'd heard rumors about from time to time.

Too old to play about with denial, he blamed himself for all this. He wished now that he had just kept the saucer secret. Maybe he should never have taught Brian to fly it. Then at least it might have been him flying the mission on the KC-135, if he had been up flying when the word came through. He dreaded having to go back to the hospital to tell Brian what happened. Though only an educated guess, he figured the military must have heard Brian's Mayday with the GPS co-ordinates and had come looking as he'd feared. Had they taken Sally to Nellis? Or worse, to Groom Lake? While he might be able to get some information from contacts at Nellis Air Force Base, getting anything out of Area 51 at Groom Lake would be next to impossible. The government still pretended it didn't exist.

47

As the helicopter lifted off, a man reached over and fastened a seat belt around her to keep her from sliding off the narrow bench. Maybe they weren't going to kill her after all. She alternated between feeling like giving up and wanting to fight back in some way. But for the moment, she conceded she could do little but sit tight. Before long, her head ached from the throbbing racket of the helicopter engine and rotors. What would Joe think when he returned for her? How was Brian doing by this time? She hoped Joe had made it to the hospital in time to save his life.

Blindfolded, her hands bound behind her, she was powerless and at the mercy of her captors, and could do nothing to help Brian at this point. The pain in her arms and shoulders soon became intolerable. No matter which way she twisted and turned, she could not ease her discomfort. "Take off these handcuffs!" She shouted, trying to be heard over the noise of the engine. But they all just laughed at her, seeming to take delight in her discomfort. Her heart jumped in fear when the helicopter gave a sudden lurch at some turbulence and the dead deer slid across the floor to rest against her legs, its body still warm, and sticky with blood.

Exhausted from little sleep, as well as the trauma of being captured and then manhandled on to the helicopter, she finally gave up and dozed off, to awaken only when she felt the helicopter descend, its forward motion cease, and go into a hover mode. She heard the whine of the winch unwind to lower its burden to the ground. The helicopter engine was so loud that she could hear none of the communications between the people on board, and thus got no clue as to what was going on at the moment or what was going to happen next. After releasing the saucer, the helicopter flew only a short distance before it settled to the ground, where the pilot throttled the engine back and shut it down. Even with the engine off, her ears were so deafened from the engine noise that she barely heard the shouted command from the sergeant for her to be brought out. When she felt her seat belt released, she realized she could finally move. One of the men still on board took her arm and guided her to the doorway. She recoiled when another man outside lifted her to the ground and made no apology for touching her breasts as he did so. She cringed. Then she heard a new voice.

"Whoa! Got some fresh meat, I see," the voice said. Sally

stiffened, unsure whether he meant her or the deer that still lay on the helicopter floor. Her blindfold denied her any visual clue as to which one he meant.

"A prisoner, eh?" The voice then said. "Take her away. You know where to put her."

Two men held her by her arms and forced her to walk with them until they entered a building. Their footsteps echoed off hard floors and walls as they descended a set of metal stairs and then along a hall. When they stopped, Sally heard a key inserted and turned in a lock, the door opened, and she was thrust into the room. There, one of the men finally snipped the plastic handcuff from her wrists and removed her blindfold. As he started to leave, Sally asked, "Could I have some water, please?"

"I'll check and see if it's allowed," he said curtly. With that, he slammed the door and locked it.

Sally took a moment to look around at her prison. The room, with walls, floor, and even the ceiling, of concrete, contained only a narrow steel cot with a thin cotton pad on it. Beside it sat a five gallon plastic bucket with an old toilet seat on top of it. A roll of toilet paper lay on the floor nearby, its edges damp and curled. A small dirty window, high in the outside wall, let in a glimmer of daylight. A tiny round window the size of a teacup in the steel door completed its decor. Overwhelmed with a combination of sadness, exhaustion, anger, and fear, Sally lay down on the cot and dissolved into tears. After a time, she drifted off into a light sleep. She awoke to the sound of footsteps in the hall and a key in the door. It opened briefly to allow a water bottle to be tossed in, which landed on the floor with a thump by her cot. Her mouth parched from thirst, she gratefully drank some of the water. But her belly remained tied in a knot, unable to let go of her fear. What's next, she wondered?

The hours passed slowly as daylight faded away. Her cot, the only piece of furniture in the dark room, offered little comfort. Before the light was totally gone, Sally relieved herself in the bucket. It sounded strangely loud to her ears. After that, the sound of her breath became her sole companion. She startled when, after a very long time, a large light bulb, recessed into the ceiling and covered by a heavy metal screen, suddenly glared into life. One more thing to make it uncomfortable for her, she thought, but maybe it was better than being in the dark.

After another long wait, she heard footsteps approaching in the hall, followed by her door being unlocked. A guard holding an automatic rifle motioned her out of the room, taking her by the arm to escort her along the hall and up the flight of stairs. There, he pushed her into a room, whose floor was covered with a dirty worn carpet. A man in a black sat behind a scarred wooden desk. No rank or insignia adorned his uniform, not even the usual name tag. He motioned her to be seated in the lone steel chair in front of the desk. Her escort stepped back, but remained within arm's reach.

"Well ma'am, I have a few questions I'd like to ask you, and which I expect you to answer. You can make this easy on yourself or hard."

"Could I have something to eat, please?" Sally asked, trying to give herself time to think. "I haven't had anything to eat all day."

"Maybe when we get through here," he said, "depending on how cooperative you are. Understand?"

Sally's heart fell. She didn't know what to say, so she said nothing.

"Understand?"

Silence.

The man, his balding and shaved head reflecting the overhead light, then leaned forward and yelled through clenched teeth, "WHEN I SPEAK TO YOU, I EXPECT AN ANSWER! UNDERSTAND?"

"Yes!" Sally said with resignation. Then gathering her courage, she said, "I am a US citizen and you have no right to hold me here. I've committed no offense. You have kidnapped me. I demand to be released so that I can go home."

"Tell us all you know about the saucer."

Sally said nothing.

"Where did it come from? Who was flying it?" Silence "We know it was an American man flying it, by his voice when he radioed his Mayday."

"I demand to be released, or at least contact a lawyer."

"You were found in the vicinity of top-secret equipment with no personal identification. Until we get a satisfactory explanation of what you were doing there and tell us all you know about it, you are going to stay right here. Like I said, you can make this easy or hard. It's up to you."

"That secret equipment that you're talking about is private property. You have no right to it."

"Brassy bitch, aren't you? Looks like you want to make this hard. You going to answer my questions?"

Something snapped in Sally at that. Her anger now overrode her fear. "If I were in the military, I would only give you my name, rank, and serial number. But since I'm not, I guess just my name will have to do. My name is Sally."

"Well now, Sally, we have ways of softening up people here. When it's a male and he tries to escape, or resist arrest, we have justification for using what is called appropriate force. With females, even brassy bitches like you, we have other ways. Ways that don't leave marks. You get my message?"

"Are you threatening to rape me?"

"We don't threaten!" He grinned maliciously, implying more than he said, then paused, "But maybe we won't need to go that far. Perhaps a little more rest and relaxation in our wonderful facilities here will loosen your tongue."

"Take her back downstairs, Sergeant."

And to Sally, "Sweet dreams!"

"Do I get anything to eat?"

"I'm so sorry," he said sarcastically, "our kitchen is closed at this time of day. I'm not even sure what time it will open tomorrow. They keep very irregular hours here, you know. We'll certainly do everything possible to make your stay here as comfortable as we can. Like I said, you can make it easy or hard. Take her away."

The guard yanked her out of her chair and hauled her back to her cell, where the light in the ceiling remained on. Discouraged and scared, did she dare hope for rescue from this awful place? Joe wouldn't know where she was, let alone be able to mount a rescue. For the first time, she faced the real possibility of dying here. She had no doubt this was some sort of military facility, maybe even the secret Area 51 in Nevada. That would be the logical place for them to take the saucer. It wasn't that far by air. The Air Force denied that such a place even existed. Brian had told her it didn't appear on any civilian air maps, though its presence was common public knowledge. They could keep her here as long as they wanted and no one would ever know the difference. She seriously doubted if her abduction had been reported to any authority that cared, unless Joe had some friends in the Air Force. Sally suspected that more than one grave marked the nearby desert, officially denied and forgotten. In her mind, she jumped back and forth between giving them what they wanted and protecting Brian and Joe. In truth, she didn't know very much about the saucer. She'd only seen it twice, the second time being only today when they rescued Brian.

But she knew for sure now how much she loved Brian, and felt fiercely protective of him and Joe. But from books she had read, she knew that every human being has a breaking point. Would she die before she broke? She hoped so.

Day Two

Sally woke long before daylight began to penetrate through the high narrow window into the depths of her cell. The overhead light still assaulted her senses and she shivered from the cold that seeped from her prison walls. No blanket had been provided for cover or comfort. She got up, used the bucket toilet again, and looked around the room for the hidden video camera she assumed must be watching her. She drank from the bottle of water, aware that she could survive a long time without food, but not long without water. At the same time she wanted to make it last as long as she could, unsure when she might get more. That might become part of softening her up too.

Curled up on the cot in a fetal position for warmth, she heard a key turn in the lock and a big man, whom she'd not previously seen, entered. A malicious grin creased his face as he said, "I've been told that you be wanting a boyfriend!"

"You've been told wrong."

"That's what it says in the official report, lady. It says that you're just begging for a little company," he said with a sneer. "I'm here to take care of you! Got it?"

Sally curled up even tighter on the cot and squeezed her eyes shut. Then she heard him yell, "Bitch!" as he grabbed her by her hair and yanked her to a sitting position. Her eyes opened wide in pain and terror. How could they do this to her? She shivered as she reminded herself that if they were willing to do this, then they'd probably never risk letting her out of here to tell her story. She decided then and there that they were probably going to kill her, one way or another. She had nothing to lose now. When the man unzipped the pants of his black uniform, pulled out his now erect penis, and stuck it in her face, she knew exactly what she had to do.

"This is yours, lady, like it or not!" he said defiantly.

As she reluctantly reached out to grab his penis with her hand, he smirked triumphantly, and thus wasn't ready for what she did next. In one swift motion, her strength magnified by all her fear and rage, she opened her mouth and bit down with all the power and strength she could muster, grinding and sawing her teeth from side to side, till in the space of one or two seconds, blood spurted in her mouth and face. Her attacker let out a hideous howl and slammed his fist into the side of her head like a sledge hammer. Sally never even knew when her face hit the floor. Mercifully, she didn't feel his furious kick in her ribs either. She wouldn't know that pain until later.

* * *

Shadows reached dark fingers across the winter landscape as Joe approached the Blanding airport in the Cub. On the flight back from the canyon where the saucer had crash landed, he played out several scenarios or alternatives for Sally's rescue. He first thought of asking an officer in the Special Forces, whom he knew he could trust, to mount a rescue, either through channels or directly on the ground. But he didn't know exactly where the saucer and Sally had been taken. If they took her to Area 51 at Groom Lake, as he suspected, getting confirmation would be nigh on to impossible. If the Air Force denied its existence, they surely would not be willing to acknowledge that any of their black ops forces had kidnapped Sally and stolen his saucer.

He thought of trying to enter the facility himself and find her. But he knew that at his age, even getting close to the place through the desert was highly unlikely. That left his third option. Call on Markel for assistance.

As soon as he landed and put the Cub away, Joe sent a signal to summon Markel. While he waited for a response, he looked up the coordinates Area 51. Not long after, he felt the miniature receiver on his key ring vibrate, indicating confirmation that his message had been received and that he should meet Markel at their usual pick up point on a mesa west of town. He had not used it since he'd brought his own Explorer craft home.

Night had already long claimed the land as Joe drove away from the airport, his headlights stabbing two shafts of light through the darkness. Not long after he arrived on top of the mesa, he heard, with relief, the familiar hum of the approaching craft. Moments later, the saucer was on the ground and its hatch lifting.

He stepped into the craft to a warm welcome from Markel. As they lifted off, Joe briefed Markel on the problem facing them. He first reported the mission that Brian had flown with the Explorer craft, taking down the KC-135 before it could accomplish its deadly mission. Then he described his search for Brian with Sally, and finally finding him and the saucer embedded in the river bank. The story of Brian's injuries and rescue, the limitations of the Cub, requiring that Sally be left behind, came next. He portrayed, as best he could, the probable sequence of events, resulting in the loss of both the saucer and Sally, his fear about Sally's fate, and the sense of urgency he felt for trying to rescue her. He worried less about the loss of the Explorer craft, but if they could do something about that too, he would be happy. By then, they were approaching the Mothership and Joe gave Markel the map coordinates that he had written down for Area 51.

Once inside the hangar bay, Markel guided Joe over to the largest saucer that he'd ever seen, nearly 90 feet in diameter. Markel said telepathically, *"This is the craft we use for retrieval missions. It is similar in function to what you call a wrecker truck on earth. If you look underneath, you'll see a large concave space into which we can fit your Explorer craft for transport. But to accomplish this and rescue Sally, I think we will need help. I'll consult with my colleagues for the* assistance we need. Perhaps you can just relax and rest a bit while I make the arrangements."

"I can't relax yet," Joe responded. "I would prefer to go with you to help work out the plan."

"As you wish. Come along. You will learn more about your own craft, and about some of the capabilities that we have for situations like this. I have asked our data technicians to pull up our records for Sally, so that we can determine how best to go about rescuing her. I did tell you that she has been with us here on the ship a number of times before, didn't I?"

"Yes, you did, but I'm really worried about her. She is in grave danger. I am sure that they will interrogate her to try to learn as much as possible about the Explorer craft. But she knows little or nothing about it, having seen it only that one time when Brian took her to the canyon. She didn't see it again until we rescued Brian from his crash. But she knows nothing about operating it or flying it. I'm afraid they won't believe her and will torture her to try to get information that she doesn't have."

Markel led Joe along a corridor, then entered a room to see two other beings similar in appearance to Markel. He introduced them to Joe as engineers who specialized in this type of retrieval mission. Joe listened and was surprised to hear them discuss the heretofore unknown capabilities of his craft that enabled it to be brought up to partial power through a remote signal from the rescue craft, that is, if it was not too badly damaged. That power was supposed to be sufficient to activate the phase change capabilities of the craft and render it invisible, making it easier to extract from its hiding place. Joe remembered that there had always been a very small trickle of power left on in the craft, which enabled the craft to identify the touch of the pilot. He learned it also maintained power to a locator chip, which, if not destroyed by the crash, would assist the rescue team in determining its exact location. Of course, they wouldn't know for certain whether those capabilities remained intact until they arrived on the scene and got closer to it. Knowing its approximate location however, would therefore be of great help. They thanked Joe for that.

"But what about Sally?" Joe asked.

One of the engineers responded, *"Our records indicate that Sally has one of our micro locator chips implanted just behind her left ear. Sometimes these were installed in one of the sinuses. But that location occasionally caused problems, such as sinus infections, and often it was expelled by extremely hard sneezes by the host. We've found that the ear location is more easily tolerated and is more stable. We don't have any indication in the records of a malfunction with her chip. If she is still alive, we can pinpoint her exact location as well."*

"But how will we get her out of there?" Joe interjected.

"We will take along some of our grays who are adept at phase change, and can even enable phase change in others, including humans, if necessary. Sally has experienced this many times over the years, beginning when she was nine years of age. She was transported out through the window of her bedroom as a child, and later on, sometimes through solid walls. We will have to see what conditions exist when we arrive."

With that, Joe and Markel proceeded back to the hangar bay to the large craft Markel showed Joe earlier. They boarded and were shortly followed by six of the small grays and the two engineers. The departure procedure for this larger craft was very similar to the smaller ones like Joe's Explorer. Even though flight time to Area 51 was relatively brief, the first hint of daylight had already begun to steal across the landscape, though the base itself remained in the shadow of the mountains to the east. Joe would have preferred the protection of total darkness. As they approached, Markel activated the sensors to try to pick up the locator chips on the saucer and Sally. He also enabled the radar protection on the craft and flew close to the mountains to reduce the risk of being picked up visually, remaining in the shadow of Bald Mountain northeast of Groom Lake. From there, it was but a short distance to the base.

Markel pointed to two lights that appeared on the instrument panel. *"Good news! We're picking up a signal from indicators from both the saucer and Sally. I'll transfer them to a map so we can see their locations."* Immediately Joe saw two red dots light up on the small-scale panel display map of the Groom Lake base. When Joe compared the screen display with what he saw by looking out the window, he assumed that the one coming from one of the old A-12 project hangars near the south part of the base came from the saucer. The other, only a short distance to the north, must be from Sally. At first he didn't see anything there when he peered out through the window, but on closer examination, he identified a small building. That must be where she was being held, though it seemed awfully small. Maybe there was more underground, like many of the installations rumored to be at the base.

"Can we try to get Sally first?" Joe signaled.

"We could," Markel responded. *"But I'm not so sure that's a good idea. If they have gone to all this trouble to obtain the Explorer craft and Sally, both are likely to be well guarded. At this time of the day, there may be fewer guards around the craft. So by going after the craft first, we may create enough of a diversion to make it easier to retrieve*

Sally with less chance of her getting hurt."

"I suppose you're right, though I'm really worried about Sally. I think time is critical here."

"I understand your concern," Markel said. "But as long as that red light is on, we know that she is at least alive. Her locator chip has to be nourished by the body in order to remain active. That's the way we can be certain the person is still alive."

"Okay, I'll concede your point," Joe said.

"I'm going to activate the phase change now on this craft, so that we can approach in an invisible mode. You will feel a slight sensation as I do this, as you know, but don't worry, it will not affect you, except that you will become invisible as well."

Joe had experienced the phase change several times in his own saucer, so he knew what to expect. When Markel switched to the phase change, he felt only a small jolt, like a mild electric shock. Beyond that, he noticed nothing else. In a few moments, Markel brought the craft in to hover close to the western-most A-12 hangar on the south end of the field. From there, he sent a signal to the captured craft to power it up enough to enable its own phase change.

* * *

Inside the large hangar, three men with automatic rifles walked patrol around the saucer under bright mercury vapor lights. A boring job, but they accepted it without complaint. They were curious about the saucer and frequently paused to study it. When they met each other as they made their rounds, the only sign of their boredom was an occasional roll of their eyes. The guard closest to the saucer startled when he heard a slight hum start to come from the craft. He knew something changed! His eyes darted around trying to make sense of it. Should he report it to his superior officer? Was this just more weird stuff in this already weird situation? He looked at the saucer carefully, but saw no other change, so he decided to just wait and watch, though he did mention it to his buddy on his next circuit. They both agreed that it was not yet worth reporting. A few moments later however, he and the others stared in shock when they saw craft rise a few inches off the wheeled dolly on which it rested and then simply begin to disappear, right in front of their eyes. Within a few seconds it was gone! They couldn't believe their eyes.

"What the hell happened?" The first one said. "Did you see that?"

"Now we gotta report!" Said the other. Then just as he was about to call out to the third guard, he received another shock. Coming right through the hangar wall in front of him were six of the small gray beings. Before he could regain his wits and bring his weapon up, the first one was already within arm's reach and touched him with a shock that rendered him immediately unconscious and numb. He crumpled to the floor. Two grays swiftly glided to the remaining two guards and similarly dispatched them. Another two went to either side of the hangar door, simultaneously pressed the buttons to engage the electric motors to raise the giant bifold door. By the time the door was high enough to allow the saucer passage, the grays, who had gathered around it, pushed its invisible form out the door to the ramp, where they made themselves invisible as well. These actions remained unseen by all, except for Joe and Markel in the large craft, which had hovered high enough off the ground to allow the smaller saucer to slide underneath and be hooked to the cables lowered for that purpose. Markel quickly drew the damaged saucer up into the well of the large craft and secured it firmly, while the grays promptly re-entered.

Unfortunately, when the hangar door was raised without initiating the proper security sequence, it set off a loud clanging alarm not only in the hangar, but also in the guard shack across the ramp to the north. Several men, armed and dressed in black, ran toward the hangar, weapons ready. All they could see was a shimmering, liquid quality to the air in front the hangar where the saucer had been stored, whose wide bifold door now hung open. They charged the hangar, saw the guards lying on the floor inside, and dropped immediately into a defensive perimeter posture, swiveling to target any potential attacker. Still, they saw nothing more to explain the situation.

By the time the guards arrived, Markel had raised the craft high enough in the air that they swept right underneath him. Had he not lifted off, they would have most certainly bumped into the large invisible craft. They would in all likelihood have been confused by that, but they also might have started shooting and possibly have caused damage to one or both craft. Meanwhile, Markel flew the craft across the ramp toward the small building which indicated Sally's location.

* * *

In a room next to the office where Sally had been interrogated, several men crowded around a small television monitor that showed Sally's cell, expecting to see her fall to the guy they called Big Mike. They laughed in great merriment when they saw what Sally did to their macho buddy. They felt sorry for the great pain he must be in, but they also thought it was incredibly funny.

"That ought to bring him down a notch or two," one man said, believing they had something they could use to tease this guy for long time to come, for he frequently bragged about his sexual conquests, often into the point of being obnoxious.

Mike had entered the office, bent over in pain, to the wild whoops of his buddies, and had just requested permission to go to the infirmary for treatment, when the alarm sounded. Well trained, they all grabbed their weapons, charged out the door and across the huge ramp to where the other guards had taken defensive positions. They also saw, through the open hangar door, that the saucer was missing!

"What the hell is going on?" Lt. Wood yelled. Then he clicked his two-way radio, its microphone attached to his shirt, and shouted with alarm, "Steve, give me a report!"

"We don't know what's happening," the leader of the hangar guards came back. "When we came out of the guard shack, the hangar door was open and the saucer was missing. I can see three men down inside. I don't know if they're alive or dead."

* * *

Inside her cell, Sally slowly regained consciousness, her head throbbed in pain from the blow she had received from the man earlier, and was now aggravated by the raucous alarm bell ringing outside in the hall. The guard stationed outside her cell, alerted by the bell, was ill prepared for what he saw next. Four aliens came right through the closed door at the end of the hall, as easily as if it were a sheer curtain. So stunned by this sight, he was unable to react before one of them reached out and touched him. The last things he saw, as he slumped into unconsciousness, were two huge black eyes staring him in the face. With the guard down, it was a simple matter then for one of the grays to retrieve the key, open the door of Sally's cell, and enter.

Sally, still groggy, stiffened with terror at what she saw coming through the now open door. She wanted to scream, but felt too weak to move or even make a sound. She felt, more than saw, two of the beings come to her side, lift her off the floor, and hurriedly carry her through the door, up the stairs, and outside. With the two beings holding her arms, she felt herself to float up. She did not see the huge craft which hovered, invisible, over her head.

Not far away, one of the guards in black turned and saw her rise up into the air. Unable to believe his eyes, he delayed a few seconds before giving the alarm.

"She's getting away! Stop her!" he finally shouted. Before he could do anything more, or bring his weapon into play, she simply disappeared.

"What's happening?" Lt. Wood yelled, turning back toward the alarm giver.

"I don't know! The woman came out of the building, floated up in the air about 30 feet and then disappeared."

"The Colonel ain't going to like this. Not one bit! We're supposed to be guarding her. Now we've lost her and the saucer too, and maybe some of the men. How in hell are we going to explain this? This is really weird shit!" Wood said.

"Yeah, she told us that the saucer was private property and that we didn't have any right to it. I guess somebody out there didn't like that. I told you we ought to take it easy on her!" The other said.

"Get in there and see what happened to Jackson. He was supposed to be guarding her." Pete, you get over to the hangar and see about the guards there! Report back to me ASAP as soon as you have reconned the situation. Move it, NOW!"

Lt. Wood stared out into the morning sky and for a moment thought he saw way off to the east, the image of a large flying saucer fading into the distance. Just as it disappeared over the mountain, he realized how big it must be to still appear as large as it did that far out.

"Oh my God!"

On board the craft, Sally was shocked, but relieved, to see Joe. When he reached out to her, she collapsed into his arms and sobbed on his shoulder, almost sliding from his grasp. Her body shook with the release of her terror. After she calmed a little, he wiped some of the blood off her face with his handkerchief. He tried to be as gentle as possible around her swollen nose, which still dripped fresh blood.

Though it wasn't a long flight back to the Mothership, Sally slipped back into unconsciousness, in spite of the throbbing in her head. Joe saw the black and blue color already emerging in the lump on the side of her head and held her as tenderly as if she were a child. When they docked in the hangar bay, the grays picked her up and carried her out of the craft to the medical care facility, where she was examined by physicians who agreed that she had sustained a severe concussion. In addition, they found some bruised and cracked ribs and a badly bruised nose.

They called in another being, trained as an energy healer, who proceeded to work on her. Fascinated, Joe watched as the being gently held her head between his hands. Joe had never seen anything like it. Gradually, the contusion and the dark color on the side of her head began to fade. She now appeared to be sleeping calmly. Next the being placed his fingers over her nose for many minutes, until the swelling went down and it too appeared more normal. When he finished with her head, he placed his hands on her rib cage, and held them there for an extended period of time, until he appeared satisfied with the effect.

After about 30 minutes, Sally's eyes began to flutter. When they fully opened, she looked around, saw the being by her side, and immediately panicked. Then she heard Joe's voice saying, "You're safe now Sally. You're okay. You're safe."

Relief flooded through Sally's mind and heart. "Where am I?" She asked.

"You're on board the Mothership, in their hospital. You've just been treated by a healer for your injuries. I've been assured that you will get well quickly. In fact, your injuries look much better already."

"What happened? The last thing I remember, I was in a prison cell, about to be raped. I knew they were going to kill me, so I fought back the only way I knew how. Then the guy hit me and everything went black. I have a vague memory of seeing aliens, but I'm not sure about that. You know anything more?"

"Markel sent some of the grays in to get you. I wanted to come too, but Markel convinced me to let them do that job. They carried you out and brought you on board," Joe said. "Then we flew here."

"What about Brian," Sally anxiously asked. "Is he okay?"

"He's in the hospital in Moab, recovering from his injuries. He has broken ribs, which punctured and collapsed a lung, as well as a broken wrist and cuts and bruises. They patched him up, but he has to stay in the hospital until that lung can heal. A week or ten days, I was told. But he's gonna be okay. It'll just take a while."

"Oh, thank God!" Sally cried, tears starting to flow down across her face. "I would have died if anything happened to him! And Joe. . . . I didn't tell them anything!"

"What?" Joe whispered in surprise.

"I didn't tell them anything about you and Brian or the saucer."

"Oh."

"They wanted to know about the saucer, where it came from and who flew it. But I didn't say anything! I really don't know much about it, anyway. They threatened to rape me if I didn't tell. But I decided that if they were gonna do that, they probably weren't going to let me out of there alive anyway. So I kept my mouth shut. Bad as it might be, I figured I was gonna die, no matter what happened. I had to protect you and Brian!"

"Thanks, Sally." Joe said, moved to tears by her courage.

"I came to realize in that moment of facing my own death, that I love Brian more than anything in this world, even my own life. Protecting him and you was the least I could do. I can't wait to get home to let him know that. You're sure he's gonna be okay?"

"I'm sure, Sally." Joe said, placing a hand on her shoulder.

"When can we go home?" Sally asked.

"By this evening. Right now would not be the best time to show up back in Blanding. Brian is well cared for in the hospital, so there's nothing we can do for him. The military doesn't know where he is. Brian and I agreed to tell hospital staff that he had fallen off a cliff, so there shouldn't be any unnecessary questions. They're accustomed to me bringing in injured parties. So, the best thing for you to do now is get some rest."

"I'm thirsty, Joe, and hungry too. I haven't had anything to eat since we left to go look for Brian. When was that, just yesterday morning? Seems like ages ago."

"I'll see what I can do to get you some food and water."

"Thanks, Joe," Sally said, gratefully.

48

7:00 p.m., January 3, 2002

After being transported back from the Mothership to the mesa top, Joe and Sally returned to Blanding in Joe's pickup, far too late to consider going to Moab to see Brian in the hospital. A sense of relief flooded Sally when she saw her Toyota pickup in the parking lot where she'd left it the morning before. So much had happened, she found it hard to believe that only two days had passed since they had flown off to look for Brian. In spite of all that, she could scarcely wait to go see Brian in the hospital, but knew she was too exhausted to make the drive to Moab this late at night. She would have to wait until morning.

When Joe saw Sally stumble and almost fall, getting out of his truck, he asked, "Sally, are you sure you're okay to drive home?"

"Yeah, I think so," Sally said, as she climbed into her pickup, amazed at how tired and stiff she was.

"But would you get my purse and keys from your office for me? I left them in the file drawer of your desk before we took off."

Joe went into the office to retrieve them for her. As he handed them to her through the car window, he said, "Be careful, Sally. Give me a call when you get home, so I'll know you're home safe."

"Okay Joe," Sally said.

"What time do you want to leave tomorrow morning to go to Moab?" Joe asked. "I'll come pick you up."

"Oh, you don't have to drive me up there."

"No, but I want to go see how Brian is doing too, so we might as well go together. I'll get somebody to fill in for me here at the airport. Besides, you've been through a whole lot and I suspect you may be more tired that you realize. So what time do you want to leave? It will take us about an hour and a half to get there."

"Can we leave by 7:30?" Sally asked.

"Fine with me. I'll come pick you up then."

"Okay," Sally said, as she started her car and drove out of the airport parking lot.

She felt so tired that it she had trouble keeping her mind focused on the road as she drove back to town. At her house, her feet felt as if they were in lead boots each step of the way between her truck and her front door. She barely had energy to go to the kitchen to get a drink of water. She then made her way to her bedroom, called Joe, and collapsed onto bed, not even bothering to undress.

When the alarm rang the next morning, Sally felt as if she had scarcely slept, but dragged herself out of bed and into the shower to try to wake up. Though she recognized the effects of the healing done on board the Mothership yesterday, which Joe had described to her, her head and her ribs still felt sore and tender. Thinking back to what had occurred, she shuddered to think what might have happened, had Joe and Markel not rescued her. She had never been so afraid for her life, not even when she was abducted as a young child. Deeply grateful, it still seemed a miracle to have escaped all of that.

She had just begun to think about something to eat when the doorbell rang. She brightened at Joe's friendly smile, glad to hear that he had both coffee and breakfast waiting for her in his truck. She had never considered breakfast from the local fast food restaurant very appealing, but today it tasted delicious. Even with a cup of coffee, by the time they reached Monticello, half way to Moab, she found herself drifting off to sleep, and wakened only when they slowed to enter the town.

Sally's stomach tightened with anxiety as they pulled into the parking lot of the Allen Memorial Hospital in Moab on West 400 North Street. She couldn't wait to get to Brian, yet was afraid to see what he might look like. Her last memory was of his face streaked with blood from his head wounds. When she and Joe entered Brian's hospital room, Sally gave a sigh of relief as her eyes took in the scene while she made her way to his bedside. The big tube protruding from his chest dripped bloody fluid into a large plastic bag hanging off the side of the bed, while another smaller one carried yellow fluid from under the sheet into yet another bag. A third ran from the bottle overhead to the IV needle inserted into his arm. He must have been sleeping. Not until she touched him gently on his hand, did he open his eyes and recognize her. A weak smile spread across his face as he said, "Hi!" He lifted a finger in greeting to Joe at the foot of the bed. Turning slightly toward Sally, he said, "Thanks for coming. I'm glad you're here."

Then taking a closer look, his brow furrowed as he noticed her bruises. "What happened to you? Looks like you got beat up," he said, never imagining how accurate his words were.

"Yeah, a little," she admitted. She didn't want to the alarm Brian, so she decided not to share anything about her ordeal yet. That could come later. It was obvious that Brian was pretty well doped up with pain medication and probably wouldn't be able to handle very much at this time. The good thing was that they were both safe for now. That would have to be enough.

Turning to Joe, Brian said, "I'm glad you got her out of there. I don't know how you do it with your Cub, Joe, but I'm sure glad you came. I don't remember much about the trip up here yesterday. I guess I was pretty well out of it."

"Yeah, you were in pretty tough shape about then. They tell me you are going to pull through just fine though," Joe said, coming up to the side of the bed.

"Thanks again," Brian said weakly, as his eyelids began to sag. Then, after a pause, he added, "I guess I'm still pretty tired. Don't have much energy." Still holding Sally's hand, he turned his head to her and asked, "Any chance you could call the girls and tell them where I am? Let 'em know that I'm OK?"

"Of course, I'll be glad to."

"Take my keys. You'll find their addresses and telephone numbers in my day timer book at my apartment."

"I'll do it just as soon as we get back there, Brian."

Then Joe spoke, "I'll leave you two alone here for a while and come back later. Just take it easy and rest."

After Joe left, Sally sat silently holding his hand as he drifted off again. A few minutes later, when he opened his eyes and looked at her, she spoke, "I was so scared, Brian. Scared that you would die and I would never see you again, that I would never get to tell you how much I love you. Before we met, I didn't think I would be able to love anyone, ever again. Then after we began dating, I started to fall in love with you. That scared me too. But it wasn't until I thought I had lost you, that I really got scared."

"I know what you mean, Sally," Brian said. "That night while I lay there in the saucer, unsure whether I would get out of there alive, thinking of you kept me going. I didn't want to die without being able to tell you how much you mean to me, how much I love you. I think that I said something about it before, but nothing like what I feel, what I truly feel."

Sally squeezed Brian's fingers, acknowledging what he had said. They held each other's eyes for long time. Then Brian spoke through half-closed eyes, "Will you marry me when I get out of here?"

"Oh yes, Brian. Yes!" Sally whispered, her eyes brimming with tears of joy and relief.

"Thanks." Then after a pause, "I'm getting pretty sleepy. They gave me a pain shot just before you arrived. You don't have to stay."

"I know. But there's nowhere else I want to be just now. I'm going to stay here with you for a while. Just rest and sleep as much as you want. I'll be right here."

With a peaceful expression on his face, Brian closed his eyes and slipped into that twilight world of drug induced semi-consciousness.

MORE:
If you have enjoyed this story, you will certainly like the 2nd and 3rd books in this series: **The General,** and, **The Star Kids Mission**, available now both as ebooks and as paperbacks at Amazon.com, where you may follow these characters and more in the continuing saga. You may preview the opening chapter of Book II, following this section. You are invited to comment or post a review of this book on Amazon.com. Go to their website, type in Sky Warriors and click on 'Customer Reviews, then click on 'Create your own review.

The author, Paul A. Hansen, Ph.D., is a licensed pilot who began flying in 1959 in a J-3 Piper Cub. He owned a 1947 Aeronca Chief, N3565E from 1962-71. In 1995 he built an experimental aircraft, a GlaStar, N43PH, which he still flies. For more information about the author and his writing, consult his website: http://paulhansenauthor.com

SETTINGS
The locales in or near Blanding, Utah are real with a few minor exceptions: Comb Ridge, Arch Canyon, Edge of the Cedars Museum, certain motels and restaurants, roads & streets exist as described. The pocket canyon where the saucer is hangared is fictitious. On old geo maps, there was an "Indian Village" site located northwest of Blanding. The FBO office at the Blanding airport was moved from the location described to a new site nearby after the time of this story. At the time of this story, the Vintage parking area at the Oshkosh, Wisconsin EAA Flyin allowed parking of experimentals. That has since been changed.

Readers who are pilots will recognize the authenticity of the stories about flight training and flying. The training manuals of the PT-17 and T-6 were researched and supplemented by interviews with a man who was a T-6 flight instructor during the war. Information about the WASP (Women's Army Service Pilots) (http://www.wingsacrossamerica.us/wasp/) has been accurately researched, including interviews with living WASP members, many of whom have died this year, 2011. Mariana, Florida was once the site of a T-6 training base, though now it is a general aviation airport. The US Army airbase near Pueblo, CO was a B-24 training base during the war, but has been changed in the story to be a primary flight training base. Though not well known, P-47s were stationed briefly during the war at Randolph Army Airfield, San Antonio, TX. (Now: Randolph Air Force Base).

The 78th Fighter Group in WW II

The **78th Fighter Group** was activated in 1942. It initially trained for combat with P-38's and served as part of the west coast air defense organization. It moved to England in November 1942 and was assigned to Eighth Air Force. The group lost its P-38's and most of its pilots in February 1943 when they were assigned to Twelfth Air Force for service in the North African campaign. The group was reassigned to Duxford airfield (*South of Cambridge, UK*) in April 1943 and equipped with P-47s. Aircraft of the group were identified by a black/white chequerboard pattern. Near the end of the war, the unit was re-equipped with P-51s.

From Duxford, the 78th flew many missions to escort B-17 and B-24 bombers that attacked industries, submarine yards and docks, V-weapon sites, and other targets on the continent. The unit also engaged in counter-air activities and strafed and dive-bombed airfields, trains, vehicles, barges, tugs, canal locks, barracks, and troops. (From Wikipedia.)

THE GENERAL

Book II: The Star People Series.

BY

PAUL HANSEN

1

6:30 a.m. Friday, January 4, 2002
Washington, DC

A thick winter fog clung to the hallowed terrain of Arlington National Cemetery and closed its shroud around Air Force Chief of Staff General Jeremy Carter as he ran in the Vietnam section. Now thirty minutes into his run, the gentle hills of Arlington pulled at his 50 year old body more than he wanted to admit. In response, he pumped his lean brown legs harder, his running shoes slapping more rapidly on the wet asphalt, until he shivered in the wind that pierced his sweat soaked T-shirt. Long undulating rows of white stones flickered past him, their alignment alternating between diagonal and straight sight lines in a surreal kaleidoscope, before disappearing into the fog. He wondered momentarily where his own stone might someday be placed.

He liked coming here to Arlington. He told his colleagues that it gave him a quiet place to think, but secretly he believed that the spirits of the dead who lay here helped him, or at least inspired him, to work out problems he faced in his job. Like now! What had really happened out in Pasadena on New Year's Day? He'd been relaxing at home watching football when the call came from General Fortner, commander of Air

Combat Command, saying a pilot of a KC-135 flying support for an F-16 training mission out of Nellis had tried to crash his jet tanker with a full load of fuel into the Rose Bowl. The two F-16s he'd been tasked to refuel had been sent to stop him, but someone or something else got there first and prevented the disaster. He didn't want to even imagine the mayhem of 25,000 gallons of fuel exploding in the Rose Bowl. He really needed the wisdom of his dead Viet Nam buddies now and silently called out to them.

Jeremy's first call had been to Colonel Stevens, Commander of the 57th Wing at Nellis AFB.

"What th' hell happened out there?"

Stevens replied, "One of the KC-135 pilots on loan from the ANG out of Lincoln, Nebraska went berserk, ordered his crew to bail out, shot his co-pilot when he wouldn't go, then headed for the Rose Bowl with the intent of crashing it there, like a copy-cat 9/11. Fortunately, he was forced down in the mountains, away from the stadium and other populated areas."

"Forced down? Who took him out?"

"We don't know."

"What do you mean, you don't know?"

"One of the two F-16 pilots sent after it, a Captain David Miller, said an unidentified craft took it down." Carter heard the catch in Steven's voice before he continued. "A UFO."

"A flying saucer!"

"Yeah. Miller got there in time to catch it all on his gun camera. I thought maybe it was some spook plane from Area 51, but I called over there and they said they had nothing up at the time. Miller insisted the pilot sounded like one of our guys when he contacted him on the radio."

"Your pilot talked to the pilot of the UFO?"

"Yes. He may not even be military. Captain Miller couldn't raise him on any military frequency. Finally made contact on civilian Guard Frequency, 121.5. We have the radio transmissions on tape as well as the video. You can see and hear them for yourself."

"That I'd like to do. In fact, if you don't mind, I'd like to talk to Miller personally."

"No problem. When do you want him?"

"Tell him to be in my office Friday morning, 4 January. And send the video and audio tapes along with him."

"I'll get it done."

Jeremy pushed harder, his running shoes mashing into last fall's wet leaves, still clustered in low drifts along the edges of the asphalt drive.

Today was the day for debriefing the personnel involved. In a couple of hours he would interview the lead F-16 pilot, Captain David Miller, and the other key personnel in the incident. Last night he'd ordered them to fly here immediately for a debriefing. He vowed to get to the bottom of this incident. The last 24 hours had been a roller coaster. His emotions had risen and plunged from relief to anger, to elation, back to rage, and then . . . even fear, though he would never admit that to anyone. Fear had been hovering ever since that morning of September 11th when it first jumped him.

Like most everyone else that day, he'd had his eyes glued to a television, watching the airliner crash into the World Trade Center, played over and over and over by the networks. When he saw the second one crash, he'd yelled, "That's no accident. We're under attack!" He frantically punched numbers into his phone to scramble fighters nearest New York City to react to the threat, knowing in his heart that it was too little, too late. He never dreamed that his own life might be at risk there in the Pentagon.

At 9:45 a.m. he felt the Pentagon shudder with the impact of the airliner crashing into the building, before the sound of the explosion penetrated to his office. In the midst of the emergency sirens blaring, he seethed in helpless rage, knowing it was already too late. Where else might they attack, whoever "they" were? The White House? The Capitol? He grabbed the phone and punched in the numbers for the fighter wing at Andrews AFB, fearing he was too late again. Indeed, he was later to learn that but for the bravery of a few passengers on United Flight 93 over Pennsylvania, the White House would have been hit too. He grieved the loss of his colleagues on the other side of the building.

Now, four months later, as he ran through the quiet lanes of the cemetery, he debated his next move. He had been jubilant two days ago when he received a report from Nellis that the Black Ops guys at Area 51 had actually retrieved the flying saucer allegedly used to take down the KC-135. Thank God for the pilot of that thing! What a disaster that would have been! He shivered as his mind played out the potential results of such a fiasco. The nearly three thousand deaths at the World Trade Center would have been small in comparison. And with an experienced Air Force pilot at the controls! Though grateful that someone, still unknown, had successfully beat his F-16's to the scene and taken the KC-135 out with that saucer, he also felt deeply embarrassed that these things had all happened on his watch. If the UFO had not succeeded and his guys had been forced to shoot down the KC-135 and splatter 25,000 gallons of flaming jet fuel and wreckage over Pasadena, it would probably have meant the end of his career. Even so, he felt perilously close to losing his job, for having "allowed" it all to happen. Wasn't he responsible for keeping this nation safe? Either result, with a nation still in mourning over 9-11, would have been unthinkable. The White House, with its current leadership, would have been equally at a loss about what to do, but not about whom to blame.

As far as he knew, his people were keeping the truth of what happened in Pasadena secret, as he'd ordered. But given the leaky nature of human beings, he knew that wouldn't last long. His high spirits over the capture and retrieval of the saucer lasted only a few hours, until they were dashed by the news that both the saucer and a woman captured with it had disappeared. How did that happen? No wonder the terrorists were able to penetrate national security and deliver such a blow to the United States. With that kind of competence, it's a wonder that things were not worse. He would get to the bottom of this, one way or the other.

Late last night, when he'd received the report that the saucer and woman were missing, he'd immediately called the wing commander again and ordered him, along with the Colonel heading up security at Area 51, all to report directly to his office by 10 a.m. this morning. He'd had his staff arrange for them to come in three separate aircraft, unknown to each other. This meant that they would have to fly during the night and would no doubt be tired upon arrival at Andrews AFB here in D.C. Fine, he thought. He was tired too. He ordered the Air Force Security Forces to meet and transport each of them to his office in separate cars, with strict orders that they not be allowed to see or talk to each other. He didn't want to give them the opportunity to coordinate their stories. He needed to know exactly what happened from those directly involved. No chain of command massaging of the information. He decided to start with the pilot of the F-16 involved in the incident with the 135. Just as well take it from the top, he thought, as he continued his run.

Later, in the shower at the Pentagon, his mind flashed back even further over the events of the past year. Like the needle of a phonograph stuck in a scratch in one of the grooves, he replayed the angry scene with Amanda, just before she walked out a year ago. She'd berated his stubborn disbelief of their son, Josh, who for years had reported being taken by a flying saucer. Josh, a gangly, frail looking youth of sixteen, began telling those stories at age four. How could anyone believe such stupid nonsense, though he reluctantly admitted to himself that the kid seemed genuinely traumatized after those so-called events? The chaos and fights that emerged with his wife over his refusal to believe Josh's stories eventually created so much distance and pain that Amanda claimed she had to leave in order to protect her own sanity. Divorce followed not long after.

He felt sad and angry about the divorce, which had only recently become final. When she first left, he'd told her that she must be insane to believe such nonsense. His own beliefs had carried him righteously until last summer, when two apparently ordinary guys flew a 40-foot saucer into the big Experimental Aircraft Association air show at Oshkosh, Wisconsin. The media had climbed all over that one. At first he'd thought it a hoax, but later had to concede that maybe it was real after he'd watched media video footage of the saucer, and especially of its departure. It went straight up and disappeared in a matter of seconds, in total silence yet! No jet exhaust! As far as he knew nothing in the current USAF inventory, or even in development at the Skunk Works or Area 51 would match what he saw in the film footage. He'd vowed then and there to get his hands on that machine, whatever it might be. Until two days ago, all efforts to find it had come up empty handed. Did those pilots have anything to do with this KC-135 incident?

Inquiry revealed that the NSA agents who tried to capture and hold the saucer and its crew at Oshkosh were so heavy handed it was no wonder the pilots decided to get away. Another one of Tony Davis' National Security Agency's glorious feats. There had long been rumors of such a craft buried deep in one of the underground hangars at Area 51, rumors that were fed by the movie "Independence Day." But that was all just Hollywood bullshit, at least as far as he could determine. Or was it? Had someone kept secrets even from him? Maybe Josh's stories held some truth after all.

He was seeing his world start to fall apart and maybe his career too. It had begun with Josh's stories and Amanda divorcing him, then the 9-11 disaster, the near miss crash of the KC-135, and now, capturing and then losing the saucer. What a merry-go-round! He shook his head, as if to shake these events out of his reality.

He finished donning his full dress uniform and gave himself a final inspection in the mirror before heading up to his office. He hoped that his interviews with Miller and the others would provide some definitive information. Miller should be landing by now and would arrive soon. He couldn't wait to see what the gun camera had captured!

He gave a little shiver of fear. Now where the hell did that come from?

ABOUT THE AUTHOR

Paul A. Hansen

From the time Paul first frustrated his parents and teachers by drawing airplanes all over his school books, flying has been a passion, culminating in the building of his own plane (1995-97), a GlaStar (above) which he still flies. He took his first flying lesson in a Piper J-3 Cub in 1959. See pictures and more details on pages in his website (http://paulhansenauthor.com, under "Flying.") Paul intends for his novels to not only entertain, but inspire his readers. A 45 year career as psychotherapist, management consultant, and minister allowed him to hone his writing while crafting articles in professional journals, training manuals, and sermons. A diverse set of hobbies: flying, fly fishing, camping, and photography help him stay grounded. Adventures in the jungles of Ecuador and Costa Rica, the pampas of Chile, the cities and countries of Europe, and flights in his plane around the US provide a rich milieu for his stories. He designed and built the passive solar home he and his wife occupy in Colorado.

A non-fiction book stems from his earlier psychotherapy career: SURVIVORS AND PARTNERS, Healing the Relationships of Sexual Abuse Survivors(1991), though still in print, is now available worldwide as an e-book for only $2.99, and eventually by Create Space books.

Made in the USA
Monee, IL
20 May 2022